Tristan's Regret

The Return of King Arthur

Jacob Sannox

Copyright © 2023 Alan O'Donoghue
All rights reserved.

Terms and Conditions:
The purchaser of this book is subject to the condition that he/she shall in no way resell it, nor any part of it, by any method, nor make copies of it, nor any part of it, to distribute freely.

This book is a work of fiction. Any similarity between the characters and situations within its pages with events or persons, living or dead, is unintentional and coincidental.

Cover by BetiBup33 - https://twitter.com/BetiBup33

Typeset by Polgarus Studio – www.polgarusstudio.com

The moral rights of the author have been asserted.

Tristan's Regret is the third book in my trilogy,
The Return of King Arthur.
If you haven't read The Ravenmaster's Revenge and Agravain's Escape, I'd recommend that you do *before* you get started on Tristan's Regret, as it's a continuing story.

Jacob Sannox

This one is for Paul Rogers, who was taken too soon,
as were so many in 2020 and 2021.
The Magic Man stood for love, family, positivity,
charity and wonder.
I made a conscious decision not to feature the
pandemic in The Return of King Arthur, but we
will never forget those who were lost.

Acknowledgements

Thank you to my first readers; Anna, Sami,
Ben and my parents.

I could not be more grateful.

Chapter One

Runbridge, England
January 2021

'Get out of my house!' roared Kayleigh Turner.

Unaware she was doing so, she unleashed a wave of power against the masked intruder, who was now standing in front of her at the top of the stairs.

The air between them flexed and crackled, then the man staggered, falling back against the wall. Kayleigh flew forward, digging her nails into his face and throwing her meagre bodyweight into him.

She did not think of her own safety, did not think of anything at all, in fact, acting purely on instinct as her amygdala, in the most primitive part of her brain, took over. One thing mattered above all in that moment, and it was so deeply ingrained in her that she need not even consciously think about it; keeping her son, Simon, safe.

She caught the intruder off guard, and the man grunted as he tried to regain his balance. He gripped Kayleigh's arms and as Simon, hiding beneath his bed, began to scream, the man fell backwards down the stairs, taking Kayleigh with him.

She took a sharp breath and held it as she fell, until her leg struck the wooden stair, accompanied by a sharp cracking sound. Searing pain radiated as she tumbled over the intruder, never letting go of him. Even as the two of them smashed into the hardwood floor of the hallway, Kayleigh could feel his fingers digging into her arms, which would leave deep bruises, as though the ghosts of his hands were still gripping her days after the attack was over.

The intruder landed on her and clawed at her throat, but Kayleigh, shock diminishing her pain, grabbed his wrists and held him away. The intruder was far stronger, and Kayleigh's arms began to shake. She screamed as desperation overcame her, but she kept fighting even as her hope faded.

She did not hear the window smash. Didn't hear the footsteps of people running down the hall.

Two men grabbed hold of her assailant and hauled him off her just as another man appeared from the living room.

'Are you alright?' he asked, extending his hands towards her as though to take her by the shoulders.

Kayleigh looked up into his grey eyes, screamed and pushed him away, feeling the blood trickling along the side of her nose. She tried to stand despite the hot, radiating pain in her leg, but it was no use - it didn't work.

Broken, she thought, as she collapsed back down, eyes wide and murmuring incoherent protestations.

She saw the other two men drag the masked intruder towards her front door and heard sirens for the first time.

'It's alright,' said the man leaning over her, withdrawing his hands, and looking her straight in the eyes, speaking calmly, but firmly. There was something reassuring about him, Kayleigh realised, even if his face bore many faded scars.

'We're friends. Trust me. You're alright,' the man continued. 'Here … '

He reached out to her once more, and Kayleigh took his hand, skin rough to the touch.

'You're alright. We can explain … ' but she no longer heard him speaking, the sounds hushed by a strange, all-pervading sensation as soon as their skin touched.

She was no longer herself, no longer injured, on the cold, hard floor of her hallway.

She knelt by a stream, looking into the water and seeing a reflection; not her own, but familiar. The hair was longer and a beard covered the lower half of his face, but she recognised the grey eyes. It was the man who had stood over her, telling her to trust him and that he was a friend. And she knew his name - Tristan.

Kayleigh watched as his hands broke the reflection, cupping water and bringing it in close to drink.

Now she was no longer by the stream. She was mounted on a horse, riding an empty path in the driving rain, with storm clouds overhead. She heard Tristan's voice telling the horse 'whoa', as another mounted figure rounded the bend, trotting slowly towards them. He sat tall in the saddle, broad-shouldered and armoured.

Lightning flashed, and Kayleigh was no longer on the road. She lay on what felt like a bed, with furs pulled up over her. She felt breath on her neck and ear. A woman whispered. She could feel the words intoxicating her mind. Something was taking hold. Something powerful.

Now she was in a car with several other people, steering as she sped away from a mansion, up the drive and through opening automated gates. She recognised the road through the woods as the car headed towards Runbridge, her hometown. She heard a voice. Arthur's voice.

And a woman's too. Nimuë, she knew. Her body shivered at the thought of her, suddenly knowing she was of her line.

Images, memories, voices, feelings … they all flooded her mind.

Someone shouted from her front garden, breaking the trance.

'We have to go! Now!'

Kayleigh pulled back her hand just as Tristan released it.

He hesitated then ran for the open door. She heard the sound of engines rise and fall as two vehicles drove away.

Kayleigh lay at the bottom of her stairs, breathing hard as a siren grew louder and louder.

'Mummy?' said Simon. She looked up and saw him standing at the top of the stairs, watching her.

'Mummy's okay, but pop back into your room, buddy,' she said, forcing herself to sound happy and relaxed, but her voice still shook. Simon didn't move, except to start sucking his thumb - an old and, she had thought, forgotten habit.

The siren grew louder, and even as she smiled at her son, she pictured the man's grey eyes.

Tristan, Kayleigh thought as she heard a car pull up, the

siren shut off and footsteps on her path.

His name was Tristan.

A pair of police officers, one male and one female, appeared at her front door, both startled at the sight of her lying in front of them. Kayleigh, still reeling from the sudden visions and awash with newly imparted knowledge, knew she had some crucial decisions to make, and quickly.

'Is there anybody else in the house?' asked the female officer as she moved into the hall, eyes on every point of approach. She must have seen Simon at the top of the stairs because she smiled suddenly, but without amusement. A gesture meant to reassure, thought Kayleigh.

'I don't think so,' said Kayleigh. 'It should just be me and Simon.'

'What happened?' asked the female officer. Kayleigh heard another siren getting louder.

Decision time, she thought.

'A man came into the house while I was upstairs with Simon,' she said.

Well, that's a start.

'Where is he now?' asked the officer.

Now or never, thought Kayleigh.

'He's gone,' she said, thinking fast, stalling for time.

'How are you hurt?' asked the female officer. Kayleigh heard the male officer asking Simon to come downstairs.

'He surprised me on the landing, and I pushed him down the stairs, but I fell too. I think my leg is broken.'

Simon appeared beside her and threw his arms around her neck.

And Kayleigh was no longer in the hall of her home.

She was under Simon's bed, seeing through his eyes, hearing herself scream 'get out of my house!' and then the sound of the fall down the stairs. She remembered being in her own womb. Knew which of his toys had meant the most to him. She acquired all of Simon's memory in that instant.

'Mummy!' he said, and once more her trance was broken.

'Mummy's okay, but her leg is sore,' said Kayleigh, smiling up at her son.

The female police officer was frowning.

'You zoned out for a second there,' she said. 'Dave, can you get ambo rolling?'

The male police officer was halfway up the stairs.

'Already done,' he called down, before shouting upstairs: 'Police! Anybody up there?' and disappearing from view.

'What's your name?' asked the female police officer. 'I'm Gemma.'

'Kayleigh.'

'Okay, Kayleigh. You're safe now. An ambulance is on the way. Are you hurt anywhere else?'

Kayleigh shook her head, although she felt bruised all over.

'Okay, just the leg and that little cut on your head,' said Gemma, as if to herself. 'Can you tell me some more about what happened?'

Kayleigh repeated her story.

'We had a call saying that there was screaming coming from your house and just before we got here, a man was dragged out?'

Kayleigh nodded, slowly, realising she had to be careful.

'Some men came in from the street while I was fighting with the guy on the floor. They dragged him off me and out into the garden. Maybe they heard me screaming?'

Gemma nodded.

'So did you recognise the man who came into your house?' she asked.

Kayleigh shook her head.

'He was wearing a mask or a balaclava.'

A paramedic appeared at the door.

'Here we go!' said Gemma. 'We'll talk more in a bit, Kayleigh, okay?'

'Okay,' said Kayleigh as the paramedic greeted her.

The life memories of both Tristan and Simon were still settling in her mind, merging with her existing knowledge.

She was the descendant of Agravain, the armoured man on the horse, and of Nimuë …

Nimuë the enchantress.

It was because of Nimuë that these powers had lain dormant within her, she knew suddenly.

And it was because of her bloodline that the intruder had broken into her house to kill Kayleigh and her son. The Order of Phobos and Deimos, under Malagant the Dread Knight, were hunting Agravain and Nimuë's descendants, and they had kidnapped Arthur's partner, Caitlyn, from her home. Tristan and the others; they had come to help her and to find clues that might lead them to the other woman before she came to harm.

It all seemed insane and yet she knew it was all true.

Kayleigh let the paramedics do their work, trying to work out how to get rid of the police as quickly as possible, without dragging Arthur and his knights into any trouble.

Then she needed time to digest, time to decide whether something really had awakened in her or if she had just hit her head harder than the cut suggested.

⁂

A while later, Arthur, armed with his ex-service Colt revolver, led Bors and Gareth on foot towards Caitlyn's cottage to search for any evidence about her kidnapping.

Ignoring the pain from the old wound in his leg, Arthur strode ahead of his knights, barely able to hold back tears, his cane a blur of movement.

He was troubled by all that had happened since his knights had saved Kayleigh Turner, and was still reeling from the shock of unmasking the intruder as Agravain, his boldest knight, possessed by Malagant, for God knows how long.

What had his knight been forced to endure? It was inconceivable, but disturbing though it was, it was the images of what came *next* that intruded on his thoughts and tormented him; Nimuë, the Lady of the Lake, turning to water and rushing into Agravain's mouth and nose, so that she could hold the malevolent spirit within her husband. Agravain, down on his knees, telling him, 'Do it', as Arthur stood over him, Excalibur in hand, unable to bear the thought of doing what he must.

He had beheaded Agravain with one stroke of his sword,

ridding the world of Malagant, but killing Nimuë as well.

He could not unsee the water, rushing from the neck of Agravain's decapitated body and pooling around Arthur's feet, soaking into the floorboards.

He had just stopped walking, almost overcome with sorrow and guilt, when his mobile phone began to ring, bringing him back into the moment. Hoping it was Caitlyn, his heart leapt, but disappointment set in when he heard Tristan, the most loyal of his knights, on the other end of the line.

'Kay just spoke with Mark Hopkins,' said Tristan, referring to the Detective Chief Inspector at Runbridge Police Station. 'Officers are on scene, but Kayleigh Turner isn't giving them much detail. Kay explained that this is one of *those* bits of business. Hopkins will call his people off, as long as we keep him updated.'

'And what of Caitlyn's disappearance?' said Arthur, his eyes fixed ahead on the path.

'He's got people on it, discreetly, but nothing has come up so far,' said Tristan. 'I'm going to pay visits to the rest of Agravain and Nimuë's descendants. We know they were targets for the Order, and it's the only way I can think of to scoop up one of Malagant's followers. Hektor Security should have people surveilling each address, but considering what happened to those in Runbridge … '

'Who's going with you?' asked Arthur.

'If I can get hold of one of them, I'll get them to talk,' said Tristan. 'I'll call when I can, sir.'

'Tristan, who's … ' started Arthur, but the line went dead.

Tristan was going alone, and Arthur supposed he should have expected it. Tristan and Agravain had been close friends until the latter had made protecting London *his* business after the Great Fire of London. A rift had opened up between them thanks to Malagant's interference. All these years, Tristan had been furious with Agravain for abandoning Arthur and the knights, and now it had transpired that he had been possessed by the Dread Knight all along. Arthur knew Tristan felt he had maligned Agravain and that his knight would protect Agravain and Nimuë's descendants from the Order at any cost.

Chapter Two

Tintagel, Cornwall
5th Century

'Insidious,' said Morgana, as she paused to examine a cluster of plants; they had green leaves and tiny, deceptively pretty, white flowers.

'My lady?' asked the soldier who accompanied King Arthur's half-sister as they strolled outside Tintagel's walls.

'Poison Hemlock,' said the sorceress. 'Mistake it for one of its innocent cousins, and one will feel no ill effect after ingestion, perhaps even for hours, and then … '

She smiled.

The soldier looked down as she turned to meet his gaze with her white, pupilless eyes, matched by her colourless hair. He muttered something inaudible.

'Will you worry when you dine?' she laughed and shoved him gently. 'What cause would I have to slip Hemlock into your bowl, Treave?'

'I would not presume to tell you your business, my lady,' said Treave. 'I'm sure you'd have your reasons.'

'You say all the right things, Treave,' said Morgana, and she shivered in the chill air, which had taken hold in the dusk, rounding off a warm day. 'Time to ready myself to dine at this Cornish king's table. I must impress him if he is to fear Mordred and to avoid more drastic measures.'

'I have no doubt that you will, my lady,' said Treave, as he escorted Morgana around the earthworks and back inside Tintagel.

―――

A merry hall, but with none of the chivalrous affections of Arthur's court, thought Morgana once the evening feast was under way. The building itself was no less grand, but the atmosphere was collegial, the folk rugged and devoid of finery.

The sorceress looked up the table towards King Mark of Cornwall, Lord of Tintagel, whose eyes were red and streaming with tears of laughter as he shared a joke with a gaggle of lords who had, briefly, solemnly supplicated before him on various matters. The formal business done, they were back to being boys at play, it seemed. She would not allow such behaviour from Mordred, Morgana decided; it did not become a king.

This Mark is a barbarian lording over barbarians, she thought, *albeit a jovial one.*

Not all of those present were making merry and as deep in their cups as the king. A tall youth, dark-haired, with a strong jaw and grey eyes, all clad for war, paced the length of the hall, keeping close to the wall and seeming to stare at each member of the assembled gathering in turn, scrutinising them.

Morgana watched him and reached out to the young man with her mind. As if feeling her gaze upon him, he turned and their eyes met for a moment, both caught in a daydream.

The young man frowned momentarily then bowed his head. Morgana returned the gesture.

'Is your meal not to your liking, Lady Morgana?' King Mark's voice broke her trance, but she did not startle easily.

She looked down at her plate, upon which lay her mostly untouched venison, feigned a smile and directed it towards the king.

'On the contrary, King Mark, the quality of your fare is as fine as your hall,' said Morgana.

'And yet you do not eat,' said Mark. 'Perhaps Arthur has spoiled his sister?'

Morgana laughed.

'Arthur's court was all finery and no substance.

You will not find it so in my son's halls, but regardless, I am simply in no hurry to finish my meal. I am enjoying your company, King Mark,' she said.

'I am truly possessed of considerable powers if I have entertained you before we have even conversed,' laughed Mark.

'True enough. You have been quite neglectful,' Morgana smiled and picked up her knife, making a show of turning her full attention to her plate.

'I shall remedy that!' said Mark, raising his goblet to her.

'That is well,' said Morgana. 'My son seeks friendship, and we have much to discuss.'

'No doubt,' said the youth who had been pacing the room. He had moved to stand before the high table, hands clasped behind his back. 'Mordred will need Cornwall's support at his back if he is to press into King Arthur's territory. Do not think us such simple folk that we cannot guess your son's intentions in sending you before our king. Cornwall has no quarrel with your brother, Lady Morgana. Do not seek to test our loyalty to him. We will not be divided.'

Morgana felt her cheeks redden as the youth spoke. She searched for a reply, but King Mark stood and interceded before she could respond.

'Come now, Tristan, let us not be discourteous. I will hear what the lady has to say and find out what Mordred would ask of me, even if I cannot give it. For now, take up a goblet, nephew, and drink to my happiness. Have I not waited over long to find a queen?'

Morgana set down her fork and reached for her own goblet, anticipating a toast to the king's happiness with his soon-to-be wife, who waited across the sea.

I pity her, thought Morgana, as she stared at the serious youth, whom King Mark had called Tristan. *She will be the overthrown queen of a fallen people before the year is out.*

~~~

'King Mark seems in no hurry to honour his word, my lady,' said Treave, nearly an hour after the king's promise to remedy his lack of conversation with Morgana.

'No, indeed, and I have had my fill of this place,' she said, standing as Treave pulled back her chair. She looked to see if the king would notice her departure, but he had abandoned his seat and was down among his men, singing and drinking.

Morgana slipped out of the hall and into the sea air.

She looked out over the moonlit waves from the cliff tops and sighed.

'Are you defeated?' said a man's voice.

Morgana looked back over her shoulder and saw the youth, Tristan, leaning back against the hall.

'Defeated?' asked Morgana.

'By the relentless cheer, or perhaps in vying for my uncle's attention. The latter is a lost cause tonight, I fear. And the former has defeated me as well. I could bear it no longer,' he smiled.

Morgana made no reply but walked towards Tristan. She saw him push back off the wall to stand straight as she approached.

'King Mark appreciates life, I can see that, but I do wonder how he holds on to all he has won while acting so frivolously, surrounded by those who covet his lands,' said Morgana.

'He is more than he seems tonight, I assure you. A great man, loved by his people no less than Arthur's love their king. And he has loyal men at his side,' said Tristan.

'Such as you?' Morgana smiled.

'Such as I,' said Tristan.

Morgana nodded, but said nothing, looking deep into his eyes, peering inside his soul. Tasting it. Tristan blinked, and she laughed.

'You are loyal, I have no doubt,' she said. 'I can see the truth behind your words.'

Tristan did not reply and folded his arms.

'I also see that you fear me, young man,' said Morgana. 'Why?'

Still he did not reply.

'No matter, I can guess,' said Morgana.

Merlin, she thought.

Tristan coughed.

'I will not lie to you, Lady Morgana. You are infamous in these parts. There are rumours that you wish to depose Arthur and place your son on his throne,' said Tristan. 'That Arthur is blind to your plots. *I* am not.'

'You sound like Merlin,' said Treave, stepping up beside Morgana. 'The old man has a wicked tongue. He speaks nothing but falsehoods. I caution you not to repeat them again lest I find cause to defend my mistress's honour, sir.'

Tristan stood all the straighter, but Morgana stepped between them.

'Thank you, Treave,' she said, with her back to him, her eyes fixed on Tristan, reading his reaction.

'Tell me, Tristan, how would King Mark respond if Mordred was to press his claim?' asked Morgana. 'If Mordred was to, say, offer the hand of friendship and yield lands along our border?'

Tristan frowned.

'King Mark and King Arthur are brothers-in-arms. No plot will sunder them, I assure you,' said Tristan.

'And would Tristan consider such an offer, even if the king would not?' said Morgana.

'That is not my role, lady,' said Tristan.

'What is your role then?' she countered.

'To protect King Mark. To follow his commands,' Tristan replied, looking away, unnerved by the appearance of her white eyes, she guessed.

'And to advise?' Morgana ventured.

'If called upon for my thoughts, perhaps,' said Tristan.

'What would it take, then, for Tristan to advise his king to accept Mordred's friendship?' asked Morgana.

Tristan laughed.

'The rumours are true about you, Lady Morgana.'

'You have not answered,' she said.

'What would it take for me to advise my uncle to accept Mordred as a friend? Why, nothing short of my belief that it was for the best and then only if it did not break faith with Arthur. I, unlike some, prize love and loyalty,' said Tristan.

'Not position or lands, wealth or influence?' asked Morgana, already knowing the answer, and beginning to smile. She saw Tristan's frown intensify in the second before he noticed.

'You toy with me,' he said, sighing, and she grinned.

'Well, you had certain expectations, and I had to play the part!' said Morgana.

Tristan grunted and once more leant back against the hall.

He feels at ease once more, thought Morgana. She decided upon her course.

'What mother would not see her son elevated? Of course I wish Mordred to take the throne, but Arthur will die in the fullness of time without my intervention. If I seek friendship in Cornwall, let it be for Arthur and for Arthur's heir as well. Merlin dislikes me and sullies my name, but he, as always, has his own motives. They are not always honourable, Tristan. Not always grounded in loyalty, difficult as it may be for one such as yourself to understand. Consider Arthur's conception; Merlin cast an illusion on King Uther so that he appeared to be Gorlois, *my* father, so that he could impregnate my mother, Igraine. A lady deceived in the foulest manner so that Uther could have his way with her and so Merlin could have his boy who would be king. My mother would not speak fondly of the wizard, Tristan. Do not take him at his word,' said Morgana, her white eyes like moons in the dark.

Tristan opened his mouth but made no reply, so Morgana continued.

'Do not forget that I am a daughter of Cornwall, young Tristan. Family, love, friendship and loyalty are not as simple as your limited experience suggests,' she concluded, turning her back on the young warrior and walking away, Treave at her side.

'Cornwall will not turn on Arthur,' her man muttered.

'Not willingly,' said Morgana, 'but let us learn from the Hemlock.'

―⁂―

Once all had eaten their fill and drank until it seemed there must be no ale left in Cornwall, Tintagel gradually fell silent, save for the snoring of those slumped over the tables or in their beds, and for the crashing waves all around.

Morgana Le Fay did not sleep.

She crept silently through King Mark's hall, her mind preceding her, peering through closed doors and around corners before she made the turn herself. Finally, she found what she was looking for. The door before her, a remnant of the Romans' time at Tintagel, was locked, but she gestured with a milk-white hand and muttered arcane words. The lock snapped open and, holding her breath, Morgana entered the chamber beyond.

Tristan, nephew of King Mark, lay sleeping in bed.

Morgana looked back over her shoulder, but

saw no one. She padded across the reed mats on the balls of her feet and stood beside the sleeping youth.

Morgana reached out and touched his eyelids with the tips of her thumb and forefinger. Tristan stirred, but she said a single word in an ancient tongue, and he settled once more.

Morgana began a chant, barely above a whisper in his ear, repeating the same words as the minutes passed. She no longer concerned herself with who might find her.

The sorceress laid a curse upon him.

'You will lose yourself in your love for others. You will fall freely, hard and fast, without restraint, devoid of caution. You will bare your heart, heedless of risk; become a champion of love and loyalty. You will love, Tristan - love your king, your family, your friends and your lovers. You will *love* until you are a slave to it,' said Morgana, and she drew back her hand.

Tristan rolled over, and Morgana shrank back a step, but he did not wake.

She stumbled as she approached the door, but steadied herself against the wall and did not wake him. Dizziness almost felled her several times as she made her way back to her own room, but she found it at last.

No need to poison any man hereabouts, she thought in the last moments before sleep overpowered her, weary as she was, *when a man can become a poison.*

Morgana slept and, outside, the poison Hemlock swayed in the wind.

Chapter Three

2021

Tristan ended the call with Arthur and set his mobile phone down on his bedside table. He had no intention of taking a device that could be linked to him on this expedition. Blood might be spilled.

The knight walked down the hallway and followed the sound of voices to a room where the door stood ajar. Kay sat at a computer, with Dagonet leaning on the back of his chair while they discussed police reports.

'Anything?' Tristan interrupted.

Kay turned in his chair, revealing his prosthetic leg.

'Apart from the initial calls about Turner's house, nothing of use,' he said.

Tristan nodded.

'I'm heading into Newtonville to meet Jack Thompson from Hektor. I'll let you know what number I'm on. Burners only now,' he said.

'I'll come with you,' said Dagonet, but Tristan shook his head and held up his hand, stopping his brother knight in his tracks.

'No, I'll be fine with Jack. Arthur wanted you and Kay here.'

He saw Dagonet frown.

'I'll be fine,' Tristan reiterated. 'But keep looking through reports, ANPR and work the phones. I'll get Hektor Security deployed.'

'Be careful, Tristan,' said Kay.

'Aren't I always?' said Tristan.

Dagonet laughed. 'Of course!'

Tristan smiled, threw the other knights a mock salute and started off down the hall, jogging down the stairs and making his way to the kitchen at the rear of the house.

Tristan ran out into the grounds of Arthur's house, heading towards the high wall that backed on to the woods. There, he unlocked a gate and, securing it behind him, slipped out through the trees, moving quickly, but stealthily, towards a hidden place.

A holloway cut through the wood, a sunken lane sloping down through the forest towards what had once been mediaeval villages. Where once cattle had been driven up to the common land that had covered the area before the trees, Tristan skulked out of view from the ground above. He knew the way well, and it was not long before he reached his destination. Tristan hauled a fallen log to one side and unlocked the disguised trap door beneath. He looked about him and pulled open the hatch before climbing down the ladder into the small cavern below, not more than a few metres in diameter.

It was a private place, known only to Tristan, dug by him

in the spirit of his former career as a Scallywagger during World War Two; a member of a secret Home Guard Auxiliary Unit, who were to be deployed as a British resistance unit in the event that the Nazis successfully invaded Britain. The bunker was a place to return to only to perform maintenance and for when things went badly wrong.

And things have, thought Tristan. Malagant had not only attacked a woman, but killed two of the Hektor Security men who had been stationed in an observation van outside her house. Tristan had deposited their bodies at the designated collection point, before returning to the mansion. There he had been told of Agravain's demise and of how his brother knight had been possessed by the Dread Knight throughout all the years which Tristan had harboured bitterness and resentment for his old friend, believing him a traitor for abandoning Arthur. And for abandoning him too, Tristan supposed.

I can never make amends. Never apologise, thought Tristan as he searched the floor for yet another, smaller hiding place. *All that time, he needed my help.*

He struggled for a while, but then found what he was looking for, and after pulling up a second, smaller trap door, Tristan fetched a plastic box from the hole in the ground.

Inside was a holdall, and, despite having already done so on a regular basis, he unzipped it and double-checked the contents. Everything was there.

Two simple mobile phones with a selection of pre-paid SIM cards.

A Third Pattern Fairburn-Sykes Commando knife,

black-bladed with a blacked zinc, cast handle.

Glock 17 L131A handgun in a shoulder holster with five boxes of 9x19mm Parabellum cartridges.

Heckler & Koch MP5K L80A1, an easily concealable submachine pistol.

Spare magazines for each weapon.

Balaclava.

Baseball cap.

Pair of leather gloves, along with face masks and several pairs of black nitrile gloves.

Hoodie.

Torch.

Ration packs.

First aid kit.

Bundle of cash, mixed notes, obtained over the years in change through cash transactions and sales.

Tristan disassembled and cleaned the firearms with a kit also hidden within, before putting them back together.

He strapped the Commando knife in a sheath to his belt and, removing his jacket, put on the shoulder holster. He placed the MP5K back in the holdall.

Tristan stood, put on the hoodie and baseball cap then slung the holdall over his shoulder before climbing back up to the holloway, where he carefully concealed the trap door and shifted the log back into position.

He was ready.

Tristan set off down the sunken lane towards the nearest village, where he had hired a lock-up, in which he had stowed a car, bought for cash, using a false identity. As he did so, he pulled a folded piece of paper from his pocket and surveyed the list of names, the remaining descendants of Agravain. Tristan made his choice and put the paper back in his pocket. He quickened his pace to a jog. There was no more time to waste. He'd call Hektor Security on the way.

~

From the top of the bank, a figure watched Tristan disappearing down the sunken track. It stood, arms folded across its chest, its antlers rivalling those of a great stag, long dark braids hanging down over its chest and back.

'Her reach is long, even in death,' said the figure to nobody at all. A robin alighted upon his antlers.

~

The vehicle, which Caitlyn presumed to be a van, stopped and somebody turned off the engine.

Muttering voices. Unfamiliar and incomprehensible.

All Caitlyn could see was dark material, bound tightly around her eyes. She had been gagged and lay trussed up with her hands behind her back, on her left side. She could feel cold metal against her arm and shoulder through the thin material of her blouse. She was breathing fast through her nose, but Caitlyn worked as a doctor in Accident & Emergency so she was used to being under pressure and coping with increased levels of adrenaline.

Breathe slowly, she told herself. *One in … one out … one in … one out …*

Her pulse was still racing, her heart palpitating on

occasion, but she felt just a little calmer and was able to concentrate on her predicament.

She heard the voices again and, listening carefully, she tried to hear what they were saying and to see if she recognised them as those of the two men and a woman who had snatched her from Hunter's Cottage.

God, please tell me Samson's alright, she thought, though she was partly reassured by the memory of continued barking as she had been loaded into the vehicle.

With the engine off and the vehicle no longer moving, Caitlyn could hear a little better, but picked up only snatches of words.

Once, she thought she heard a man say 'Arthur'.

What's this got to do with him?

Caitlyn shifted to relieve the pressure on her left side.

The voices started up again, and this time Caitlyn recognised a degree of panic in the tone. Were they squabbling? What might that suggest?

Something's gone wrong, she thought, *but what?*

Caitlyn could feel panic rising in her once more, but she refused to let it overwhelm her, and she lay still, not making a sound.

Right, Doctor, she thought to herself, *let's see if that Oxford education has any use in the real world. Symptoms. Testing. Differential diagnosis. Further tests. Diagnosis. Prognosis without treatment. Possible treatments and likely prognosis for each. What else is there to do with your time?*

Well, let's start with taking a history. Any history of being dragged out of the house and into vans? No. So this is unprecedented. Any grievances with anybody? No.

Symptoms?

Dragged out of the house by two strange men and a woman.

Restrained, but not assaulted, physically or sexually, at least not yet.

No injuries.

Hands tied tightly. Legs bound together. Blindfolded and gagged.

Put into a vehicle and taken away from the house, but not to another location. The van has stopped, but they aren't getting out.

Tense, bickering kidnappers.

And they mentioned Arthur.

Caitlyn listened intently for a while. Low voices, but also the sound of cars nearby, but not right outside.

She counted the seconds between cars passing by the rise and fall of engine noise. Vehicles were passing almost constantly, but the van didn't rock at all, nothing was rushing by.

Parked just off a main road, but impossible to say where.

So, no history of similar incidents and no apparent motives relating to me specifically, but they mentioned Arthur, so perhaps this is to do with him and this isn't something that personally involves me, Caitlyn surmised. *I'm the girlfriend of a wealthy man. I haven't been wounded or sexually abused, yet. So, perhaps, they don't intend to harm me.*

Provisional diagnosis then? Kidnapped so they can extort Arthur. They want him to pay a ransom.

Prognosis?

Here, Caitlyn's lack of experience let her down. She'd seen a lot of films, watched the news and read books, but she had no idea of the ratios when it came to how many hostages were released if ransoms were or were not paid. How many kidnappers just asked for more and more money before finally killing their victim? Caitlyn had no idea.

Prognosis uncertain. Impossible to say whether she could expect complete recovery, life-changing injury or whether her situation was terminal. And there were factors beyond both the control of her and her kidnappers. Would Arthur pay? Would he involve the police?

If that diagnosis is correct, best to assume the worst. They would kill her.

Okay, possible treatments, thought Caitlyn. *Perhaps if my condition is terminal, I can delay death by complying, resisting, befriending or becoming complicit? But they're probably not stupid*, she thought. *Who knows how they will react?*

One possible diagnosis. Differential diagnosis?

They're tense, which is probably to be expected, but why are they arguing? And why have they parked up? Something may have gone wrong, but what? Too many possibilities to know, but either way, it may lead to a diagnosis of a botched kidnapping with intent to extort Arthur. Possibly more serious than the first scenario, especially if they are panicking and become desperate.

What else could this be?

Caitlyn tried to think outside the box.

Differential diagnosis. Arthur is behind the kidnapping?

She dismissed that immediately. It did not fit with their life together. There was no possible motivation.

Differential diagnosis. Kidnapped with the intent to harm me for some unknown reason. To hurt Arthur?

Possible, but they hadn't hurt her so far. Perhaps they would though, at a time and place of their choosing.

Insufficient data for a definitive diagnosis, decided Caitlyn. Time to order tests and investigate.

She paused for a moment. Did she really want to take the risk of annoying them or making herself seem like trouble? What choice did she have? If the prognosis of doing nothing was potentially fatal, she needed to take action and fast.

Caitlyn began to gradually reposition herself, shuffling and sliding, and once knocking her head against the wall or the door of the van. She ended up on her back, parallel with what she assumed was the wall of the van, given where the voices were coming from. She shunted feet first towards the sound of the voices until her slippered feet touched another wall, hopefully one between her and the cab of the van.

She hesitated, breathing hard, wondering if she could really do what she was planning.

Caitlyn drew up her knees and kicked the wall of the van hard; one, two, three, four times, stopping only because she heard a voice, the muffled sound of a door opening and felt the van rock beneath her.

Test ordered, she thought. *Stay cool. It's okay.*

The door to the back of the van opened, light visible through her blindfold.

Silence.

Chapter Four

Tintagel, Cornwall
5th Century

'May God watch over your voyage, nephew,' said King Mark, grasping Tristan's hand in both of his. 'Return safely with my bride, and I will be ever in your debt.'

The two men stood alone upon the cliffs of Tintagel, watching as the final preparations were made aboard the ship that would carry Tristan to Ireland; clinker-built, with a single, dyed green sail, bearing the rampant golden lion that was Tristan's symbol.

He looked into his uncle's eyes, as he had a thousand times before, and felt a swell of emotion.

Perhaps it is the gravity of the task he has set me, thought Tristan; *the trust he is bestowing upon me.*

'I will do all in my power, Uncle,' said Tristan, not breaking eye contact to bow his head as once he might have done. He saw Mark narrow his eyes momentarily as the king smiled.

'I know it. I have chosen well,' said the king.

⁕

'About time! I thought your fear of the sea had got the better of you,' said a slightly older, sharp-featured man as he hauled Tristan aboard, his long blond hair tied back into a ponytail.

'Hold your tongue, Lucan,' Tristan laughed, clapping his friend on the shoulder. 'I wager you'll spend the voyage emptying your stomach while I look on and laugh.'

'We shall see who is the better man,' said Lucan. 'And do not forget I have made this journey before.'

'Are we ready to set sail?' asked Tristan.

Lucan nodded.

'The wind is as favourable as we can hope. Now's the time,' said Lucan, growing serious.

Tristan turned his back on the great rock of Tintagel and looked out across the grey expanse of the sea, its horizon blurred by piles of grey clouds.

Tristan shivered. He was, in truth, fearful of the voyage. He had prayed for their success that morning, but when he looked out at the water, he wondered if he would not be better off invoking the name of some abandoned sea god, maybe Neptune or Lir, or perhaps he should call out for the aid of a bucca, a sea spirit, so that it might drive away storms.

'Tristan?' said Lucan.

'I am afraid, Lucan,' said Tristan in a whisper, so that the crew could not hear.

'You'd be a fool if you weren't, brother, with nothing but planks between us and the depths, but we'll pull through together, you'll see. We'll bring the princess home safely,' said Lucan.

The men hauled on their oars, driving the ship out into open waters, and Tristan looked back at Tintagel, despite his determination not to do so, wishing to look to the future without succumbing to his longing for the shore behind them. He soon saw the cause of his weakness, though he knew it not. Standing beside the imposing King Mark was Lady Morgana Le Fay, with her white hair plaited over her shoulders. Tristan could feel her white eyes upon him, and he shuddered.

He turned his gaze on his uncle, and once more his determination renewed. He owed Mark much, and he would complete his task for love of his mother's brother, whom he looked upon, privately, as his father. Tristan took a deep breath, raised one hand in farewell and then turned his back on Tintagel, resolving not to turn again.

'To Ireland,' said Tristan.

'God willing,' said Lucan. Tristan looked at his friend, frowning, but after a moment, both men grinned. And the anticipation of adventure stirred Tristan's heart.

※

The first days at sea passed without incident, though the weather worsened, forcing them to head farther west than planned. As the wind picked up, the sail filled, and Tristan clung to the mast, showered with sea spray, uttering whispered prayers until he caught Lucan, his hair soaked, pointing at him and grinning. Tristan stood as straight as he was able, but mere seconds later, he ran for the side and hurled his breakfast into the water below, the laughter of the crew only subsiding when he turned back to them, raising an eyebrow in challenge. They returned to their duties, grins fading to smiles.

'Bastards,' muttered Tristan, wiping his mouth on his sleeve, but he couldn't blame them. He'd have laughed in their place.

'Oh, every one of them,' said Lucan. 'I don't like the look of those clouds.'

'Nor I,' said Tristan, before once more running to the side while Lucan looked on, laughing.

※

The brothers-in-arms may have harboured fears during the journey, and the winds *did* harry their little ship, but they eventually sighted the coast of Munster, and Tristan found his waning hopes restored.

As they drew close to the shore, Tristan spied a company gathering beyond the tide wrack, armed warriors encircling three figures.

'Is it …?' asked Tristan.

'Aye, the King of Munster,' said Lucan, 'his queen and … '

'His daughter,' said Tristan, his eyes fixed on the slender figure standing beside her mother, but as tall as her father.

'I bid you welcome, nephew of Mark,' said the King of Munster, and Tristan, kneeling before him, lifted his gaze to meet the older man's eyes. He rose and bowed his head.

'I am honoured to set foot on your shore for the first time, my lord,' said Tristan. 'King Mark sends his greetings to you, your queen and your daughter. He wishes you joy of the peace between us, and gives his word that his bride will know nothing but happiness in her new home.'

'I will hold him to it,' said the queen, and she wrapped an arm around her daughter's shoulders before leading her forward.

'King Mark's bride she may be, but she was our daughter first, and she will remain so,' said the king. 'Tristan, I commit Isolde to your safekeeping. It is with a heavy heart Ireland bids her farewell, but may her parting strengthen the bond between Munster and Cornwall. Let her children lay claim to both our countries when my time is done.'

Tristan bowed his head once more to the king and moved to stand before Isolde, a statuesque woman a few years older than himself, but still younger than Mark, her long hair braided, and a torc of gold about her neck. Her expression was grim and for a moment, Tristan was lost for words. Isolde was not what he had expected. He was attracted to her, sure enough, but his heart stirred at the bidding of Morgana's curse.

Eventually, he took her hand and kissed it. He felt his spine tingle.

'I am honoured to escort you across the waves to Cornwall on behalf of my uncle. He is a good man, and a just king, and he awaits you upon the rock of Tintagel.'

She nodded, slowly.

'May the journey be swift,' she said without feeling.

The king stepped forward.

'Your men must be tired,' he said, addressing

both Lucan and Tristan. 'You will return with me to my hall, for I desire my daughter to spend one more night under my roof before she is lost to us.' At this, he took the queen's hand.

'We will feast you,' she said, 'and see that you have all you need for the return journey.'

'I am grateful,' said Tristan, smiling, but as the king, queen and princess turned their backs, he took a moment to cast his eye over the Irish warriors, evaluating the quality of their armour and in what manner they were armed.

Tristan sat at the high table during the feast, the Princess Isolde beside him. He ate in silence for the most part, thankful that Lucan was holding the king and queen's attention, regaling them with stories of King Mark and of the lands their daughter would soon rule over beside him.

Tristan looked up from time to time, and he could not help but notice the serious expressions on both the queen and the princess's faces. The queen feigned a smile whenever it was required, telegraphed by Lucan's inability to stifle a grin whenever he found some point in his story amusing or impressive, but Isolde would only look down at her barely touched food.

She is as taciturn as I, thought Tristan, *but who can blame her, sent away from all she knows, taken overseas by strange men, to wed a strange king in a land she does not know? No doubt my appetite would suffer if I were in her place.*

His sympathy for Isolde spurred Tristan to rally. He sat up, cleared his throat and tried to think of something to say that might comfort the girl, but instead found he was sitting mute, staring at her. She turned and caught him when his mouth had just opened to speak words he had yet to find, looking like a dead fish.

Isolde raised an eyebrow and, Tristan thought, looked slightly affronted.

She's mistaken my intentions, he thought. *Say something, for God's sake. Offer her succour.*

'My lady,' he started, but faltered when her eyes met his. He felt a shiver run through him, not entirely unpleasantly.

She raised both eyebrows in expectation, but when he said nothing more, her mouth opened a little, and she gave a little shake of her head as if to say, 'Well?'

Tristan coughed.

'My lady,' he said again.

You fool, thought Tristan.

'I think we have established that you consider me your lady,' said Isolde, 'but is there more?'

She was smiling. A little victory, even if it was entirely unplanned.

Tristan rallied once more and coughed.

'Not *my* lady, my lady,' he said, and sighed, his shoulders dropping. Isolde laughed.

'Ah, one step forward, one step back. I am not your lady, but I am your lady, it seems? You may as well have never spoken at all,' she said, but not unkindly.

'You looked unhappy,' said Tristan, his eyes fixed on the remains of his meal, but looking up to discern her reaction. She nodded slowly, a reluctant admission in the gesture.

He continued.

'I wanted to offer words of comfort, but what is there to say?' said Tristan.

Isolde smiled at him then smiled at a passing warrior who acknowledged her as he went by.

'Have no fear of giving offence, my lady,' said Tristan, and Isolde snorted quietly as he once more addressed her by title. She rounded on him.

'Do not fear offending the man who I must trust to carry me safely over the sea, away from my kind and all that I know? Someone in whom I must place all of my trust, and who has the ear of the man I must marry? I should not fear offending that man?' she asked.

'Not I,' said Tristan. 'I know what it is to lose one's parents and be taken from one's home, though my father and mother are dead, not over the sea. And as for King Mark? He will hear no report of your words to me. I know the truth of it already, if I guess well. Indeed, my lady, any with a heart could imagine how you must surely be feeling at this moment, on the last night in your father's hall.'

Isolde snorted once more.

'I am filled with sorrow at the thought of tomorrow's parting, and I do not relish being joined with an older man whom I have never met and who I may never love,' she admitted.

'The sorrow will fade with time, my lady,' replied Tristan, 'and you will not be alone in this adventure. I will be at your side, and I hope you will call me friend before we set foot in Cornwall.'

Her face softened, and she looked him in the eye.

'I hope that too,' she said, 'but I would not be entirely alone, in any case. I travel with my handmaidens. I already call them friends.'

'Then all is not lost,' said Tristan, thinking of his own lonely journey to King Mark's court when he was a boy.

'Tell me of King Mark,' said Isolde.

Tristan could not suppress a smile at the thought of his uncle.

'A kinder, bolder husband you could not wish for, my lady, and though I cannot speak to the fairness of his countenance as though I were a maid, I think he is not ugly,' he said.

'Ah, not ugly,' said Isolde laughing. 'That is something, at the least!'

Tristan felt heat in his cheeks, but Isolde waved his embarrassment away.

'It is the least of my concerns,' she said, 'though not unimportant. And who can tell what another might consider handsome or beautiful?'

Looking into Isolde's eyes, now that her guard was dropped, Tristan felt his heart reach out to the Irish girl. He could not tell what she might think of Mark, but for the first time, considering her face and drawn in by her eyes, he knew what he considered beautiful.

And fear rose in him.

Chapter Five

2021

Arthur, Bors and Gareth rounded the curve in the path that led through the woodland to Hunter's Cottage and found Caitlyn's home as they had left it.

Arthur's desire to turn the place over looking for clues had cooled a little since his conversation with Tristan, and rather than charge up the gate, he halted the others there.

'I'll take a look around the surrounding area,' said Bors, but Arthur grabbed him by the shoulder as he turned away. His knight looked back at him, and Arthur shook his head.

'Cordon Investigations are bringing a dog as well as the CSI team. We don't want to mess up the track, if there is one,' he said, and Bors nodded three times, deliberately, blowing air through pursed lips as if saying, 'yes … close one.'

Bors leant back against the gatepost while Gareth stood, hands clasped in front of him like a bodyguard or a bouncer, Arthur thought, as he paced a small circle outside the house. His feet were the only sound apart from birdsong, the creaking of swaying trees all around and the occasional, distant sound of traffic.

An unpleasant coldness washed through Arthur as he thought of all that could follow if they did not locate Caitlyn quickly. Police. Press. Investigation and exposure?

Exposure, thought Arthur, perhaps not, in terms of the greater scheme of things, but to Caitlyn? Could he avoid telling her the truth any longer and how on Earth would she respond to discovering her boyfriend was King Arthur? She'd think he was insane, surely. They could not continue.

But it was the least of his concerns at that moment, even if he felt frantic at the mere thought of losing her. He had to find her, had to get her home safely.

Two Cordon Investigations vehicles pulled up, a van and a 4x4 from which Arthur saw a Cordon dog-handler emerge. She disappeared behind it for a moment, and when she returned, she was preceded by a very eager brown and white spaniel, tugging at a long lead.

Arthur told the woman all he knew and where they had walked. The dog-handler frowned disapprovingly as if to say 'how dare you walk the hallowed ground before me? Are you an idiot?' before setting her dog to work, beginning from the front door of Hunter's Cottage.

Arthur and the knights regrouped by the CSI van, watching as the investigators pulled on boot covers, paper suits, masks and gloves. The lead technician pulled out a PDA, and Bors briefed him.

The area around Hunter's Cottage was busy as it had never been before, but Arthur stood alone and silently watched while Gareth pointed out some tyre tracks on the path, possibly her kidnappers, possibly Arthur's own vehicle when they had first attended and found Caitlyn gone.

⁓⁂⁓

The dog-handler drove away first, and the CSI technicians, having found little of use, were packing up when a contractor arrived to repair the door of the cottage.

How long before the hospital raises the alarm? Arthur wondered. *How long before her parents wonder where she is? Did she have plans with friends?*

He felt helpless, as he so often had since the First World War. His leg ached more than usual after his pounding walk from the mansion, and it acted as a reminder of his physical limitations and the psychological problems that had emerged immediately after sustaining the injury at the Battle of the Somme. The flashbacks had never gone away. Sometimes, unexpectedly, he would return to that battlefield, and come back to his senses sweating and breathing hard, his pulse racing. He had not been able to fight in the Second World War, and since then, hobbling about with a cane, he had often wondered if he had lost all of his value.

King Arthur, the most famous of the Britons, and what was he in 2021? A suit with a dwindling company of loyal servants? Tristan was out hunting down the Order. The other knights were contributing, but him, their valiant leader?

He missed Merlin deeply at that moment. The old man would be able to set him straight, but he was gone, along with so many of the knights.

Arthur told Gareth and Bors to stay put until the contractor was finished and to get out of sight, maintaining a watch over the cottage until they heard otherwise. They objected when he set off alone, but he stared them down, and their ancient subservience facilitated his escape.

They are better men than I, he thought, unhappily.

Arthur's phone rang, and he retrieved it from the inside pocket of his coat.

'Hello?' he said.

'Arthur?' A woman's voice on the line. Quiet. Uncertain. Strained.

'Who is this?' said Arthur, trying to keep his tone level. 'Caitlyn?'

'Er, no. Sorry,' said the woman.

Arthur said nothing.

'Is that Arthur? Arthur … Grimwood?' said the woman, with an upward inflection.

Definitely not Caitlyn, Arthur realised. Perhaps one of the Order? One of Malagant's people, maybe?

'Grimwood speaking. Who is this?' he demanded, forcing himself to sound calm.

The woman didn't reply.

Arthur looked at the phone screen and confirmed that no number had been displayed.

He returned it to his ear, looking all around him, and seeing nothing as he left the cover of the trees and crossed the road to his mansion.

'This is Arthur Grimwood,' he confirmed. 'Who's speaking? How can I help?'

Another pause, but then …

'I can't believe I'm even making this call,' said the woman, sighing.

Arthur considered telling her he was hanging up, but decided to give her the benefit of the doubt.

'You came to my house today,' said the woman, and suddenly Arthur realised who had called him. His mouth dropped open, unsure what he should say and unable to guess how she had got his name, let alone how she had obtained his phone number. Had the Order returned after he and his knights had dragged Agravain and Malagant away?

'Kayleigh Turner?' asked Arthur.

A relieved sigh on the line was the only response. What could she want? Was this a sign of good or ill fortune, Arthur wondered.

'I … don't understand what's happening to me,' said Kayleigh. 'I didn't understand any of it to begin with, but now I know too much.'

A sneaking suspicion began to form in Arthur's mind.

'Where are you, Kayleigh?' he asked.

'I'm at the hospital. Waiting. My leg is broken,' she said.

'I'm sorry to hear that. Are you alright otherwise?' said Arthur.

'I'm not sure,' said Kayleigh, 'but I think we need to meet. Soon.'

Arthur was about to suggest he come to the hospital, but common sense kicked in.

'Are you with anyone?' he asked.

'No. The police were here, but I sent them away,' Kayleigh replied.

'I'll come to you then,' said Arthur, and he had started asking exactly where she was at the hospital when Kayleigh cut him off.

'No, I don't think so,' she said. 'My leg needs properly seeing to, and it wouldn't be wise for us to be seen together. The police may be gone for now, but they are very suspicious about what happened. We can't risk exposing you or the rest of your … friends.'

There was a new confidence there, but was that disbelief in the final word?

'Very well,' said Arthur. 'If you are safe, call me once you are finished, and I'll collect you, if that's acceptable?'

'I think so. Yes, that's okay, I think,' said Kayleigh. 'Be careful, Arthur. The Order could have eyes on you even now.'

She ended the call.

Arthur looked at his phone in disbelief, watching the call drop and the home screen reappear before the device went black as the light died.

How can she know about the Order?

Arthur tucked his phone away, took a deep breath.

If only Merlin was here, he thought as he passed through the gates of his home.

⁘

'You can't go alone, sir,' said Kay, leaning down to stroke Nimuë's Border collie, who lay at his feet. 'The Order could be waiting for an opportunity to strike.'

Arthur shook his head.

'Even if that's true, the whole point in kidnapping Caitlyn was to draw fear from me. They might not know that Malagant is dead and can no longer benefit. Not yet. There's a chance they won't harm me.'

'It wasn't their only goal though,' said Bedivere, who had just got back from a business engagement that had kept him occupied throughout the day. 'Malagant wanted Agravain and Nimuë's descendants dead. The Order may not know that the Dread Knight is no more, that's true, and they likely don't know that Agravain and Nimuë have fallen as well, but should you come between them and their prey, and with no direction from Malagant, who's to say how they will respond, sir? We don't know much about the Order or what they want.'

'Nevertheless, my priority is finding Caitlyn,' said Arthur. 'Tristan is working the list of descendants with Hektor Security, Bors and Gareth are watching Caitlyn's cottage, and I need the three of you working ANPR, analysing the phone data and liaising with the police, Hektor and Cordon, as well as anybody else who might be of use. Keep researching the Order, see if you can find any incidents that might link to them, work social media and try to find out who their members are … let's get Cordon out checking CCTV. Have we managed to contact Gawain, Lucan and Ector yet?' Kay shook his head, and Arthur continued, 'I will see Kayleigh Turner alone.'

'But sir,' started Dagonet, stopping when Arthur held up

his hand, standing straighter as he did so.

'No, I've decided, though I thank you for your concern.'

Kay, Bedivere and Dagonet exchanged glances, and Arthur sighed.

'Kayleigh Turner knows of us and of the Order, knows my name and how to contact me. She sent the police away. As far as I know, she has never had any contact with Merlin, Nimuë, Agravain, Malagant or any of us. I must find out what she knows and how. We need to know what she wants from us.'

He snatched up his cane and headed for the door.

'Maybe she can help us find Caitlyn.'

Chapter Six

Tintagel, Cornwall
5th Century

Morgana finally found a way to secure time with King Mark.

She had her man, Treave, spread the word among Mark's folk that a white hart with silver antlers had been sighted nearby, and that he would ride out in search of it, if his duties allowed.

The Cornishmen coveted such a prize, a creature straight out of legend, and some of them pleaded to join Treave on the hunt, but he said that he alone would bring down the creature, and when they laughed, telling him that perhaps they would assemble their own party, he would only give them a wry smile and wish them luck. When pressed, Treave would reply, 'Only my mistress knows where the hart may be found, for she knows its mind and sees through its eyes when she sleeps', and they believed him and fell silent, for Morgana Le Fay's name was well known throughout the lands.

It did not take long for word to reach Mark's ear. A keen hunter, as was well known by all, particularly by Morgana, Mark laughed when he heard of Treave's pride, and he sent for Morgana the moment his mirth had subsided.

The sorceress did not attend him hastily, tarrying in her chamber, arranging and rearranging her hair for a while before setting out to go before the King of Cornwall.

King Mark greeted her with a smile, sitting back on his wooden throne, his fingers interlaced over his stomach.

'Ah, I thought perhaps you had fallen from the cliffs, my lady!' he laughed. 'I have been watching the hairs on my arm turn grey while I waited for you.'

Morgana smiled sweetly at the king.

'I thought not to hasten my arrival, knowing how reluctant you have been to give me an audience, lord,' she replied.

'And you know why!' said Mark. 'Do you think Tristan kept your conversation a secret?'

Morgana feigned shock.

'An emissary from a neighbouring land attempting to curry the favour of a foreign king? An ambassador attempting to make gains for her own kin? Truly these are novel ideas, lord, for all courtiers and nobles are driven purely by altruism. I am *clearly* not to be trusted.'

She sat on a long bench, asking no leave to do so, and resisted the smile that threatened to emerge as she saw Mark's jovial countenance darken momentarily.

'But I jest, King Mark. I beg for forgiveness. Pray, tell me, why have you summoned me?' she continued, sparing him the trouble of devising a prompt and witty rebuke.

The king unclasped his fingers and draped one hand over the arm of his chair and the other over the pommel of his sword.

'Your man is bragging of his intention to hunt a white hart, claiming you and only you have a connection with the beast. Is this so?' he asked.

'Is what so, that Treave boasts or that I have a connection with the hart?' asked Morgana, but she sensed the king's patience had reached its limit, and she smiled at him.

'It is true that I know of such an animal, lord,' she said.

'And what price would you ask for its location?' asked Mark.

'Only the pleasure of your company on the hunt,' said Morgana, her smile fading.

Mark remained still, appearing to consider her words, but eventually he nodded.

'That is but a small favour, Lady Morgana,' he said.

'Do not mistake me, lord,' she said. 'I ask for the pleasure of *only* your company on the hunt. We ride alone.'

'That will not please your man,' said the king, smiling, and, she perceived, sensing he had been drawn into some trap, though its nature might be unclear to him.

'Treave has led a very disappointing life. He's accustomed to it,' said Morgana.

The king stood.

'To where do we ride, lady?'

Morgana, too, stood, and she strode towards the door.

'Never fear, King Mark, we will return in time to greet your bride,' she called back over her shoulder, and even when he raised his voice in protest, Lady Morgana Le Fay would say no more and was gone.

On the same day that Morgana and Mark rode out, Tristan took Princess Isolde's hand and led her aboard the ship that would carry her away from home to her new country.

Lucan walked behind them and even as Tristan enjoyed the touch of her skin, he knew his friend was scrutinising him. He did not release her hand though, both for what it might convey to the Irish and because, well, why should he? There was no harm in the gesture, and what man would not be moved by the soft touch of a woman's hand upon his own? He felt a pang of annoyance at Lucan, though he knew it was probably unwarranted.

The ship departed with little ceremony, but Isolde stood and watched her family lingering on the beach. She cut a lonely figure, turning aside Lucan's attempt at making light conversation with her until he gave up and went to stand beside Tristan.

They must feel the parting keenly, thought Tristan, *for who knows when or if they will ever set eyes on one another again.*

Soon, though, Tristan became occupied with keeping the contents of his stomach where they belonged, and as the journey wore on, he thought he had finally won his sea legs until the wind picked up and dark clouds swept in. The ship pitched and rolled as the waves battered it.

Tristan lingered near the side for a time, thinking he would vomit again, dreading it all the more for knowing Princess Isolde would see and might think less of him. But he mastered himself and joined Lucan and Isolde, who were sitting, blankets over their shoulders and smiling at him, clearly amused by his predicament.

'And how are we feeling?' asked Isolde.

Tristan grunted, his ability to remain civil much reduced by his torment.

Lucan punched him on the arm and tousled his hair.

'The king's nephew is no sailor!' he laughed, and Tristan scowled at him, but hearing Isolde laugh, his heart softened, and the trio fell into what gradually became easy conversation.

Lucan told Isolde of Cornwall and of King Mark, and she listened, enraptured. All the time, Tristan's glance shifted towards Isolde. His eyes traced the line of her neck, and he contemplated the blue of her eyes. She turned towards him, and he quickly looked elsewhere and was troubled by a sinking feeling in his stomach that provoked him to consider whether he should keep his distance from his uncle's betrothed, but Isolde spoke to him, asking of his life.

As the storm raged, they put up their hoods against the rain, and he told her of his early life in Cornwall, the son of King Mark's younger sister, who died in childbirth. Tristan spoke fondly of his late father and of his guilt for considering Mark a father now when he had such love for his own. Isolde laid a hand upon Tristan's shoulder as his voice wavered, and he caught sight of Lucan raising an eyebrow, but was distracted as Isolde told him of how she pitied him for the loss of his parents, knowing how important hers had been in her life. She sighed, and Tristan asked about Ireland. As the two of them spoke, Lucan joined in less and less, until finally he got up, making his excuses, and went off to speak with the navigator.

Tristan and Isolde talked long after nightfall, and he learnt of all that she cared about, all that she would miss.

It is a pity, thought Tristan, *that I have found a woman with whom I can speak so freely, a woman so beautiful, and to whom I am drawn, when she is promised to another.*

He took a sharp intake of breath, realising he was verging on disloyalty to Mark, if only in his heart. He struggled with his own impulses, his love for Mark and this new, burgeoning affection for Isolde, as Morgana's curse worked and took hold.

'I should check on the men,' said Tristan, getting to his feet and staggering as the deck lurched. He felt Isolde's hands on his hips, and he saw that she had reached out to steady him. He felt his cheeks redden and mumbled thanks.

A peal of thunder rolled all around the churning ocean and lightning flashed just as Tristan was stepping over a coil of rope. Startled, his foot caught, and he lumbered forward, smashing into the gunwale, and his momentum tossed him over the side.

He heard voices cry out in the second before he plunged into the sea and went under, all sound suddenly deadened. He closed his eyes and thrashed his limbs, desperately.

Men abandoned their oars, and Lucan dashed across the deck, pushing his way through. The ship yawed suddenly as its crew lost concentration.

'He can't swim!' he yelled in a panic, unable to help, for he too was not a swimmer.

He could not see Tristan among the furious waves.

Tristan coughed into the salt water as he fought to get back to the surface, kicking his booted feet, his hood pulling at his throat. He held his breath, but there was no air left in his lungs as he tried to swim, kicking and clawing at the water, his eyes now wide open.

He began to sink.

I'm going to die, thought Tristan.

But then a hand grasped his hair and yanked so hard that it felt as though his scalp would be ripped off. Tristan let out a silent cry and breathed in sea water. The pain on his head lessened as another hand took him under the armpit. He felt himself drawn upward as his rescuer released the hand holding his hair and hauled him to the surface.

Tristan coughed up water as he was pulled on to his back and cried out as a kicking leg struck him in the calf. Thunder boomed again as he continued coughing, but he turned and saw that it was Isolde who had hold of him. She was lying on her back, with him tucked under her arm, and she began hollering to the ship, which was nowhere to be seen.

He could do nothing but cough and try to keep his head up, utterly dependent on the princess for his survival.

'My lady!' said a man from out of view. He felt a loop of rope drop over his head, and he slipped his arm through it.

The ship's crew began to haul them aboard.

'I owe you my life, lady,' said Tristan, his teeth chattering and his whole body shivering. The princess was in no less a state, despite the furs, cloaks and blankets that had been thrown over them.

'Don't forget it,' she grinned, looking straight into his eyes. There was no deference there, not of the kind expected of a woman of that time, nor the kind reserved for those who had high standing in a new place where one had yet to carve out a niche or establish oneself. He saw openness and honesty on her fair features, and Tristan fell for her; fell hard.

※

Lying beside a campfire, many miles away, with King Mark snoring an arm's length away, Lady Morgana Le Fay looked up at the stars, passing a Hemlock leaf from hand to hand.

Chapter Seven

2021

Arthur drove towards Runbridge Hospital, but would have no memory of the journey, his mind was so occupied with other things. He thought of how to find Caitlyn and, when he reached an impasse, his mind was drawn back to Agravain's long torment over more than a century.

No, he corrected himself. He may have been possessed by Malagant since the late 1800s, but he had been tormented for far longer, abandoned by Nimuë and watching his children and then his children's children, and so on, grow old and die. How could he have thought so little of his friend and knight, Arthur wondered? But then, how could he have known? Arthur had no inkling that the Dread Knight had occupied his friend, but then, Agravain had walked away from the company to watch over London long before that, and Arthur had never truly understood. It hurt even then, as he thought of it, driving his own automatic car through the streets towards Runbridge, rain now falling heavily from darkening skies.

Arthur had been intending to park in the multi-storey

opposite the main hospital building, but as he drew close to the turn, he saw a bedraggled figure on crutches, half hiding in a bus stop. Was that Kayleigh Turner? The woman had seen him and left the shelter, swinging awkwardly between her crutches. Arthur pulled up at the side of the road and heaved himself, groaning, from the driver's seat before heading round to open the front passenger door for the woman. She approached slowly, ignoring the rain that ran off her brow and down her cheeks.

Arthur saw her nod to him, but then, as she balanced herself and gathered her crutches, she grunted and shook her head, looking down at the floor.

'This is ridiculous,' she said.

Arthur could think of nothing meaningful to say, so he offered her his gloved hand to help her drop down into the seat. He knew how hard a manoeuvre it could be from the pain he felt in his leg every time he entered or exited a vehicle.

'I'm Arthur,' he said, and Kayleigh sighed through a worn-out smile.

'I suppose you are,' she said, 'and I have *completely* lost it.'

Arthur laid her crutches across the back seat, beside his cane, and made his way round to the driver's seat.

Arthur drove, and they maintained an awkward silence until they could bear it no longer.

'My home is not far from here. You must be hungry, and we can get you a cup of tea or a mug of hot coffee,' he said.

But Arthur saw Kayleigh shake her head out of the corner of his eye.

'No, I need you to take me to my friend's house. Sarah's looking after my kid.'

Arthur said nothing, making a conscious effort not to let his frustration overwhelm him to the extent that he made an outburst, but he must have given something away, perhaps shifting in his seat.

'I just need to check on Simon, that's all. We can talk on the way and later too, after I'm sure he's okay. Calm down,' said Kayleigh. Arthur turned to look at her, this young woman of the 21st century, whose life had been turned upside down in the course of one evening, who dared to speak to him so candidly.

'Very well,' said Arthur. 'Where do we begin?'

'Turn around,' said Kayleigh. 'You're going in the wrong direction.'

Arthur pulled up at the side of the road and put on his hazard lights, the orange lights blinking on and off at each corner of his car to warn other motorists it was there. He brought up the satnav on the dashboard console and set the destination postcode when Kayleigh provided it. Half an hour until they arrived. He nodded, silently, and, checking over his shoulder, Arthur pulled back out into the traffic.

'This is all impossible,' said Kayleigh suddenly. 'But I know it's all true, right down in my bones. Everything I've learnt today is as ingrained in me as memories I've had all my life. We've never met, but I know you, know things about you that even you don't know. I don't get how, but it's real. Either the world just got a little crazier or I did, but either way, what choice do I have but to accept it?' She laughed. 'Nuts!'

'The world is no crazier than it has ever been, I'm afraid. You've just been alerted to much that is hidden from most,' said Arthur, then he added, 'what do you know of me that I don't?'

'That during World War Two, Tristan punched Agravain for calling you a coward for not fighting. That was what finally drove him away. Tristan never told you what passed between them,' said Kayleigh, her words becoming softer as she realised their impact.

Arthur did not reply, driving silently.

'He didn't want to hurt you,' Kayleigh offered, by way of making reparation, Arthur assumed. 'He kept it from you as he knew how much Agravain's words would get to you. Perhaps I shouldn't have said anything. That was stupid.'

'Not stupid,' said Arthur, though he did not know what else it might have been. Insensitive? Naive?

He sighed.

'Agravain was not himself at that time. We know that now, after today,' said Arthur, and even he detected the weariness and sadness in his voice. He realised he was slumping forward, and he straightened his back to sit up while steering.

'What do you mean?' asked Kayleigh.

Arthur turned to look at her briefly then returned his eyes to the road.

'What do you know about Malagant?' asked Arthur.

'I know what Tristan knew when he touched me at my house,' said Kayleigh.

'That was before we found out the identity of your

attacker,' said Arthur, nodding. 'The man who broke into your house today was Agravain, but we have discovered that Malagant had possessed him since the 19th century. He was not himself,' said Arthur.

'And Malagant wanted to kill me to punish Agravain,' Kayleigh nodded, 'because I'm his relative. His great-great-great -great-whatever-granddaughter?'

'That's correct, as far as I understand it, Miss Turner,' said Arthur. 'You are the result of a line that began with Sir Agravain and the enchantress, Nimuë.'

'Nimuë,' said Kayleigh, almost in a whisper, and Arthur caught her looking down at her hands, turning them over as though they were glowing. They weren't.

'Which brings me around to my questions,' said Arthur. 'How long have you known of my knights and I? Your phone call earlier, well, it took me by surprise, to say the least.'

Kayleigh pointed suddenly at a road on the right.

'That way's quicker, ignore the satnav,' she said. 'Sorry. You were saying?'

'How do you know of me, Miss Turner?' asked Arthur.

'I hoped you'd know more than me about that! But it's obvious that whatever went on at my house when Agravain or Malagant attacked, something happened to me. I'd never met Tristan before, but when he touched me, I knew what he knew, I started seeing his memories like they were mine. I saw Agravain, Nimuë, you, Isolde … '

Arthur blew air between pursed lips.

'What?' asked Kayleigh, stopping mid-sentence.

'If I were you, I would not mention Isolde to Tristan, if ever you should meet him. We do not speak of her,' said Arthur.

'I can understand that, I suppose,' said Kayleigh, 'even if it was such a long time ago.'

'Some wounds never heal,' said Arthur. 'Tristan's regret will never fade.'

Silence fell between them momentarily, and it seemed to Arthur that neither of them truly understood why they had come together. He knew he had to protect her, of course, to honour his word to Agravain, if for no other reason. But what of these powers of insight she was developing? Would all who shared Nimuë's blood have a share in her abilities?

'So what happens now then?' asked Kayleigh.

'That … is a very good question,' said Arthur, raising his eyebrows and drumming the steering wheel with his fingers.

Silence again for a few moments while Arthur gathered his thoughts. Kayleigh beat him to it.

'I guess there are two issues. First, there are psychos trying to kill us … me, Simon and whoever else is left. How do we keep safe? And how do you protect the rest? You have a list of names, but can you really watch over them day and night? You tried doing that, but they still got to me, didn't they?'

Arthur nodded as he indicated left and turned on to a country road. The headlights swept across hedgerows and lit up an animal's eyes, staring back at them.

'My company and I must put the Order of Phobos and Deimos down,' said Arthur. 'Not only to protect you and those like you, but because Malagant has kidnapped my partner.'

'Caitlyn,' said Kayleigh, softly. 'Yes, of course.'

Silence once more.

'Can you help me find her? Do your abilities stretch that far?' asked Arthur.

'You mean the abilities I've had since dinner time? Those abilities?'

He heard the edge to her tone and fell silent.

'I mean, bear with me, for God's sake,' said Kayleigh. 'One minute I was washing the dishes, and the next I was fighting off a possessed knight from a storybook. And then I find that with a single touch, I've learnt everything of a former immortal's long life. A quick jaunt to the hospital with a broken leg later, I'm getting a lift to my best mate's house in King Arthur's car. I mean. Give me a minute, yeah?'

'My apologies,' said Arthur, 'but although I appreciate the difficulty you may have processing all of this information, you must understand, Caitlyn's life is at stake and neither she nor your family is safe until we catch up with the Order.'

'Well, I don't see what I can do,' said Kayleigh. 'There's not much I can do by stealing memories at a touch.'

'There is much you could achieve with such an ability,' said Arthur, 'but I agree, for now, if that is the only power that has passed down to you from Nimuë, the best plan would be to see you to a place of safety.'

'Like where? I can't just up and leave! Simon has school and friends! And his dad is expecting him at the weekend. I've got work, too,' said Kayleigh.

'I understand, and I'd prefer to keep you close by, anyway, though it would be a risk to send Simon to stay with his father at this point,' said Arthur.

'You want us to stay with you?' asked Kayleigh.

'For now,' said Arthur. 'My home is not a fortress, but I can think of nowhere safer for you, especially as it remains to be seen how your powers might develop over time, now that they have come to you.'

Kayleigh let out a long sigh.

'Are you alright?' asked Arthur, but Kayleigh did not reply, instead turning away from him to look out of the side window at the world as it rushed by.

A few seconds later, he heard her beginning to sob.

Arthur drove on, biting his lip, frustrated that Kayleigh could not help him, and he despaired at the time he was losing in taking her to fetch her son.

Caitlyn's chances dwindled with every passing second.

Arthur pressed down on the accelerator and forced himself to take long, deep breaths, in through the nose and out through the mouth.

He had to find Caitlyn, but how?

Chapter Eight

Cornwall
5th Century

Morgana Le Fay and King Mark of Cornwall rode side by side under a web of interlacing branches, through which the moonlight poured. The two of them, woman and man, appeared alike to ghostly woodland sprites as they emerged from the wood on to undulating grasslands.

'We will soon be upon it,' said the sorceress, but the king laughed.

'I gave up hope of ever seeing your white hart long ago,' said Mark in answer to her quizzical expression.

'Have you no faith in me?' asked Morgana.

'Faith in what? I have every confidence in your ability to get all that you desire. You wanted me alone, and here we are, riding alone, after some proffered spectral stag that you knew I could not resist,' said King Mark.

'You think me a deceiver, then?' asked Morgana,

quietly, her eyes fixed on the path ahead.

'Do you deny it?' asked Mark.

'A difficult question. Would you accept such a thing of yourself? Can you say you have never deceived another? No. Who could make such a claim? But are you a 'deceiver' or one who has deceived?' said Morgana.

The king said nothing, but smiled.

'You think me nothing but a plotter and a manipulator? A twister of words, who means to bring down Arthur and elevate our son?' said Morgana.

'Your son,' repeated Mark.

'Our son,' said Morgana.

'Fathered by Arthur,' stated Mark.

'That is so, though he outright denies it to some and accepts it was true to others, but claims that he was bewitched when he committed the fateful act,' said Morgana. 'Deceivers are everywhere, it seems.'

'Arthur is an honest man,' said King Mark. 'You will not divide us, Morgana.'

'I could if I so wished,' she replied, 'but that is not my way.' She reined in her mare and looked straight at Mark, who also slowed his mount.

'Arthur is the father, and he came to my bed willingly,' she said, her face serious. She saw the unease in the tension of Mark's features. 'I doubt I have ever met or will ever meet a truly honest man or woman either, for that matter. You are not unwise, my lord, so I will understand your words, thus: Arthur tells the truth more often than he lies, and you feel he does not lie to you about anything that you care about.'

King Mark did not reply. He just stared at her.

'Now, you asked if I denied being a deceiver? Yes, I deny it. Have I deceived? Yes. Will I again, oh yes! But I am not a deceiver. Look yonder,' she concluded and pointed over Mark's shoulder.

Across the grasslands, standing on top of a rocky outcrop, stood a great white stag, a terrible beast, with shining silver antlers that seemed to hold the full moon in its grasp.

Mark turned in the saddle and brought his palfrey round, his eyes wide and his mouth hanging open.

'The hunt continues then, lord,' said Morgana.

King Mark did not take his eyes from the white hart, and Morgana knew that in him, the desire to bring down the beast strove with a need to prostrate himself before it in awe, as a primitive presented with a new god, hitherto only a rumour.

'I apologise, my lady. I should not have

doubted you,' said King Mark, and she laughed, amused by his inability to remove his gaze from the animal, perhaps held by some supernatural power or maybe just afraid that it would bound away and be lost to him forever.

'Then this was not a trick? A way to secure the time necessary to whisper in my ear until I turn against Arthur?' whispered King Mark.

'Oh no, it *was* a trick,' said Morgana. 'But why would I try to turn you against Arthur, when I can make you love and fear me more?'

She wondered if he would turn and scold her, remonstrating against her tone and her boldness, but the king did no such thing. He sat in his saddle, and he stared.

The white hart stared back.

The simple stone fort at Tintagel, high up on the cliffs, could have been a shining fairy palace of silver and gold, for all the pull it had on Tristan's heart, and yet, the sight of it filled him with dread.

He had woken depressed on the final morning of the voyage, knowing full well that soon, he and Isolde would be parted. He knew he should keep away from her, that it would be for the best if he distanced himself mentally and physically, but still he tended to her needs, offering her fresh water and sustenance before any other member of the crew even noticed that she was awake. She received his ministrations gratefully, with a smile, and as she reached for whatever was offered, sometimes the skin of their fingers would touch, and the young man and woman exchanged a lingering glance, but no apology. The seeds of destruction had been sown, Tristan knew, and he wondered if he courted disaster by allowing such little moments of affection, but he told himself that no harm would come of them, as long as they did not continue ashore and that he had done nothing that his uncle would not forgive. He was, after all, a young man, and Isolde a young woman, and their, he believed, mutual attraction was understandable. She had saved his life, they had spent time with one another, and this was but a passing attachment, he knew. His duties at Tintagel would keep him occupied, and Isolde would be swept up in preparing to become a queen.

He would deliver Princess Isolde to King Mark and all would be well.

⁓⁓✦⁓⁓

'Where is he then?' asked Tristan, scowling at Tintagel's castellan, the governor of the fort.

'The king rode out in pursuit of a white hart with Lady Morgana Le Fay, my lord,' replied the man.

What possessed his uncle to accompany the

sorceress when his true allegiance was with Arthur, and Morgana so clearly meant to come between them?

'Did he leave word of when he would return? I had thought he would wish to greet his bride?' asked Tristan.

'Lady Morgana told the king they would return before now,' said the castellan.

Tristan made no reply, pondering what this meant for Isolde. He was all too aware as he strode to meet her at the shore, that she had departed Ireland a princess, with an honour guard and her royal family waving her off, but that Cornwall would receive her with little ceremony, only the castellan and some of the household guard lined up, standing to attention, with the standards of both Tintagel and Cornwall flapping in the sea breeze.

He guided Isolde away from her handmaidens and spoke softly.

'The king has been called away, Princess,' he told her.

Her mouth formed a tight line, and he felt for her, knowing how she had steeled herself for this moment, drawn together all her courage in preparation for meeting the man she would wed, not for love, but out of duty. He knew she hoped to come to love King Mark and this was not a promising beginning.

'Called away?' she said quietly.

Tristan nodded and looked back over his shoulder at the castellan's group to buy himself just a few more seconds.

'Indeed, lady. He has business with an emissary of Prince Mordred's court. He rode away with the Prince's mother, and it seems they have been delayed, but he will return soon, if I am informed correctly.' He hesitated then added, 'I am sorry, Isolde.'

Tristan noticed Isolde's hands had scrunched into fists, but she relaxed them and after a moment contemplating his shoes, she looked up and nodded.

'Kings are busy men, I know it well,' she said. 'I will have to impose on his nephew a little longer it seems, for I would not wander Tintagel unguided.'

Tristan quailed, his heart foreseeing the danger even if his mind did not acknowledge it. But what could he do? His first duty was to King Mark, in whose place he must make Princess Isolde welcome, surely? And did he not owe the princess his life, quite aside from any obligation the depth of his affection for her might lay upon him?

'I would be honoured to welcome you to both Tintagel and to Cornwall, my lady,' said Tristan, bowing low. When he straightened up, he saw

Lucan standing a short distance away, arms folded across his chest, his face serious.

⁂

'I cannot fathom what Mark was thinking,' hissed Lucan while he and Tristan watched the folk of Tintagel dancing in the great hall. The two men had worked tirelessly all day to make up for the lacklustre welcome, consisting of Princess Isolde being escorted up the fort, watched by the fisherfolk and small folk as they went about their business.

'And the castellan,' said Tristan. 'I could have killed him. I could still kill him. How must she have felt at the moment of her greatest vulnerability, in a strange land, with the prospect of taking a king to her bed, to be so forgotten and disrespected?'

'She seems happy enough,' said Lucan.

Tristan watched Isolde dancing with a local lord, a smile fixed on her taut face.

'We did all we could in Mark's stead,' he said, clasping his hands behind his back.

He could feel Lucan's eyes on him, scrutinising, but he did not turn to face him, keeping his eyes fixed on Isolde, wishing he could save her from the feast he had thrown in her honour. Surely she would want to retreat to her chambers, take a breath and some time to herself?

'I fear for the king, out alone with Morgana,' said Lucan, breaking Tristan's rumination.

Tristan nodded, folding his arms across his chest, leaning back against the wall and turning his full attention to Lucan.

'I, too. She is not to be trusted,' said Tristan. 'I am minded to send a company after them.'

Lucan nodded.

'Will you lead them?' asked Tristan, making eye contact in earnest.

'I ... ' started Lucan and bit his lip.

Tristan waited, but when his friend did not continue, he asked him to speak his mind. Lucan sighed, rubbed his eyes with his thumb and forefinger, pinched the bridge of his nose, sighed again and then met Tristan's gaze.

'Forgive me, brother, but is it wise to send away all your allies and leave you here with Princess Isolde with nobody you can trust at your side?' said Lucan, and it seemed to Tristan that the words had cost him a deal of effort.

He was about to reply about the castellan, the fort's defences and his own ability to lead the men remaining at his disposal, but Lucan's honesty deserved nothing less in return, Tristan decided. He, too, sighed before speaking.

'I have fallen for her,' he admitted, 'but I will not fail my uncle. She is to be his bride, and I will love her as an aunt, not as a woman.'

'That would be quite the feat,' said Lucan. 'Are you sure you are up to it?'

'Do you really question my loyalty to King Mark? Or do you doubt my resolve?' said Tristan, and he saw that Lucan thought carefully before replying.

'If there is a man alive whose loyalty is beyond question, it is you, brother, but a change has come over you since we departed Ireland, and it worries me. You are different, but I cannot tell how. You are somehow laid bare, and I heard you speak with Isolde aboard ship. Your heart was unguarded. You gave too much of yourself. And I saw how both your gazes lingered upon the other. The gestures. Tristan may be the truest man in all Cornwall and all the lands ruled over by King Arthur, but if ever his honour is in peril, it is now. You have not known love before, not this kind of love, which strikes hard and without mercy,' said Lucan, not unkindly, and Tristan's rising anger abated quickly, perhaps all the faster because, though he would not admit it, he heard the truth in his friend's words.

He glanced over at Isolde.

'It is easy to be loyal when there is nothing at stake or nothing to compromise oneself,' Tristan said. 'I will test my honour here and look after Isolde in Mark's stead. Have no fear,

Lucan. All will be well. And besides, I would trust nobody but you with the pursuit of the king.'

Lucan sighed once more.

'Very well, Tristan, but I caution you, be careful. King Mark is a kindly man, but harsh when need requires it.'

'I have no need to fear my uncle, whom I love beyond all else, as a father and my king,' he concluded.

Thus it was agreed. Lucan would ride out in the morning. He excused himself and set off to order the necessary preparations.

Tristan hooked his thumbs into his belt and watched as the dancing ended. The lords and ladies returned to their seats, and Isolde was left alone for a moment. Tristan saw her smile fade, but then she caught sight of him, and she came alive again, but this time, the smile was genuine.

Tristan walked forward to meet her.

Chapter Nine

2021

Arthur checked his watch for what must have been the hundredth time since Kayleigh had gone into her friend's house. He sighed and, once again, checked his phone.

No messages. No updates.

How much longer would she be? Every second he waited was a moment he was not spending on finding Caitlyn, but then, what use was he in that regard? He had no idea where Malagant had taken her. He didn't know where to start.

Finally, after what felt like a century, but, was in actual fact, no more than about fifteen minutes, Kayleigh Turner appeared through the gate between high hedges at the front of her friend's house, her son, Simon, walking too slowly in front of her as she swung between crutches.

He looks happy enough, considering, thought Arthur. He groaned as he levered himself out of the driver's seat, offering Simon a smile when he saw the boy stop in his tracks, immediately frowning.

'This is Arthur,' said Kayleigh, beating Arthur to the introduction. 'He's Mummy's friend, and he's letting us stay with him for a few days.'

The boy muttered something that Arthur could not make out, but Kayleigh's ear was better tuned.

'It's too late tonight, so let's get you to bed, and we can pick up your toys and clothes in the morning, right, Arthur?'

'Right,' said Arthur, unused to being around children. 'A pleasure to meet you, Simon.'

'Say hello to Arthur,' said Kayleigh, quietly.

'Hello,' came the reluctant response.

He couldn't blame the child, thought Arthur, as he opened the rear door to the car, and Simon clambered inside on all fours, totally unnecessary, but in the way children did.

He's been through something quite traumatic this evening and is now being taken to a stranger's house by a stranger, introduced to a world not his own. And he has a target on his back, just like his mother.

He held the door for Kayleigh, eased himself into the driver's seat and set off for home, while Kayleigh feigned a breezy attitude as she asked about Simon's day and fielded questions about her broken leg.

⁂

The car slipped between the automated gates of the mansion, and Arthur chuckled as Simon, his initial nerves apparently wearing off, called out,

'Mum, it's a castle!'

'Not quite, but it's not far off!' she laughed.

'Does he live here?' Simon whispered, leaning forward as Arthur parked the car.

'Ask him yourself. He won't bite,' said Kayleigh, and Simon repeated the question to Arthur.

'Got it in one, lad. This is my home. I live here with some friends,' said Arthur.

'Kids?' asked Simon.

'No children, no,' said Arthur. 'I'm sorry.'

'That's alright. But what about games?' Simon continued, pressing a button so that the front passenger headrest dropped down. Arthur unclicked his seatbelt and opened his door slightly.

'Scrabble, I think. Monopoly … I'm not sure. One of the others will know,' he said, as he started to pull himself out of the vehicle to stand below the oak that dominated the courtyard before his front door.

'He means computer games,' said Kayleigh, as Arthur helped her out.

'None of those,' said Arthur, opening the door for Simon. 'Sorry.'

'That's alright. TV though?'

Arthur nodded and waved a hand towards the front door.

A short time later, once Bors and Gareth had arrived back, Dagonet, Arthur, Kayleigh and Bedivere were seated around the round table in the dining room, each with their drink of choice, waiting.

'I should go and check on them,' said Kayleigh, but as she pushed back her chair, Arthur heard Kay making slow progress down the stairs. His knight pushed open the dining room door.

'I've set him up on Fortnite,' said Kay, easing himself into his seat and resting his crutch against the edge of the table. Too many of them were walking with aids, thought Arthur.

'We won't see him for hours then,' said Kayleigh. 'Good shout.'

'What did I miss?' asked Kay.

Arthur summarised Kayleigh's account of the attack on her earlier in the day, but asked her to take over, and she once again explained what she had experienced when Tristan had touched her, the insight she had been given into his memories.

'I just called him,' said Kay. 'He's been to two local addresses and is keeping in touch with Hektor. They're reeling after the loss of the men outside Miss Turner's, but they're still on board.'

'Too bloody right - we pay them enough,' said Bors.

'Wait, what do you mean, the loss of the men outside mine?' said Kayleigh, but as she spoke, the words tapered off. 'The men in the van, watching out for me. Malagant killed them.'

'Unfortunate, yes, but Hektor will be more vigilant now,' said Arthur.

'That's a bit heartless, isn't it?' asked Kayleigh.

Arthur expected one of his knights to speak up on his behalf, but none of them did so.

Bors broke the silence, speaking to Kay, who had been coordinating their efforts.

'Where are we up to then?'

'Nothing useful turned up at the cottage,' Bedivere cut in.

'Tristan's working his list, but no luck yet. In short, we have very little to go on,' said Kay.

'She could be anywhere by now,' said Arthur, looking at Kayleigh.

'What?' she said. 'Why are you looking at me?'

Arthur felt heat in his cheeks.

'I'm not Nimuë. I can't help in *that* way!' she said.

'As far as you know,' said Bors, 'and you didn't know much until today. Maybe you'll know more in an hour, or tomorrow or next week.'

'I don't have any answers,' said Kayleigh. 'You lot are the immortals. Don't *you* have *any* ideas?'

An uncomfortable silence passed before Arthur replied.

'I am ashamed to admit that we have always been somewhat dependent on the expertise of first Merlin and then Nimuë, to a lesser extent, when it comes to matters of the arcane. We are soldiers, first and foremost, Miss Turner, not wizards, sorcerers or enchanters.'

'Like you,' said Dagonet, quietly.

'Not like me. I don't know anything about magic. All I did was touch Tristan's wrist and … '

She stopped and lowered her pointing finger to the table, and Arthur thought she'd been hit by a realisation.

'What is it?' he asked.

'That isn't all,' she said. 'I didn't even realise I was doing it, but when I first saw Malagant at the top of the stairs, I unleashed a wave of … I dunno … something, against him. It knocked him back.'

'Told you,' said Bors.

'Shut up, you ass,' said Gareth. 'Give her time to think, won't you?'

Bors grunted, and, before Arthur spoke, he noticed Kayleigh was chewing her lower lip.

'It seems the confrontation unlocked something in you,' he said. 'Maybe you will gain more insight and new abilities as time progresses. This is something you can try to develop on your own, but in the meantime, it raises the question: how many others on Tristan's list might also have abilities? And would those individuals be willing to help us?'

'Sure, but in more practical terms, Arthur, if we could just get our hands on one of the Order, we can throttle it out of them,' said Bors.

'So we have two avenues to explore, the arcane and the mundane.' said Gareth. 'How best to go about it?'

'Tristan's got the mundane covered already,' Kay said, 'but we could help him work his way down the list?'

Arthur nodded.

'Start at the bottom and work our way up, I … ' but a thought struck him. 'If Hektor are watching the addresses, can we trust them to make the enquiries on our behalf?'

He regretted suggesting it before the words were out of his mouth, and the shaking of the knights' heads only confirmed his opinion. Hektor Security could be trusted, but they did not know his company's true business or their origins. This was beyond their remit and their capabilities.

'Alright, perhaps we can help Tristan, but what about the arcane avenue? Is there anything we can do? Anyone?' asked Arthur, looking around the table as desperation mounted.

Silence.

'Really? Nothing at all?' asked Kayleigh, and Arthur saw only blank faces.

'All I can suggest,' said Bedivere, 'is that you test the bounds of your new abilities while you are here. Perhaps some of the others will allow you to touch them to see if you can perceive their memories, as you did Tristan's? Maybe your abilities are not confined to people, but objects as well. Perhaps if you were to lay a hand on Excalibur, you could … '

At that moment, the door creaked open and Arthur turned to check if Simon had crept downstairs, but instead he saw Caitlyn's Rottweiler, Samson, nosing his way inside.

He reached out a hand to him and the dog wandered over, looking very sorry for himself.

'Excalibur,' said Kayleigh, shaking her head. 'I'm still not sure I'm not in a coma or something. I did fall down the stairs after all.'

Arthur heard Bors snort as Kayleigh made a show of pinching the back of her hand.

Gareth pushed back his chair.

'I'll fetch it,' he said and slipped out of the room, returning a few minutes later, holding Excalibur before him. He laid it on the table, and Arthur stood, beckoning for Kayleigh to approach, not saying a word.

'Here goes nothing, I guess,' she said, standing, and Arthur passed her the sword, hilt first.

He watched, his eyes flitting between her outstretched fingers and her face, anticipating the moment of contact and the reaction to come.

It seemed at first as though Kayleigh would tentatively brush Excalibur with her fingers, cautious of potential harm, but at the last moment, she grasped the grip.

Arthur stepped back, scrutinising her face, looking for a change, but the woman just held up the blade before her.

'Anything?' whispered Gareth, and Kayleigh shook her head.

'Shut up and let her concentrate!' said Bors.

Kayleigh took the sword in both hands, letting the edge of the blade rest against the table so that the furniture took the weapon's weight, and she closed her eyes, brow furrowing.

Arthur waited. Nobody spoke. Someone shifted their weight, causing a chair to creak.

Kayleigh opened her eyes.

'Anything?' asked Arthur. Samson nudged his leg until Arthur scratched behind the dog's ear.

Kayleigh only shook her head, pursing her lips slightly, Arthur noticed, before she handed back the sword.

'Sorry. Don't think I can help,' she said.

'Not in that way, it seems,' said Arthur as he crossed the room to stow Excalibur.

He heard Bors say, "So what now?" and Kay reply, "Back at square one, and we've …" before the knight's sentence cut off prematurely and the others gasped. Arthur turned and saw Kayleigh leaning down, hand touching Samson's head. The dog was looking at her expectantly, but she did not stroke or scratch. Instead, Arthur noticed, the woman appeared to be in a trance, staring through the dog.

'Kayleigh?' he tried to rouse her as he crossed the room,

waving a hand for the gathering knights to back away.

He need not have worried. A few seconds later, Kayleigh seemed to come to, blinking and taking three deep breaths that seemed to go on forever.

Arthur offered a hand, and she almost took it, but remembered at the last second.

'Are you alright?' asked Arthur, searching her face.

She chuckled, raising both eyebrows.

'I'm okay, but that was … different. A dog's eye view,' said Kayleigh.

'You're joking!' said Bors, and Arthur shot him a look to immediately silence him.

'Anything of use?' asked Kay.

Kayleigh stooped, reaching out for Samson, out of instinct, it seemed to Arthur, but she stopped short and then, perhaps wondering if she should test the bounds, she gave the Rottweiler's head a scratch. This time, nothing happened.

'Well, I've seen who broke into her house and locked the dog away. Agravain, a big man and a woman. She struggled, but they locked Samson away after he bit the big man's leg. I didn't see any more.'

Chapter Ten

Cornwall
5th Century

Morgana rode beside King Mark, whose eyes were fixed on the white hart. The beast, appearing ethereal in the moonlight, would sometimes disappear from view ahead of them, over a hillock or into a group of trees, and Morgana sensed Mark's fear that it would evade them. He need not have worried, for no sooner had they drawn closer or traversed the obstacle, there the hart would be, standing, waiting for them, as she knew it would be.

Morgana smiled and rode on.

Before long, the land rose up before them and the way was barred by a wall of stone, but the hart's silver hooves found a path that led into a cave, from which a stream ran, its waters utterly clear, devoid of fallen detritus, and its bed seemingly composed of white sand.

Morgana watched the white hart disappear

into the gap in the rock face, and, for a moment, she and Mark sat upon their horses in silence, save for the gentle singing of the stream and the breath of their mounts.

'Shall we dismount and follow, my lord?' Morgana prompted, and she saw the king lick his lips, as he stared into the darkness before them.

'My lord?' she said again, pleased with his evident discomfort. He was drawn forward, Morgana knew, but desired not to enter, though he knew not why. She could have dismounted, but she wanted King Mark to decide for himself; she wanted him to go willingly.

Finally, Mark took a deep breath and dropped to the grass. Morgana did the same while he tied his horse to a tree that grew a little way off.

The two of them stood side by side on the stream's bank before the darkness of the chasm. Morgana avoided looking directly into it, as she remembered how her stomach had lurched the last time she had been there. She recalled the sensation of falling from a high place and, sure enough, Mark staggered and righted himself.

'What is this place? And what manner of creature is the hart that leads us here?' asked the king.

'A place like no other,' she replied. 'Merlin brought me here when I was just a girl, not long after Arthur was born. As for the hart, you will see. None can find this place without one such as he. Will you enter?'

King Mark met her gaze, and she saw the doubt in his eyes. This had begun as a simple hunt, but the king seemed bewitched by the mere sight of his quarry. He felt it, she knew, but would he resist and turn back? If so, their business together was done, and she had failed.

Mark sighed and started forward.

'Will you not fetch your bow, my lord?' asked Morgana, but Mark shook his head.

'You know full well we are beyond that now,' he said, and the display of insight impressed her. She followed the king as he walked into the dark chasm, his sword hanging at his side in its scabbard.

Morgana felt her way into the chasm, leaning against the wet, lichen-covered rock walls. Before long, all light had faded, and she heard Mark stumbling and sometimes his boots splashed into the stream. Once, he cursed, and she spoke harshly to him, cautioning him to speak and act only with respect, there in that hallowed place.

The tunnel turned to the right, and as it did so, she walked into Mark's back.

'There is a light up ahead. A green glow,' whispered the king. 'And I hear something. Voices, I think. Is this some kind of trap, Morgana?'

She smiled, unseen, in the dark.

'For a king, isn't everything a snare, one way or another? But I mean you no harm,' she said.

Mark moved neither forward or back, and as her eyes adjusted, she could see him silhouetted by the distant green glow.

'Come now, you have gone this far, Mark. I would show you, if you are not too cowardly to go on where I, a mere woman, have trod before you,' Morgana said, and she scolded herself for her loss of composure. That outburst seemed to have the desired effect though, and she heard Mark grunt then step forward, his boots making ripples in the stream.

They walked on together, creeping nearer and nearer to the end of the tunnel, with the voices and also the sound of animals echoing between the walls, accompanied always by the sound of the stream. She could see now, by the light ahead, and she saw King Mark walking before her as they reached their destination. The light emerged from a cave ahead, the tunnel widening into its entrance. Mark stood before a curtain of what looked like kelp and vines, through which the light poured as if there was no obstruction at all.

Morgana stood behind him, at his shoulder, and whispered,

'He is waiting for you.'

Mark straightened up, took a deep breath and pushed through the curtain.

Morgana pushed Mark forward as she emerged through the curtain of hanging plants, for he had stopped just on the other side, no doubt awestruck.

The voices stopped.

They stood in a vast cavern that rose to a rough high dome above them. A great lake, glowing green, filled almost the entire space, its farther reaches disappearing into the distance. Little islands broke its surface here and there, and upon one stood a small keep constructed from white stone. Morgana spied a single boat out on the water, a lone man seated within, fishing as always, she realised, seeing him cast out a line.

Before them, the stream ran down a gentle slope, from a beach of white sand, and it was the strange gathering upon it that had left King Mark with his mouth agape.

A collection of all manner of birds and beasts congregated, seemingly without fear, around the great white stag, its silver antlers gleaming, lit by the green glow of the lake itself as it stood by the water.

Mark started to speak, but the stag looked up, catching his gaze, looked at Morgana and bowed low. It turned and stalked into the shallows of the green lake, sinking deeper and deeper with every step, until half of its great body was submerged. The moment the stag left the beach, the collection of animals dispersed along the shore, and some of them ran back the way Morgana and Mark had travelled, avoiding the two humans as they did so.

'What is this place?' asked King Mark, but Morgana did not answer, instead walking down to the water. By now, only the hart's antlers, head and neck were visible above the water.

The sorceress crouched down and trailed her fingertips across the surface of the preternaturally still lake while she waited for Mark to join her. It was important that he took the first step at each stage. She would walk ahead, but not lead. Mark would be his own champion or downfall, whatever occurred. She could feel her own excitement building, but was well practised at masking her emotions.

The king's boots appeared beside her, disturbing the white sand.

'We'll lose him,' whispered the king. 'He's going under.'

'It won't harm him. Haven't you realised that by now? Beside, my lord, this is no longer a hunt,' said Morgana. 'He has honoured you by bringing you, a mortal, to this place, where only those who were unbidden and unwelcome have come before. You are, to my knowledge, the first to be invited.'

She stood, fingers dripping, and joined Mark in watching as the tips of the white hart's antlers disappeared into the lake, yet seemed not to disturb the water's surface. All fell silent, and they looked out towards the island castle and the man fishing in the boat before it.

Mark looked all around, before turning back to Morgana, and when he spoke, it seemed to her that he had composed himself.

'Lady Morgana, what is this place? What is the hart and who,' he nodded out towards the small boat, 'is that out there on the lake?'

'I will explain everything when we get there,' said Morgana, and as she spoke, she kicked off her shoes and paddled into the lake, the glowing green water covering her feet and lapping at her ankles.

'Come,' she said, beckoning to King Mark, then waded farther out.

She knew he would stand for a moment, bewildered, upon the shore of the eerie underground lake. She knew he would quail and doubt her motives, but just as surely, she knew he was, even now, pulling off his boots and laying down his sword belt, she knew that …

Morgana heard splashing behind her and, knowing he would follow, she began to swim..

They trod water, facing one another, some distance out, but still far from the island with the castle upon it and not yet within calling distance of the fisherman, who seemed to pay them no heed at all.

'We are at the first of our destinations,' said Morgana.

'In the middle of an underground lake,' said Mark, spluttering, struggling to keep himself afloat.

'No ordinary lake,' said Morgana.

'I can see that, but can we not discuss this ashore,' said Mark. Water lapped into his mouth as he sank a little, and he spat it out then began to cough.

Morgana shook her head, satisfied to see him struggling and content that she had brought him so far. She swam closer to Mark, and wrapped an arm around him, helping to keep him afloat.

'Not long before the lady arrives. The message will have been relayed,' said Morgana.

'A lady?' asked Mark, sounding a little less desperate now that she was aiding him. Before she could answer, the dark-haired head of a woman broke the water, no more than an arm's length away from them. She frowned at Morgana, regarded Mark for a moment, bowing her head slowly, but cautiously, in acknowledgement, before turning her head back to the sorceress.

'Is it time?' she said.

'Nearly. I would introduce you to an honoured guest,' said Morgana, 'Mark, King of Cornwall.'

The lady, as was her way, seemed less than impressed, but then, thought Morgana, what was Cornwall to her, one who had yet to venture beyond the cavern.

The lady nodded her head to the king once more, but although she kept her eyes on him, she spoke to Morgana.

'If I take him down and through, will you keep your promise and take my child out of harm's reach when the time comes?'

Morgana smiled.

'Of course. Take him. Show him.'

'Very well,' said the lady, and she began to drift through the water towards Mark.

'Take me where? Show me what?' he said, clearly beginning to panic. Morgana tightened her grasp on him, and he struggled, but to no avail. The lady dove down before him, offering a brief glimpse of her swollen pregnant belly, bare back, behind and legs before disappearing.

'Morgana, I demand … ' began Mark, but then he cried out as he was pulled down. Morgana released him, and the king clawed at her, but she fended him off easily, then pushed down on his shoulders.

Mark, King of Cornwall, disappeared beneath the water.

As silence fell and the water stilled, Morgana swam towards the little boat and its lone occupant.

Chapter Eleven

2021

Tristan saw his destination from a mile away. As he drew closer, the block towered above him, some 25 floors high. He could see tiny balconies crammed with children's push-along cars, plastic slides and garden chairs, their railings decorated with drying sheets and clothing. Some windows were boarded up or broken.

He pulled his car into a small parking area, half-filled with working vehicles, but also an overflowing refuse skip, a burnt-out motorbike in a pool of melted tarmac and several cars up on bricks, their wheels missing.

Tristan pulled on the handbrake and checked the next name on his list.

Charles Merton.

Tristan centred himself for a moment, scanning the other vehicles in the car park for occupants, but he saw nobody. There were no vans parked on the streets that afforded a view of the front entrance, and although there were people around, he saw nobody that he should obviously be worried about. But where were the people from Hektor Security?

He left the holdall in the boot of the car and set out across the grass verge to the snaking footpath towards the building, remembering his counter-surveillance training, attempting to appear as inconspicuous as possible, while taking in his surroundings.

He reached the foot of the building and circled it, finding there were two ways in, the main door and an exit into a small car park at the back. Tristan approached the front door and made note of the intercom, a tarnished metal panel with buttons, numbers for flats underneath each of them, some worn away. No names.

There was a single button at the bottom, marked 'Trades'. He pressed it and pulled the door, but there was no movement. Broken or deactivated, it seemed.

He moved to the rear of the building and found a similar arrangement, noticing a needle cap on the ground among the other litter.

He pressed the 'Trades' button and found that it too was broken or deactivated.

Postman is out of luck then, thought Tristan.

No immediate way in.

Short of forcing entry, Tristan could go back to the mansion or call Hektor to bring him a fire key, used by the fire service to open communal doors, he could start pressing buttons and blag his way in or he could wait for an occupant to approach the door and rely on good old English politeness to follow them in. Somewhere else, perhaps somebody in that situation would challenge him, but in Tristan's experience, he was just as likely to have somebody hold a door open for him.

He paused, his finger outstretched, ready to start pressing buttons, as a realisation dawned.

Call Hektor to bring him a fire key.

His sorrow for Agravain had clouded his judgement, he realised. He would have to be careful.

He should not need to call Hektor Security. They should be there already. Watching.

And he'd already let Hektor know to send more people to back up their first unit after the attack on Kayleigh Turner, but there was no sign of anyone. Perhaps they'd already gone in?

Tristan stepped down from the communal door and pulled out his mobile phone. He called Hektor Security's control room and passed his identity and his codeword.

The call took less than a minute.

The Hektor units should be on scene and backup had apparently arrived some time ago. Two double-crewed units that had been checking in on schedule. Tristan made a note of the registration numbers of the Hektor Security vehicles and searched the immediate area. He found one, a nondescript car, in the same car park where he had left his vehicle. The second, a van, was parked in the next street. They must have walked across to meet their colleagues, rather than park another vehicle so close to the building.

But where were they? The Hektor control room operative told him they had just responded to welfare checks on their radios.

'Send more units, something has gone wrong,' said Tristan.

He ended the call and headed straight back to the Hektor

car and looked it over. No sign of a struggle. The doors were locked. Nothing out of place. Nothing on the ground around the car. Nobody was showing any interest in the car or the area, and people loved to stick their noses in, Tristan knew. Nothing obvious had happened in the street.

Which means what?

The Hektor Security people, four of them, had somehow been kidnapped without any sign of a struggle or anybody noticing or they had gone inside. But why would they? Perhaps they had seen somebody enter the tower block and were concerned enough to follow them.

And yet no updates about it to their control room?

It didn't make sense.

Tristan circled to the rear door of the building. The 'Trades' button didn't work there either, so he started hitting buttons on the intercom.

Number 1. No answer.

Number 2. No answer.

Number 3. Didn't work.

Each attempt cost him at least twenty seconds, as there was no way to end the call prematurely.

Number 4.

'Heelllo?' a woman's voice. Tristan estimated fifties, but maybe thirties or forties if she'd had a hard life.

'Hello, I'm sorry to bother you,' said Tristan. 'Nothing to worry about, but could you buzz me in?'

'Who is it?' said the voice.

'Police,' said Tristan, 'but I'm not coming to your address.'

'Fuck off,' said the woman and hung up.

Number 5. No answer.

Number 6. No answer.

Number 7.

'Yeah?' A man's voice. Gruff.

'Hello, I'm sorry to bother you,' said Tristan. 'Nothing to worry about, but could you buzz me in?'

'Who is it?'

'Police,' said Tristan, ' but I'm not here for you, mate.' He laughed.

Silence then a loud, irritating buzz.

Tristan hauled on the communal door, and it swung open.

'You're a gentleman,' called Tristan to the open intercom as he stepped inside. He took a pen from his inside pocket and used it to wedge the communal door open, so if he needed help, Hektor or the knights would have less trouble getting in.

He called Kay and told him what was happening.

'Dagonet's going to come and meet you,' said Kay.

'No, it'll take too long, and Hektor are sending more people. But if I call, you know where I am. Touch base with Hektor and have their control room update you. I'll stay in touch with them.'

Next, he called Hektor and told them he was going in. In return, the operator told him that backup was fifteen minutes out. Tristan checked they had picked up a fire key.

Satisfied, Tristan entered the tower block alone.

Silence.

Caitlyn held her breath as the van doors creaked open.

'Whatever you're doing, stop it,' said a man's voice.

Here goes nothing, test ordered, thought Caitlyn, as she mustered her courage.

'I need the toilet,' she said, but the gag rendered the speech incoherent.

She heard a sigh. Somebody climbed up into the van.

She flinched as fingers pressed hard into her cheeks, digging the gag up and prising it out from between her teeth.

'What?' said the man.

'I need the toilet,' said Caitlyn and was surprised at how forceful she sounded.

'You'll have to hold it,' said the man.

'I *have* been holding it,' said Caitlyn. 'I can't for much longer.'

Silence.

Not good, she thought, *but he hasn't left me. Initial test results are indicative of what? A human with actual feelings? Somebody indecisive? A person under orders that don't cover such an eventuality?*

'Well you can't go here,' said the man.

Was that an accent? She decided to concentrate on his voice despite the blindfold also obstructing her ears.

'I'd rather not,' she admitted, less forcefully than before.

Try for humour? Not yet, she thought. *Tests inconclusive.*

'I'm going to wet myself,' said Caitlyn. 'Please.'

The man sighed.

'Can you hold it for a few minutes more?'

Bingo. A human being with real actual feelings, thought Caitlyn. *Could still be under vague orders, but still, he made a decision based on compassion. And it's either an Irish or a Scottish accent.*

'I'll try. Thank you,' she said, trying to sound grateful and maybe a little pathetic.

The man grunted, put the gag back into place, looser than before, she realised, and he slammed the doors after climbing down. What little light had made it through the blindfold went out. She was alone in the dark once more.

The engine started up, and Caitlyn rolled as the driver manoeuvred the van. It stopped. She rolled the other way and then it was clear from the backward pull and the sound of the driver working their way through the gears that they were accelerating forward.

She considered her predicament in light of the new information.

Kidnapped, likely because of something to do with Arthur, by at least one male with a Scottish or Irish accent, who has enough compassion not to let me lie in my own urine. Well, either that or he doesn't want me to piss in his van, she thought.

Still insufficient information for a diagnosis, and there were a lot of unknown factors. The man who'd spoken to her was not working alone. She had been snatched by two men and a woman.

The van slowed, and Caitlyn slid feet first towards the front of the van as the driver hit the brakes a little too hard. This time two doors opened. The van rocked, and she heard footsteps either side of it.

The rear doors screeched and clunked as they were pulled open, and once more the rear was flooded with barely perceptible light.

She heard air expelled, and the rear of the van dipped as somebody stepped inside.

She felt a hand seize her foot and heard the snip of scissors on plastic, and she realised her legs were no longer bound.

Hands seized one arm and one shoulder before pulling her up into a sitting position.

'Stand up, but watch your head,' said the man with what she was now sure was an Irish accent. And feelings.

She stood, half-hauled to her feet by the Irishman, and he guided her towards the doors. He stepped down, the van shifted, and then he took hold of her right arm in both of his hands. Another pair of hands took her left.

'Step down,' said the Irishman, and Caitlyn did so, crouching and then swinging her leg forward. She started to pitch forward and yelped, but the hands holding her stopped the motion. Her foot hit what felt like dirt, and she stepped out.

There was no time to think about tests and symptoms and diagnoses, but she was out, her gag was looser and her legs were free.

'What about her trousers?' said the Irishman, and the words provoked an instant panic in Caitlyn.

They won't undress me? Surely not ...

'Let's take her over there, by those trees,' said a woman's voice. Hers was unmistakably a local accent. She sounded exasperated.

Caitlyn tried to protest, but the gag was still in place, and this time, the Irishman made no attempt to hear her better. They propelled her forward, and she tripped over a root.

'Stand very still,' said the woman. 'If you move, we'll kill you. Understood?'

Caitlyn nodded, wondering what would happen next.

'Move her hands to the front,' said the woman.

The hands on her right arm let go, then she felt fingers grip her left forearm and heard the same snipping sound.

Her hands were free, but Caitlyn, still blindfolded and totally unaware of her surroundings and what level of risk these people posed to her, stood obediently.

'Turn to face me,' said the Irishman, and Caitlyn did so, shuffling around, guided by the woman's hands on her left upper arm.

'Put your hands together,' said the Irishman, and she did as she was told. Within seconds, her hands were secured with a cable tie once more, but this time, in front of her.

'I'll face away,' said the Irishman, and he stepped back as he did so. 'Can you manage?'

'How?' said Caitlyn through the gag, bewildered and aghast at whatever manoeuvring she was about to have to do in front of and possibly aided by two strangers.

'You'll work it out,' said the woman. 'Hold my hands and squat if it helps, just hurry up.'

So this is where an Oxford education gets me, thought Caitlyn, taking a deep breath and fumbling to undo her jeans.

Chapter Twelve

Tintagel, Cornwall
5th Century

'What news?' asked Isolde, looking up as Tristan, soaked from the rain, entered her chamber. He shook his head, wet hair sticking to the back of his neck.

'Lucan sent a rider. They're still searching, but so far there's been no sign of the king or Morgana,' he reported and was about to remove his sodden cloak when Isolde stood.

'Well then,' she said. 'I've waited long enough.'

Tristan tilted his head, puzzled.

'I'll not sit idly by while my future husband lies injured in some ditch or murdered by some treacherous sorceress,' said Isolde, and she set her handmaidens scurrying to pack her belongings.

'You cannot mean to ride out?' asked Tristan, but a fierce glance from Isolde told him otherwise, and he stood watching her until she looked up, eyebrows raised, and scolded him.

'Will you stand there till you take root, my lord?' she asked. 'Or perhaps you could send word to the stables that the Irish mean to ride out and show the Cornish how it's done.'

Tristan laughed at her audacity.

'I forbid it,' said Tristan. 'King Mark would have me flayed if I allowed his bride to roam the land, here and there, with little thought for her own safety. Nay, lady. You'll stay at Tintagel until the king is found or returns of his own accord.'

'Will I?' She stood, planting her hands on her hips. 'And who is Tristan to command the Princess of Munster and soon-to-be Queen of Cornwall, tell me that?'

'Your appointed guardian and commander of Tintagel in my uncle's stead,' said Tristan, quieter than before, aware of not only Isolde's anger, but the eyes of her handmaidens upon him.

'Guardian, is it? This princess remembers plucking her guardian from the sea, not so very long ago,' she said.

'Even so,' said Tristan, and it pained him to be firm with her, going against his every instinct to acquiesce to her wishes, to make her smile rather than frown. While she stood, defying him, her pale cheeks reddening and her anger radiating across the room, he could not help but think of going to her and taking her in an embrace.

'Even so,' she spat, turning her back on him.

'Isolde … ' Tristan started, but she held up her hand and said,

'If you'll leave me in peace then, *my lord.*'

He stood for a moment, regretting his words, but then left her to stew.

He'd known she would not heed him, though he could not have explained why, beyond feeling that there was some connection between them, and he just … knew. He felt as though he'd known Isolde all his life and yet had been waiting for her. They'd spent only a small amount of time together since they met in Munster, and yet Tristan felt about her as he had no other. The word love crossed his mind when he thought of her, berating himself inwardly when it slipped past his guard.

In the early hours of the morning, all who dwelt at Tintagel were silent and still, save for the guards who made their patrols and for the Irish princess who Tristan knew would all too soon creep from her chamber.

He waited, resting back against the stone wall and, sure enough, he heard the hinges creak before an hour had passed.

Tristan listened to her feet padding towards him and stepped out so that when she rounded the corner, he barred her path. Isolde jumped when she saw him and let out a gasp, but no more. They stood, looking into one another's eyes, saying nothing for a time.

'He's to be my husband and king,' she said when the silence wore itself out.

'And so he'll expect to find you here when he returns,' said Tristan. 'What difference can you make out there in lands you know not at all?'

'More than if I sit here and play the helpless maid!' said Isolde.

Once more silence fell between them, but neither looked away from the other's eyes.

Once more, Isolde spoke first.

'I would not have it said I stood by and left the king to his fate. I will go, Tristan, if not now, then when your vigilance fails, but I hope it will not come to that. I am not a prisoner at Tintagel, am I?'

'No, lady,' Tristan conceded, 'and though I could lock you away, I could not live with myself. If you are determined, I will allow it.'

He reached for her hands and saw her hesitate before taking them in her own.

'You are of the greatest importance to me, Princess,' he said, caressing the back of her hands with the pads of his thumbs. He looked down, watching the motion momentarily, and when he looked up, he saw uncertainty and was that ... anxiety?

'I ... ' he began, but thought better of what he had been about to say, as he felt her gently trying to withdraw her hands.

'I ... will see to it that you have a company with mounts and provisions so that you may join the search in the morning,' he concluded, releasing her. He could have sworn he saw her sigh in relief. Surely he had not frightened her? It was all too apparent to Tristan that there was a bond between them, so he doubted she would fear him. Perhaps the prospect of their growing affection alarmed her, just as it did him? Perhaps she did not trust herself?

He stepped back out of respect for whatever she was thinking and feeling.

She smiled and thanked him before asking,

'Will you ride out with us, Tristan?'

Ah, so she is not ill at ease if she is inviting me to join her!

'I will, thank you, lady,' he said, 'but not before I escort you back to your chambers, lest you are missed and all of Tintagel is woken by the cries of your outraged handmaidens!'

Once more, she smiled, and Tristan took her hand. Again, she hesitated, but allowed him to walk with her. Tristan felt his heart beating as they approached her chamber, unable to dismiss the image of him rounding on her, sweeping her into that longed-for embrace before giving in and kissing her.

He did not act on the impulse, knowing they must resist one another.

Tristan and Isolde are not destined to be lovers, he told himself as she opened the door to her chambers, his eyes taking in every inch of her before she disappeared, offering him the thinnest of goodnights as she did so.

My loyalty lies with my uncle and not with my heart's desire, thought Tristan as he set off for his own room.

He tried to sleep, knowing he had a long day ahead of him, but he could not stop thinking of Isolde, imagining a future together that he knew could never happen, not without betraying his king and his country. The hours before dawn passed all too slowly, and as the morning's light covered Tintagel, Tristan despaired of composing himself when next he saw Isolde.

He must not give himself away, must not act like a foolish boy.

'Easier said than done,' he whispered, his forearm draped across his eyes as he lay in bed.

❦

He must have fallen asleep eventually, as he was woken by knocking on his chamber door.

'Beg pardon, my lord, but Lucan has returned, and he has brought Merlin with him.

The wizard demands to speak with you,' said the guard, after Tristan bade him enter.

'Merlin? See that they are given a meal in the great hall,' said Tristan, jumping up, several thoughts and feelings coming to him at once; concern for King Mark, disappointment and relief at the delay in riding out with Isolde, but comfort at the news of the wizard's arrival. 'I will be down directly.'

He dressed in a hurry, wondering what news Lucan would bring of his uncle, running a score of scenarios through his mind, not a few of which resulted in him becoming king and taking Isolde to wife. He hated himself for the thoughts when they came, unbidden, and he muttered chastisements as he pulled on his boots before making for the great hall.

There he found Lucan's company seated at a long table, looking weary, but, when Tristan counted them, all intact. There was no sign of Merlin. Lucan stood and met him halfway across the hall.

'Good morrow, brother,' said Lucan.

'What tidings?' asked Tristan, watching Lucan lick his lips.

Speak, thought Tristan. *Let me know of my uncle's fate. I can wait no longer.*

'We have not found them,' said Lucan. 'We've followed every trail worth following, scoured every shelter and searched far and wide with no luck, save for stumbling upon Merlin.'

'What has she done to him?' said Tristan. 'By God, if she's hurt him, Mordred will feel the wrath of Cornwall, I swear it.'

He felt like a hypocrite, offering up such threats in the name of honour and vengeance while privately coveting his uncle's bride, scheming against him, even if it were only in his dreams.

'Merlin doubts Morgana would have done so, cousin,' said Lucan.

'And why is that?' asked Tristan. He did not know Merlin well, but had met the wizard several times when he visited Tintagel.

'Because I have a brain, knowledge and crafts beyond your ken, young lord,' said Merlin from behind him. Tristan turned and bowed low to the wizard.

'You are welcome, Merlin,' he said. 'You could not have come at a better time, if you are willing to lend aid. But what brings you to Tintagel? We were not expecting you.'

'I was not so far away when a messenger reached me, bringing troubling news of the King of Cornwall seen in the company of King Arthur's sister, Morgana,' said Merlin. 'I thought more of Mark than to fall for her schemes, but Lucan tells me that he rode out with her of his own volition, in search of a white hart. I would speak plainly, but it is bad luck and ill manners to speak of the idiocy of a king in his own hall,' he concluded.

Neither Tristan nor Lucan replied.

'He has still not returned?' asked Merlin, and Tristan shook his head.

'Another search party was to ride out this morning,' he said, but Merlin scoffed.

'A waste of time, boy, a waste of time. He is with Morgana, and if she does not wish for him to be found then he will not be, not by the usual means, though I may be able to assist,' he said.

'I ... we ... fear she has bewitched him, Merlin,' said Tristan, feeling foolish at the suggestion.

'Lucan told me as much, and though she is not above dabbling with enchantments and bewitchment, if she has led King Mark to the white hart and the beast is complicit, there are greater matters at hand and much more to worry about.'

'What is the significance of the white hart?' said Isolde. Tristan realised for the first time that she had come up silently behind him.

'And who is this?' asked Merlin.

'May I introduce Princess Isolde of Munster, Merlin? She is promised to King Mark, and they are to be married when he returns,' said Tristan.

'If he returns,' said Merlin, but he bowed to Isolde before continuing,

'The significance of the white hart, my dear, is debated by the wise, but I have spoken with him and know the truth of it. While others contend that he is of the Otherworld, I know better. The white hart is *of* this island, Princess, one with it, but he also travels between it and the Otherworld. He knows the way there. And there is only one mortal, other than myself, who knows the way - Morgana Le Fay.'

'And you think this is more than a coincidence?' asked Lucan.

Tristan folded his arms over his chest, taking his eyes from Isolde and focusing on Merlin.

'A sorceress attempting to position her son to usurp King Arthur takes the King of Cornwall, Arthur's ally, on a quest to hunt the white hart, a legendary being who passes between this land and the Otherworld, with which she too has connections, just as an alliance between Munster and Cornwall was about to be assured by marriage. How can this be a mere coincidence?' asked Tristan.

'It is not, boy,' said Merlin.

'Then what has become of King Mark?' asked Isolde.

Chapter Thirteen

2021

Tristan stood alone in the tower block's lobby, the reek of urine filling his nostrils. Grime and neglect were apparent wherever he looked, from the pile of split bin bags spilling their contents on to the floor, notably a banana peel and a used nappy, to the bare concrete stairs, upon which various small puddles and stains could be seen.

Agravain's descendant lives here?

Charles Merton's flat was up there somewhere, high above Tristan's head, through floor after floor of flats.

He had two options, take the stairs all the way up to the top floor or risk the, no doubt, dilapidated lift car. He glanced towards the metal doors and saw a sign bearing the words 'OUT OF ORDER' on them.

One option then.

Nevertheless, Tristan pressed the call button for the lift, just in case. No movement.

He set off up the stairs.

Up and up he went, his Glock 17 still in its shoulder holster, his Commando knife still sheathed on his belt. He considered the angles of exposure, where he was vulnerable to attack from the landing he was approaching, as well as the stairways above and below.

Close angle on approach to a landing, mid angle as he checked the next stair up and high angle, looking up at the landing they led to, he worked floor by floor, as stealthily as possible, keeping a steady pace, not hurrying to problem angles and pausing, but working from muscle memory, in routine, as he moved.

He wanted to draw his firearm, but this was a residential building with any number of witnesses and although his gut told him that there was something amiss, he had no solid proof of its nature yet, so arming himself seemed premature.

He knew the time might come before long.

Tristan paid attention with all senses, feeling for vibration under foot or in the walls, listening for noise all around him, trying to differentiate between relevant sounds and the hubbub from the flats, trying to detect unusual odours in the air that might give him cause for concern.

Tristan had reached the tenth floor, and he was feeling it in his legs.

The door to his right opened, and he stepped to one side, dropping one hand to his knife, but it was a couple manoeuvring a pushchair with a sleeping infant inside. He relaxed somewhat, apologised when the woman jumped upon seeing him, then started up the next set of stairs.

'Don't give us a hand then,' said the man.

Tristan looked back and saw the couple begin the long journey down the stairs, her holding the pushchair's handles and him holding up the front.

'Next time,' said Tristan, quietly, as he carried on up the stairs.

He heard the man say 'wanker' under his breath, but ignored it.

Tristan began to tire, his leg muscles aching and his breathing laboured.

He crossed the thirteenth floor, breathing hard of the urine-tainted air, and as he was heading up to the fourteenth, he heard a door open just behind him. Before he could turn back to look, he was frozen to the spot, unable to move at all, not even his eyes.

'Follow me, mate,' said a man's voice, rough, like a lifetime smoker.

Tristan felt his limbs begin to move without a command. He could not draw his Glock or go for his knife, he just turned and walked slowly back down the stairs towards the man who was holding open the door that led to the flats on the thirteenth floor, all movement out of his control.

The man was in his fifties, with days' worth of stubble and lank greasy grey hair. His cheeks were hollow and his eyes sunken. He wore a cheap tracksuit, but expensive trainers on his feet. His bent body shook, but his eyes were fixed on Tristan as the knight walked meekly towards him.

Tristan, not knowing why, took hold of the open door, and the man shuffled around and set off down a corridor. Tristan followed a few paces behind.

They reached the door to one of the flats, and the man knocked.

A chain jangled on the other side of the door, and it opened a crack. A woman, also in her fifties, was just visible through the gap.

Two junkies in less than a minute, thought Tristan. *Not surprising in this locale, but a junkie with mind control? That's interesting.*

It would be if it was true, said a new male voice in his head.

Tristan's mind went blank from the shock, but then, unbidden, his normal internal voice returned, considering his options, laying bare his tactics and plans, even as he tried to resist doing so.

Battling with his own mind, Tristan elected to recite the alphabet silently in the real world, but at a holler inside his mind, drowning out all other thought or attention.

The woman opened the door, and the man in the tracksuit looked up at Tristan, seemingly confused, then disappeared back towards the stairwell without another word.

Tristan sidled into the darkness of the flat beyond, as if side-stepping into an oven, the heat was so extreme. He took in all the detail, but kept mentally chanting letters, so he had no ability to consider what he had seen or heard until later. His feet sunk into what felt like wet brown carpet, something that would not have been out of place in the 1970s. He travelled down a narrow hallway with a single bare light bulb hanging overhead and peeling wallpaper either side of him. As he passed the kitchen, a monstrous dog leapt up, barking, and smashed into two baby gates, fixed in the frame to bar the way. Tristan's recitation ended as his adrenaline spiked, but he did not react bodily, simply continuing to walk towards a half-open door at the end of the hallway, through which he could now hear a voice.

―⁂―

Well, that was fun, thought Caitlyn as she finished pulling up her jeans and fiddled with the button. She kept her head down to hide that while she had been positioning herself into a crouch so that she did not get urine on her clothes, aided by the woman, she had managed to nudge the blindfold slightly off her left eye.

Partial vision in one eye, less tightly gagged, muffled hearing, legs free and hands bound to her front.

Progress, thought Caitlyn.

'Here, let me,' said the woman. Caitlyn paused then held her arms slightly apart as the woman finished securing her jeans.

'Thank you,' said Caitlyn.

No response from the woman.

'Alright?' said the Irishman.

The woman grunted.

'Wait a minute,' said Caitlyn, as she heard the Irishman start walking back towards her and felt the woman's hand on her arm grip tighter.

The Irishman paused.

'Come on,' said the woman, pulling forward, but Caitlyn pulled back, just enough to check motion, not to fight.

'Are you going to hurt me?' she asked, hoping to put her

kidnappers on the back foot. Given the woman's humane behaviour during the peeing episode, she felt newly confident that both of these people weren't hardened sociopaths, even if they weren't very pleasant.

'No, love, you'll be fine,' said the Irishman.

'Not if you shut up and do as you're told,' said the woman.

Caitlyn stumbled forward a few steps as the Irishman grabbed her other arm.

'Is this about Arthur?' she blurted, desperate not to go back into the van and lose all of the progress she had made.

They kept dragging her forward. She had no way of digging her heels in, so she dropped suddenly, no doubt yanking their shoulders. They both exclaimed, her a yelping sound and him, more of a 'Hey!'.

'I'm just his girlfriend,' said Caitlyn, unable to disguise the fear in her voice. 'He's not going to pay you anything for me. Please, I don't have anything to do with this.'

The woman dropped her, and pain shot through Caitlyn's knees as they thumped into the dirt. A second later, and she felt the woman's left hand grip her upper arm and then a punch to the left side of the head, just behind the temple.

Caitlyn, caught completely unawares, let out a guttural groan, not a noise she had ever made before, and head spinning, she collapsed forward and to her right, then hung suspended by her right arm, the Irishman having never let go.

'For fuck's sake, Sandrine, we're not meant to hurt her,'

said the Irishman, but extricating a name through this reverse form of torture gave Caitlyn no pleasure. In fact, she barely registered it for a moment, she was so close to losing consciousness, her vision blurred and an instant headache dancing all over her skull.

'Get up, love,' he said.

'I wonder about you,' spat the woman, helping haul Caitlyn up. They dragged her forward, her knees occasionally grazing the ground.

'Please,' managed Caitlyn, opening her eyes to find that the blindfold had shifted so that it no longer covered either of her eyes.

She was being dragged through woodland, back towards the open rear doors of the van, seemingly alone in a very small car park.

'I'll give you whatever you want,' said Caitlyn, the tears coming now, 'tell you whatever you need.'

'Look,' said Sandrine, her voice sharp. She dropped Caitlyn once more, and this time she hit the dirt face-first. Sandrine grabbed a handful of Caitlyn's hair, lifting her face slightly, squatted low and hissed at her. 'We've got enough on our plates without you starting to be a stupid bitch, got it? We don't have to hurt you if you behave, but I bloody will if you don't. You've got nothing we want and you *are* coming with us. Got it? Now stop pricking about and get back in the van.' She slammed Caitlyn's head forward.

Caitlyn's face smashed into the dirt, and she howled as her nose mashed against a stone. Blood started running over her top lip and dribbled into her mouth as her whole face began to feel like it was pulsating.

Sheer panic took over, and Caitlyn began to scream, long and hard and loud.

Another blow to the back of the head, and Caitlyn began to sob as the Irishman tried to pull her up, telling Sandrine to stop. Caitlyn's knees cleared the ground, and she found her feet.

'Get her in the van,' Sandrine ordered.

The Irishman obeyed, and Caitlyn, sobbing, nose broken, blood dripping down her face and her whole head in pain, made no more attempts at resisting or persuading.

The woman seized her arm again, the two of them walked her up into the van then forcefully sat her down.

'Lie on your back,' said the woman, and Caitlyn, composing herself, but still with tears rolling down her cheeks, did as she was told. She found herself looking up at a slight, dark-haired woman with tanned skin and black hair tied back in a ponytail.

Sandrine dropped to one knee.

'For fuck's sake,' she spat, and hauled the blindfold back over Caitlyn's eyes. 'You told her my bloody name and now she's seen my face.'

The Irishman made no reply.

Together, they retied her legs, re-secured her gag and blindfold and once more moved her hands behind her before cable-tying them together.

They climbed down out of the van, and Caitlyn heard the doors creak.

'You've seen my face,' said Sandrine. 'You know my

name. You aren't going home, you might as well accept it.'

'Sandrine … ' said the Irishman in a chiding tone.

'Let her stew on that,' said the woman. 'Malagant will feed all the better for it.'

Caitlyn, her whole body shaking, heard footsteps down the side of the van.

The door to the cab opened, and she heard the engine start up. A shudder ran through the vehicle, and she felt the ongoing vibration through the metal floor.

The van doors creaked as though someone was about to close them.

'I'm a doctor,' said Caitlyn. 'I have family.'

'Don't we all,' said the Irishman.

One door slammed shut.

'Help me,' said Caitlyn.

'I would if I could, love,' said the Irishman, 'but there's big business going on.'

The other door creaked.

'And the boss has to eat,' he concluded, before slamming it shut, and the last of the light faded.

Caitlyn lay in the dark and cried.

Chapter Fourteen

Cornwall
5th Century

'You can't stay silent forever,' said Morgana to the figure, swathed in robes, sitting in the stern of the boat and quietly fishing.

He turned his head, and she could feel his eyes upon her, but then he turned his attention to the depths once more.

'I *will* be back,' said Morgana, smiling, 'I always get my way in the end.'

'I suspect I will not see you again,' said the voice from within the robe.

Morgana frowned, but recovered quickly from the moment of apparent prescience ... or was he just taunting her?

'Maybe so, but you spoke,' she concluded, before turning her eyes back to the water and the green glow coming from below.

'How long will they be?' she said to nobody, shivering in her wet clothes, but the robed figure answered.

'Days, weeks, months, years,' it said. 'How long were you gone, Morgana, when Merlin sent you in?'

Morgana did not reply, but she remembered all too well. The temptation had been too much. A day in the Otherworld had cost her many, many years.

'Row me to the shore? No, not that way. To the island,' she said. The robed figure sighed and did as it was bade, pulling slowly. The boat's progress caused ripples in the still water and the merest of sounds in a near-silent cavern.

'Why do you keep coming here if you only wish to leave every time? There are wonders below and life beyond measure,' asked the figure in the boat.

'I have business with the Britons, Fisher King,' said Morgana. 'Merlin uses his magic to exert sway over these lands, meddling where he should not. He ensured my father's death, allowed Uther to rape my mother and brought about the birth of my half-brother, Arthur, who now rules much of the land. And with honour, they say! Chivalry, they will say! A warlord destined to become a legend. The wizard cannot be allowed to succeed. We both know what this land will become. Green fields will be replaced with black roads with mechanised carts and smoke fouling the air. The trees? Gone. Peace and harmony? Gone. My kind will run rampant, separated from their bonds with nature, and the land will suffer. I cannot allow the harmony that Merlin seeks, and the means to thwart him lie below. I cannot allow his vision for humanity to come to pass, and I will die before I give up.'

'You will, lady,' said the figure, giving Morgana pause, and he kept on rowing.

'You saw the white hart?' she asked, a few moments later, as the boat neared the shore.

'Cernunnos aids you, I know,' said the Fisher King. 'Although I cannot fathom why.'

'I shared my visions of the future, and he does not wish to see such destruction.'

The Fisher King sighed.

'When you have lived as long as I, you will see the folly in attempting to slow the inevitable, lady. I am surprised you have earned the support of the Horned God, but he will regret his part in time, I have no doubt.'

'We will see,' said Morgana.

'Not you, my lady, you are not long for this world now. Merlin is not the only meddler, and meddlers make for young corpses. Be warned. There is time to turn away, but you won't, I know,' the Fisher King concluded, as the prow of the boat ran up against white sand.

'We will see,' said Morgana once more. She

jumped from the boat into the clear, cool shallows and, feeling a tingling in the air, she looked up at the looming castle walls while she made her way up the slight incline to the open portcullis.

The Fisher King shook his head as the boat floated back on to the surface of the lake, and once he was far enough out, he fetched up his rod and line once more.

There was time. For him, at least.

Morgana passed through the gate of Corbenic Castle, and the hairs on the back of her neck stood up. The air seemed to crackle around her as she walked into the silent, deserted courtyard. She passed by the well and made for a door in a corner tower, opening it silently and passing into the dimly lit interior, green flame burning in sconces on the walls. Morgana entered a stairwell of bare stone, almost impossibly steep to her eyes, but she knew from experience that she could scramble down it if she went backwards and used her hands to steady her as she followed the tight twists down and down. She did so now and an eternity seemed to pass before she reached yet another door at the bottom.

Morgana reached out, but the door creaked open and a light sprang up in the dark cave beyond. The sound of dripping met her ears, as though she was hearing the dwindling count of her life's remaining seconds; a steady, relentless drip of water into a pool.

She exhaled loudly, realising she had been holding her breath despite her exertion on the stairs. It had been such a long time since she had ventured down here and the last occasion had been with Merlin, as a girl, when the bond between them was strong, and he still thought it wise to share his knowledge with her.

All was as it had been. The small cave was almost entirely taken up by a great iron cauldron that came up to her chest. That was different. Merlin had lifted her to see inside when she was little, but now she could see the shimmering water within, all on her own. She needed nobody now.

Only the drops of water broke the surface, falling directly into the centre and sending never-ending ripples towards the edge like tiny waves. A plain wooden cup of an ancient and simple design bobbed within the cauldron, and Morgana chuckled at the sight of it.

She looked up at the source of the dripping and saw a curl of iridescent root of many colours, emerging from a crack in the rock and twisting down from the roof of the cave. Water ran along it before reaching the lowest point and falling into the cauldron below.

Morgana licked her lips, her heart beating fast.

As much as she despised Merlin now, she would do as he had done, so many years ago. She hurried to the cauldron, showing no reverence, and, ignoring the cup, she reached in to take up a handful of water. Most of it escaped before it reached her lips, but she hurriedly drank what was left, and shivered as it passed through her, making her body tingle. She closed her eyes and brought more and more water to her lips then licked every last drop from her skin, sucking it from each finger and her thumb in turn. She exhaled, bit her lip and tried to control her breathing, fighting the euphoric high that threatened to consume her.

She reached for her waterskin, hand shaking, and emptied it out on to the moss at her feet and then plunged it into the cauldron until it had filled.

It would be enough, she thought, to treat her plants accordingly.

∽∾⊹∾∾

When Morgana returned to the lakeside, she saw only the Fisher King out in his boat, and when she called to him, he simply shook his head. Spying nobody on the far shore, Morgana sighed and returned to Corbenic Castle, kicking the pebbles at her feet petulantly as she did so.

She wandered the halls and the courtyard. She tried every door she came across, poked around empty rooms, sat in chairs by unlit fireplaces and wondered at the purpose of the place, who had built it and if anyone had ever lived there.

Hours passed in this way, broken only by her trips down to the shoreline, each fruitless.

What if he does not return? What then? How will Cornwall react to their king disappearing with Mordred's mother? All my plans will have led to worse than had I never set them in motion at all, she thought, in her weaker moments.

But she did have faith, and the worries passed.

Malagant would not fail her. He would show King Mark what was being prepared and convince him to join with Mordred. Her memories of communing with the Unseelie fey spirit across the barriers between his world and hers kept her company for a while, until her concentration was broken when she passed through yet another nondescript door and found an orchard, nestled within the castle walls, perfectly protected on all sides.

Scattered all around between the trees were grassy hillocks. Burial mounds, she realised, but for whom?

The castle's builders, perhaps, but if it were so, from which side did they hail? Surely the Otherworld, given the advanced nature of Corbenic itself, far beyond any halls humans had so far constructed.

Morgana reached the nearest mound and lay upon it, face down, her arms outstretched as though embracing the ground. She closed her eyes and reached out to whatever or whoever lay within, but although something stirred in her, the faintest of connections, she received no reply.

She did, however, hear a call echo around the cavern, and she smiled as she set off to find King Mark - hopefully, her latest ally.

―⁂―

Morgana stood at the entrance to Corbenic Castle, her eyes fixed on the Fisher King's boat. The old man himself sat silently, oars at the ready, while King Mark clung to the gunwale, his long hair loose and drenched. She saw him pause for a moment and then with a great heave he pulled himself up and propelled his body over and into the boat.

The Fisher King handled the oars with skill,

turned the boat's prow towards her, and he began to row. Morgana watched King Mark settle in the stern sheets. She saw his serious face dissolve into an uncharacteristic grin, and he raised a hand in greeting. She returned the gesture cautiously, though her heart was leaping.

She made a great effort not to fidget, as drawn as she was to shifting her weight from foot to foot and wringing her hands. Morgana forced herself to remain composed as she waited to see the outcome of King Mark's visit through the portal to the Otherworld.

She watched him jump into the shallows and wade on to the beach, looking all around him. She saw him exchange words with the Fisher King, who simply shook his head and began to take his boat a little farther out.

Mark stood on the white sand and looked up, seemingly marvelling at the castle, but then stopped, his eyes fixing on Morgana. The grin returned, and he walked up to meet her, and she to him, never taking her eyes off him. Something was wrong.

'Lady Morgana,' said King Mark, still grinning, but he bowed his head slightly.

'King Mark?' she asked.

'He dwells within,' said the spirit wearing the man before her. 'You were true to your word.

The king was a powerful man, physically and politically. If all is as you say and this place is devoid of magic, I will feast like a great lord in your world with him as my host.'

'This was not what we agreed, Malagant. You were to show him all that will one day come through, under my son's command, then send him back,' said Morgana.

'King Mark was not persuaded,' said Malagant. 'So rather than have him as a pawn in your game, he will be a vessel for me to cross into your world.'

Morgana said nothing for a moment, rethinking her strategy, and pondering her next moves, closing her eyes as she did so. It came to her and she opened her eyes.

'You will play the part of King Mark and bring Cornwall under our control,' she said.

'A mortal dares to command me?' said Malagant with King Mark's mouth.

'A mortal no longer,' said Morgana, 'and one who dared to reach between the worlds and offer up a king, it seems, so that we might bring down a greater one and install a greater one still, in my son, here in a world where you need not fear your previous masters, Malagant. You will work for me or I will send you home, spirit. And when my goals are met, when my son sits upon King Arthur's throne, and I have banished

Merlin's evil from this land, your hunger will be more than sated.'

A red mist seeped from around Mark's eyes, forming a cloud about him, and for a moment, the king was himself once more.

'You betrayed me,' said Mark, as the mist began to float towards Morgana. She ignored the king, held up a hand and extended her grasp with her will, checking the spirit as it advanced upon her, not yet fully abandoning the king.

'Do not test me, Malagant,' she said and extended her fingers, partially dissipating the mist. King Mark was backing away from her, but the mist gathered together and sank back into him. Mark stood still and bowed his head.

'Together then,' said Malagant.

Morgana nodded.

'Let us go. We have work to do and much to discuss.'

Chapter Fifteen

2021

Tristan gave up resisting as his body was compelled to walk towards the room and the voice at the end of the dimly lit, dank corridor, his boots squelching on the wet brown carpet.

He heard the ill-looking woman close the front door behind him.

A catch clicked. A chain jangled.

Tristan forced himself not to think of how he might resist or escape, knowing all too well that the voice in his head was listening. He forced thoughtlessness upon himself, seeing what he saw, smelling what he smelt, hearing what he heard. He made no mental comment upon it.

He reached the mostly open entrance to the living room beyond and saw his hand rise then push the door wide.

Tristan stepped inside, his eyes still locked dead ahead, and though he could make out a figure to his right in his peripheral vision, all he could focus on was the stained, ripped and peeling wallpaper directly opposite him. It bore a rose pattern, something ostentatious, but outdated and perhaps, thought Tristan, indicative of a previous tenant.

'No idea,' said the voice in his head, but this time aloud, presumably from the figure on the right. He wanted to turn towards it, but he still had no control over his body.

'Why you here then, eh?' said the man's voice. 'Well?'

Still, Tristan could not move, his eyes fixed dead ahead.

How am I supposed to answer?

The man to his right laughed.

'Sorry fella! What a twat.'

Tristan was carried as a passenger in his own body as it walked into the room, and he took in the view as he turned. The wallpaper was in the same condition throughout, except for a section where it was entirely missing. Three dirty, bare mattresses were pushed up against walls and a scattering of empty plastic bottles, dog-ends and various detritus was littered across the carpet, stained in places and inexplicably wet throughout. The dog started barking again.

Tristan wheeled and a balding, diminutive man in his fifties came into view, his back to the knight. Expensive trainers again, generic grey tracksuit trousers and a white polo shirt. His arms were heavily tattooed with tribal designs. He stood, hunched, at the window, bracing himself with a forearm against the glass, while he looked out over the council estate below and greenery farther afield.

'Go on then, talk,' said the man.

Tristan frowned then realised he *could* frown. He cleared his throat, tried to move his arms and was about to speak when the man cut in, never turning to look at him.

'I can feel you trying. Don't be daft, yeah? You can only

do what I let you do. My turf, this. You're here for me. I know that much.'

'Charles Merton?' asked Tristan, relieved to hear his own voice again.

The man nodded.

'For my sins,' he muttered, 'but call me Charlie.'

'I'm not here to hurt you, Mr Merton,' said Tristan.

Silence for a moment, and Tristan realised that Merton was … what? Probing his mind. Poking about in his thoughts and intentions.

'Seems not,' said Merton, straightening up and turning towards Tristan for the first time. His face was clean-shaven and unremarkable, and his clothes were clean. He seemed incongruous in the grotty flat. 'Let's be sure though, eh?'

Tristan felt himself draw his Glock and unsheath his Commando knife. He walked towards Merton and handed them both over, before stepping back to his previous position.

Fuck.

'Yeah, fuck,' Merton laughed, but did not look amused. 'You're alright though, and so are your friends.' The man nodded towards the far side of the room, behind Tristan, and, suddenly able to, the knight turned and saw the four men from Hektor Security, facing the wall, with their fingers in their ears.

Tristan turned back to Merton.

'How much do you know?' he asked.

'Bits and pieces from what crosses your mind. You're here for me. You're in a hurry. You've got other people to check on. You thought I might be dead, but you're relieved

I'm not. That's good, innit?'

'It's a lot to explain, but you are in danger, Mr Merton. There are people who may be coming for you. You're related to somebody important to them.'

'Agravain?' spat Merton, frowning. 'What kind of name is that?'

But before Tristan could answer, Merton continued.

'An old one,' he whispered, then, louder and increasingly doubtful, 'One of Arthur's knights. He just died? You feel guilty about it. Woah, don't get angry, son. I'm just saying what you're thinking.'

Tristan bit his lip and, finding he was now free, he folded his arms across his chest, but kept his hands free, so that he was ready if an assault should come.

'Can we try this the usual way, Mr Merton?'

'Go on, son,' said Merton, scratching behind his jaw. 'I assume I'm right in thinking you're on your own?'

'Yes, but it won't be long before others arrive.'

'I've had these fellas check in whenever their radios went off or their phones rang,' said Merton. 'Can do the same for you if needs be.'

Tristan didn't reply, but watched as Merton stepped out of the room, and took a look into the kitchen.

'I fancy a tea, but not made here,' he said.

'This isn't your flat?' asked Tristan.

'No, I heard these guys when they turned up, all their thoughts turned to me and my flat. I thought I'd better make myself scarce until I could figure out what was up. Can't be too careful in my game.'

'What game is that?' asked Tristan.

A wry smile crept on to Merton's face.

'I've … borrowed … this flat from some … customers.' He raised an eyebrow and tilted his head towards the hallway. Tristan looked down towards the front door and saw the woman still standing there, like a still zombie, track marks up her arms. She, too, was under Merton's control, he realised.

'That's right,' said the man at the window. 'Comes in handy. Can't switch it off. Awake, asleep. I see and hear everything from up here. It's amazing what I can get away with now.'

Merton turned the Glock over, inspecting it.

He doesn't know how to use it, thought Tristan, but was unable to stop the images of the weapon's operation popping into his mind.

'Glock 17? Good to know,' said Merton then laughed, but in a good-natured way, Tristan acknowledged, when the knight sighed.

'You're alright, son, don't worry. But let's be having it, yeah?' said Merton.

Tristan sighed and began at the beginning. The story sounded ridiculous, even to him, but he persisted, his cheeks reddening and his brow furrowing all the more with every grunt, chortle, laugh and expletive Charlie Merton displayed or put forth.

'So, you may be in danger from Malagant's people,' Tristan finished.

Silence.

' … the Order of … what was it?' said Merton, smirking, eyebrows raised.

'The Order of Phobos and Deimos,' said Tristan, maintaining eye contact, feeling foolish, but determined to persist.

'The Order … of Phobos … and Deimos,' Merton repeated. He turned to look out of the window.

'I know it sounds … ' Tristan began, but Merton cut him off.

'I know it's true, or at least, you believe it's true.'

'So you think I'm insane? I'm not,' said Tristan.

'No, no you're not. You haven't lived until you've dipped into the mind of a schizophrenic. Her out in the hall? She's a treat to have screaming in your mind while you sleep, trust me on that,' muttered Merton. 'I know you're telling the truth, but it's bloody hard to believe, all the same!'

Tristan nodded.

'They're coming for you. We can keep you safe,' he said, but Merton just smiled a patronising smile.

'If I can keep the Old Bill, you, Hektor Security and my competitors at bay, I ain't gonna worry about some nutty cultists, am I?' said Merton.

'We don't know who they have working with them or what abilities they might possess. You might find yourself outmatched, and besides ….' Tristan looked around the flat and raised his eyebrow, 'we can get you out of this dump.'

'My place is a lot nicer, and I've got all I need,' said Merton, frowning.

Tristan didn't reply.

'I'm set up for life,' Merton continued.

Tristan said nothing.

'Well, what do you know?' said Merton, waving a hand dismissively at Tristan.

'I didn't say anything,' said Tristan.

'No,' said Merton. He returned to staring out of the window.

Tristan looked at the man's back, feeling a desperate need to help, not for Merton's sake, but for Agravain's. Here was his friend's descendant. The part of Agravain that lived on and what, he was a drug dealer in a rundown block of flats? King of the tower?

How to make Merton see things could be better? And that he could help Arthur find Caitlyn.

Merton punched a wall and strode out into the hall. Tristan tried to follow, but his feet were rooted to the damp carpet.

He had to do something. He owed it to Agravain, Caitlyn needed help and there were others to see, to check on, others who may not be able to look after themselves like Charlie Merton.

'Go then!' shouted Merton, erupting back into the living room, spattering Tristan's face with droplets of saliva. 'Take your fucking gun and your fucking knife and piss off. Go save someone else.'

'I want to save all of you,' said Tristan.

'Past that point, maybe.' Merton's volume dropped.

Tristan shook his head.

'You can start again. We have resources,' he said.

Merton locked eyes with Tristan.

'I can get anything I want. Make anyone do anything,' he said, tapping his temple.

'But you shouldn't. Not like this. Let us help you find another way. You can contribute. Help the rest of your family,' said Tristan.

'I don't have any family,' said Merton, and Tristan heard bitterness in the man's voice.

You do, he thought, *you just haven't met them yet. And if you don't come with me, they might not live to meet you.*

Merton maintained eye contact, tilting his head slightly.

'What's in it for me?' asked Charlie Merton, and Tristan felt the hold on his body release.

He raised his hands, clenching and unclenching them into fists, cracking his neck and adjusting his posture.

'We will make it worth your while. I promise. We have money. We can set you up with a new life. All I ask is that you let me help you, not for your sake, but my friend's memory. You come from a great line, Mr Merton, a line that the Order is trying to extinguish. You can help us keep your last living relatives safe. Leave this shithole and let me help you.'

Merton smirked, once more turning to look out across the shabby estate below.

Tristan crossed the room and retrieved his Glock and Commando knife.

'It's time we got you out of here. Let them go too.'

Merton licked his lips, and Tristan heard sharp intakes of breath behind him.

'It's alright,' he said to the four men from Hektor Security, 'I'll explain later.'

Tristan holstered his Glock and checked on the Hektor security men. They were a little dazed, very confused, but all of them had worked with Tristan before, and when he began issuing orders, they didn't question them. They set off back to their vehicles, ready to meet the backup when it arrived.

'Is there anything you need from your flat? Anything you can't live without?' Tristan asked Merton.

'I'll grab a bag,' said Merton, nodding and heading for the door.

Tristan stepped from a grotty hallway in through Merton's front door and was surprised to find the other side looked more like a flat in Mayfair or an apartment on Park Avenue, at least in terms of the decor. He wandered from room to room as Charlie Merton busied about, gathering all that he couldn't leave behind into a type of battered old leather suitcase that Tristan had previously thought went extinct in the eighties.

'If you can afford all this, why do you stay on this estate?' asked Tristan.

Merton grinned.

'I'd explain, but it's probably easier to just think of me as Jenny from the Block.'

'You've lost me,' said Tristan.

'This is where I'm from. It doesn't matter where I go or what I do or how I live, this is always where I'm from, right?

You can't escape your origins. Why try?'

Tristan frowned, uncomfortable, but unsure why.

'You can honour your past without living it,' he said after a moment.

Merton harrumphed.

'We'll find out. That's everything. Go, go, go, yeah?'

Tristan led him out into the hall and noticed Merton pause for a moment as if saying a silent goodbye to his home before closing and carefully locking the door.

'This place will be in chaos before the day is out without me running it,' Merton muttered.

'They'll make their own choices. People *need* to make their own choices,' said Tristan.

As soon as they stepped out of the block and his phone had reception again, Tristan's phone registered several missed calls from Kay.

'Excuse me, I … ' Tristan started, but Merton held up his hand.

'Yeah, yeah. Gotta call Kay,' he said.

Tristan nodded, but didn't step aside to make contact, knowing full well that Merton would hear the whole conversation one way or another.

'Tristan?' said Kay. He sounded excitable. Either a really good or bad thing.

'I had no signal. Bringing Charles Merton back to the house. He has abilities you can use,' said Tristan. 'Why were you calling?'

'We've had a breakthrough looking at the phone data. A phone just activated that Malagant called from Caitlyn's phone before he went after Kayleigh Turner in Runbridge,' said Kay.

'And?' asked Tristan.

'And that same number was in the vicinity of Hunter's Cottage not long before. We think it's one of the kidnappers' phones,' said Kay.

Tristan licked his lips.

'Alright, is it on the move?'

'Stationary at the moment, at what looks like a farm or an industrial unit not far from you now,' said Kay.

'I'll head straight there, give me the location. Address? Postcode? What3words code?' he asked, knowing the website allowed narrowing of position down to a three-metre square.

'Phone data isn't that precise, but I can give you the postcode of the buildings. They're out in the country. We're getting ready to head out now, but you're closer.'

'I'll call in when I get there. I'm sending Merton back with Hektor,' said Tristan, and he ended the call.

He saw that Merton was frowning.

'I could use you, but you're one of their targets,' said Tristan, walking up to the Hektor car. Merton remained quiet. 'I have to go,' said Tristan to the nearest operative. 'Get Mr Merton back to the house. I'm going after Caitlyn. There isn't a moment to waste. I know what just happened was outside your experience, but this was the job you signed up for. I know I can trust you to do your duty,' said Tristan.

With that, Charlie Merton got into the back of the Hektor car.

Tristan watched as it pulled out of the car park, and he headed for his own vehicle.

Chapter Sixteen

Tintagel, Cornwall
5th Century

Isolde plagued Tristan's thoughts at night, so that he struggled to fall asleep until the early hours. When he woke, he experienced a brief moment of lightness, and felt content until his thoughts turned to Isolde, and he pictured her walking on the clifftops, looking out towards Ireland. He sighed, his heart suddenly heavy, and he wondered if he should seek her out, after all, she was to be the lady of the castle if Mark returned.

King Mark. Tristan readied himself for the day and asked the guard outside his door whether there was any news. Told there was none, the king's nephew, duty done, set out to find Isolde.

They ate together at the high table, separated only by King Mark's empty throne, drinking small beer and picking at their food. Tristan struggled to take his eyes from her, but when he did, he noticed Lucan frowning at him. Momentarily perturbed, he remembered to be more discreet, as Isolde was not destined for him, even if she was rapidly becoming his heart's desire. He knew he must remain above his own desires, remember his station and his foremost loyalty to his uncle. He would protect her. He would do her bidding. But nothing could ever come of it.

But it was no good. His appetite gone, Tristan stood and offered Isolde his apologies.

'You have not finished eating,' she observed.

'My joy at your company diminished the fear for my uncle,' admitted Tristan. 'I must not forget how I should be spending my days while he is gone, and it is not in levity. Forgive me, but I must away and find meaningful pursuit.'

Isolde looked down, failing to hide a small smile, and Tristan realised he had spoken carelessly.

'Spending time with Lady Isolde is, of course, meaningful and I would bask in her company all day, if my duty allowed it. I struggle to think of anything else.'

She looked up at that, and Tristan's cheeks grew hot. He started to say something, he knew not what, but bowed to the lady before taking his leave.

'Meet me in the training yard when you have

finished your meal,' he said to Lucan, as he strode by, not stopping to hear a response.

―――

They sparred hard for hours, sometimes with weapons and sometimes just with their hands, until Tristan's entire body ached and sweat was dripping from him, the exertion successfully keeping his errant thoughts at bay.

Their training was interrupted by a messenger from the gate.

'Apologies, my lord, but King Mark and Lady Morgana Le Fay are drawing near.'

Tristan and Lucan both threw down their arms and, still drenched in sweat, they ran to the Tintagel's gate. Sure enough, Tristan could see King Mark and Morgana both sitting up straight in their saddles and laughing with one another, as though they had arrived early instead of being long overdue and the cause of much concern.

Tristan realised he was scowling. He turned to Lucan.

'I'll warn Isolde and then receive the king in his hall. Pass the word for folk to gather for the king's first sighting of his bride,' said Tristan, unable to assess how he felt, as there was such a mixture of relief and joy at seeing his uncle safe, but also overwhelming dread at the thought of relinquishing Isolde. Morgana's curse gnawed at his mind and heightened his love for both kin and the woman he had so recently encountered, with whom he had developed such a bond. Perhaps it would have been mere appreciation or kindled interest if it had not been for Morgana, nobody would ever know, but whatever had hooked Tristan pulled the line taut, and he felt the piercing barbs.

He ran to his own chambers, quickly changed his clothes then went to find Isolde. Her own room was empty, and the guard told him that the lady and her maids had departed for the chapel. Tristan took the news like a punch, but simply nodded and walked away in a more collected fashion than he felt.

He considered running to her, taking her by the hand and asking her to flee with him, feeling in that moment that there was nothing he would not do for her and nobody he would allow to stand between them. Then he thought of King Mark and guilt overwhelmed him, knowing all his uncle had done for him, believing with all his being that Mark was a good man and a kind ruler, deserving not only of Isolde but of his loyalty … loyalty that Tristan did not question. He loved both Mark and Isolde beyond question, and he knew not what to do.

He could not go to her, he decided, so he

made for the hall as originally planned and saw that an honour guard stood to receive the king.

Merlin was waiting on the dais, before the high table, and Tristan went to stand beside him.

'Isolde?' asked Arthur's wizard.

'She awaits the king in the chapel,' said Tristan under his breath. He could feel Merlin scrutinising him, but he kept his eyes on the closed double doors at the opposite end of the hall.

'She, at least, knows her duty,' said Merlin, in an unusual tone, but Tristan resisted the urge to turn and question him. He knew the wizard was testing him, but not how much the old man knew. He would play his part and show the old man that he too knew his duty.

Tristan spent the remaining time composing himself.

'We will see what mischief Morgana has been orchestrating,' said Merlin, perhaps to himself.

Eventually, the doors swung open, and Lucan led the king and Morgana into the hall. Mark looked quite different to the jovial figure Tristan had observed on the approach to Tintagel. He looked weary, pale and ready for a good meal and other comforts of home.

Tristan recognised a tired but affectionate smile when King Mark saw him standing on the dais, and, spying Merlin, his uncle raised a hand in greeting. Tristan noted Morgana was smiling, walking beside the king as he traversed the hall.

'Sire,' said Tristan, bowing his head, wanting to say more and yet unable to bring himself to offer what he feared would sound like hollow expressions of relief, even if they were mostly genuine.

King Mark took him by both shoulders, a foolish grin on his tired face.

'Did you think me dead, nephew? Quite a time we had of it, but I am intact. Be cheered!'

Tristan offered his uncle a weak smile as the king shook him ever so slightly. He felt his heart sinking and became overwhelmed with guilt as he looked into the older man's open, honest face.

'You had us all worried, sire. What delayed you? Did you take the hart?'

Mark laughed.

'The damn thing near took me! No, I caught no sight of the beast. And I suspect it was merely a ploy of Lady Morgana to secure my ear for a few days uninterrupted. Is it so, my lady?' asked Mark, still grinning.

'You have me, sire,' the sorceress replied, and Tristan saw that she never took her eyes from Merlin. The wizard stood silently, still waiting to be greeted, and once the pleasantries were exchanged, the king turned to him.

'And I have an honoured guest from Arthur's court. I hope I have not kept you waiting too long, Lord Merlin,' said Mark. 'You are welcome! It seems Tintagel draws only the most mighty in the lands these days.'

'You honour me, King Mark. I am glad to see you safe, well and whole,' said the wizard, not sparing Morgana even a glance, 'but perhaps you should rest a while before we speak further. You are weary, I deem.'

'Truly, you are a seer,' said Mark, and Tristan wondered if his uncle's words were meant as a slight. Merlin did not react negatively, however, simply bowing and stepping back.

What was Merlin playing at? He knew Isolde was waiting. And as to that, Mark had made no mention of the princess, Tristan's journey or the wedding. The realisation troubled Tristan, and he stepped forward, interrupting the king as he exchanged words with Lucan.

'Sire, your bride awaits you in the chapel,' said Tristan, quietly.

'She is eager to be wed, it seems!' said Morgana. Tristan felt her eyes upon him.

'Her wedding was delayed, lady. She would already be queen were it not for Morgana and her tale of a white hart,' he snapped.

Mark hushed him.

'No matter, no matter. I had quite forgotten the princess. A bath and a meal would have been welcome, but perhaps Isolde is right, and I will not displease her any more than I already have. Tristan, will you set about organising a feast? The queen and I will return once married,' he said, smiling and walking away. Tristan heard him sigh.

'There is no hurry, sire,' said Morgana. 'Perhaps it would be best to consummate the marriage before the festivities. As the princess is so keen to forge your bond.'

Tristan stepped towards her, clenching his fists, but if anybody noticed, they did not react, save for Morgana who smiled at him, only turning her attention to Mark when he looked back, looking puzzled.

Will he not chastise her for such talk?

Mark shook his head, but he gave a weak smile, and Tristan could have sworn his eyes flashed green momentarily. A trick of the light, no doubt.

'I will not keep the lady waiting,' said Mark. He looked at Tristan. And winked.

The younger man felt his mouth drop open at the blatant disrespect to Isolde, but Mark continued on his way, and he was left silent on the dais with Merlin, who finally turned his attention to Morgana.

'You've been busy, girl,' said the wizard.

'It's our way, is it not?' she replied.

Without another word, they both went their separate ways, heading out of the hall. Tristan saw Treave emerge from the gathered crowd and fall in step behind the sorceress.

Where has he been all this time? Lurking in the shadows, no doubt, thought Tristan.

'Are you unwell? You look pale,' said Lucan.

Tristan could not reply. Mark was gone from sight. Soon he would enter the chapel and, without a single feeling for her, marry the woman Tristan loved.

And then they would retreat to the king's bed.

Tristan bit his lip and swallowed hard.

He could stand it. He'd have to stand it.

'Tristan?' asked Lucan.

Broken from his trance, Tristan nodded.

'Yes, I'm alright.'

But the images he tried to banish continued to plague him.

Chapter Seventeen

2021

Caitlyn rolled across the floor, slamming against the wall as the van swerved around a tight bend. The engine roared and the whole vehicle jerked as whoever was driving made a rough gear change.

Got to be Sandrine, thought Caitlyn. *She drives like she talks.*

She had mastered her panic by now, even if her heart rate was still way above normal. She was used to adrenaline, after all, working in Accident & Emergency. Resus was no cakewalk, and she didn't think you could ever truly wash out all of that blood. She'd saved so many, couldn't help others and, no doubt, given up on some who could have made it, though never by intent. Caitlyn lived with that, and she knew how to cope in traumatic situations. Her current predicament was quite different, but she was adapting nevertheless. She listened, trying to glean what she could while the journey lasted - possibly her last journey, it occurred to her.

Survival was all that mattered now, and Caitlyn resolved

that she would do whatever it took, short of costing someone innocent their life. She was already fantasising about just how she could down Sandrine, her memory poring over old anatomy textbooks, interspersed with scenes from action films, although she knew that served little purpose and remembering such conflicts only served to raise her heart rate. She'd never been in a fight, and she doubted she could do much.

Caitlyn felt her body slide towards the front of the van as it braked and then the sensation lessened as the vehicle came to a stop.

The sound of a chain and creaking metal.

The van moved again, but pulled up less than a minute later, during which it made a left then two right turns.

A door opened up front, but didn't close.

Footsteps.

She recognised the sound of a metal roller shutter going up.

Footsteps.

The van shifted to the left and then the door closed. The van moved forwards for a few seconds and then stopped. The engine died, both doors opened, the van shifted right then left, the doors slammed shut and then the roller shutter screeched as it came down. After that, she could hear nothing but the murmur of hushed voices and then footsteps echoing.

Echoing could mean an industrial unit rather than a garage, she thought.

Caitlyn wondered whether she was in some kind of

private complex or if there might be other people nearby, businesses and customers or the like?

She tried to remember as much detail as possible, lying there with the smell of oil filling her nostrils.

All was silent for a few minutes, but then Caitlyn heard the rasping flint wheel of a lighter, again and again, as though whoever was standing outside was struggling to light a cigarette.

Caitlyn shuffled towards the double van doors and kicked at them lightly, trying to sound as far from petulant or bad-tempered as she could.

One of the doors opened.

Fingers pried the gag from her mouth.

'What's up?' asked the Irishman.

'I heard someone trying to light a cigarette,' Caitlyn replied.

The flint wheel turned again.

'All used up,' he said.

'For the best,' said Caitlyn. 'Those things will kill you.'

The Irishman snorted.

'Why would that bother you?' he asked.

'Well, unless you're going to drop dead in the next few minutes, it would hardly help me, would it? I'm a doctor. I care about people's health. Even if they have kidnapped me,' said Caitlyn.

'Impressive job, that. You must be smarter than the average bear, so? Here, take a look at this,' he said and he shifted the blindfold from her eyes.

The Irishman put one foot inside the van and Caitlyn

saw his trouser leg was torn and bloodied. He pulled it up and revealed what looked like a makeshift bandage, possibly a T-shirt, soaked in blood.

Well done, Samson, she thought.

'You'll need that cleaning out, antibiotics and stitches too,' she said.

The Irishman grunted.

Caitlyn felt a little burst of adrenaline as he sat down on the edge of the van, looking in at her as, once more, he tried and failed to light a cigarette. He obviously felt comfortable. She had something to build upon.

'What about you, what do you do?' she asked him.

He grinned at her.

'Are you joking?'

'I assume you don't put "kidnapper" in the occupation box on forms!' Caitlyn smiled back at him, and he dropped his chin and snorted quietly.

'No,' he said.

'So what do you put?' asked Caitlyn.

'Trying to find out about me?' asked the Irishman. 'Preparing your move?'

Caitlyn felt her cheeks flush.

'Well, I am smarter than the average bear. What would you do, just lie here and wait?' she asked.

He looked as though he was weighing it up and shook his head.

'I'd do whatever I could,' he said.

'So no hard feelings then?' she asked.

'No, no hard feelings. Gonna hold this,' he nodded his

head towards the van interior, 'against me?'

'That depends on if I get out of this unscathed. Can you make that happen?' said Caitlyn, her breaths coming faster.

The Irishman's eyes were rooted on the lighter that he turned over in his hands.

'That's brave, asking me … '

Sandrine's voice cut him off mid-sentence.

'What in the hell are you doing?' she shouted.

The Irishman sighed and got to his feet as Sandrine stepped into view, looking first at the Irishman as he straightened up and then into the van, scowling as she saw Caitlyn's gag and blindfold were off.

'You two want some wine and candles? Fuck's sake.'

Caitlyn said nothing, but she saw the Irishman give Sandrine a condescending smile.

'There's no harm done. Relax,' he said.

'Relax. Sure. You need to get inside and get an update. I'll watch her.'

The Irishman nodded, winked at Caitlyn and stepped out of view. She caught Sandrine's gaze, and the two women stared into one another's eyes as his footsteps faded away.

'Getting cosy with the big man?' Sandrine asked, her voice a little less harsh than usual. She pressed the power button on a phone and stared at the screen as it loaded up.

'Trying to work out what's going on,' Caitlyn admitted. 'I think I deserve to know, even if it isn't going to end well.'

Sandrine continued to stare at the phone, frown intensifying. She sighed and rounded on Caitlyn.

'I don't know how this is going to end for you, but my

guess? You aren't leaving this building alive. But if you think he's going to help you? If you think he's the good guy or the gentle giant, you are *so* wrong. You don't know him at all, okay? Just stay quiet, and we'll see how this plays out.'

'I didn't do anything,' said Caitlyn, desperation overcoming her and her calm mask beginning to disintegrate, the disappointment of her wasted efforts on the Irishman only exacerbating the spiral.

'I know, but it doesn't matter. None of this is about you. If you have *any* chance of surviving, it's in staying quiet and doing as we tell you with no fuss. Got it? You aren't going to talk your way out of here, the big man isn't going to help you and nobody is going to come for you. Unless you're some secret ninja or something, you aren't going to fight your way out. So save your energy, make your peace with leaving the world, and I won't hasten your departure, doctor.'

Caitlyn said nothing.

Sandrine sucked her teeth, sighed once and slammed the van door.

Darkness.

Chapter Eighteen

5th Century
Tintagel

Tristan's wait for King Mark and Queen Isolde to return to the feast seemed like hours, even with the distraction of readying the great hall and sending out invitations to nearby guests.

They were longer than anyone could have expected, even if Mark wished to consummate the marriage, a thought that made Tristan light-headed, and he felt cold sweat forming on his brow.

A hand on his shoulder. Tristan flinched.

'You were in another world,' said Merlin, smiling kindly, but Tristan detected something, possibly concern, but maybe just curiosity behind the expression.

'Another version of this one, perhaps,' he replied.

Merlin's facade dropped.

'I am troubled, too. It is unclear what

influence Morgana has over King Mark, but we will see before long,' said Merlin.

Tristan nodded slowly, and there was a moment of silence amid the preparation before Merlin spoke again, quieter and in a kindlier tone.

'What think you of Lady Isolde?' asked the wizard.

Tristan raised his head, and when he met the old man's eyes, he could see Merlin knew what was in his heart. The wizard nodded.

'A difficult thing, but you are not the first and you will not be the last to face such a predicament,' he said.

―⁂―

The great hall was ready, decorated with flowers, garlands and candles. Common folk shared the same long tables with those of higher status, albeit at opposite ends, with the more important people nearer the dais. Tristan stood, hands clasped behind his back, while Merlin and Morgana, without invitation, had taken up seats at the dais, with only the king and queen's chairs between them. Tristan did not consider the significance however, as he was too busy staring at the door through which the newly-weds would emerge, his liege lord and his queen.

He thought of her walking the halls, standing on the deck of the ship that took her from home, laughing with him while they ate on the various evenings since arriving at Tintagel, despite their worries. Did she feel the same? Could she? And what of it if she did?

Indeed, he reminded himself, *what of it? Ours is a love that would never be realised.*

Was it so? Did he love her? How could he, after so short a time?

She was brave, funny, challenging, she had beauty, grace and wisdom. He felt consumed by her. Whenever he tried to concentrate on other endeavours, to prioritise anything else, she was always there, just out of view, but he could feel her eyes upon him. And her face appeared before him.

One of the king's men opened the door behind the dais and through it appeared King Mark, then, her arm intertwined with his, stepped Isolde, smiling.

'May I present my bride, Queen Isolde of Cornwall, Princess of Munster,' announced King Mark to the gathering.

'My Queen,' said Tristan, dropping to one knee, and then others followed suit, led by Lucan.

'Rise,' said Isolde, still smiling.

Applause filled the room, and Isolde beamed naturally at the response. But Tristan was still worrying as they all took their seats. His place was next to Merlin, infuriatingly close to Isolde and yet too far for conversation.

During the feast, he could only pick at his food.

He felt Merlin's elbow in his ribs and turned to face the wizard, whose expression was grave.

'Eat. You will need your strength, Tristan,' he said. 'Something, I know not what, is amiss here.'

Tristan did not reply. Could the wizard discern the connection between Tristan and Isolde? There was no time to question him, as Merlin had turned to speak with the bride. He heard her laugh quietly and that heartened him, but deep down, Tristan knew that something was very wrong at Tintagel.

Later in the feast, Isolde slipped from the hall and Tristan stood, intending to follow her. Before he had taken more than a few steps, Lucan called out to him, then went to meet him, speaking in a hushed voice.

'Where are you going? Do you not think he will notice?'

'And what of it? I wish to check the queen is well. To pay my respects,' said Tristan.

Lucan, unsmiling, raised an eyebrow and sighed.

'You do not fool me, and if you seek her out,

you won't fool the king for long either, Tristan. They are married now. Let it alone,' said Lucan.

'But something is wrong, I can feel it,' Tristan replied.

'You are not yourself, kinsman,' said Lucan. 'All is well except for your own troubled heart. Isolde is not troubled in kind, I assure you.'

Tristan dropped his gaze at his friend's words, but Lucan took him by the shoulders and forced eye contact.

'Stay and drink through it,' said Lucan, smiling. 'Lord knows we've all had our hearts broken at one time or another, but let's not turn this into a tale for the ages, eh?'

Tristan smiled and allowed Lucan to lead him back towards the hall.

All was well for the remainder of the evening, and the two men fell to reminiscing and laughter. Even so, he looked for Isolde's return and was relieved to see when she returned to the high table, even if Morgana succeeded in moving to the chair beside her while Merlin was talking to a gathering of local lords elsewhere on the dais.

'Tristan,' chided Lucan, and he held up his hands in surrender.

'Another drink,' he said, and Lucan grinned.

The night wore on, and Tristan kept his back to the high table, so that he might keep Isolde out of sight if not out of mind.

Chapter Nineteen

2021

Tristan drove fast along country roads, rarely hitting the brake except in the run-up to corners, which he traversed at steady speed and from which he powered away; in like a lamb and out like a lion. In control, despite the need for haste.

As he approached a small village, Tristan spotted a petrol station, but drove past it, parked in a side street then walked back to avoid his car being picked up on cameras or index plate grabbers on the forecourt. He pulled his baseball cap down low and headed into the shop. It took less than a minute to find the shelves dedicated to screenwash, hanging air fresheners, engine oil and local map books.

He plucked out a map book and headed for the checkout, paying with cash before returning to the car. He opened the book and took a moment to find the right location.

The industrial unit where the phone was located wasn't far out of town, yet was still isolated, surrounded by what Tristan suspected were arable fields. He picked out some nearby roads which could be of use.

It wasn't a lot of information, much less than he usually gathered before attempting, well, whatever he was going to attempt when he arrived at the industrial unit, but the Order were on the move, and Caitlyn's life was ticking down.

Tristan tossed the map book on to the passenger seat, started the car and set off, alone, towards the unit.

He thought of Arthur's pained expression as he drove, knowing all too well the torment of fearing for a loved one. Tristan had deliberately spent very little time with Caitlyn, as he tended to avoid women he found attractive, but she seemed pleasant enough from their few, brief interactions, though he decided that was meagre praise. She had treated both Arthur and the knights with nothing but respect, never saying a word, as far as Tristan knew, about the unusual living arrangement of several apparently middle-aged men, not only living together platonically, but working together as well. She had accepted that they had all served together in the military, and her relationship with Arthur had been nothing if not unobtrusive for over a year now. Arthur seemed happier and, until recently, at peace. So why did Tristan detect resentment deep down within himself?

A proprietary feeling towards Arthur rose up in him, and it was uncomfortable, inappropriate, and it alarmed him, so he centred himself, concentrated on his driving and thinking through various scenarios.

His phone rang from the centre console and, reminding himself to put it on silent, Tristan snatched it up, answered the call and put it on speaker.

'Go ahead,' he said.

'Where are you?' It was Kay's voice emerging, tinny, from the cheap phone.

'About five minutes out. What's the news?' asked Tristan.

'I think Charlie Merton just arrived. There's a van pulling up. Hektor says all the other addresses on the list appear secure.'

Silence for a moment.

'What are you planning, Tristan?' Kay was quiet. Cautious.

'I'm going to get Arthur's squeeze back, that's what,' said Tristan and was surprised at his own vitriol.

Silence again. He knew Kay was thinking how to persuade him out of tackling the Order alone.

'We don't have a choice,' said Tristan, rounding a bend and seeing the entrance to a sloping drive up ahead on the left, between high hedges.

'It *is* a narrow window of opportunity,' said Kay.

'Get to me when you can,' said Tristan, casting his eyes left as subtly as he could manage as he passed the turning. A short drive, sloping upwards, the top of a high gate was all that was visible, all else concealed over the brow of a hill.

A pause and then Kay spoke.

'God be with you, Tristan.'

Tristan shook his head.

'Good luck,' he said, and he ended the call.

The industrial estate seemed accessible across fields from many directions, but only via the driveway in a vehicle, which was a strange choice, thought Tristan. He'd have expected more security, but perhaps it was only a staging point. He got the impression that the gate was there simply to prevent vehicles driving on to the site, likely an existing precaution from before the Order had acquired the location.

Tristan slowed on approach to a roundabout, just beyond the driveway, and turned left, keeping the complex to *his* left, but hidden from view by a thin line of trees. He passed a small cottage and pulled into a layby, where he parked up. Tristan turned off the ignition and sat for a moment in silence, interrupted only by the sound of a car and the far off neighing of a horse, before retrieving his holdall from the boot and stepping into the trees.

Tristan stopped walking only when he was confident he was out of sight from the road. Positioned in a narrow copse, he could just make out the cottage to his left. Ahead of him were a paddock, in which five horses were grazing, and beyond that a stretch of field cut off from the industrial unit by dense bushes, beyond which Tristan could make out a couple of shipping containers and low buildings with corrugated iron roofs sloping down towards him. There wasn't much in the way of cover, but also no obvious enemy vantage points. This was no fortress, and Tristan's instincts told him this place had never been intended as somewhere to make a stand. Just a staging point, as he suspected.

Tristan could think of three options, and he was drawn to the most risky.

He could walk back along the road and cut across behind the gate. This would minimise his visibility from the complex, but he'd be seen clearly from everyone on the road.

His next option was to drive up to the gate and either talk or smash his way in, but in doing so, he would lose the element of surprise.

Finally, he could quit sitting on his hands, cross the open ground, taking a gamble that the Order's main strength was currently deployed and that with no obvious vantage points and no expectation of attack, the fields remained relatively unwatched.

Do or die, thought Tristan, as he removed the hoodie and knelt to unzip the holdall. He threw the strap of the MP5K submachine pistol over his shoulder so that the weapon hung at his back. He drew the Glock 17 from its holster, checked it over and then returned it before pulling on and zipping up the oversized hoodie once more, disguising all he was carrying as best he could. He put a spare clip for the Glock in his left jeans pocket, black nitrile gloves in his right, stuffed the balaclava in his rear jeans pocket and pulled the baseball cap on with the curved peak down low. In the cap, hoodie, jeans and army boots, he'd never pass for a hiker or anyone who had any business in the countryside, but if he was seen, that would be the least of his concerns.

Tristan snatched up the holdall and returned to the car.

Nobody about. He stowed the bag and headed back into the trees. Once he was as sure as he could be that nobody was watching, he sent a text to Kay just saying, 'going in', before setting off, walking briskly, but casually across the strip of grassy ground between him and the paddock. Rather than cut through, he took the longer walk round it, just in case anyone from the cottage to which it belonged was watching, and having successfully traversed the first obstacle, he jogged across the narrow field and ducked into a gap in the bushes, through which he could make out the blue steel of a shipping container. He stopped there, caught his breath and listened.

Chapter Twenty

2021

Arthur was standing at an upstairs window overlooking the courtyard, with the old oak at its centre, when the gates swung open and a car drove in.

He was ready for Charlie Merton's arrival, had felt him drawing closer and closer, a pulsing energy akin to the steadily strengthening waves on a beach, signalling the passage of a vessel much farther out. Arthur had never felt anything like it, not even from Merlin or Branok. He had never even suspected Malagant was anything but human back in ancient days or while he was possessing Agravain.

'What have you sent me, Tristan?' asked Arthur. He watched a slightly built, balding man in his fifties climb out of the van, a white polo shirt showing off his tattooed arms. The man looked all around, nodding, before turning his gaze, quite deliberately, on Arthur, who shuddered as the man smiled.

An image of Merlin flashed before his mind's eye for an instant, even though Charlie Merton didn't resemble the wizard in the slightest. Arthur caught himself frowning as he took in the man's trainers, tracksuit bottoms and the tattoos.

That's shameful, thought Arthur, *judging a man like that. I don't know where he came from or his story. And what of his clothes? What does his sense of style tell me, apart from his socio-economic class and perhaps what kind of family he is from? He is Agravain's blood and, so, one of my people now.*

Arthur felt a sharp pain between his eyes and as though someone had pinched the base of his neck between sharp talons.

What do my clothes tell you? Not as much as your first impression tells me, said a man's voice inside Arthur's mind, even as the former king kept his eyes locked on those of Charlie Merton, who stood looking up at him.

Arthur opened his mouth to speak, but remembered the man could not hear his voice. Merton smiled at him, a humourless little grin, devilish, and allowed himself to be escorted up to the door by one of the Hektor Security men, disappearing from Arthur's view.

'Well,' said Arthur, aloud and to nobody.

Well what, said the voice in his mind.

'We have yet to be introduced,' said Arthur.

Better come down then … sire, said the voice in his head.

A sense of foreboding overcame Arthur, and he felt light-headed, so steadied himself against a wall. This didn't feel right. What had he allowed into his home?

Charlie Merton. Soon-to-be reformed drug dealer, apparently, said the voice.

Stay out of my mind, thought Arthur. *I'll be down presently.*

He continued looking out of the window for a few

moments, watching as newly arrived Hektor Security people took up stations around the perimeter of his estate, preparing for a possible attack, then he took up his cane from where it was propped against a table, and he started towards the stairs, trying to keep his mind clear, focusing on re-creating the image of the courtyard oak in his mind, not entirely successfully. He could hear Merton laughing quietly somewhere between his thoughts.

Arthur thought the house eerily quiet, despite all of the activity within and without. He limped, leaning on his cane as he started down the stairs, hearing only the ticking of the grandfather clock in the hall below, the hall where Percival had died over a year ago.

The hall through which his men had carried Agravain, struggling with Malagant's possession. The hall Nimuë had crossed following her husband and which she would never cross again.

This place, thought Arthur, is full of ghosts.

Nothing from Charlie Merton in his mind. Either he was respecting Arthur's request, had his own reasons for not listening in or he was there, lurking, but silent.

No matter, thought Arthur, *I have nothing to hide.*

Bors stepped into view in the hall below.

'Tristan's moving in on the unit. Are you coming?'

Arthur nodded.

'Kit up, and we'll head out in due course. First, I must speak with our latest arrival,' he said, heading for the drawing-room.

'Your boy, Tristan. There's something up with him. Something not quite right,' said Merton, staring into the flames as Arthur entered. Bedivere, who had been watching over him, went up to check on Kay's progress.

'In what way?' asked Arthur.

Merton shrugged.

'I'm no expert, but when I'm in his noggin, he's there. He's … malleable. But his thoughts aren't quite his own,' he said, after a moment's pause.

Arthur stood, leaning heavily on his cane.

'A malign influence? Any sign of another's presence within him?' he asked.

Merton laughed.

'What a place! Casually chatting about possession and malign influence with King Arthur when we have barely introduced ourselves!' he said, when the laughing subsided. Arthur watched, patient and unmoved.

He watched as Merton's smile faded and the other man shifted somewhat uncomfortably.

'Nah, I didn't feel anyone else, but there is, what did you call it?' asked Merton, less cocky now, Arthur noted.

'Malign influence?' he suggested.

'Yeah, that,' Merton nodded. He sat in the same chair by the fire Merlin had once occupied and looked up at Arthur, as if waiting for a conversational steer, but the former king said nothing, just looked up at Excalibur, pondering the nature of the malign influence on Tristan. How far did it extend? What was its purpose? Were any more of his company not themselves? He had discovered that two were … or had been, he reminded himself of Agravain, in a single day.

A knock at the door.

'Come in,' said Arthur, and Dagonet stepped into the room.

'We've just heard from Hektor's control room about the other addresses on the list. Gareth and Bors are readying to head out after Tristan with some of the Hektor lads. Kay, Bedivere and I will stay here to look after our guests.' His eyes flitted from Arthur to Merton and back to Arthur.

'Go on,' said Arthur, seeing Merton smile.

'Yeah, mate. Tell us everything's golden and that there's no sign of movement yet.'

He just can't resist getting a dig in, thought Arthur.

Dagonet frowned, but nodded.

'Exactly that. Hektor deployed more units to the other addresses, but as of yet, no sign of anything to worry about, sir.'

'Thanks, mate. Worth the effort coming downstairs, eh?' said Merton.

Dagonet stared at Merton, whose smile broadened before he said,

'Who do I think I am? I think I'm the bloke who knows what you're thinking before you do, bud.'

'Thank you, Dagonet,' said Arthur, sighing before addressing his guest, barely holding his temper in check. 'And Mr Merton, if you could refrain from poking around in my comrades' minds, it would be appreciated. If you cannot resist, at least keep a civil tongue in your head. Understood?'

'Yeah, yeah,' said Merton, waving his hand and looking back at the fire. 'Thanks Dag, mate.'

'Can I do anything for you, sir?' asked Dagonet of Arthur.

'No, nothing more, but please tell Bors I will be going with them.'

'Sir, I … '

Arthur was about to interrupt, but Merton got there first.

'He's not gonna leave saving his missus up to his lackeys, is he? Not very bright, your knights, are they Arthur?' said Merton, pretending to look disappointed.

Dagonet took a step forward, but Arthur held up his hand and his knight left the room, closing the door behind him. A barely audible click and a soft thump was all that disturbed the silence.

Arthur stood and fetched Excalibur from its mounting on the panelled wall. He checked over his Colt revolver. As he did so, he asked his guest,

'Have we done something to offend you, Mr Merton? Your words are harsh and disrespectful, and you seem almost unwilling to be here. I appreciate we've dragged you from your normal routine, but with only your best interests at heart.'

Arthur holstered the pistol.

Merton grinned then replied,

'Never cared enough to track me down before they took your missus though, did you? What's got you sending blokes in vans to watch over Agravain's relatives now?'

Arthur frowned.

'We were unaware that Agravain and Nimuë had children until recently.'

He saw Merton go to speak, but close his mouth again. Arthur wondered if he had been caught off guard, his narrative undermined. Perhaps Merton thought of himself as abandoned, but now knew it wasn't true.

'No?' said Merton.

'Couldn't you tell if I was lying?' asked Arthur.

Merton did not reply, but scowled at him.

Arthur sighed, mentally ticked off everything he needed and turned to Merton.

'I don't have time to discuss this further at the moment, but we will, at length. And I assure you, you will be looked after if you choose to remain among us or connected with us. If not, you are free to go back to your old life, but even if you do, you will be taken care of. We are not without means.'

Arthur opened the door and extended a hand towards the hall. Merton took the hint and exited the drawing-room, but not without mumbling 'I'd say not. Entitled bastards,' under his breath, just loud enough for Arthur to hear as he passed by.

Gareth and Bors were helping load up two plain Hektor vans. Arthur saw Kay making his way, slowly, down the stairs, assisted by Bedivere. Dagonet appeared on the landing and followed them down.

'Good luck, sir,' said Kay, breathlessly, when he reached the ground floor, and Arthur shook each of the assembled knights' hands.

'To us all. You'll keep working here?' he asked Kay, who nodded.

'Bedivere will watch over security while Dagonet and I continue to work on ANPR, phones, CCTV and such.'

Arthur nodded.

'Thank you both, but please make sure you look after our guests. Perhaps Mr Merton could help Miss Turner explore her abilities?'

Arthur started towards the door, not bothering to speak to Charlie Merton.

Arthur limped to the nearest van, through the passenger window of which he could see Gareth in the driving seat.

Make yourself at home, Mr Merton, and be kind to the others. They are your family, and as bewildering as that may seem to you now, there are good times ahead. With your potential, you could contribute more than you currently realise, now that Merlin and Nimuë are gone. Think on it.

But Arthur received no reply.

He climbed up into the van and with a nod to Gareth, he signalled it was time to depart in the hope of finding both Tristan and Caitlyn, alive and unharmed.

Chapter Twenty-One

The Order's Industrial Unit
2021

Suspiciously quiet, thought Tristan. But what did it mean?

The unit was poorly situated, unfortified, exposed and apparently devoid of guards.

From the cover of a shipping container, he surveyed the surrounding area and saw nobody.

A small brick outhouse stood a little distance away, and Tristan bolted across to take up position behind it. From building to wall, to shipping container to whatever cover he could find, he made his way deeper into the complex until low brick buildings formed a square before him, accessible through gaps on both corners. Through the closest gap, he could see that the buildings formed a square with a yard in the centre, and another exit on the other side. There was probably vehicle access at all four corners. From his position, he could see straight down one side of the yard's interior and only the tops of trees over the roofs of the buildings ahead of him.

Tristan considered entering the yard, but it would leave

him vulnerable and visible, so instead, he ran from his hiding place, keeping low, until he was up against the wall of one of the low brick buildings. He checked left, right and behind him, listening carefully and scanned his eyes over the brickwork until he found an area where he felt confident he could pick out enough hand and foot holds.

He smiled wistfully as he placed his foot on a protruding brick and his fingertips in the mortar-filled gaps, thinking of when he and Agravain had scaled a cliff to fight Malagant and Morgana with Merlin, so many centuries before; the confrontation in which the wizard had killed the sorceress. The thought of his friend pained him, but he put the memory aside and climbed swiftly, hauling himself over a loose gutter and on to the sloping roof in just a few seconds. Once up, he lay still, listening, and he could make out people talking over the crest of the roof, presumably down in the courtyard below, as he had come to think of the space within the square of buildings.

Tristan crawled up the roof, pausing twice as tiles shifted under his weight. Eventually, what seemed like hours later, he was able to lift his head just enough so that he could see down into the courtyard.

Two vans, facing him, one closed up with two men sitting up front. The other van's rear doors were open and folded back against the sides. Three people, dressed nondescript, were standing around at the rear, smoking cigarettes, while a man sat behind the wheel with a woman beside him. Tristan's eyes darted to the building behind them as a mechanical scraping and whirring started up, and he saw a metal roller shutter begin to descend to cover the entrance to one of the units.

He started to look away when a movement in the dim space within caught his eye, and he saw Caitlyn, hands tied in front of her, being led by two men out into the courtyard and towards the vans.

'Fuck,' Tristan whispered. 'Okay. Okay.'

He licked his lips, pulled out his mobile phone and sent a text to Kay containing the vans' index plates, as well as their make and models. After each vehicle he included, '2 up. No visibility rear' and then concluded with '5 on foot.' He'd have to clarify later as things changed, if time allowed. At least this way, if he failed, Kay could attempt to track the vehicles. But for now, Tristan had a narrowing window of opportunity for action.

No less than nine opponents, but he could surprise them. He began turning over possible approaches, but two thoughts were foremost in his consideration of the situation.

First, he had to consider the risk to Caitlyn of harm from him or those who held her if he moved against them. Secondly, she was, even then, being loaded into one of the vans.

He had to move. To attack or follow, he had yet to decide.

Did he have time to cut them off? Should he go for her now? How many were already inside the vans? He didn't have enough information.

No more time. Tristan began sliding back down the roof as quietly as he could manage without losing too much time.

He dislodged a couple of tiles, causing a grating noise, but, he hoped, not loud enough to draw attention.

Tristan dropped down to the grass and, certain now that this area was not being watched, he cut right between the low buildings until he reached soft ground underfoot and sprinted back to the car, breathing steadily, in through the nose, out through the mouth, all the time worrying that he could be losing his opportunity, wondering how he would face Arthur if he lost Caitlyn, or worse. He pushed the thoughts aside, knowing he had to focus, put his head down, and, never looking back, he ran, no longer caring who saw him.

Definitely not as young as I was, thought Tristan, as he threw himself behind the wheel, turned the key in the ignition and drove back down the road the way he had come.

He got his breathing under control, considering his options as he headed back towards the drive up to the farm.

Tristan indicated right, waited for a few seconds while a line of cars passed by in the opposite direction then darted through a gap in the traffic and on to the drive. It sloped upwards steeply and Tristan could see the top of the gates, which were shut, and the roofs of the first buildings over the crest, but the view of the remainder of the drive up to the gate was obscured by a ridge.

He parked almost diagonally before the ridge, enough to block the drive, with the trees providing natural obstacles on the grass banks either side of it. He was confident that neither van could squeeze through. He popped the bonnet and then ran round to prop it open, revealing the engine, before darting into the trees, where he checked he had not been seen from the farm. Satisfied that he remained undetected and that the car couldn't be seen from anyone coming from the farm until they were through the gate and nearing the ridge, he headed up the slope using the cover of the trees, still unsure exactly what he would do. Tristan had no plan, just an opportunity.

He heard the engines kick in. Tristan pulled out one of his two burner phones and texted Kay.

They're on the move. Going in.

He tore off his hoodie and, happy that the MP5k was accessible, he waited, Glock in hand.

The engine noise grew louder.

Keep calm. Keep moving. They won't see it coming, he told himself.

If the first driver had half a brain, he'd see the car with its bonnet up and assume an ambush, but there would be nowhere for him to go. Tristan made his best guess at where the van would stop, guessing he'd pull up immediately, as soon as the lower slope of the drive became visible. The knight took position accordingly and waited.

The vans appeared around the trees and trundled up to the gate. Tristan saw two men in the first vehicle and nodded to himself, again licking his parched lips, conscious that his mouth was now drying out. A man got out of the front passenger seat of the first van and unlocked the gate, swinging it open. The vans drove through and Tristan cursed inwardly as he realised the lone cultist on foot was closing and locking the gate. Would there be enough room on the drive for them to pull up and for him to get back in without seeing the obstruction? He hoped so, but wasn't sure. He shifted on to one knee, ready to go. Sure enough, the vans pulled up once they were through and the man at the back began securing the gate, just a few metres from Tristan's position.

Here goes nothing.

He raised the Glock, aimed and fired.

16, he thought, counting down his remaining rounds, as the bullet took the man at the gate through the side of the throat before he had secured the padlock.

Time slowed.

Tristan flicked his eyes from the rear doors to the front of the vehicle and on to the first van and back.

The driver's door of the rear van opened.

Tristan, midway down the length of the vehicle, moved the Glock right. A big man with a bloody trouser leg stepped out, wide-eyed and looking all around him, fumbled with a handgun, his hands shaking.

He looked Tristan dead in the eye, the trembling gun hand started to rise, and the knight fired again, taking him in the chest.

15.

The dust hadn't settled, and Tristan knew the cultists had yet to process what was happening, but doors would start flying open any second, so he dropped back into the trees. He couldn't afford for a swarm of armed cultists to appear out of the rear of the front van while he was still visible.

He cut left and bypassed the gate, as he heard doors opening. Tristan looked back and saw the driver's door of the other van open slightly, a face appear and then duck back in, presumably as the person within saw his fallen comrade. The van pulled forward, engine roaring. What were they doing? Getting clear? Repositioning? Making a break for it?

For a moment he regretted that he had blocked the way, as the first van's brake lights lit up red. They'd seen his car.

He heard the squeal of a door opening on the second van, but could see no change. The front passenger was out then.

Tristan raised the Glock and began to sidestep to the left around the rear of the van, losing the view down the right of the vehicle.

The rear doors stayed closed, and Tristan, still on the other side of the partially open gate, stepped out to the left, gaining a view down the van for a millisecond, just long enough to see a tanned woman, with dark hair in a ponytail, raise her own weapon. Tristan dashed back to the right as the boom hit his ears. Tristan pulled the insecure gate open and ran straight at the van, smashing into the rear door shoulder first.

He fired off a shot to the right to put off anyone who might be approaching that way.

14.

Another shot to the left to stall the woman who had seen him.

13.

The knight burst around the left side of the van to find the woman gone, but he saw four of the cultists approaching from the first van.

And they saw him too, raising their sidearms.

He ducked back behind the van's rear doors, despite the risk that whoever was inside would fire through them.

They'd split up and come round at him from both sides now. If he fought from his current position, he could only cover one angle and they could approach from behind him. He could step out and advance towards them, but he'd be totally exposed, even if he might take a couple of them down. He could run, but from there, anything was possible, and he'd be abandoning Caitlyn, even temporarily.

They could kill her at any time.

That decided it.

Tristan stood behind the left door, grabbed the handle of the right and flung it open, ducking back for a beat before stepping out of cover to get a view of the van's interior, Glock raised, fully expecting these to be his last moments.

Caitlyn was sitting, shaking, against the wall, gagged, blindfolded and with her hands tied.

She was alone.

Tristan heard shouts and footsteps coming up towards him. There was only one thing for it.

The knight jumped up into the van, hauling the door closed behind him. He threw himself down on the floor, blocking as much of Caitlyn as he could if the doors were opened, then snatched up the MP5K, and, set to full automatic, he waited until he heard the door handle creak, then sprayed a line of rounds from left to right, deafening himself.

The screaming started and Tristan heard a thump. The door didn't open.

The knight waited, leaning back against Caitlyn. He could feel her shaking beneath him.

'It's okay,' he said quietly. 'It's okay.'

He ran his tongue across his lips and might as well have been licking sandpaper.

If they were going to kill Caitlyn anyway, the bullets would start to fly through the van any second now, he guessed. If not, well, this was a siege situation, and the knights would be on their way.

'Tristan,' a woman's raised voice came through the side of the van, pretty steady, given the circumstances.

How did she know him? Tristan didn't reply.

'We will kill you both if we have to, don't think we won't,' she said, and Tristan believed her.

What should he do?

He could make a stand, but what was the point? There was little chance of success, and he'd just end up getting them both killed.

'I surrender,' he shouted.

No reply for a second.

'Then open the doors and throw out your weapons,' said the woman's voice, from another direction.

'You'll shoot me,' said Tristan, still stalling for time. He had no choice.

'Not unless you make us,' said the woman. 'Arthur's knights are prizes in themselves.'

Swallowing, he got to his feet, squatting in the small space, knowing that at any second, it could all be over.

Tristan called out,

'I'm opening them now,' before flinging open the right door, allowing him some cover. He saw nothing but a view into the farm and a man writhing, bleeding out on the ground.

'Throw out your weapons. You have a pistol and a machine gun,' said the woman's voice.

Tristan did as instructed, throwing out the MP5K and the Glock 17, sending them skittering across the ground in a cloud of dust. He backed up to Caitlyn, standing between her and the open door.

The woman stepped into view, her own pistol raised, aiming into the van.

Tristan held up his empty hands.

Sandrine smiled.

Then fired.

Chapter Twenty-Two

Tintagel, Cornwall
5th Century

'Were you bored without me, Treave?' asked Morgana, reclining on her bed.

'Every moment was a living agony, my lady,' Treave, sitting by her feet, replied without conveying a hint of emotion.

Morgana smiled.

'Did you keep busy, at least?' she asked.

Treave shrugged.

'I've passed the time in the lands hereabouts. I've watched and I've listened, learnt a little, perhaps, nothing compared with your accomplishments, returning home with the King of Cornwall in the palm of your hand. All went to plan, then?' he asked.

Morgana frowned and kicked Treave's armour, between his armpit and hip, just enough to rock him.

'Does anything ever go entirely to plan? We

are where we are and that is, perhaps, in a stronger position than expected, though I must keep an eye on Malagant,' said Morgana.

She saw the question forming on Treave's lips.

'Not all went to plan. The water woman fulfilled her end of the bargain. When she gives birth, I will see that her baby will be raised in our world and, in time, join us so that she might escape predation in the Otherworld. The lady took King Mark down and, once through the breach, I assume Malagant showed him the forces amassing there. It may be years, even centuries before they are ready, but Mark did not know that, and we have time.' Her eyes darted to the waterskin, filled with the cauldron's waters.

'What went wrong?' asked Treave.

'Malagant tells me Mark was not impressed, or he may have been, but he was not cowed as I hoped. At best I had hoped he would join with Mordred to save Cornwall and at worst, I thought he might distance himself from Arthur and lend no support when the war begins. But Malagant tells me the king is made of sterner stuff and that he remained defiant, even in the face of the gathering horde. So the spirit, the fey, the ghost, whatever he is, rode the king's body back through the breach and remains in control of it. Mark is our puppet now.'

Morgana neglected, purposely, to tell Treave of Malagant's little rebellion in the cave, and how she had put him back in his place, but her man was astute, of course, or she would not keep him so close.

'And now he has a body from our world, Malagant is less inclined to play the willing servant?' asked Treave.

'I'd have thought less of him if he hadn't tried,' lied Morgana. 'He knows his place now, but still we remain watchful.'

'As always,' said Treave. 'What next?'

Morgana sat up and crossed her legs.

'Tell me what you have observed of Tristan and Isolde since our return,' she asked.

'The curse has very much taken hold and with Mark absent, I hear Tristan has spent much time with his new aunt. They have grown close, but it is clear to more than I that he would have them closer still, though he shows restraint. There has been nothing untoward, and as for the queen, her handmaids tell me she appreciates his company, and there is a bond there, but I do not think she would allow it to develop. Isolde is dutiful and loyal. She will honour her marriage vows,' said Treave. 'Tristan was visibly distressed after Mark's return.'

Morgana nodded. So many strands to this web, but which to pluck?

'My hope is the young man will be forced to distance himself from the royal couple lest he dishonour himself and betray the king or that he will be unable to resist the curse and chaos will ensue. Either way, the bond between Mark and Tristan will weaken, and cracks will begin to emerge at Tintagel. The question is what to encourage and what to leave alone, letting things play out in time. Now that we have complete control of King Mark, what need is there to play these games at all, aside from torturing Tristan, which I am not inclined to do, for he has never wronged us? A little insolence does not deserve such torment without significant reward for us.'

Treave stood and moved to the door. He opened it and checked there was still nobody in the corridor, then stood with his back to it so he might talk and yet listen for interlopers.

'If King Mark begins to act out of character, how sure are you that his court and the people of Cornwall would support him? If it becomes clear that there is something wrong, might there be rebellion? There are already whispers about what you might have done to him or what powers you have exerted while you were away together.'

Morgana sat silently for a moment, thinking over all that she had put into motion and how best to turn things to her advantage.

'You have a point, Treave, as always. If King Mark suddenly turns against Arthur, there may be an outcry and blood would flow, no doubt. Men do *so* love the sight of it. Give them a hint of an opportunity, and they will turn the grass red.'

'And the outcome would be uncertain. The Cornish might rally to another's banner and overthrow the king, only strengthening the alliance with your brother,' said Treave.

'And to whom would they rally, Treave?' asked the sorceress.

Her man hesitated and he smiled.

'Tristan, my lady,' he said. Morgana nodded.

'Just so. It may well serve us then, to sunder the unity here and bide our time before bringing Cornwall to Mordred's side.'

Treave nodded and checked the hall once more.

Morgana stood and smoothed her dress.

'If you believe Isolde will not dishonour herself, perhaps it is time I paid the queen a visit. Besides, if it is not Tristan alone who acts in the coming scandal, Cornwall's alliance with the Irish may be jeopardised as well. We could turn it to our advantage. Manage the aftermath subtly, and we will have Cornwall in our grasp.'

'You would lay a curse upon Isolde as well?' asked Treave.

Morgana nodded.

'Shall we consider this a trial run for Arthur's own court, I wonder? When Malagant is done here, we can send him to my brother and wreak havoc from within.'

'Would it not be simpler to simply possess Arthur and have him cede the throne to Mordred?' asked Treave.

Morgana laughed.

'If this was truly about land, territory and thrones, perhaps, but where would be the fun in that? Where would be the sweet revenge upon Merlin and the boy the wizard's foul meddling produced? I would see my mother's honour restored and avenge my poor murdered father. I would have Arthur and Merlin watch all they have built crumble before them. Perhaps at the last, we can use Malagant to seize the throne decisively, but not until the wizard and his boy king are defeated in heart, mind and soul.'

Treave did not reply, and Morgana set out to find the king and queen of Cornwall. She had business with the lady, and somehow doubted her husband would, nay, could, intervene.

The next morning, the very same curse laid upon both Tristan and Queen Isolde, Morgana announced to the company breaking their fast in the king's hall that she would be departing before noon, that she wished the marriage well and hoped to visit Tintagel again before too long.

Malagant, wearing King Mark, thanked Morgana for her visit and told her that she was always welcome in Cornwall and that he looked forward to working towards lasting peace between all of the peoples of the island they all inhabited.

Morgana led Treave across the hall so that they might prepare for their journey, and it took all her will not to smile as she felt the eyes of Isolde, Tristan, Lucan and Merlin upon her. She had them vexed, and it was oh-so-sweet.

Once on the road, Morgana turned in her saddle, shivering in the biting rain, and turned to Treave.

'I have a task for you. A long one.'

She tossed him the wineskin and explained as they rode.

Chapter Twenty-Three

2021

Sirens, just audible over the sound of the roaring engine. Arthur cast a glance towards Gareth at the wheel. His knight was concentrating hard, overtaking the vehicles in front whenever he got the opportunity, despite the fast-moving, narrow and winding country lanes, and Arthur thought better of disturbing him.

He jumped a short while later when Gareth shouted 'one minute out', banging on the panel behind him.

Please let her be safe, thought Arthur as the van drifted round a final corner on two wheels and entered the final straight to the industrial unit.

He was thrown forward, saved from hurtling through the windscreen by his seatbelt, as Gareth slammed on the brakes. A line of traffic was backing up towards the last bend. The knight dumped some of the speed and expertly avoided the car in front, carrying on, still fast and on the wrong side of the road where nothing was coming from the other direction.

'Gareth!' shouted Arthur, as a car in the line pulled out to do a three-point turn to avoid the jam.

Gareth threw the van through the gap the car had left, the side of it disappeared into the hedgerow, and for an instant, Arthur thought that was how it would end, but somehow Gareth kept her on the road, accompanied by blaring horns and inaudible shouts from outraged motorists, the sirens growing louder in the background.

Arthur saw the obstruction for the first time, a car with its bonnet up and its side stove in, completely blocking the oncoming lane and partially obstructing the other. Vehicles were slowly pulling around it up ahead of them, using the entrance to the farm driveway as a passing place.

Rammed, clearly.

'Turn in,' said Arthur, seeing nobody in the damaged car. His heart rate was up, his mouth drying out.

'Sir?' asked Gareth, bringing the van to a crawl on the approach.

'Turn in! We have to get up there,' said Arthur, keeping his eyes dead ahead.

'Surely we're too exposed, sir. Lots of eyes-on and the police will be here soon?' said Gareth, and Arthur detected the cautious but insistent tone to his voice, but he snapped back nonetheless.

'We're not missing the chance that we could help Caitlyn and Tristan,' said Arthur. 'Turn in.'

He saw a van with both cab doors open, then his eyes dropped as they crested the hill, and Arthur saw a man lying in a pool of blood by the driver's door.

'Right up there,' he hissed.

'Sir?' asked Gareth.

'Do it,' Arthur hissed, readying his Colt.

A few more seconds and Gareth threw the wheel over, bringing the van to a halt.

He pummelled the wall behind him, shouting "Go, go, go!" before bursting out of the door himself. It took Arthur a few moments longer, his leg screaming at him and he found it had seized up throughout the tense journey.

Arthur limped forward with his Colt raised, but Bors and the Hektor operatives swarmed past him, clearing the area.

Nobody was in the cab, the driver was dead on the floor. Arthur didn't recognise him, but noted his trouser leg was torn and bloody.

'It's alright!' Bors's voice from the rear of the van. 'We're here to help. Jesus Christ. Arthur!'

Arthur rounded the open back door, stepping over another fallen cultist, his blood pooling on the ground, and saw yet another by the gate, shot through the neck. He looked into the van, and saw two more dead cultists, one of them a tanned, dark-haired woman with a Commando knife in her neck, and he let out a breath as he saw Caitlyn, loosely gagged and with a blindfold over one eye, kneeling over another.

No, not another.

Tristan was groaning, writhing and bleeding profusely from one wound in his chest and another in his shoulder.

'Caitlyn,' said Arthur, pushing past the Hektor operatives.

She looked up, face stern, and barely showed recognition, dry blood around her swollen nose and staining the front of her shirt.

'Cut me loose!' she shouted into the gag, which distorted

her words. She held out her bound, bloody hands. 'Get me a first aid kit and call an ambulance.'

Tristan strove in vain to speak, blood bubbling from his mouth.

'Do it,' said Arthur, and Gareth cut the doctor's bonds while one of the Hektor operatives handed Arthur a first aid kit contained in a pouch on his belt. Caitlyn immediately turned back to Tristan.

'Stay with me,' said Caitlyn, before looking up, eyes cold and fixed on Arthur.

'Plastic, sheeting, a bag, a credit card if you can't find anything else,' said Caitlyn. 'It's a sucking chest wound. Have to stop air getting in. Scissors?'

Bors pulled the knife from Sandrine's neck and handed it to her. Arthur marvelled that she barely reacted, just cutting open Tristan's T-shirt. Arthur could hear air being sucked into Tristan's chest as he breathed. Caitlyn used her hand to partially seal the wound.

'Sir, we have to go,' said Gareth.

The sirens were getting closer.

'Agreed. Let's get out of here before any more damage is done.'

'Arthur, he needs treatment! We need an ambulance.'

Arthur began to climb into the back of the van, and Bors helped him up.

He opened up the first aid kit, searching the contents and handing over an occlusive chest seal.

'This should do,' he said quietly and turned back to his men.

'Gareth, get the bodies in our vans and regroup at home. Bors, we're taking this one, get us out of here and fast.'

Caitlyn ripped open the chest seal and started to apply it.

'Arthur, he needs an ambulance!'

'We've got people,' said Arthur, unable to meet her gaze as she looked up at him and two Hektor medics climbed in with them.

'Let's go,' said Arthur, as Caitlyn lowered her head and began giving instructions to the medics.

The doors slammed shut and a few moments later, the cult's van set off down the driveway, followed by the two Hektor vehicles. The three vans turned left around Tristan's damaged car, avoiding the traffic jam, and set off in the opposite direction to which they had come.

Arthur watched Caitlyn work, admiring how calm and collected she seemed to be, her precise instructions easily interpreted and followed by the medics.

Arthur, sitting by Tristan's head, braced himself as they began to slide to the side.

'Tristan, can you hear me?' he said, leaning in close.

Tristan's eyes opened and fixed on Arthur's. He tried to speak, but Arthur watched as the words failed to form and his knight lost consciousness.

'Where are we going?' asked Caitlyn, rounding on him. He'd never seen her look so quietly angry, a cold fire burning in her eyes.

'Can you keep him alive?' asked Arthur, feeling as though his relationship with this woman was now a lost cause and any pretence was a folly.

'Until we get to a hospital, maybe,' she said.

'We're not going to a hospital,' said Arthur. 'We're heading home.'

'He needs a fucking hospital, Arthur!'

But Arthur did not reply.

Chapter Twenty-Four

Tintagel, Cornwall
5th Century

Tristan stood on top of the earthworks with Lucan at his side, watching Morgana and Treave ride away from Tintagel, but he felt no relief.

The sorceress had arrived without warning, taken the king away then returned with apparently no harm done, with perhaps the only unusual consequence being that King Mark had offered an open invitation for Mordred and his mother to return, where previously his uncle had been cautious and kept Arthur's sister and son at bay.

'She's done *something*,' said Tristan.

'Perhaps she just wants us to worry about it,' said Lucan. 'After all, she's just had an effective diplomatic visit. A bond has been forged between the sorceress and the king. What more could she want?'

'I suppose,' said Tristan. 'More, I think. She does not like to be too direct. We will have to keep careful watch over the king and queen. And who knows what mischief her man, Treave, got up to while we were away. He may have employed some of our own as spies.'

Tristan felt Lucan's eyes burning into him.

'It's possible,' said his friend, 'but just as likely that Morgana wants you distracted and fearful. Discord in Cornwall would only strengthen Mordred. We must be cautious, of course, but not to our own detriment.'

Tristan nodded, but he could think only of protecting Isolde, King Mark and even Lucan. The fear became so overwhelming that he could think of nothing else and sweat formed on his brow, and he blinked away dizziness.

―⁂―

Tristan was on his way to find King Mark when he saw Queen Isolde, dressed for riding, heading for the stables. She was accompanied by guards and though he longed to go to her, he was determined to check on his uncle and put plans in place to deal with the aftermath of the sorceress's visit. He had to be wary. Watchful.

'Good afternoon,' said Merlin, who was walking beside him as though he had materialised. Tristan jumped, smashing his left shoulder into a wall, and he clutched it, scowling as he turned on the wizard, who put up an appeasing hand before he could be scolded.

'If you seek your uncle, I will accompany you, boy. I have not had a chance to speak with him until now. Morgana has been like an odour hanging in the air whenever I was near him.'

Tristan nodded slowly, anger fading.

The two men were admitted to the king's chambers, and they found Mark sitting at a table, poring over a map which Tristan recognised as showing the borders between Cornwall and both Mordred's and Arthur's lands. The king looked up as Tristan closed the door behind them.

'Merlin, you are most welcome, as are you, nephew. Come in, there is much to discuss,' said King Mark, not rising and barely taking his eyes from the maps for a second.

As Tristan approached, the king began to rub his temples, and once Merlin had pulled up a chair, Tristan standing beside him, Mark sat back, sighed and smiled wearily at both of them.

'She is gone then,' said the king. 'Now our work begins.'

'As you say, King Mark, Lady Morgana has departed, and there will be work to be done, but of what kind? Your nephew and I are …

concerned … about her visit.'

'Rightfully so,' said Mark, and Tristan saw nothing but earnest concentration and concern on his uncle's face. 'Where Morgana rides, trouble is sure to follow. She poured honey in my ears, cajoled, seduced, threatened and soothed me, subtly, of course, but her message was clear enough. She wants Cornwall's forces either beside Mordred in the coming fight or far behind the lines, safe in their homes.'

'She was that blatant?' asked Tristan.

'Of course not, but the purpose of her visit was clear before ever I laid eyes on her. I wished only to see how she would go about her business. I am only a little wiser, but I am sure that war is coming. We must prepare. Merlin, I must ask that you cut short your visit and take word to King Arthur that it will not be long now before his sister makes her move,' said Mark.

Merlin said nothing, and Tristan moved beside the king to get a better view of the wizard's face. His eyes were closed, and he was breathing steadily.

'Merlin?' asked King Mark.

The wizard opened his eyes, but his gaze was focused on another place or time, looking through the walls of Tintagel.

'Merlin,' said Tristan, and the old man came round, frowning and looking at the king.

'You would have me depart so soon, when I might offer counsel in this matter?'

'There is no time to waste. Our peoples must be made ready. Mordred could strike at any time. I played Morgana's game, assuring her that diplomatic channels would remain open, and that this is not our war, nevertheless, she knows my allegiance to Arthur and that Cornwall is unlikely to remain neutral. Arthur must be warned, and I must ready my lands for attacks from without and from within. Who knows who she has in her employ? Will you do as I ask, Merlin?'

The wizard muttered something unintelligible, and Tristan hoped the old man would use his famed magic to draw the truth from Mark, but Merlin eventually nodded.

'I will do as you ask, for I am a guest at Tintagel, and Arthur must be warned, but I caution you King Mark, and I warn your nephew while in your presence. Morgana may have laid traps here before leaving, so be watchful,' said Merlin. He held out his hand towards Mark and Tristan's heart leapt. He stepped forward, realising his hopes were coming to fruition, but he saw only the wizard frown in concentration and King Mark grin momentarily, before his face went slack, and he looked around the room as though he had just arrived. Less than a second later, he was back to himself once more, and Merlin ceased his efforts.

'She has done *something* to you, King Mark, but I cannot discern exactly what. It is as though when I look, an influence or a presence hides farther back inside your mind,' said Merlin. He pushed back his chair and leant on his staff, looming over Mark from the other side of the table.

Tristan stepped forward, ready to throw himself in front of the king or at Merlin if required, but the wizard spoke on, intoning the words as he released them.

'War may be coming, and I deem that you are right, King Mark, Cornwall is at risk not only from Mordred but from within. Seeds of anarchy have been planted here, I deem. Be cautious,' said the wizard, and the king stood.

'You say I have been influenced and yet you claim to be at a loss, unable to help me despite your famed arts? Does Lady Morgana surpass you in ability? Surely not. Perhaps you are simply unwilling, and it would serve Arthur better to have Cornwall fall into disarray so that he might extend his realm and hasten the united kingdom of which he so often speaks? Perhaps Camelot will be built on the rubble of Tintagel?'

Tristan could not believe what he was hearing.

'Sire,' he objected, and saw his uncle's face was not stern, but almost amused. He cast his eyes at Merlin and for a moment, it seemed as though he was looking through a green haze that gradually dissipated.

Merlin said nothing, simply nodded.

'It begins,' he said. 'You are compromised, King Mark. I will take my leave of Tintagel and bear word to Arthur.'

'Compromised? You think so little of me, Merlin. I will have to consider whether my borders should be maintained rather than join Arthur on the march when the time comes,' said Mark.

'He does not mean it, Merlin, as you've … ' said Tristan.

'Do not speak for me,' Mark bellowed over him.

The room fell silent.

'It is time I was leaving,' said Merlin. 'The alliance stands, King Mark, and I will seek the means to help … Cornwall.'

'We will see. Send Arthur my love when you return to his hall. May this war be averted or won swiftly, so that all of our minds might remain at rest and peace reign, rather than any one man. Tristan will escort you to the stables.'

The king sat and returned his attention to his maps, and without further discussion, Tristan walked with Merlin back to the wizard's chamber. When all was readied, they made for the stables and found Lucan on the way, regaling him of their encounter while the wizard's horse was readied.

'He's banishing you?' asked Lucan.

'That's not what we said. Not at all. The king would not do that,' said Tristan sharply.

Merlin hushed him, smiling kindly as he did so.

'He … or rather … Morgana — wants me gone, but I do not doubt he would allow me to return if it suited him. I sense, perhaps, things will move faster than that and my attention will be elsewhere. I am sorry to see that already King Mark is dispatching more men to the gate and see how he has sent away any of the small folk he can do without? Cornwall will become a land of paranoia in the weeks to come, I fear. You must hold true to one another, but accept that what happens here may be partly Morgana's volition.'

The wizard turned his attention to Tristan and his already quiet voice dropped to a barely audible whisper.

'I fear that you are most at risk. That you have been … positioned … in some way. Your affection for the queen is dangerous, and I wonder if it is quite natural. Perhaps Morgana has influenced you, I cannot tell. Morgana has dabbled in arts different to my own. With Mark potentially compromised and watchful for betrayal, I would advise you to leave Tintagel and take up a command on the borders,' said Merlin.

Tristan shook his head, hearing sense, but not accepting it. He could not be parted from her, even if he must love her from afar and through only the exchange of glances. And he could not leave his uncle at his time of need nor abandon Lucan when Tintagel was under siege.

'I cannot go,' he said, annoyed at Merlin's suggestion that his feelings for Isolde might not be genuine, 'but I do heed your words. I will stay away from the queen and focus solely on my duties. We will secure Tintagel and be ready when Mordred's forces make their move.'

Merlin sighed and exchanged a look with Lucan.

'Watch over him as best you can, boy. I sense this will not end well for him. But know, if things go wrong, you will always have a place at Arthur's court.'

With that, Merlin mounted his horse and rode out from Tintagel, seeking the road back to King Arthur, leaving Cornwall to its fate, along with Lucan, King Mark, Tristan and Isolde.

Chapter Twenty-Five

2021

Kayleigh Turner explored the ground floor of the mansion, passing from empty room to empty room, accompanied only by the steady tick of the grandfather clock in the hall, sometimes distant, sometimes nearby, as well as the sound of her crutches thumping against the hardwood floors. There was a stillness about the place, she felt, as though it existed outside of time.

Kayleigh passed the grandfather clock, then, taking a breath before beginning, she made her way up the stairs, following the sound of muffled voices coming from a room above; Kay and Dagonet working in the office, still trying to find Arthur's missing girlfriend.

It occurred to her that she should check on Simon, who should be napping in the room they were sharing, with Bobbi the Border collie laying beside him.

A voice from behind stopped her in her tracks.

'Caught ya.'

She jumped slightly and let out an 'oh', but when she saw a balding man in a tracksuit grinning up at her from the bottom of the stairs, she laughed and clutched her heart.

'You scared me!' she scolded, and the little man bowed, not taking his eyes from her.

He was not dressed anything like Arthur or his knights, and he looked even more out of place than she did. She didn't recognise him from any of her visions, either from touching Tristan or Samson.

'Got ya good!' he pointed at her, wagging his finger.

'You did. Watch your back. You're next,' Kayleigh joked, caught between the desire to exit the interaction and go to her son, and that fundamental British need to complete a social transaction as politely and properly as possible.

'Oh, I'm used to that, love,' said the man. 'You live here or just visiting?'

Kayleigh kept the smile on her face with a little effort, though she felt it fade from her eyes. The man didn't seem to notice.

'I'm visiting. What about you?'

'Dunno yet, love. Dunno. Been invited to stay, but they aren't really my kind of people, you know? Arthur's got a stick up his arse, you know?' said the man.

The smile faded a little more. She had no particular affection for Arthur, but insulting the man in his own home after he'd just helped her? She drew a line there.

'He seems alright,' she said. 'I've got to … '

And she couldn't move, her body slightly twisted in the turn she had started to make. Kayleigh tried to move, half afraid she would fling her limbs in some bizarre display, but panic was setting in.

Nothing.

'Alright or not, his time's up. With the boss dead, it's time I put this lot down. I'll make it quick, yeah?' said the man. Kayleigh tried to turn her head at the sound of footsteps approaching from the direction of the office, and she realised she could no longer hear Kay and Dagonet around the same time as she realised she could not move her head.

I'm Charlie Merton, by the way, said a voice in her head.

She tried to speak, but her lips wouldn't move. But it seemed that Merton heard her anyway.

'We've got mixed up in something here, but we've ended up on different sides,' said Merton, and as he did so, Bedivere led a group of Hektor men through the front door and filled up the hall behind him. They stood, hands by their sides, staring immediately forward, unmoving.

They're under control too, thought Kayleigh.

Kay and Dagonet made their way downstairs and stopped a few steps up, facing down at the Hektor operatives and Merton.

'Right, that's everyone, I think,' said Merton.

What about Simon? Kayleigh couldn't help but think it.

'Simon?' asked Merton, frowning, and to her horror, Kayleigh realised what came next.

'Your son. There's a boy in the house?'

Still frowning, Merton closed his eyes and opened them again a few moments later. He shook his head.

'He ain't here now, luv. Let's get on with this, shall we?'

Bedivere and one of the men from Hektor raised their

sidearms and pointed them straight at Kay and Dagonet's heads.

No, oh fuck, no, thought Kayleigh.

She didn't flinch, physically at least, when the shots rang out and both knights collapsed to the floor.

Trapped inside her own mind, Kayleigh Turner was screaming.

Merton walked up to stand beside her, chatting inanely, but she was unable to look away as the men below began to execute one another, each time with a single shot between the eyes to a man who just stood, blank-faced and waiting.

When they're done, am I next?

'Probably for the best, love, after all, you did see all of this, didn't you? And you weren't supposed to live this long. The boss might be gone, but yada yada continue his work yada yada. They'll still want you gone.'

Simon, where is he?

A final shot rang out and Bedivere slumped atop the other corpses, a bullet wound through his temple.

'I told you, he's not fucking here, is he!'

He must be, she thought.

Merton shook his head, bent to pick up a pistol, and he came up the steps towards Kayleigh, who found herself releasing the crutch on her good side and taking the pistol from him.

'Sorry about this,' he said, 'but if you wouldn't mind dying now?'

'Mummy?'

There, on the landing, rubbing his eyes and standing

barefoot in his pyjamas, was Simon, Bobbi growling at his side. She saw him look down at the carnage on the stairs and in the hall and at his mother holding a gun, and he screamed.

Merton nearly jumped out of his skin. For a moment, Kayleigh had control of herself. She started to bring up the gun after realisation dawned, but then Merton regained control. Simon ran back out of sight, but Bobbi remained on guard.

'How?' spat Merton. He closed his eyes, frowning intensely and pinched the bridge of his nose.

When he looked up, Kayleigh saw fear written clearly over his face.

'Plan B then,' said Merton.

And Kayleigh tucked the pistol down the waistband of her trousers as Merton stooped and handed her the fallen crutch. She turned, slowly, and continued up the stairs.

'Simon,' she heard her voice call out, but robotic and not comforting as she would have sounded had she been trying to soothe her son.

No, I won't let you, she thought and tried to wheel, tried to summon that same force she had used against Malagant in Agravain's body when the Dread Knight had attacked her in her own home.

'None of that,' said Merton. 'Find your boy and put him down, yeah?'

Kayleigh Turner, trapped in her own head, paused on the landing, drew the pistol and fired into Bobbi's head before beginning the hunt for her son.

Room by room, she stalked the upper floor of Arthur's

mansion, swinging between her crutches. She called out to Simon as she went, all the while fighting to regain control, but only managing to slow herself down enough to draw Merton's attention, at which point he would overwhelm her defences, and her body went about the task of removing from the world what it had brought into it.

Mummy.

She heard Simon's voice in her head as she had Merton's not long before.

Get out of the house if you can, but if not, hide like before, she thought. *Mummy's coming, but a bad man is making her do things.*

None of that, said Merton's inside her head. Kayleigh felt like a consciousness, devoid of body, conversing with spirits as she watched herself move through the house.

She tried to occupy her mind, tried to block her thoughts, but the best she could manage was to think the same words over and over.

Please, leave him alone. Please, leave him alone.

Mummy. Simon again. *The bad man is searching for me. He's hurting my head. I can hear him, but he can't hear me.*

Please, leave him alone. Please, leave him alone.

She was approaching their bedroom when Simon stepped out into the corridor. She dropped the crutch and pulled out the pistol. Kayleigh resisted with everything she had, her whole arm shaking, pointing the weapon just in front of her son's feet.

'Mummy,' said Simon, his voice shaking.

Oh God, help, thought Kayleigh as the gun began to rise

again, it was aimed at his pyjama covered legs, then his stomach, then his chest. Tears rolled down her cheeks.

Run Simon! The boy turned to run back into the bedroom.

Her index finger squeezed the trigger, but as it did so, Kayleigh managed to flinch ever so slightly and the shot went wide, just missing Simon's back.

The little boy screamed as Kayleigh hopped forward, turning into the bedroom, leaning against the door jamb.

Simon rolled over on the floor, his hand outstretched towards her, his eyes wide. He looked up as she brought the gun to bear.

Kayleigh felt her trigger finger moving once more and then …

She froze, horrified, as Simon's eyes rolled back in his head.

Everything fell silent. Even the voices in her mind.

Kayleigh drew from her inner reserve and found she could, slowly, begin to move.

She dropped the pistol, and it clattered on the hardwood floor.

She tried to get to Simon, but the movement was so, so slow.

And then she fell forward, hitting her head on the door as she went down. She cried out and had never been so happy to hear herself expressing pain, realising she was in command of her own body again.

She crawled to Simon and took hold of his shoulders. He was shaking, beginning to seize, a low moan emerging from his mouth as his head began to twist and his hands clenched into fists.

'Simon. SIMON,' she screamed, but there was nothing and still no voices in her head; not Merton and not her son.

She could only think of one more thing to do.

Kayleigh managed to crawl out into the corridor and stood with an effort once she had retrieved her crutches, putting down their rubber ends and lightly swinging forward to set off as quietly as she could.

She reached the top of the stairs and saw Merton backed up against the front door on the ground floor, amid the fallen. He too was seizing, only the whites of his eyes visible, drool hanging from his mouth and dripping to the floor.

She passed Bobbi's fallen form and made her way down the stairs, manoeuvring around the corpses of Dagonet and Kay. Merton did not react.

Once Kayleigh reached the ground floor, she stooped and picked up Bedivere's pistol.

She pressed the muzzle against Merton's forehead, crying and shaking as she did so.

She had intended to pull the trigger, but hesitated and reached out with her other hand, touching his cheek.

Kayleigh was elsewhere. In Merton's memories. She saw the good, the bad, the horrors, the cult making contact with him, bringing him onboard, and she saw Simon. She saw through Merton's eyes, heard the screams and the battling within the heads of both man and boy. And then the connection broke.

Kayleigh was in the hall of Arthur's mansion once more. She began to wail and the sound turned into a roar.

She pulled the trigger.

Chapter Twenty-Six

Tintagel, Cornwall
5th Century

'You jest?' asked Lucan, issuing an incredulous little laugh as he turned his attention away from the parchment in his hands. Concern was written across his face.

Tristan shook his head.

'King Mark rides out tomorrow to gather his forces and you are to go with him.'

'Leaving you in command of Tintagel and alone with Queen Isolde, which is exactly what Merlin advised against,' said Lucan, incredulous.

Tristan nodded, but said nothing.

'It cannot be a coincidence,' Lucan persisted. 'Whatever Morgana's hold over the king, she is steering him to put you in this position, surely you see that? It is clear you are drawn to the queen, and I believe it is due to the sorceress. We must do something to disrupt the plans,' said Lucan.

'What *can* we do? We have the king's orders,' said Tristan, and he heard the affront in his own voice. Did Lucan think as little of him as Merlin? Did his friend not think he was strong enough to resist the impulses he felt?

'I could feign illness so that you must needs go in my stead?' asked Lucan, but Tristan shook his head.

'If my uncle is set upon this course by fair means or foul, such a pretence will not dissuade him. He would ride out and leave us both, taking another with him.'

'At least I would be here too. What other possibilities?' asked Lucan.

'There are none,' said Tristan, glum, and yet, was he not a little excited, deep down inside, to know that he might spend more time with the queen, even if his head knew it would be the wrong course? He should assign another to tend to her needs and to watch over her if he was to remain at Tintagel. 'I spoke at length with King Mark and argued against his decision, but he would not be swayed.'

Lucan began to speak, but stopped short.

'What is it?' Tristan frowned, and Lucan hesitated.

'It's just, forgive me, but I wonder how hard you argued, brother,' said Lucan. 'You are in a dangerous position, Tristan, and neither my words nor Merlin's can reach you. You nod and agree, but deep down, I fear you are not as concerned as you should be.'

'I listen well enough and I take heed, but I cannot help but feel I am the victim of an injustice here, that my kinsman and the wizard would think so little of me, a supposed man of honour,' said Tristan, throwing up his hands and turning his back on Lucan, his subconscious internal battle between right and wrong manifesting in anger against those who would watch over him. His thoughts argued against his feelings, but then changed tack and sought to justify them. Ever Morgana whispered, unheard, but heeded, deep down in the depths of his mind, where there was no light.

Lucan laid a hand on Tristan's shoulder, but he did not turn.

'Tristan, you *are* a man of honour, but the sorceress toys with us all and you are only human. You are fallible, no matter how loyal. We can all fail,' said Lucan, barely above a whisper.

'I will keep my distance from the queen in your absence and as she has never sought me out since her marriage, I believe that will suffice. I will give Mark no cause to doubt my loyalty. I bear the king and queen great love, no less one than the other. If I cannot unfeel, I will suffer from afar,' said Tristan. 'Morgana cannot use me to cause strife at Tintagel.'

Lucan did not reply, but patted his friend on the shoulder.

⁕

That evening while they dined in the sombre hall of Tintagel, a place where caution and paranoia were now taking hold, with warriors, advisors and servants all briefed against one another, Tristan was troubled, and it seemed King Mark had noticed.

'Who pissed in your wine, nephew?' said the king, but there was no humour behind his words and he did not laugh, though Tristan thought he caught wry amusement on his uncle's face for a moment before all expression deadened.

'It saddens me to hear such brooding silence in this hall that only recently was a place of merriment and contentment. I wish you would not ride out, uncle. I fear for all of us,' said Tristan.

The king nodded.

'These will be trying times with war looming, but I would be neglectful if I did not command wariness in my people when the sorceress is abroad.'

Tristan thought the king's eyes flashed green momentarily, which he dismissed as a trick of the light.

The king continued.

'You are as a son to me Tristan, and I love you well. You have always served me faithfully. I could have asked no more of a nephew or a warrior in my service. We will prevail. There is nobody else to whom I would entrust the care of my keep and my queen while I am abroad.'

Tristan's heart swelled to hear such praise and expression of mutual love, appreciation and affection. He could not help but smile. Of course he would do right by his uncle! He bore love for Isolde, it was true, but he was a man of honour. What was there to fear?

The curse whispered to him, *what risk is there? You love your uncle no less than you love Isolde? They are both worthy of your love and you are worthy of their trust.*

Tristan raised his goblet, smiling at the king.

'A toast to the peace on the other side of war, Uncle. Long may you reign.'

King Mark grinned and raised his own.

Once the king's company had departed, Tristan reviewed plans for the defence and security of Tintagel with the castellan, whom he had still not forgiven for Isolde's lacklustre welcome when they returned from Ireland. Slight alterations made and orders decided upon, he was satisfied, if saddened by the extreme measures, and he decided to ride out to clear his head.

Despite the cold and the rain, being out of Tintagel and alone immediately began to invigorate him, and he relished the water on his skin, cooling his passions. He took in the coast, the rolling moorland and the woods. Tristan felt the weight lift for a while, and he made the rides after meeting with the castellan part of his daily routine.

He assigned a guard to the queen, gave command of Tintagel itself to the castellan and busied himself with considering Cornwall's wider concerns. He ate in his chambers and kept away from Isolde, though he much desired to spend time with her. Part of resisting temptation, though, he decided, was knowing where not to be and who not to be around.

Days passed and all seemed well. Riders from the king's company brought regular news, the workings of Tintagel went on as they usually did. Tristan, though conspicuously absent from gatherings, got about his work and enjoyed his rides, vital for keeping him wakeful, as he slept poorly at night, disturbed by dreams of trysts with Isolde and conflict with his beloved uncle.

Awake, Tristan remained true to himself and to his allegiances.

One morning, he had dismounted at the edge of the woods to rest his horse when he heard approaching hooves.

He looked up and realised it was not a messenger bringing news, but Isolde, riding alone.

Fear struck him, mingled with desire. She had made no attempt to find him since the king's departure, and now she put herself in danger to do so? Something grave must have happened, thought Tristan.

She loves you, fool, whispered the curse. *She can deny it no longer.*

'My queen?' he asked as she dismounted, her hair all in disarray and her cheeks red from the cold.

No hesitation. She drew close and kissed him. Caught off guard, never expecting Isolde to act in such a way, so blatantly and for all to see, he returned the kiss.

They broke apart, and he saw that she was crying.

'I have been torn in two,' she said, 'but I cannot deny my heart.'

Isolde's behaviour was so different that Tristan should have paused and considered, but he too was under the influence of King Arthur's sister, and the curse whispered away all concerns. In Isolde's company, thus impassioned, he did not think of the king.

He led her into the woods and there, under the cover of the trees, they made love for the first time.

As they dressed, the enormity of what they had done hit them both, and they brooded in silence, but still could not help stealing glances at one another. Readied, they drew close once more and embraced, both of them sighing and feeling the weight of the betrayal, for Tristan loved his uncle deeply, and Isolde admitted she respected Mark as a good husband, who had made her welcome and treated her kindly since their marriage. The couple remained in one another's arms, quietly thinking, regretting, relishing, hoping and scheming, unaware that their actions would become legend, knelling through eternity.

Mark was not there. Tristan and Isolde had each other, and their love came to the forefront.

'You must return to Tintagel, and I will follow later,' said Tristan.

'Will you tell Mark?' she asked. 'He would have our heads.'

'Perhaps we owe them to him,' said Tristan gravely. 'We cannot tell him, for more harm would be done than our parting, Isolde. Cornwall must remain strong, as must our alliance with your father.'

Isolde nodded.

'This was always more an alliance than a

marriage. Have I not the right to choose who I love if a husband is forced upon me? No harm is done here, if we remain discreet,' she said, and she appeared to be genuine in her belief. Tristan sighed, knowing full well he was betraying his uncle and king, but Isolde was right and, the curse told him, *what right does any power in this world have to sunder two loving hearts? You can serve him well, honour your king and queen, and yet continue to love the lady.*

'We must be careful,' he said. 'I will do my duty to him and to Cornwall, serving him more fiercely than ever. In loving his queen, I will protect her all the more ardently.'

They held each other tighter and agreed, the affair must not continue within the walls, though they bore each other great love and it would pain them to remain aloof or apart between encounters. They would indeed have to be careful.

Isolde mounted her horse and rode back to Tintagel, where she would no doubt be scolded by her guards. Tristan entered into the woods and emerged elsewhere, continuing his ride so that he might return by a different route. As he rode, he remembered their lovemaking and a fierce flame ignited within his heart.

Lovers can only be so careful.

Their absences at night were noted, sometimes his, sometimes hers, sometimes both. And before long, the days between trysts were fewer until Tristan and Isolde, strangers driven by a malevolent curse, crept from Tintagel nightly and made love in their glade.

One night, they lay beside one another, staring into each other's eyes, lying upon their laid-out cloaks and drifted off to sleep.

When Tristan awoke, it was still dark, but a shard of moonlight glinted between them.

King Mark's sword lay between the lovers.

Tristan leapt to his feet, naked though he was, and looked all around, listening carefully, but he heard nothing except the sounds of the woods and the beasts therein. He dressed, whispering Isolde's name until she stirred, and she questioned his haste to ready himself, but fell silent when her eyes fell upon her husband's sword.

Tristan breathed hard, panic rising. All was undone. Merlin and Lucan had warned him.

He had allowed himself to get close to her and now, what? What did the sword portend?

'Why hasn't he seized us or killed us while we slept?' asked Tristan as Isolde came to stand beside him.

'He is a better man than that,' said Isolde,

eyes sad and her tone flat. Tristan nodded, realising it was true.

'You can escape,' he said. 'I will go with you and see you safe before returning to face my uncle.'

Isolde shook her head.

'We will face him together,' she said and sighed, covering her eyes with her hands. 'And face all of those who saw us here together. This news will spread, no matter how good-hearted your uncle may be.'

They walked back together in silence and received hard stares from those at the gates as they made no attempt to return by the secret ways they used to facilitate their meetings unseen, though Tristan wondered if perhaps they had been observed, if Mark had found them so easily.

The castellan met them, his face grave, and told them the king awaited them in his chambers.

There they found Mark, seated behind his table with the same maps spread out before him, and Lucan sprang up from a chair as the lovers were shown in.

Mark bade the castellan leave the four of them alone.

Silence fell after the door closed.

Tristan's whole body shook and his mouth went dry, his lips feeling as though they were cracking more by the second. He looked at

Lucan, who appeared desperate, tilting his head with a sad expression on his face, before anxiously returning his attention to the king.

'How long?' said King Mark.

Tristan spoke without hesitation.

'I fell for the lady at sea, Uncle, but kept my love in check until a few days ago. I have betrayed you, my king, and I deserve death, but spare the lady. She is new to these lands, and I gave her no choice,' said Tristan, but Isolde interjected fiercely and loudly.

'That is NOT true,' she insisted. 'I was fond of Tristan, but after your departure, I thought of him more and more. I could not deny I had grown to love him, and I sought him out, though I knew he was staying away from me, to preserve his honour and out of loyalty to you. I am at fault, *not* him.'

The lovers fell silent, the room filled with the sound of the crackling fire. Tristan looked down at the floor, his hands clasped before him. Now he was with his uncle once more, the guilt and regret was unbearable. How had he been so foolish? The affair could only have ended one way.

It isn't over, said the curse. *You are armed. Strike him down. You are the better swordsman.*

The words were not heard by Tristan's conscious mind, but he began to consider whether they might make their escape and continue the story of Tristan and Isolde, but the curse spoke again.

He is your uncle. He raised you. A noble king and a good man. He does not deserve it. Better you die than him. Save Isolde if you can, so that they might have one another. And yet maybe in time, she will slip away from him and come to you. If you bide your ...

'I cannot look at either of you,' said King Mark, raising his head, showing the tears running down his cheeks, but he kept his eyes on the table. 'You have both betrayed me, which perhaps I could understand of the queen, new to these lands and not married out of love, but you, Tristan? You abandon all loyalty to me after all I have done for you, on a whim of your heart and at the call of your stirring loins?'

Tristan's heart felt like stone, his guts churning. Mark was right, of course. He was a traitor, nothing more than a lovestruck fool who had wandered into treason.

Tristan looked over at Lucan, who was still watching the king intently as Mark stood and, clearly with an effort, looked up at the lovers, his eyes red and his face seeming gaunt.

'You have cuckolded the King of Cornwall,' his voice was shaking.

Tristan swallowed hard, wanting to fall on

his knees to beg his uncle's forgiveness.

'Part of me wants to throw you from the cliffs on to the rocks below, but what good would that do? I would have killed those I love in anger and be seen as nothing more than a jealous, vengeful husband. Your sins against me are grave, but all too human,' said Mark, straightening up and appearing more kingly.

'My queen,' said the king, beckoning Isolde to his side. She went and he took both of her hands in his.

'You have betrayed our vows, but not your heart. I will forgive you in time and perhaps you will come to truly love me. The alliance with your father will remain strong and perhaps, in time, our marriage will become the same. Let the people say what they will, but all loving hearts are in jeopardy.' He turned to his nephew, his eyes cold. His next words clearly cost him.

'You, Tristan, I will try to forgive in time, but I will not be made to look a fool in my own halls. Let it be known that I granted you mercy. You have until morning to depart Cornwall. Do not return unless I send word or you will face swift, harsh justice at the hands of those who remain loyal to King Mark.'

Tristan felt his knees go, but before he could fall to the floor, Lucan grabbed him under the arms and kept him up.

'Uncle, I ... ' said Tristan, but Mark held up his hand.

'I am nothing to you now,' said the king. 'Lucan, get him out of my sight before I change my mind.'

'Mark, have mercy on him, he is no more at fault than I,' said Isolde, but her husband shook his head.

'If his exile torments you, then that is the price you pay for disloyalty. It is not as costly as it could have been for you, my queen,' said Mark.

The last Tristan saw of Isolde as Lucan manhandled him out of the royal couple's chambers, her eyes were locked on him and streaming tears.

'Come *on,* Tristan, there is no time to waste,' hissed Lucan, hauling at his friend's arm, Tristan barely staggering forward.

'We must go!' said Lucan and that brought Tristan round.

'We?' he asked.

'I will not abandon you. If you are banished then I will be at your side. Morgana is behind this somehow, I know it, and *you* are not at fault.'

Tristan heeded his friend, and the two men quickly snatched up what they could with all the eyes of Tintagel upon them.

They rode out before dawn, Tristan looking back only once, tears streaming down his cheeks as he thought of his uncle teaching him to ride as a boy and of Isolde, her quick wit and the touch of her skin.

Chapter Twenty-Seven

2021

'Hold on, Tristan,' said Caitlyn. 'Stay with me.'

Arthur watched, helpless, massaging his mouth with one hand and bracing himself against the wall with the other.

The van made a tight turn, slowing as it did so, and parked up a few seconds later. The doors were thrown open and Arthur clambered out as Caitlyn directed the Hektor operatives in moving Tristan.

The other two vans were also present, and Bors overtook Arthur on the way to the front door. There was no sign of Kay, Bedivere or Dagonet, nor anyone from Hektor. Gareth ran to Tristan's side.

Ahead of Arthur, Bors tried to open the front door. Arthur saw the big man force his shoulder against the wood, as though something was preventing the door from being opened on the other side. Bors drew back, pulled out his pistol and held up a hand, signalling everyone to stop.

Arthur drew his Colt and moved up beside Bors. The scent of iron and death drifted through the crack in the door, and Arthur could make out somebody's legs across the hall floor, not far from where Percival had fallen two years before.

'There could be more of them,' whispered Arthur, as Gareth ran up beside them and Bors backed away.

'Go in through the kitchen?' asked Gareth, but as he did so, Bors sprinted forward smashing into the door and wedging himself into the gap. He forced it open, and Gareth slipped in behind him.

'Wait here,' said Arthur to one of the Hektor men.

Gareth opened the door and closed it behind Arthur once he stepped inside the mansion.

Carnage everywhere.

Bedivere and the Hektor operatives lay dead on the hall floor, Charlie Merton now lying to one side by the front door, which bore a single hole, the inches-thick oak just managing to stop the bullet from disappearing outside.

'Arthur … ' said Bors, his tone strained.

Arthur turned and saw Dagonet and Kay for the first time, part way down the stairs, crumpled up and lifeless.

Numb, he was about to order a sweep of both floors when he heard a child's crying start up, suddenly muffled and then, as the three of them headed up to the first floor, passing Bobbi, he heard Kayleigh Turner's voice calling his name from up above.

Bors took point, heading towards the sound.

'It's alright,' called Kayleigh. 'He's dead.' The sound came from her room, and Arthur followed the knights down the corridor.

Inside, Kayleigh was sitting on the floor, wild-eyed and

shaking, clutching Simon to her while he rocked back and forth. The boy looked up when Arthur entered.

'The bad man is gone,' said Simon, 'but he killed everyone.'

Arthur frowned, not understanding, battling to contain his tears and his rage.

'Who?' he asked Kayleigh, as he holstered his Colt and knelt down before them. He took both of Simon's hands in his and said quietly, 'It's alright. You're alright now.'

'Charlie Merton,' said Kayleigh. 'He made them kill each other. Made me try to kill … ' she tipped her head towards her son, leaning into his hair, 'but Simon fought back enough for me to … to … '

'I know. We saw,' said Arthur. 'Don't say any more.'

He got to his feet and, asking Bors and Gareth to look after their guests, he made his way back downstairs in time to see the medics carrying Tristan out of the hall and into an anteroom. Caitlyn stepped in from outside, visibly shaking and her mouth dropping open as she took in the horrors within. Arthur took a deep breath as he went down to her.

'What the fuck is this, Arthur? Some private war? He needs an ambulance!' she said, pointing towards the room where Tristan had been taken.

'A private ambulance is on the way. We can't call 999, Caitlyn. It's a complicated situation. I'd better explain.'

'There's no time for any of that. Your friend … I thought he was your friend … has been shot, Arthur. Shot! Maybe you are used to this, but I'm not. He needs to go to hospital.'

Arthur placed both hands on her shoulders, meaning to reassure her, but Caitlyn swept them away and stepped back.

'Don't touch me,' she snapped. 'Don't touch me. What the fuck is even going on?'

Arthur straightened up and said nothing for a moment.

'Well?' she demanded, but held up a hand dismissively as she disappeared from the hall, following the medics.

Arthur looked around him at the gore and stepped out of the house to address the remaining Hektor men, asking them to load up the bodies into the van and get the vehicles off the property.

He made his way to the room where the medics were treating Tristan, with Caitlyn overseeing.

'Where's the ambulance?' she snapped at Arthur. He looked at the medic, who called the Hektor control room.

'Fifteen minutes out,' he said.

Caitlyn rounded on him.

'What the fuck is this about?'

Arthur looked into her eyes.

'I know you've had an ordeal, that this is frightening and distressing. I know I've not been as honest with you as I could have been, but I need you to trust that it was for good reasons. Can you do that?'

Caitlyn held his gaze then looked back at Tristan.

'Caitlyn, I'm sorry, I am, and I'll give you all the answers you need once Tristan is stable. And you should probably check in with work or your family before someone reports you missing.'

She shook her head and returned to tending Tristan.

Arthur retreated back into the hall, now devoid of corpses, but blood still covering the walls and floor.

Chapter Twenty-Eight

5th Century

Tristan and Lucan rode in silence much of the time as they put Tintagel, King Mark and Isolde farther behind them with every hoof laid upon the muddy road.

Tristan's heart was heavy, and he rebuffed his friend's attempts at raising his spirits, feeling all the more guilty for knowing that Lucan had given up everything to accompany him and that his friend's exile was of his own choosing.

The two of them were alone in the world now, without allies and without a home, wandering the road with nothing but a few meagre possessions and their mounts, which were already showing signs of needing to rest and take water.

Tristan asked Lucan to keep an eye out for streams and a good place to stop, and before long, they had dismounted, led the horses to water and let them drink.

Both men knelt by the stream and drank the cold water with cupped hands. Tristan splashed his face and scrubbed at his skin then dipped his head into the stream, bringing up his hair, drenched. He shook it out like a dog, spraying Lucan, who laughed.

Tristan turned to him, surprised by the mirth, as sullen as he felt, and saw Lucan was smiling.

'How can you be so merry?' asked Tristan.

Lucan sat cross-legged on a tussock, sighed and looked up at the clouds overhead. He spoke without looking at his friend.

'At least we are away with our heads still on our necks, eh, brother? For a while there, I thought you and the king would come to blows,' he said.

Tristan sighed and nodded his head, but he could think only of Isolde, and the pain in his heart was all too real.

'It will get easier,' said Lucan, but Tristan did not reply.

'Have you given much thought to our destination?' asked Lucan, after a while.

'What does it matter?' asked Tristan, but heard the petulance in his voice, and he apologised to Lucan then swept his hair back behind his ears, taking a long breath and rallying somewhat. Isolde was behind him, and even if his heart belied his friend's words, he knew they were true. It would get easier, but what manner of life would he have now, as an exiled, disgraced noble seeking a life with little coin in new lands? Where should they go? And how could he live with dragging Lucan along?

'I've made quite enough decisions for us both. And I am ever in your debt for standing by me. *I* will follow *you* from now on,' said Tristan.

Lucan grinned.

'We'll see how long that lasts!' he said and both men chuckled, a little levity creeping into that new phase of their lives.

'As it happens, I do have a destination in mind,' said Lucan, and Tristan thought his voice was a little restrained or perhaps just strained.

'Oh?' he asked.

'Before Merlin left, he bade me tell you that he would speak for you if we crossed the border. He knew all that befell King Mark and those around him was not of your making, Tristan, as do I,' said Lucan. 'You are not entirely at fault, I am sure of it.'

Tristan stood tall and tucked his thumbs into his sword belt, his friend's assertion riling him somewhat unaccountably, perhaps because he knew the truth, or at least the curse's version of it as he understood it.

'I led her into that glade, Lucan, my king's bride and my own aunt! I threw away all loyalty to my uncle in the face of love's challenge. How am I innocent?' His voice rose as he spoke, but Lucan did not seem affected.

'I knew the man you were before you met the lady Isolde. You are not that man today. You were staunch and stalwart, quiet and watchful. You would never have acted with such abandon before her, and she was not the first pretty maid to cross your path,' said Lucan, smiling, but Tristan did not join him in his amusement.

'Never had I been forbidden from pursuing one I loved,' he said. 'Perhaps this was the first true test of my character. I fell for a woman destined for my king, and I held that love above bonds of friendship, of country, of kin and of fealty. I am no more than a common cur, who besmirched a lady's honour and threw away my own.'

Lucan shook his head and stepped forward, putting a hand on Tristan's shoulder.

'You are fierce in your loyalty and your love, brother, and you always have been. You always will be. It is, in truth, your greatest strength. Perhaps it has led you astray when the path forked this time, but all men fail at times. You cannot cast aside all love for yourself over this matter. All is well. King Mark and Queen Isolde reign in Cornwall, and we will make new lives for ourselves, away from such memories. There is glory to be found in the court of King Arthur, I am sure of it. But still, I am not convinced that Morgana did not play a part in this drama. Merlin said it himself, she seeks to drive a wedge between Arthur and his allies for her own son's gain, and perhaps causing strife within his ally's court aids her in ways we have yet to fathom. Who knows, but for my part, I forgive you your role and believe if you must do anything now, it is not to mope and lament, but to atone for your actions by being all the more loyal, loving all the more and making a great name for yourself. The world will forget that the names Tristan and Isolde were bound together in haste for only a small time in the greater story of the lives you each will build. We go on to new challenges, and I still have hope,' Lucan lightly slapped Tristan's cheek, 'for both of us! So buck up, let's rest awhile and tomorrow, we ride to seek King Arthur.'

As the days passed, the memory of Isolde never faded, nor his uncle's hurt expression, but if Tristan could not forget what he had done, or forgive himself, he began to realise he could accept his failings and take Lucan's advice. He would strive to do better in the years ahead and serve Mark's ally better than he had his own uncle, if King Arthur would have him.

Both men had not travelled that road many times before, but they remembered enough to know they were approaching the border.

Dark clouds were gathering overhead and heavy rain fell on the evening when they spied a rider up ahead, rounding a bend in the road and heading towards them, which was nothing in itself, for the road was much used by those who lived nearby and travellers from farther afield. But then they noticed a troop of armed men following behind.

After a moment's consultation, Tristan and Lucan agreed to continue cautiously, for bandits were uncommon so close to King Arthur's lands.

As the two companies drew close together, Tristan spied the lead rider was a broad-shouldered, armoured man with grey-flecked black hair.

'Good evening,' he called, reining in his great horse, his face serious, but not unkind or threatening, for which Tristan was glad, having decided he would not wish to fight the imposing warrior.

'Good evening, sir,' he called. 'Do you have

business with us or shall we step aside and let you pass?'

'That depends on your names,' said the big man, who waited, expectantly, his eyes locked on Tristan.

'We are travellers from Tintagel, sir, invited by Merlin to visit King Arthur's court. I am Tristan and this is my kinsman, Lucan. May I ask your name?' said Tristan, sitting up as straight as he could in the saddle, all too aware that they were outnumbered if he had spoken too plainly. He heard Lucan clear his throat.

The big man nodded to each in turn.

'Merlin sensed your approach on this road, and King Arthur sent me to escort you to his hall. I am Sir Agravain, and I am at your service.'

He spurred his horse on and came between the two men, offering each his hand.

'If you mean to join us, ride with me and pay respect to your new king,' said Agravain, and Tristan took an instant liking to the man, his heart stirring once more.

'You have my gratitude, Sir Agravain. Lead on, and perhaps tell us more of what to expect from Arthur's halls.'

Chapter Twenty-Nine

2021

The Hektor ambulance arrived, and Arthur stood in the hall listening to Caitlyn briefing the paramedics in the anteroom and the sound of crying coming from upstairs.

He took in the scent of iron and, feeling light-headed, he staggered forward. He sat down on the third step up and placed his hand where Dagonet and Kay had lain a few minutes before. He began to sob and covered his face with his hands, as memories overwhelmed him. So many of the knights were gone now; Geraint, Gaheris, Galahad, Lamorak, Percival, Agravain, Dagonet, Bedivere and Kay — all dead. Only Tristan, Bors and Gareth remained by his side, with Lucan, Ector and Gawain out of contact for months, off living their own lives, as he had allowed them to do.

And now what? They had retrieved Caitlyn, though Arthur may have lost her in so doing, and gathered new folk to them, but what else was to come in this age where they had so little relevance?

A door banged, and Arthur stood as the paramedics

wheeled Tristan out on a stretcher, covered by a blanket and with an oxygen mask over his nose and mouth. They hurried out to the ambulance, and Arthur watched from the doorway.

'Arthur?'

He turned, startled, and saw Caitlyn wiping blood from her hands on a cloth at the bottom of the stairs. She was looking up at him, a cold expression on her bloody, swollen face, hair hanging in front of her eyes, but she sighed, blowing out her cheeks when she realised he had been crying.

'Will he be alright?' asked Arthur. He cleared his throat and wiped tears on his coat sleeve then stepped towards her. She didn't back off, which he found encouraging.

'I don't know. He's critical,' she said.

'Thank you for tending to him,' said Arthur, wanting to say so much more, but sheltering behind formality.

'Are you kidding me? That's all you've got to say? Don't I deserve some answers? And I'm fine by the way, thanks for asking!'

Specks of her saliva landed on his cheek and caught in his beard.

'I will explain everything,' he intoned, perhaps mustering a forgotten version of himself from ancient days, but she held up her hand.

'You know what, I'm too tired to hear it right now. I'm going home,' said Caitlyn.

'You can't, it isn't safe,' said Arthur. She rounded on him.

'Don't tell me what to do. Don't you dare, after everything

I've been through today being somehow down to you! I mean, what have you got me into? No, never mind.'

The hand came up again and she strode to the front door, Samson, who had been found shut in the drawing-room, following at her heels.

'I'm going home.'

'Please wait,' said Arthur.

She was already outside, but whirled and pointed at him.

'Keep me updated about Tristan, but other than that, I don't want to hear from you.'

'Will you go to the police?' asked Arthur.

Caitlyn glared at him, but said nothing.

'You'll need this,' said Arthur, and she snatched her phone from him.

She marched across the courtyard towards the gate, Samson following behind, and Arthur watched her go then pushed the door closed and shot the bolts.

Later that evening, after he'd received news from Hektor that Tristan was critical, but stable, Arthur woke to the sound of knocking on the drawing-room door. He grunted, almost dropping his empty glass as he sat up in the wingback chair by the fireplace.

Merlin's chair, as he had come to think of it, though the wizard had only spent a short time sitting there, was empty, and Arthur sighed at the sight of it.

'Come in,' he croaked, then licked his dry lips.

Gareth stepped into the room, hands clasped behind his

back, and he bowed his head slightly.

'Cordon have dealt with the floors, sir. Bors has gone to sit with Tristan. The Turners are resting in their room. I told them we'd all speak in the morning. Hektor sent more men, though God knows where they found them,' he said, mournfully.

Arthur straightened up and looked around for the whisky bottle, eventually spying it on his desk.

'Would you mind? Get yourself a glass too,' said Arthur. He watched the logs burning in the fireplace, not looking away when Gareth refilled his glass, only when the knight sat in Merlin's chair.

'To Dagonet, Kay and Bedivere,' said Arthur, reaching out with his glass. Gareth clinked his own against it and both men drank deeply.

'They've earned their rest,' said Gareth, quietly.

Arthur looked up, frowning, wondering exactly what his subordinate meant by that, but thought better of questioning it.

'We're lucky Tristan's still with us, sir,' said Gareth. 'He went above and beyond.'

Arthur just nodded, his head swimming. Tristan could always be relied upon, it was a given, but the future of his relationship with Caitlyn was less than certain.

Arthur sighed and took another gulp of Scotch.

'Gareth, what do I tell her about all of this?' he asked, setting down his empty glass on the table beside his chair.

'You want *my* opinion?' asked Gareth.

'Is that so surprising?' asked Arthur, laughing.

Gareth didn't answer his question, but said,

'You owe her the truth, especially after the events of the day. She deserves to know. Lord above, if she isn't permanently traumatised, it will be a miracle, sir. You need to lay it all out before her so she can deal with reality. We've hidden for too long.'

'Hidden for too long?' asked Arthur, and Gareth nodded.

'We can't forever remain in the shadows, sir. How many people saw us today? Somehow we escaped the Branok situation without public attention, but how long before Agravain's escape comes back to haunt us, and how many people saw us today at the farm? Will Caitlyn say anything? What about Charlie Merton going missing? Christ, how many did Hektor lose on our account? Those poor families. How will Hektor explain it? This could all catch up with us.'

'I paid them over the odds for their work and their families will be taken care of. They knew their duty,' said Arthur.

'That's just it though, sir. They didn't know who we truly are or what any of this was all really about. They knew we ran a covert operation here, but not its significance.'

Arthur's frown intensified as he watched Gareth finish his drink. When the knight spoke again, he grew more animated and his words were hot.

'We're attracting trouble now. Hurting people who otherwise would not be bothered. It's time we drew this to an end. Whatever the Order is up to, let's finish this and move on from … well, from all of this and from each other.'

Arthur couldn't believe what he was hearing from

Gareth, normally so reserved, and he was about to react when another knock interrupted them.

Bors's head appeared around the door, and he thumbed back the way he had come.

'They think he's going to be alright, Arthur.'

Chapter Thirty

5th Century
Two Years After Tristan and Lucan arrived at
King Arthur's Court.

A stranger to King Arthur's firelit hall might have thought the three men to be conspirators, if he saw them leaning in and speaking in hushed tones at the round table, until, that is, one of them made a jest and the trio fell about laughing.

Tristan, Lucan and Agravain, the closest of friends, passed most of their evenings in that fashion, being men without family; their only responsibilities were to their king and the folk in their charge. They were weary on that particular night, having ridden a sortie against one of Mordred's closest camps, but they had returned victorious with mercifully few lives lost, and the merriment made them forget their sorrows for a time.

Tristan finished his wine and looked around

for a serving girl, but the many tables in the great hall were packed and the servers were scurrying about and dripping with sweat.

The doors at the far end opened, and a page announced King Arthur, who wore plain clothes, no armour and only a simple gold circlet upon his brow. Excalibur hung at his left hip. Ector and Gawain, a green band tied around his upper arm, followed the king into his hall.

Everyone leapt to their feet and dropped to one knee, bowing their heads as he passed them by, paying them little heed individually, but nodding and smiling as though he was acknowledging them all.

The knights, too, paid their respects by genuflecting.

'Rise,' said Arthur, smiling, 'lest you dirty your knees!'

Arthur strode towards the round table and took up his customary seat, which looked no different to any other. Ector and Gawain settled into their own.

'What tales of the day then, my knights?' he asked, slapping Tristan on the shoulder. 'What mischief did you cause our foes today?'

Tristan felt his heart swell with affection at the king's attention, and he smiled warmly as the king sat back in his chair. The remainder of the hall resumed their meals and the minstrels started playing so that the hall was filled with music and the sound of feasting.

'We gave them swift ends, sire,' interrupted Agravain. 'No more, no less.'

'What else could I expect from my finest knights,' said Arthur, becoming more serious in the face of the weighty response. 'You are right to have mercy on those Mordred has rallied to his banner. I must remember few of them fight willingly. They were all my subjects after all.'

'And will be again, sire, once Mordred is brought back into the fold,' said Ector.

'Hear hear,' said Tristan, holding up his goblet as a serving girl approached. She filled King Arthur's before attending to the knight.

'It may not be so easy as all that,' said Arthur. 'Morgana will see to it that this ends with either my death or my son's. There will be no reconciliation.'

The round table fell silent.

'Honour in battle then,' said Tristan. 'Your word is law, sire, and if we have to fight a thousand battles, we will bring peace to Briton once more. You are the one true king.'

Arthur smiled, Agravain drank deeply, lowering his eyes, and Tristan felt Lucan watching him. Heat rose in his cheeks, and he coughed uncomfortably, breaking a short silence.

'I am ever grateful for your loyalty and faith, Tristan,' said Arthur, raising his goblet to his knight before drinking, 'but enough of such trivial matters.'

'Kings, war and honour, sire?' chuckled Gawain.

'The merest of things!' laughed Agravain.

'In the face of the test our friend here faces tomorrow, perhaps!' teased Arthur. 'Do you mean to go through with your plan, provided Mordred doesn't keep us occupied?'

Tristan recovered from his embarrassment, cursing himself for the thousandth time for wearing his heart on his sleeve.

'I do sire, if I still have your blessing. If you would prefer I remain devoted solely to the defence of your realm, I ... ' said Tristan, but Arthur held up his hand.

'Friend, you will not escape your fate with my assistance. You have my blessing,' said Arthur, and Tristan laughed as he saw his king and brother knights were all happy for him.

He nodded his head, sipped his wine and swallowed hard.

'I will ride out at dawn and ask Rozenn's father's permission to marry her,' he said.

Arthur, Agravain, Lucan, Ector and Gawain all cheered.

'The wine has gone to my head,' said Tristan,

suddenly awash with emotion. 'I'll get some air. Sire,' he said, bowing his head as he left the round table. He heard one of them saying something he could not quite make out in a jovial tone and all five men were still laughing as Tristan made his way out into the moonlight, sadness beginning to overwhelm him.

He wandered into the darker spaces between low buildings and stopped in a narrow passage, where he finally allowed his tears to fall.

He knew Rozenn very well and loved her with all his heart. He could scarcely wait to gain her father's permission before asking her hand in marriage, and yet, he felt conflicted, knowing his wife would require his love and attention when until now, he had been able to devote himself utterly to his king and his brother knights. And there was Isolde, always Isolde, in the back of his mind. The touch of her lips on his a constant memory, burning even brighter when he thought of Rozenn or of his duties. The women's faces both appeared before him. He wanted to rush away to seek out the Queen of Cornwall, to propose to Lady Rozenn, to spend all his time in service as a knight and yet to watch his brother's backs at the cost of even the realm. Ever they plagued him, the conflicting loves and loyalties he had accrued since Morgana's curse had taken hold, and sometimes, such as that moonlit night, Tristan struggled to keep his many passions in balance.

He wiped the moisture from his cheeks and eyes with the back of his hands before heading to the hall again. Up ahead, he noticed one of Arthur's soldiers enter the hall and passed him a few minutes later as the man exited once more, making for the gate.

'News?' asked Tristan.

'Aye, my lord,' said the soldier. 'Word from Tintagel.'

Tristan froze and before he could ask more, the soldier bowed his head and took his leave, hurrying back to his post.

Fair news or foul, wondered Tristan as he crossed the hall. The music and feasting continued, but the men at the round table now appeared grave.

Tristan stood behind his chair and nodded to Arthur.

'Tristan,' said Lucan, standing.

Tristan licked his lips, his tongue feeling like parchment and his entire mouth suddenly dry.

'What news?' he asked, barely louder than a whisper.

Arthur stood.

'I am sorry, brother, but we have just received word from Tintagel,' said the king, but then he paused.

'What news?' Tristan repeated, knowing before he heard.

'Mordred's forces have taken Tintagel.'

'Impossible,' whispered Tristan. 'How?'

'There must be some treachery,' said Agravain. 'I am sorry, brother.'

'Survivors?' asked Tristan.

Agravain looked at Arthur then back at Tristan, before shaking his head.

He felt Lucan's hand on his shoulder and when he looked into his friend's eyes, he knew what would come next.

'Your uncle is dead, Tristan,' said Lucan. 'I'm sorry.'

Tristan staggered and leant against a chair.

'And … Queen Isolde?' he could not help but ask.

'Mordred has sent her back to Ireland to appease her father.'

Tristan's legs went from under him. It could not be so. He slumped forward, but Agravain and Lucan caught hold of him, and he just retained his consciousness.

'It will not stand, Tristan,' said Arthur. 'It is time to take the fight to Mordred.'

King Mark dead, and yet in Tristan's misery, his regret at all that had befallen them and his part in it, he could not help but wonder if he should seek out Isolde now that she was free to wed him. And then he remembered Rozenn. And his friends. And his king.

◈

Before a month had passed, Tristan and Rozenn were married, and a group of Cornish refugees arrived at Arthur's border, led by a warrior called Malagant, who claimed to have been at Tintagel when it fell.

Arthur and his knights offered aid, and before long, having joined the king's army, Malagant was knighted after he held a pass open for Gareth's defeated company to escape a disastrous battle, personally felling thirty of Mordred's men.

Sir Malagant took up his seat at the round table, seated at Sir Tristan's right hand.

Chapter Thirty-One

2021

By the time Caitlyn had crossed the road and was on the path through the woods to Hunter's Cottage, her slippers were more mud than material and reality had begun to sink in. She felt eyes on her from all around, but could see nobody no matter how often she checked, sometimes walking backwards for a few seconds or using her peripheral vision. Samson had always been a comforting presence at her isolated home and when out walking in the woods that surrounded it, but now, she felt no safer with him by her side than if she had been alone. He had bitten the Irishman, it was true, he'd tried, but her kidnappers had locked him away with little trouble after that.

God knows how, thought Caitlyn, shivering, coatless and buffeted by cold wind.

The unease grew greater as she approached her cottage and even when she had retrieved a key from its hiding place in the garden and was safely behind the door, she felt no calmer, heart still beating fast.

It will just take some time, she thought, but couldn't help

feeling she was in danger. What was to stop more of Arthur's enemies coming for her again?

She kicked off her slippers and made a tour of the ground floor, noting where the CSI team had not cleaned up after themselves, and the mud on the floors. Flashbacks of her struggle with the two men and the woman troubled her as she moved from room to room, and she didn't need to go upstairs to know that she could not stay at Hunter's Cottage, not yet. But where to go with so much on her mind and a swollen nose? Questions would be asked, and she knew all too well that lying about it would lead to accusations against Arthur. How many times had she heard women tell her their injuries were sustained by walking into a door or falling down the stairs? People never believed that, not these days, and had they ever really, or was it just easier to nod and accept what went on in people's homes was a private matter?

Caitlyn didn't want to be around anyone, couldn't stand the questions and needed time to process the events of the day, so it was staying at home or perhaps getting an Airbnb at late notice, so she could take Samson with her.

She fetched a knife from the kitchen and went round the house, followed by Samson, checking all of the doors and windows were closed and locked, before heading upstairs and sitting on the edge of the bed, by that time, feeling almost numb.

Caitlyn pulled out her phone and checked in with friends and family where required, making excuses about a low day and sorry if they were worried.

She checked Airbnb, but given how late it was in the day

and the remoteness of the area, there was nowhere suitable that would allow dogs. She could take him anyway, of course, and the thought crossed her mind, but that wouldn't be right.

She wondered about Tristan's condition, and a thought struck her.

She typed out a message to Arthur.

I'm not ready to talk, but I want to check on Tristan. Where is he?

He must have been checking his phone constantly, as the reply was almost instantaneous.

I understand. In a private hospital. The staff are first-rate, don't worry about him. He's receiving the best care. How are you?

'That doesn't answer the question, Arthur,' said Caitlyn as she typed her response.

If you don't want me calling the police about this, give me the address and make sure they'll let me in. And Samson too, I'm not leaving him alone.

A few minutes passed and an address came through, accompanied by,

I'll meet you there and we can talk.

Her reply came off harsher than she intended.

If I see you, I will walk away. Don't come. If we're ever going to talk, it will be when I'm ready and not before. Don't ask again or we're done.

Another couple of minutes, and Caitlyn watched as the app indicated Arthur was typing, stopping, typing, stopping. Eventually a message came through.

Understood. In your own time. I am sorry, and I will tell you everything.

Caitlyn pocketed her phone and set about putting a bag of essentials together. Before half an hour had passed, she was in the car and on her way to the hospital on the outskirts of Runbridge.

─────

She drove past the small hospital twice before realising where she needed to go. There was no signage at the front of what looked like a large country house in an elevated position beside a quiet country lane. As she turned into the drive and slowed before the gates, looking for an intercom, they swung open, which she found reassuring, knowing that Arthur had been good to his word.

A narrow path led round to the back of the building where a small car park, mostly full, was tucked out of sight from the road. Caitlyn took a few moments to gather her nerve, opened the rear door and put Samson on a leash before heading towards the back door to the house, discreetly marked, 'Reception'.

She pushed the door, but it was locked. Caitlyn pressed the button of an intercom on the wall and a male voice came through, just asking 'Hello?'.

'Dr Caitlyn Farley to see one of your patients. Arthur Grimwood rang ahead?' she said, guessing, and realised she didn't know Tristan's surname.

The intercom buzzed and when Caitlyn pushed against the door, it opened.

The reception area was small, modern and neat, its desk manned by what looked like a security guard, young and tough. He gave her a perfunctory smile as she entered, eyed Samson, but didn't object.

'Take a seat, Dr Farley. Someone will be with you shortly. Tea or coffee? Water for the dog?'

Caitlyn settled into a neat leather armchair beside a low table stacked with magazines.

'Tea would be good, thank you. Milk and two sugars. Water would be good too, thank you.'

The guard nodded and picked up a phone.

'On its way,' he said as he set down his phone and returned to monitoring CCTV cameras.

'Thank you,' said Caitlyn, realising she had now said so three times in less than a minute.

Calm down.

She sat for a moment, taking in the empty waiting area and the walls devoid of the usual health posters.

'What is this place?' she asked and the guard smiled apologetically.

'A private hospital,' he said.

She started to ask more questions, but he held up his hand.

'That's as much as you'll get, Dr Farley, I'm sorry.'

'Thank you,' said Caitlyn, cheeks feeling hot with embarrassment, or was it anger?

After a few minutes, the mug of tea and bowl of water were delivered by another security guard and a few minutes after that, a woman wearing scrubs, looking about fifty, came into the waiting area through a frosted glass door, which swung open with a hiss.

'If you'll come with me, Dr?' she said and passed over a reusable ice bag. 'For your nose.'

Caitlyn stepped through the door and the older lady showed her into a private en-suite room immediately to her right, with a bed and an armchair, a television mounted on the wall and a chest of drawers. All in all, Caitlyn decided she had seen worse hotel rooms.

'I've come to see Tristan,' she said, confused about why she was being shown into an empty room.

'He's in surgery at the moment, but Mr Grimwood asked us to provide you with a room for as long as you need it. Just let us know if you're hungry. Food isn't great, but we could order in for you if you want.'

'Whatever you've got would be good, to be honest. I've not eaten since breakfast, and,' she sighed, 'it's been a day.'

The same apologetic smile as the security guard had given her.

'Mr Grimwood asks that we keep things purely professional for the duration of your visits, I'm sorry,' said the older woman.

'And how about Tristan? What's his condition?'

'He's in surgery, but we'll let you know when he's out and awake,' said the woman, whose patience seemed to be wearing thin, her words coming out a little clipped.

'You can't give me any details?' asked Caitlyn, frowning.

'You aren't related,' said the woman. 'I'll bring you some of whatever's left from tonight's menu and let you get some rest. We'll let you know how he is once he's out of surgery. I will say it could go either way for now, but saying anything else is more than my job is worth. Sorry.'

Caitlyn closed the door, set down her bag and the water bowl then lay down on the single hospital bed, suddenly so, so tired. She started to ice her nose, but was asleep before the nurse returned with food.

───※───

Caitlyn woke to the sound of knocking on the door and Samson barking. It took her a moment to orient herself, and she comforted her dog before going to the door, opening it a crack.

'Good afternoon, Dr Farley,' said a male nurse, who backed up a step, eyeing Samson.

Caitlyn looked at her watch and saw she had slept through the night and the whole of the next morning.

'Any news?' she asked, rubbing her eyes.

'It went well. He's out of surgery and in recovery. We thought you and your dog might want some lunch?'

───※───

Several hours later, yet another nurse brought news that Tristan was in and out of consciousness and that she could sit with him if she liked.

Once she had eaten, Caitlyn brushed her teeth and showered, then decided to head out and find Tristan.

Her door was locked. Instant panic. She knocked on the wood then remembered she could buzz the nurse from her bed, but the door opened before she had got there.

The same nurse stood in the doorway.

'You locked me in?' Caitlyn demanded, as she walked towards her.

'Nobody told you? It's a secure facility. You'll be escorted anywhere you need to go,' said the nurse. Caitlyn shook her head and started out of the door, but the nurse raised a finger.

'I'm afraid your dog will have to stay here. You understand,' said the nurse.

Caitlyn did and, reluctantly, she fussed Samson and left him in the room.

She followed the nurse down a short corridor and was shown into another room, almost identical to her own. There she found Tristan lying in bed, hooked up to monitors, machines and a drip. His eyes were closed.

'Buzz if you need anything,' said the nurse, shutting Caitlyn into the room, and, she supposed, locking her in.

She knew she should sit and let him wake of his own accord, but couldn't wait any longer. Caitlyn stood at the bedside.

'Tristan,' she said quietly.

Nothing.

She placed a hand on his shoulder, just lightly.

He stirred, his eyelids flickering.

'Arthur?' he said.

'Is it the beard?' she asked at a normal volume, surprised to hear herself cracking jokes again already. Tristan's eyes opened.

'You'd suit one,' he said, closing them again for a few seconds. Then he frowned and was looking first at her then around the room.

'What happened?' he asked.

'I get to ask the questions,' said Caitlyn. 'What have they told you?'

'Two gunshot wounds. I remember the gunshots,' he said. 'Surgery to fix some of the damage, and they said it's gone well. Should be alright.'

Caitlyn nodded, knowing the details would have to wait.

'You came after me,' she said.

Tristan opened his eyes and looked at her, licking his lips. She poured him a cup of water from a jug on the table by his bed and helped him drink.

'How is it you're here?' asked Tristan.

'Least I could do, considering you saved me. Even took a bullet for me. I feel like the President or something,' she said. 'I kept you alive long enough for an ambulance to get to you, so I guess we're even.'

Tristan smiled wistfully and thanked her. Caitlyn couldn't resist pushing further.

'I do need answers. I can't speak to Arthur. Not right now. Will you tell me?' she asked.

Tristan frowned and Caitlyn felt his hand take hers. She stepped in closer as he tried to sit up. When he spoke, his grey eyes locked on to her, and a strange look came over him.

'Arthur's a good man. The best of men,' said Tristan, unblinking, his gaze constant. She couldn't think how to reply, but he continued. 'There's a good reason for all of this.

Trust him,' he said. 'Give him a chance to explain.'

'I'm not ready,' she tried to say, but it came out as a whisper.

'You won't ever be ready. Nobody could be,' said Tristan, giving up and lying back down, but not letting go of Caitlyn's hand. She pulled it back, slow, but insistent.

'Talk to him,' said Tristan.

'We'll see,' said Caitlyn. 'But there's a better chance I will if you give me some answers. I know I owe you, but I deserve the truth.'

Tristan smiled.

'You owe me nothing, my lady,' he said, and she noticed his cheeks had flushed.

'My lady? They better ease you off the pain meds,' said Caitlyn, but she felt uncomfortable. There was something different about the way Arthur's friend was looking at her. And she realised he had yet to be told of the murder of his friends. She cast her eyes to the monitor to check his stats.

⁂

She is quite something, thought Tristan as Caitlyn frowned, taking in the information on the screen, *caring for me even though we have barely spoken before, checking on me before even my brother knights or Arthur have come.*

And as it had so many times before when a close connection was formed one way or another, Morgana's curse, outliving her, sent neurotransmitters swirling and focused his attention on Caitlyn's scent, the line of her jaw, the briefest glimpse of her clavicle. She had kept him alive, using her arts and her mind to keep his body going.

Her owe *him*? He was nothing but a pawn of Arthur. An instrument of war. A solution to any problem. Despite all that had happened to her and her anger towards Arthur, her lack of answers and her confusion, here she was tending him. Watching over him.

His angel.

He thought back to that day, a millennium ago, when he had fallen overboard on the crossing from Ireland to Cornwall, and of how Isolde had pulled him from the sea. He remembered looking into her eyes and something, stirring, deep down in his soul. A need. An insatiable desire. A powerful and sudden attraction turned even faster to a heedless, feckless, ridiculous, heated love.

'I need to know what's going on. If you don't tell me, I *will* just walk away, and never see Arthur again. Maybe even call the police, I haven't decided.'

Tristan swallowed, marvelled at her ferocity. She was a fighter, worthy of their company.

But no, she was with Arthur. He couldn't allow himself to feel such things.

And yet, private thoughts were just that. Feelings could not be helped, could they?

But he had suppressed such secrets before, hiding them even from himself. Duty mattered above all. Duty and loyalty to his king. He had, after all, sworn an oath.

As you did to King Mark, Morgana's curse taunted him. *You tried to resist, and the whole world knows how that turned out, doesn't it? Tristan & Isolde.*

Tristan sighed.

'It's not my place to give you the answers you need,' he said. 'You should hear them from Arthur.'

Caitlyn nodded, pursing her lips. She leant down, pressed the buzzer and went to stand by the door.

'Think about it,' she said and then the nurse escorted her away.

Tristan realised he may have done Arthur some harm. Momentarily guilty, he wondered why Arthur hadn't been to see him and once more he thought of Caitlyn, the only person who had cared enough to visit. He remembered the touch of her hand and the new beauty he saw in her eyes that sparked his heart afire.

Chapter Thirty-Two

5th Century
The Aftermath of the Battle of Camlann

The great war between King Arthur and Mordred had come to an end, father and son having mortally wounded one another.

Mordred had followed his mother, Morgana, killed by Merlin not so long before, into the afterlife. Not so King Arthur. In desperation, Merlin used a taboo enchantment to preserve the king on the verge of death's embrace, so at the allotted time, he would rise again.

The wizard offered the knights the opportunity to slumber beside their liege lord until his resurrection, and not one of Arthur's knights turned his back on the king.

They set out to Stonehenge, bearing with them Arthur's body, accompanied by Merlin and an armed escort.

TRISTAN'S REGRET

Sir Tristan walked beside the cart that bore the king's coffin, draped in the Pendragon standard, his mind in so many different places.

'You look a thousand miles away, boy,' said Merlin, breaking the knight's daydream.

'I was, Merlin. There is so much to dwell on, so much to regret. I cannot believe Arthur is dead. We never united the land as he hoped,' said Tristan.

'As I hoped,' said Merlin, quietly.

'What was that?' asked Tristan.

'Nothing, boy, nothing,' said Merlin. 'Only that you are not the only man here with regrets, I assure you. Things have not turned out as I foresaw, and there is much that I meddled with that led to the events of the day, may the land forgive me.'

'May God forgive us all,' said Tristan.

'Yes, God,' snorted Merlin. 'God, indeed.'

They walked in silence for a few minutes.

'You are giving up more than most to go with Arthur, I understand that. And it is not the first sacrifice you have made for the sake of your duty and love of a king. Twice now have you been compelled to turn your back on a woman you love,' said Merlin, carefully.

Tristan sighed, for he had taken to banishing Isolde from his mind whenever possible, erecting barriers to withstand his thoughts and desires. Now, he thought of her again for a moment, then pushed the raging emotions down and behind their wall. It was not so simple with his feelings for Rozenn, which he had, until now, allowed to grow and flourish.

'It is not an easy decision, Merlin,' said Tristan, 'but I have a duty as an anointed knight. There is nowhere Arthur can go that I will not follow. He has my heart and my sword.'

He wished he felt as resolute as his words sounded, but it became apparent Merlin was not fooled.

'I know you, boy. You love your wife dearly, and have not even had the chance to bid her farewell. Are you sure you wish to abandon her? To choose your king over your beloved?' asked Merlin.

'Is Arthur not beloved too? Not only by me, but by his people and by my brother knights? And what of them? Would I send Agravain and Lucan into the dark future without me by their side?' asked Tristan, desperation manifesting as anger that warded off Merlin's questioning for only a moment before the wizard said,

'Lady Rozenn walks into the future without you, in a land without Arthur. What of her fate?'

Tristan wanted to turn and walk back the way they had come, wanted to run back to his wife, with whom he had yet to start the family they so desired. What would she think of him for leaving? How could he live without her? How could he bear knowing that she might feel betrayed?

But if he was to turn his back on Merlin, Arthur and the knights of the round table, how could he live with himself, even if Rozenn was by his side during the day and in his bed at night?

He was torn, racked with regrets, unable to decide where his duty lay, but in the end, even if he was tormented until the end of days, he knew that Rozenn believed him a man of honour. He thought or hoped she would understand. Arthur's code bound him to his brethren. He could not turn aside from this quest, escorting his friend and king into the ages that were to come. She would know that. She would.

Rozenn would survive and pass on when her time came. He could not influence her life any longer and their time together, he knew, was over. So too was the time of following his affections, he decided as Merlin fell back, seeming to realise he needed time to think. To decide.

From here on out, Tristan decided, *there will be no more distractions. I will give my all in service to my king. I will be his right hand and his protector.*

Rozenn, he thought, hoping that somehow

she would hear him, *I love you, my darling, but the wars are not done, and Arthur needs my sword, as he has these years past.*

Please, my love, forgive me, and live a long and happy life. Find a man who can cherish you and not forever be torn in two. Goodbye.

He stood a little straighter and considered his duties in the here and now, namely getting Arthur to the place of Merlin's choosing. He set about deploying scouts and reorganising the escort, wondering as he did so what was in store for these warriors now that there was no king to lead them and Mordred had fallen.

He found Merlin walking alongside the men, muttering to himself and distracted by passing birds while Tristan moved closer.

'Merlin, what will happen to Briton in our absence?' asked Tristan, and he was relieved when the wizard actually answered his question rather than prying into his decision-making.

'There will be no unity for this land for a long, long time,' said Merlin. 'My prescience extends no further than that in this matter. Arthur, I knew, could unite the land, but in orchestrating his birth by providing Uther Pendragon, his father, with a means to deceive the woman of his choosing, I caused Arthur and yet angered Morgana, which would prove to be my undoing. Morgana deceived Arthur in kind to create

Mordred, and blood has undone all.' The wizard sighed. 'Perhaps in the future, he will be able to do more, when the time is right, now that Morgana and Mordred are gone. We shall see.'

And so it was that the company arrived at Stonehenge, and Merlin set the king and the knights of the round table to slumber, sealing them underneath the henge itself.

They would not wake again until Branok the Ravenmaster persuaded Merlin the time was right over a thousand years later.

And as Tristan closed his eyes, drifting off to sleep for centuries in the company of his friends, his last thoughts and his dreams were of Rozenn.

And of Isolde.

Chapter Thirty-Three

2021

Despite her threats, Caitlyn could not bring herself to go home nor to approach Arthur for answers. She called in sick to work and told friends and family she had gone away for a break on the coast. In truth, she remained at the hospital, going over everything that happened in a neutral environment, walking Samson in the grounds and checking on Tristan, whose recovery was going remarkably well.

Arthur did not message her again, which annoyed her, though she realised he was respecting her wishes and was probably going out of his mind. Any sympathy was short-lived, however, as she remembered her ordeal and how much she had learnt of his secret life. The enemies. The guns. The private hospitals and the secrecy.

She spent some of the next day with Tristan, and the two of them came to know one another. He was an odd man, extremely earnest and offering such profound insights at times, and yet he remained guarded, Caitlyn thought, increasingly with an effort. His attempts to get her to speak to Arthur became more and more insistent.

On the second morning at the hospital, Caitlyn was Beginning to wonder why Arthur's friends had not visited Tristan, and she meant to ask him if he knew why, but when she arrived at his room, she was surprised to find him sitting up in bed, at an obvious cost to himself, and insisting he was going home.

'They can set me up on the ground floor. I need to be home,' he insisted. 'I told the doctors you would check in on me.'

Caitlyn didn't know what to say, Tristan's words were so presumptuous.

'I will, will I?' she asked, half-amused, half-annoyed. He blushed then and she pitied him.

'I'm sorry,' he said. 'I just assumed. I value your company, and I'm sure it has aided my recovery.'

'You haven't recovered yet, my friend, so go easy. You should be staying here or moving to a *proper* hospital.' She shot the nurse a look.

'I'll be fine. I'm going home,' said Tristan.

I guess I am too, then, thought Caitlyn. *No more excuses for putting it off.*

Arthur was in the drawing-room later that morning when an ambulance, followed by Caitlyn's car, came through the gates and parked in the courtyard.

He heard the front door open and just a few seconds later, the drawing-room door burst open and Caitlyn strode in.

Arthur stood, using his arms for leverage.

He caught a glimpse of paramedics wheeling Tristan on a stretcher through the hall towards the anteroom allocated for his recovery before Caitlyn closed the door behind her.

She stood with her arms crossed, scowling at Arthur, visibly shaking.

'Let's hear it,' she said.

Arthur offered Caitlyn a drink.

'We have a lot to talk about, after all, and this won't be easy to tell or to hear,' said Arthur.

'No, I'm good, thanks. Let me just hear it, Arthur,' she said.

'Take a seat?' he offered her Merlin's chair by the crackling fire.

Caitlyn crossed to the whisky decanter and poured herself a drink and leant on the back of Merlin's chair.

'I'll stand,' she said. Arthur sighed. He supposed he deserved this. He refilled his own glass, before returning to his own seat. He groaned as he eased himself down, his leg aching from overuse. It had been a long few days, and he felt it in his bones.

As was his way, he stared into the flames while he mustered his thoughts, torn between deception and the truth, considering how Caitlyn would react.

'Please take a seat,' he said again, and it sounded pitiful even to him. Unbecoming of a king, he thought and smiled.

'What's so funny?' Caitlyn asked, and Arthur saw she had settled into Merlin's chair.

'Nothing,' he said. 'Just a passing thought. Caitlyn,

you're shaking,' he said and started to stand, but she held up a hand.

'Don't even think about coming over here. You are the last person in the world I want comforting me right now. What I need from you is honesty,' she said, then took a sip of her drink, her eyes focused on him over the glass.

Arthur nodded slowly and looked back into the fire, not knowing where to begin.

'Any time today,' she said.

Arthur's temper rose up, but he breathed through it and gave Caitlyn his full attention.

'I'm not sure where to start,' he admitted, and her expression softened a little.

'Let's start with how I ended up dragged out of my house and thrown into a van. Who the hell were those people and why are you and your mates acting like the God-damned A-Team?' she asked.

Arthur took a drink, rallied his courage and replied.

'Those people work for an organisation that we have gone up against in the past, a long time ago. Their leadership wanted to hurt me and somehow knew about you. They know how much you mean to me, so they took you away, to scare me, to put me on the backfoot, to weaken me and for revenge. I don't know what they intended for you ultimately, but you were at risk. It was unthinkable and unacceptable. I've been going out of my mind ever since,' he said.

Caitlyn sat back in her chair. Arthur rubbed the bridge of his nose and persevered.

'Once we discovered you were taken, we began an investigation, and Tristan managed to intercept you before you were moved, thank God,' he said.

'Thank Tristan, more like,' said Caitlyn.

'Just so,' Arthur agreed. 'I owe that man more than you will ever know. He has been loyal to me and by my side since we were very young.'

'So who the hell are you? I loved the man I knew, but you, I don't recognise,' said Caitlyn, and the words cut Arthur to the quick.

'You *knew* we were veterans,' he said, frowning. He'd kept things from her, for her own good, but did she need to be so sharp with him?

'Veterans or still serving in the military?' She shot back at him. 'Are you even allowed to have all these guns? Christ, what am I doing coming back here! I'm going to end up in prison, aren't I? That's what comes next!'

Arthur didn't interrupt as she vented her fear and frustration for a few moments longer before coming back to him and waiting for his answer.

'Everything is licensed. We have many friends in many places, but we do try to keep our heads down. Tristan and the others, those who have adopted aliases to hide their original identities, we were a specialist unit fighting for the UK. We retain certain privileges, but officially, we do not exist. We have served all of our lives, since we were young, but we'd been retired from those activities for some time when I met you, with our various other interests ticking over in the background, businesses, charities and more. I know you thought it strange that Tristan and the man you know as Robert continued to live in my house, but the truth is, it's *our* home really. Our place, together. Not mine alone. We have kept each other alive this long, and it has not been easy to let go of who we once were, though since meeting you, I have wanted nothing more than to put the past behind us and to move forward in your company, Caitlyn, please believe me.'

She said nothing for a moment, swigging her drink before replying.

'So what went wrong? Who were those people?'

'All that was left of a terror organisation that the man you've heard me call John Gravain brought down, or so we thought, long ago. Their leader recently reached out and threatened John's family. But we caught him, and what happened the other day was his plan to hurt me petering out as those working for him floundered in the wake of his demise. I had no way to know this could happen, Caitlyn, and I am so sorry I could not tell you the full truth until now and also that you have been caught up in the chaos of our lives from way back when,' Arthur concluded.

The two of them sat in silence for a while. Caitlyn emptied her glass, and now it was her turn to stare into the flames. Arthur watched her, trying to get a read on what she was thinking, but she began to sob, shaking more as she did so. The tears came and she leant forward, burying her head in her hands. Arthur stood and went to her, but she pushed him away.

'Not yet,' she said. 'I need time to process all of this and get my head together.'

'I understand,' said Arthur, though it pained him; the rejection, the fear she would not come around and the knowledge that things between them would remain tenuous for some time to come.

He returned to his seat and waited for her to compose herself. Once she had wiped away the tears and sat back in the chair, she looked at him once more.

'I have *some* idea of what's gone on now then,' she said, but seemingly not to anyone but herself. 'Tristan couldn't go to a normal hospital because?'

'Because if we … '

'Because this is some secret spy shit,' said Caitlyn. 'Yes, you said. Got you.'

She ran her finger around the rim of her empty glass, looking lost in thought.

Eventually she looked up.

'I'm going to need some time, Arthur. I'm going home, if I can face it, and I'll be in contact, but I need you to give me space, alright? Your people will look after Tristan and get him to hospital if need be?'

Arthur nodded.

'We can put in cameras and alarms at Hunter's Cottage, and I have our people watching the area. Not closely enough that you have to worry about privacy though.'

He thought she would object, but instead she said,

'I may come by to check on him when I can. I do owe the man my life. God forbid he takes a turn for the worse.'

She stood and motioned for him to remain seated.

'I'll see myself out.'

And then she was gone.

Arthur remained still until he heard the front door close then, roaring, he hurled his whisky glass into the fireplace so that it shattered among the flames, shards coming to rest on the rug at his feet.

He didn't visit Tristan that day, unable to muster the strength as he thought of the loss of Dagonet, Kay and Bedivere and the near-miss with Tristan, as well as his hopes for the future dwindling.

It would be Bors and Gareth together who told Tristan of their losses, while Arthur lost himself in the privacy of his drawing-room.

Chapter Thirty-Four

2021

Kayleigh Turner's sleep was fitful that night, and she woke early to the imagined sounds of thunder and Simon screaming, certain there were intruders in the house. But when she opened her eyes, the house was still, and her son slept beside her, content despite the events of the previous days.

The sun was not yet up, and Kayleigh lay awake, thinking, staring out of the window at the tops of the trees in the garden and beyond the walls of Arthur's estate, considering all that had happened over the last couple of days and whether she was better off going home or staying with Arthur and his remaining knights.

If they were to leave, she and Simon had nothing to protect themselves but their own little-understood abilities, but hadn't they been enough on both occasions, just about, when they were under threat? Caught alone, Merton might have defeated either one of them, but the knights thought he was possibly the greatest untapped resource of her generation, neglected for too long and clearly recruited by

Malagant's people. An outlier, maybe, but what else remained of the Order of Phobos and Deimos?

Yes, Malagant was dead, as were those who had kidnapped Caitlyn. But a van full of cultists had escaped, heading God knows where, and presumably there was still someone calling the shots, somewhere out there, given that Malagant had been hiding within Agravain while he was in prison for years. The threat, she realised, was not over, and it was perhaps best to stay close to these men for the time being, for their sake, her's and her son's.

Her bladder insisted she get up after a while, and she pulled on a jumper then swung on her crutches down the hall to use the toilet.

Emptied, she decided to fill up with something hot, as the house was chill, and she knew she would not sleep again that morning.

She searched the kitchen cupboards and a face appeared in her mind when she found an open box of peppermint tea bags. Percival - another of Arthur's knights who had been killed recently by an enemy from the distant past.

Kayleigh cradled the warm mug in her hands and wandered the repaired and cleaned ground floor, passing the time and thinking. She paused before entering the room where Tristan was recovering, but then opened the door as quietly as she could.

The dark-haired knight seemed to be sleeping on his back, one arm slung over his eyes. He was snoring softly.

Not so loud it would disturb his lover, thought Kayleigh, shocking herself. *Where did that come from?*

As she stood in the doorway, listening to the light rasping of his breath, she saw before her a man of great passions, who had loved greatly, was fiercely loyal and brave too, as the events of the previous days had shown. Kayleigh felt the stirring of affection within her and, feeling like a stalker or a creep in the shadows, she closed the door and continued exploring.

'Shit me,' said Kayleigh, a little louder than she meant as she turned on the light to the cinema. 'They're loaded.'

She moved on to the next room, and whistled as she entered.

Floor to ceiling bookcases.

She was about to close the door, not being a big reader, when a thought struck her, and she moved through the library, scanning the shelves. It took her a few minutes, but she soon confirmed her suspicion and found a section devoted to the myths and legends of King Arthur and his knights, recognising first of all Sir Thomas Mallory's, *Le Morte d'Arthur*, between T.H. White's, *The Once and Future King* and John Steinbeck's, *The Acts of King Arthur and his Noble Knights*.

Kayleigh plucked out *Le Morte d'Arthur*, found a comfy chair with a convenient lamp, and she began to turn the pages.

Arthur woke early, though not as dramatically as Kayleigh, with his heart heavy both from the loss of his knights and knowing that his hopes for a new life with Caitlyn were fading fast. He could accept and bear the latter, he decided, but it saddened him. He *had* hoped to enter a period of retirement and peace, with her by his side.

Perhaps it isn't to be, and my long suffering will continue, he thought.

He thought a walk in the morning air might help, but his leg protested at the idea of the effort, and Arthur decided to delay by fetching a coffee and reading the morning papers if they had arrived. They had been delivered ever since Percival had died. Every morning when he stepped out of his room, the absence of the coffee and papers waiting for him was a painful reminder of the loss.

A door creaked open, and Arthur saw Simon put his head out into the hall, first looking away and then locking eyes with him, unsmiling, but not at all surprised.

'Good morning, Simon,' said Arthur, in a hushed voice to avoid waking anyone else.

Simon nodded.

'Is your mother sleeping?' asked Arthur, but the boy shook his head.

'She's in the library, reading about you,' he replied.

'And what are you up to, young man?' Arthur shuffled forward and stooped to lower his eyeline.

'Just looking,' he said.

'Hungry?' asked Arthur, and when Simon nodded, he set him up with a bowl of cereal and some toast, before taking his coffee down to the library. He checked on Tristan on the way, but his knight was dead to the world, snoring softly. Arthur felt guilty at the sight of his injured friend, but heartened to see him sleeping peacefully.

I really must see him later.

Sure enough, Kayleigh was curled up in an armchair in the library, reading what appeared to be *The Matter of Britain* by Harold Moreland. Arthur remembered it well, particularly the introduction by Kathleen Raine, a prominent poet in the mid-20th century.

Dagonet had once told him that she had cursed the author Gavin Maxwell by laying her hands on a rowan tree and speaking fell words. His knight had seemed convinced the author's later woes were more than coincidence.

But now Dagonet is gone, Arthur remembered.

He sighed then coughed quietly to draw Kayleigh's attention, and she looked up.

'I hope you don't mind,' she said, closing the book on one of her fingers to mark the page.

'Not at all. Simon told me I'd find you here,' said Arthur.

'But he doesn't know,' said Kayleigh, frowning.

'That boy is full of surprises,' said Arthur. 'Found anything interesting in there?'

Kayleigh blushed.

'Feels like you've caught me reading your diary. I've just been skimming through a few of these. Put them all back in the right place though, don't worry,' she said.

'There isn't much of a system,' he replied. 'What do you think?'

'It's all mismatched and out of sequence. All of it. People disappear and appear, motives change, allegiances change. So many discrepancies. What's the truth?' she asked.

'I can scarcely remember any more,' Arthur confessed. 'These are stories, nothing more, Miss Turner.'

'Based on truth, though,' she persisted.

'If you go far enough back and take many twists and turns.'

'Like, Mordred for instance. From Tristan's memories, I gathered you fathered him with your sister, Morgana,' she said, not meeting his eyes. 'But in there … ' she pointed to *Le Morte d'Arthur*, it said you had two sisters, Morgana and Margawse … but it's Morgause elsewhere, and that Morgause was Mordred's mother.'

'Just stories,' said Arthur, unable to speak the full truth to her. 'There was only ever Morgana, my half-sister. Our union was not of my consent. She disguised herself as a woman named Margawse with her arts, perhaps to get revenge on Merlin for doing the same to her mother, enabling my father, Uther, to sire me against her wishes.'

'Wow. Rapey,' said Kayleigh.

'It was a different time,' said Arthur, knowing full well it was no excuse.

'Bet you're glad Twitter wasn't around back then. You'd all have been cancelled.'

'Merlin and Morgana are both dead, so you don't have to worry. As far as I know, the only people remaining with any arcane ability are you and your son. So perhaps *we* should be wary of *you*,' said Arthur.

'There might be something in these to give us a clue what comes next or who else might be involved with the cult,' said Kayleigh.

Arthur nodded. 'By all means, see if you can find anything. The library and my people are all at your disposal. And when you have time, perhaps read what history makes of your forefather, Sir Agravain. He was the best of us,' said Arthur, heading for the door. Saying so provoked guilt, and he determined to stop in to wake Tristan.

'Where's Simon?' Kayleigh called after him.

'Eating a bowl of cereal at the latest round table. Mallory is turning in his grave, no doubt.'

⁂

Tristan stirred and found Arthur standing over him, both hands leaning on his cane. The knight yawned, covering his mouth with the back of his hand.

'I'm sorry, sir,' he said. 'This week has taken it out of me.'

Arthur smiled.

'You are too humble. You nearly died. I can't thank you enough for risking your life to save Caitlyn on my behalf. I'm sorry I didn't come to see you sooner, but so much was going on. You've been told about Kayleigh Turner's abilities, Merton's betrayal and … about what happened to Kay, Bedivere and Dagonet?'

Tristan nodded.

'And I sent him to you. A death sentence. I'll never forgive myself, but we've got to put the Order in the ground. No more ghosts rising up to haunt us, sir,' said Tristan, his face grave.

Arthur nodded.

'You weren't to know about Charles Merton,' said

Arthur, but the knight replied,

'How is Caitlyn?'

Arthur sighed, and his eyes drifted to the window, perhaps spying a man from Hektor Security patrolling the interior of the estate, as Tristan had done on occasion.

'Bodily, she is fine. But she is confused and furious with me. She thinks I betrayed her, no doubt,' said Arthur.

Tristan did not reply. Thoughts unbidden slipped into his head.

If she was done with Arthur, perhaps he could spend more time with … but no, what was he thinking? He scarcely knew her. How could he think of betraying Arthur?

But Tristan knew how to betray a king.

He'd done it before, a long, long time ago.

Chapter Thirty-Five

*1666 - The Great Fire of London
The Tower of London.*

Merlin had sealed Branok the Ravenmaster within the White Tower while the knights gave battle to his raven familiars, at the cost of Sir Geraint, and Arthur's company were ready to escape down the Thames from the Tower's water gate, were it not for a short delay.

Tristan remained watchful as he stood on the bottom step above the water at Traitor's Gate with one hand on the gunwale, still not confident that the guards paralysed by Merlin would not spring to life and attempt to waylay the company, most of them now waiting in the boat below, with Geraint's corpse, but there was no sign of movement.

Where had Agravain taken Arthur and what could be so urgent that could not wait or be discussed with them all?

Frustrated, suspicious, impatient and

heartsore, Tristan looked once more at his fallen friend, surrounded by the other knights and Merlin, who seemed to be muttering to himself, slumped in the stern sheets, no doubt exhausted from his encounter with Branok.

Tristan heard footsteps and turned to see Arthur appear at the top of the steps.

'Sire?' asked Tristan as Arthur paused, looking down at the waiting knights.

'Agravain will not be joining us. He feels the pull of other causes here in London. He could not face you all,' said Arthur, walking slowly down the stone stair and climbing into the boat, sitting down beside Merlin.

'He's abandoning us?' asked Tristan, louder than he intended, drawing Arthur's full attention.

'I am as surprised as you, Tristan, but he made it clear he does not wish to take leave of my service, but of the company for a time. He feels a connection to the people of London and a ... sense of responsibility,' said Arthur. 'I granted him leave to go, so do not blame Agravain. I sense he has found his calling.'

Tristan climbed into the boat, still fuming as he took up an oar. They shoved off, and the boat drifted out through Traitor's Gate, out on to the open Thames, leaving behind one of Tristan's closest friends, who had not even had the courage to face him and say goodbye, *and* when they had just lost a brother knight.

The loss of Geraint mingled with his sorrow at losing Agravain, and Tristan poured the emotion into his oar strokes, hauling along with his brothers.

The curse whispered to him.

How can he leave Arthur? Leave his brothers? Leave you?

It stoked his hurt and anger like a fire until his own thoughts ignited. Had he not left behind Rozenn to stay with Arthur? Sacrificed his marriage and a lifetime of happiness with his wife? His chance to have a family? Had he not walked away from Isolde, eventually, when it came to it, out of love for his uncle and king? Wasn't love and duty about sacrificing one's wants and desires? He had thought better of Agravain, considered him the best man he knew, along with Arthur and Lucan, who too had given up his home at Tintagel to stand by a kinsman.

Tristan doubted very much that he would ever forgive Agravain the betrayer.

The company passed down the river and, in time, out of London. It would be many years before Agravain and Tristan were united again.

In the wake of the Interregnum, Charles II reigned while Branok slumbered. Arthur continued to establish himself, influencing people's hearts and minds with the power of his voice, supported by his knights. Friendships, employment, partnerships, businesses and alliances followed, and in time a subtle organisation sprang to life, overseen by Arthur and the knights, who commanded an army of managers, solicitors and accountants.

But those who ruled would not slip into relative obscurity and financial security. Arthur had come to think of himself as the unacknowledged protector of the islands. He took on the alias of Arthur Grimwood, and Tristan was ever at his side.

The long watch began.

༺༻

1724
King George I of the House of Hanover reigns. The era of Stuart monarchs, those manoeuvred to the throne by Branok, is over, though the Jacobites aim to restore them.

It was on the same day that Agravain first met Nimuë, far away in London, that Tristan and Arthur were out riding with their dogs, and they first saw Lady Penelope Fitzroy promenading in the park, escorted by her grandfather.

Arthur brought his horse to a halt as they approached and spoke to Tristan, quietly, before dismounting.

'Lord Fitzroy is prominent within the East India Company. This is a connection that is long overdue.'

The former king dropped to the path and bowed his head to the lord.

'My lord, permit me to introduce myself. I am Colonel Arthur Grimwood. I believe we have a mutual friend in Viscount Lowrie?'

The older gentleman harrumphed, tapped his cane twice on the floor and extended a hand.

'I am pleased to make your acquaintance,' he said, his tone haughty.

Arthur wasted no time.

'I understand, my lord, that you are … '

Tristan's attention, rarely held by talk of financial opportunity, drifted, and he nodded to Lady Penelope, smiling, to convey respect. She smiled back, never breaking eye contact, and Tristan felt that familiar stirring in his heart. He immediately looked down and cleared his throat, paying attention to Arthur's conversation once more — something about exporting goods to the Thirteen Colonies through Boston.

―⁂―

Some weeks later, Tristan was reading in the parlour of the manor house when Arthur entered the library holding a glass of brandy and held it out to him.

'I have a favour to ask, brother,' said Arthur.

'This sounds ominous, sire,' said Tristan, accepting the brandy and emptying the glass in a few gulps.

'You remember Lord Fitzroy? We encountered him and his granddaughter, Lady Penelope, in the park?'

'I do,' said Tristan, still dubious.

'I have secured a lucrative deal with Lord Fitzroy, and it seems he has friends not only within the East India Company at Crosby House, but in Parliament. I believe it necessary to … strengthen the bonds between us.'

Tristan said nothing and caught himself before he started glaring at Arthur. He knew what was coming.

Arthur continued,

'I'd like you to propose to Lady Penelope, Tristan. Bring the Fitzroys into the fold.'

Tristan looked down into his empty glass, excited by the possibility and yet determined.

'Tristan?'

'Perhaps one of my brothers, sire,' said Tristan, and he saw Arthur frowning. The king's reaction annoyed him. Had he forgotten all he had sacrificed already? And he asked him to marry again?

'Sire, I had to walk away from Isolde for the sake of my uncle and was lucky enough to marry my Rozenn, but I left her behind to grow old without me, so that I could remain by your side. I have seldom asked you for anything since you knighted me and took me into your service, and I have never regretted my years with you. But do not ask me to marry. My heart belongs to you, and I will not share it. I will not … risk it,' said Tristan. 'I cannot be torn in two again.'

He could feel Arthur's eyes upon him, but tears threatened, and he could not raise his head. His chest began heaving as he struggled to control his breathing.

Arthur stood and patted him on the shoulder.

Tristan waited for the apology or, finally, acknowledgement of all he had given up.

'Very well, brother,' said King Arthur. 'I will speak to the others.'

With that, Arthur walked away, leaving Tristan feeling more than a little hard done by.

Chapter Thirty-Six

2021

Tristan's frustration grew throughout the day, being unable to assist Arthur, Bors and Gareth in deciding their next course of action and investigating what remained of the cult, their efforts now hampered by the loss of both Kay and Dagonet's technical skills. They were forced to use Hektor's resources to fulfil that function.

He tried to read, tried to watch old films, tried to sleep.

Nothing worked, his mind was too busy, his inner monologue working with, struggling against and being coerced by Morgana's ancient curse.

He'd known Caitlyn for over a year now, but not well. True, he had deliberately avoided her. After all, she was an attractive woman, but it did Arthur a disservice even to think about her in that way. Tristan had learnt from long, hard experience, heartache, loss and the diminishment of faith in himself that it was best that he remained focused on his duty and his love for Arthur and his brothers. It was safer. It meant, he admitted to himself, that he could avoid getting hurt.

Or hurting anyone else.

But time and again, he remembered Caitlyn's face, her form, her eyes and her scent. He held his breath at the memory of her skin touching his while she tended to him, and this in turn brought forth the memory of Isolde saving him from the sea, which stirred the guilt he felt in remembering Rozenn last, she whom he had forsaken.

For Arthur.

Time and again, he had acted upon or ignored his own instincts for the sake of a king. But no, he told himself, he had no rights here. He meant nothing to Caitlyn. Caitlyn meant nothing to him. Where was this desire coming from?

The hours passed slowly and painfully, interrupted, to his relief, by the occasional visit from Arthur and the other knights. They kept him apprised of their investigation, but there were few results and only one real lead.

A satnav located in the Order's abandoned van indicated that their destination was a postcode linked to a small village in Cornwall, not so very far from Tintagel.

The consensus among the knights was that it could not be a coincidence that the Order were heading back to their ancient stomping grounds and that the company's troubles with the past were far from over. The investigation was continuing, including a search for the first van, but nothing had come of it yet.

※

Around eight in the evening, Bors told Arthur that Caitlyn was at the gate, and Hektor had buzzed her in, so he went to meet her at the front door.

Watching her come towards him, hands in her pockets, shoulders hunched against the cold, he hoped for a kind word, but all he got was a weak smile.

'How was your day?' he asked.

'Busy,' she replied. 'I'm here to check on Tristan.'

'Very well,' said Arthur, as she approached and he stepped back to let her in. He watched, desperate, as she took off her boots and hung her coat and scarf on the hooks in an anteroom, hoping she would have more to say to him, but she disappeared towards Tristan's room. Arthur sighed, closed the front door and went down to the library to find Kayleigh and Simon.

Tristan heard the door handle turn, and he could not disguise a broad smile as his heart leapt when Caitlyn stepped into view.

Your saviour, the curse told him.

How beautiful she is, worthy of a role in legend, thought Tristan, seeing more in Caitlyn than he had before.

She looked pensive at first, but apparently his smile was contagious, and her face lit up too, perhaps more amused than happy to see him. But Tristan did not forget her thoughtful frown, and he guessed at the reason for it, finding himself jealous of any interaction she might have had with Arthur.

He doesn't deserve her, withholding truths as he does, thought Tristan.

'How's the patient this morning?' she asked.

'Bored,' said Tristan. 'And tired. I've barely slept. How fares the doctor?'

Caitlyn shook her head, smiling faintly.

'You and Arthur are both the same. "How fares the doctor?" Such a strange way of putting it,' she said as she began to remove his bandage. Tristan grimaced at the pain, but the touch of her fingers on his flesh sent a thrill throughout his body.

He panted slightly as he answered,

'We came up at a different time, I suppose,' said Tristan.

'You're no older than me!' said Caitlyn as she checked for signs of infection. 'It's looking alright.' She launched into a medical interrogation for a short while, and when she was done Tristan answered.

'You're younger, I've no doubt,' he said.

'Smooth,' said Caitlyn. 'Next you tell me I can't be a day over twenty-one, right?'

Tristan felt his cheeks heat up, and the doctor's smile widened. She set about replacing the dressing.

'If I didn't know better, I'd say it was less about your generation and more about your background. Did you boys all go to the same private school or something? Did Mummy and Daddy pay your way in the world?'

Tristan's smile faded a little.

'What?' asked Caitlyn.

'My parents died when I was so young that I do not remember their faces. I was raised by my uncle,' said Tristan.

'I'm sorry, I was teasing, but it was thoughtless. I had no idea, Tristan. I *am* sorry. What an idiot,' said Caitlyn and now it was her turn for a red face.

Tristan reached out and took her hand, replying,

'Think nothing of it, you could not have known.'

Caitlyn blew air between her lips, rolled her eyes and mimed putting a gun to her temple and pulling the trigger, which set Tristan's heart racing and not in a good way.

'Arthur and I. All of us. We've all been together for an extremely long time and, yes, you could say we have privileged backgrounds, although not quite the sort you are thinking of,' said Tristan, yearning to tell her the truth. Didn't he owe his saviour that much?

'Go on,' said Caitlyn, growing serious, which brought Tristan to his senses and his mind floated up above the level of the curse's fog.

'It's not for me to say,' said Tristan.

'He's already told me about your military background together. The sneaky spy stuff,' said Caitlyn. She paused then added, 'Is there more he hasn't told me?'

Tristan stayed silent, thinking. Wanting.

'I deserve to know,' said Caitlyn. 'And it isn't wise to annoy your doctor,' she added, smiling.

'There's more,' said Tristan then breathed hard, the words having slipped out faster than he could frame a reply, 'but it's not my story to tell. And you wouldn't believe it if I did.'

Caitlyn sat on the edge of the bed. Her right thigh against his, were it not for the blanket. He was oh-so-conscious of that proximity, imagining he could feel the heat of her body. His heart rate crept up as she looked down into his eyes, perched on the edge of the bed.

She does deserve to know, said the curse, indistinguishable from his own thoughts.

He wanted to tell her more with every passing second, all the time battling with his loyalty to Arthur, his obligation to him and this new, overpowering … what? Could it really be love that he felt for Caitlyn? How had he not realised what she meant to him before? All thoughts of Isolde and of Rozenn faded in comparison in that moment, as did the brotherly love towards the knights and his adoration for Arthur, though in truth, he thought, what had there been to adore for a century now?

Arthur is a ghost of his former self. An irrelevance, thought Tristan, and was surprised to find that no challenge arose from within.

'We are far, far older than we seem,' said Tristan, taking up Caitlyn's right hand and holding it in both of his. 'My heart won't allow me to withhold anything from you,' said Tristan. He saw she was looking at him strangely now, frowning. She reached out and placed the back of her left hand against his forehead.

'You don't feel hot,' she murmured. 'Why are you talking like this? What the hell is going on in this house?'

Tristan bit his lip, wanting to shout out the truth, *all* of his truths, at once.

'What isn't he telling me, Tristan? I want to know,' said Caitlyn, frowning and staring deep into his eyes. He could feel himself disappearing in that gaze. He tried to find words that would not make him sound insane.

'My brothers and I, we have served together, under Arthur, for longer than you have been alive. We served before Camlann, we took on the Jacobites and the French. We were in Crimea and at the Somme,' said Tristan. 'We serve him still, those of us who remain.'

Caitlyn's frown intensified, her hand tensing within his. She searched his face while he regretted his words and felt as though a burden had been lifted at the same time.

'What year is it?' she asked.

'2021,' replied Tristan. 'I'm not afflicted.'

'And where are we?'

'My home,' said Tristan.

'Who am I?'

'Caitlyn.' The word was honey on his lips.

'47 plus 59?'

'107. No, 106,' said Tristan after a moment.

'Are you taking the piss out of me? It's not funny, if you are,' said Caitlyn, and her disapproval pained him.

He shook his head.

'I know how it sounds, but it's true. Arthur was once King of the Britons. And I served by his side until he fell, only to be set to slumber until the land needed him again,' said Tristan, mournfully. 'We were woken during the English Civil War and did not age until 2019, when Merlin died. Now we are men like any other, just older and with memories lost to time except in us.'

Caitlyn pulled her hand away.

'I needed to be honest with you,' he said while she stared at him as if searching for the truth on his features. Frowning all the more, he guessed, when she could find no hint of deceit or jest.

Caitlyn stood.

'I'll see you again at some point,' she said.

'You're leaving?' Tristan asked.

'I can't work out if you're mentally ill, a liar or mocking me,' she said.

'I know it's hard to believe. We live in a world nearly devoid of magic. But I spoke the truth.' Tristan sighed, feeling his cause was lost. But he had done as honour demanded and had been honest with his lady. He looked up suddenly.

'I can prove it. Help me up,' said Tristan, dismissing her objections, as he pushed himself up to a sitting position. She helped him swing his legs out over the edge of the bed.

He hobbled through corridors, Caitlyn holding him up by one arm, and Arthur stepped out of the library with Kayleigh and Simon behind him.

'Should you be … ' the king started, but Tristan saw him look at Caitlyn and his face grew ashen. 'What's happening?'

Guilt rose up in him, his loyalty competing with a deep-set resentment for Arthur, to whom he had devoted his life, turning aside his own passions, loves and chances.

'We must gather at the table, Arthur. All of us. You and your boy too, Kayleigh,' said Tristan.

'Miss Turner, would you take the boy and show Caitlyn to the table? I need to speak to Tristan,' said Arthur, quietly.

'No, I want to hear this. No more secrets,' said Caitlyn.

'I am seconds from walking out of here and never coming back, so this had better be good, I warn you.'

Beside the round table, Kayleigh hung back, holding Simon's hand, intending to let Arthur and the knights sit before finding empty chairs, but Arthur seated them both, all the while looking deadly serious.

And no wonder, thought Kayleigh, given that Caitlyn looked furious as she took up a chair beside her, directly opposite Arthur. Tristan took his place at his king's right hand. Kayleigh scrutinised his face and saw he was wild-eyed, whereas before he had been calm and collected. His fists were on the table, his back stooped, probably in pain and he was breathing hard.

Bors and Gareth took up their seats across from one another.

'Can I play Fortnite?' whispered Simon.

'In a little while. Stay quiet for now and you can though, I promise,' said Kayleigh, leaning down to speak softly in her son's ear.

'Well?' said Caitlyn, looking at Tristan with eyebrows raised, clearly mad at him, but why?

'Tristan, what is this about?' asked Arthur, his voice low.

'Tristan told me an interesting story about your past,' said Caitlyn. 'And apparently he's about to prove he's not mad.'

'What story?' said Arthur, staring at Tristan.

Kayleigh saw Tristan straighten up in his seat before announcing,

'I told her the truth, Arthur. All of it,' he said, raising his voice as he continued. 'She deserves better than half-truths and lies!'

Bors stood, pushing back his chair fast, he leant forward, fists on the round table. Gareth did the same, but slowly and deliberately, Kayleigh noticed, watching all of the men.

Arthur gave Tristan a hard stare then focused on Caitlyn.

'What did he tell you?' he asked.

'You tell me, King Arthur, is it?' said Caitlyn, almost laughing.

The room fell silent, and it was Caitlyn's voice that broke it a few seconds later.

'You're either all mad or in on the joke. It isn't funny,' said Caitlyn, looking from man to man and then to Kayleigh.

'It's true,' Kayleigh heard herself say, and as all eyes turned to her, she felt as though she were shrinking and burning all at once.

'Ow.' Kayleigh realised she was crushing Simon's hand.

'Sorry, buddy,' she said, kissing the top of his head. When she spoke again, she kept her voice level and, with lots of loaded eye contact, signalled to all around the table that things were to remain civil with her son present.

'I'm sorry, I'm not clear on who you are,' said Caitlyn.

'I'm Kayleigh and this is my son, Simon. We're guests. I didn't know any of these guys until a few days ago, when they saved us from an intruder. Arthur invited us here so we'd be safe. Which with hindsight … '

She looked over at Arthur, smiling, but he was staring

down at the table top — through it, if that were possible.

'And you believe he's King Arthur?' Caitlyn made pinching motions with her fingers, level with her temples, closing her eyes as she did so.

'I don't have any choice now. Something happened to me when I was attacked. I've gained a new ability. When I touch someone, I can see all of their memories.'

'Bullshit,' said Caitlyn, then snapped an apology, holding up a hand towards Simon without looking at him.

'Let her prove it,' said Tristan. 'We know how it sounds, characters from myth wandering into your life, but we are just men who've been influenced by arcane arts.'

Caitlyn huffed.

'I can show you what I can do, if you let me touch your hand,' said Kayleigh, looking from Caitlyn, who was now rubbing her forehead, to Arthur, who remained silent and staring.

Nobody said anything for a moment.

'This should be good,' said Caitlyn, moving round the table to stand behind Simon and beside Kayleigh. She held out her hand. 'I'll play along, but then I'm going home.'

Arthur leant forward on his elbows, his hands clasped together, peering over them as he observed the two women.

He nodded once, slowly, so Kayleigh reached out and took hold of Caitlyn's hand.

―――

The room fell away as that strange all-pervading sensation began with a crackle across the skin of her fingers and up her arm, all sound dropping to nothing.

Kayleigh was no more.

She was someone else, looking out over a small snow-covered garden, looking at a middle-aged woman building a snowman.

No, said a young voice in her mind. It sounded familiar, but very far away.

Now she was in a lecture hall, with rows of desks dropping down to the main floor, where a professor was guiding a class through some aspect of human anatomy.

Mummy, the lady wants to hear her secrets, said the voice again and now she knew it was Simon.

Kayleigh couldn't reply. She wasn't there. She couldn't feel. But it was as though she was Caitlyn, turning inward, towards the things she kept hidden, even from herself.

She - Kayleigh, Caitlyn or whoever she was - found dark pits and she slipped over the edge to descend.

⁕

Kayleigh gasped as she withdrew from Caitlyn's mind, still bearing the memories she had unearthed. She rocked back in her chair so hard she would have fallen if Arthur had not been standing behind her, which momentarily threw her, as he had been seated what seemed like only a second ago, but then Caitlyn took a pace back, pulling her hand away, her whole body shaking.

'Are you alright?' asked Arthur, putting an arm around Caitlyn's shoulder. She shrugged it off as discreetly as she was able, Kayleigh noticed, and wiped sweat from her own brow.

'I don't know. I thought I was going to faint,' Caitlyn replied, her hands trembling.

Kayleigh watched her steady one with the other before their gazes met.

'Well?' said Caitlyn.

Kayleigh looked down at Simon. He was so pale and when she touched his skin, it was cold and clammy.

'Sweetie, are you feeling alright?' asked Kayleigh.

Simon nodded slowly, and she heard his voice in her mind.

I saw her secrets, Mummy.

Kayleigh pulled Simon into her chest, wrapping her arms around him.

'It's okay, sweetie. Just silly dreams,' said Kayleigh. She kissed his wet forehead and cupped his face in her hands, looking deep into his eyes.

'Memories,' he said, and it frightened her how old he sounded for a moment.

'Let me check him over,' said Caitlyn, but Kayleigh stood and took her by the arm.

'I have your proof,' she said. Caitlyn looked at her with a quizzical expression on her face.

'You see!' said Tristan, as he struggled to stand, bracing heavily against the table. 'Tell her. She needs to know. It's not right that *he* kept it from her.'

Kayleigh was shocked to hear the venom in the knight's words as he pointed at Arthur.

'Tristan,' said Gareth quietly, as Arthur's mouth fell open and Bors shouted, 'shut your damn mouth!'

'Enough!' said Kayleigh. 'There is a little boy sitting here with you. I'd say act your age, but that seems ridiculous. You're behaving like boys in a schoolyard.'

The men fell silent, all save Tristan, who murmured, 'I owe her the truth. I can't shy away this time, not out of loyalty to a king!'

'Quiet,' Kayleigh snapped.

He can't help it. Simon's voice in her mind once more. *There are two voices in his head.*

Kayleigh crouched down to him as best she could, her leg in agony.

'Gareth will look after you for a minute. Maybe play some Fortnite together?'

'I … ' Gareth started, but he chose not to utter that particular death sentence after Kayleigh shot him a look.

'Fortnite it is,' said Gareth, but Simon shook his head and folded his arms. Kayleigh half expected a foot stomp.

'We'll talk in a moment, okay?' she said. 'First I need to talk to the lady about what we saw in her head.'

Eyes turned towards the boy as she said it.

'Now you're bringing him into this?' said Caitlyn. 'I've had enough.'

She strode towards the door, pulled it open and slammed it behind her, ignoring Arthur's plea for her to wait.

'Let me,' said Kayleigh, following Caitlyn out into the hall.

Chapter Thirty-Seven

2021

As the door closed behind Kayleigh, Gareth grabbed Bors by the shoulder as his brother knight started to shout.

'Give us the room,' said Arthur, his eyes locked on Tristan.

'I'm not leaving you alone with *him*,' said Bors, as Gareth offered Simon his hand, but Simon, still regaining his colour, ran from him, backing up against the wall.

'It wasn't him!' Simon shouted.

'It's alright,' said Arthur, distracted from his staring contest with Tristan, who was now standing as tall as he could manage, occasionally steadying himself against a chair, still looking resolute.

'It's not alright! She's speaking! Not him! Don't be mad at him!'

With that, they heard the sound of the front door slamming and a few seconds later Kayleigh returned. She went to Simon.

'What's wrong?' she asked, leaning down to wrap an arm around the crying boy's shoulders.

'They won't listen, Mummy. They won't listen,' Simon sobbed into Kayleigh's shoulder.

'We're listening, we're all listening, sweetie. Go ahead. What do you want to say?' asked Kayleigh. She sounded comforting, but Arthur could hear that she was holding back tears herself, remaining stoic for her son.

'I can hear her in his mind,' Simon pointed at Tristan. 'He doesn't mean it, but he's getting in trouble.'

'Caitlyn's gone?' Arthur asked. 'What happened? She didn't believe?'

Kayleigh still held Simon, who was calming somewhat, his sobs guttering out like a candle flame. Her face was deadly serious as she met his gaze.

'No, Arthur. She believes now, but it came at a price. I told her things about her past that she had forgotten herself. She's reeling. Give her space.'

Arthur nodded. He was reluctant to let Caitlyn go, but there were other matters at hand. A movement caught his eye, and he realised Tristan was going for the door. Arthur barred his way, holding up a hand.

'Leave her,' he commanded, and for the first time, he saw Tristan wrestling with whether to heed the word of his king. He did not recognise the wild-eyed knight before him.

'I must go to her, Arthur,' he growled, and Arthur could only stare at him in response, his world falling apart now that his most loyal knight had seemingly turned against him. The thought sent a word speeding from his mind to his lips before he could stop it.

'Lancelot,' said Arthur. The name hit Tristan like an

arrow to the shoulder, and there was a moment where Arthur was unsure whether his friend would stagger back from the impact or come forward, through him.

'Arthur … ' Tristan said, but Arthur shook his head.

'First your uncle and now … ' he did not finish the sentence, as Tristan stepped forward.

A tension, invisible but undeniable, grew between them, stretching taut, ready for regrettable actions to commence and cascade towards final doom and retribution. Arthur shifted his weight, Tristan's fist clenched and then …

Arthur could not move nor take his eyes from his knight, who appeared similarly afflicted.

'Arthur?' he heard Bors say and then felt the knight's hands on his shoulders .

Gareth checked Tristan.

'It's not him, it's the woman in his head,' said Simon. 'No more fighting.'

Arthur wanted to ask what the boy meant, but he could not speak.

Listen, said Simon's voice inside his mind, and Arthur's vision faded away.

༺⚜༻

Tristan's voice in the dark.

This is the boy! He's like Merton, but more powerful. What does he mean 'the woman in his head?' What's he talking about?

Arthur listened, unable to call out when he tried.

He could feel Tristan resisting Simon's hold over him like swimming against a current, but Arthur, and, he assumed, Tristan too, was powerless. He listened as Tristan's inner narrative struck up again.

Maybe it's for the best — one more moment and you might have struck Arthur.

It was true, Arthur had felt it coming, and he had been ready to respond in kind.

Simon's voice welled up around his consciousness.

Listen!

Arthur tried to shut off his own thoughts and pay attention, as he caught a hint of quieter words beneath the forefront of Tristan's mind, below the surface.

He doesn't deserve to be betrayed. For the love you bear him, man, walk away. Avoid attachments as you have for so, so long. You owe him your allegiance.

This was the Tristan that Arthur recognised, though to hear his friend thinking of avoiding attachments surprised him, and he was wondering what the knight meant when another voice spoke up, even quieter, barely audible as a whisper.

How can it be a betrayal to follow your heart's desire? If Arthur was a true friend and leader, he would not stand in the way of true love. How has he repaid your loyalty? You are his servant. Not an equal. You call him 'sir'. And you would choose your employer over a worthy woman, who brought you back from death's door?

Arthur recognised that voice, though it had been many centuries since he had last heard it.

Arthur took a sharp intake of breath and staggered, almost falling, before he steadied himself with his cane.

'Did you hear her?' asked Simon. Arthur coughed and looked at Tristan, still frozen in place.

'Yes, I heard her. You have some incredible powers, Simon,' said Arthur.

'Heard who?' asked Bors.

'Morgana,' said Arthur, and nobody spoke for a few seconds.

'So he's not in trouble?' asked Simon, his eyes flitting to Tristan.

Arthur smiled, but he felt no less anger for the knight who had dared to challenge him, even if there was some magic at work.

'No, he's not in trouble. It's not his fault,' said Arthur.

'She's a bad lady, like the bad man from before?' asked Simon.

'She was, but you don't have to worry. She died a long, long time ago,' said Arthur.

Simon shrugged off his mother's hand and stood between Tristan, still frozen in place, and Arthur.

'The dead shouldn't speak,' said Simon.

His eyes rolled back in his head, and he threw what looked like a petulant punch towards Tristan.

A blast ruffled the knight's hair, but he did not move at all for a moment, but then he staggered, clutched his head with both hands and began to scream.

Blood dripped from his eyes and ears. He spat droplets of gore from his throat while all present stood stock-still, mouths hanging open and eyes wide.

'Simon, no!' screamed Kayleigh, and she made to grab him, but the little boy lowered his head, only the whites of his eyes visible, and his mother stopped dead.

Tristan's screaming tailed away and he stopped thrashing his head when he fell back and lay prone on the hardwood floor.

Chapter Thirty-Eight

December 31st 1999

Tristan woke in his mostly bare room, alone. He lay on his back, one hand beneath the pillow and looked up at the ceiling.

'Good morning, my loves,' he whispered to Isolde and Rozenn as he imagined their faces.

He forced himself up and opened the curtains to be greeted by the sight of the gardens and the woods beyond, all white with snow, which brought a smile to his face. Rozenn would have loved it. She'd have complained bitterly about the cold, but Tristan was pained by the memory of his joy at wrapping her in a blanket and warming her.

He showered, exchanged sleepy good mornings with Percival, who was off to fetch Arthur's newspapers from the village shop, and he dressed while the others slept.

Tristan performed his various duties, maintained his weapons and took exercise around the grounds while the others made merry inside, celebrating New Year's Eve. He would join them later, but duty came first. He had to be ready for whatever threatened those he cared about.

'It's unbelievable,' slurred Gareth, nursing the remains of his drink.

A chorus of laughter and objections sounded out from around the table.

'You've said. You keep saying,' said Tristan.

'Enough!' said Bors.

'But we're … about to become the only people in history to have lived in three different minnellia.' said Gareth. More laughter.

'Millennia,' said Arthur, smiling.

'Minnellium,' said Gareth and gave up.

'He's right, of course, and what better time to take stock than on the brink of the 21st century and our third,' said Arthur. He stood and raised his glass.

'Warlords in the 5th century, we slumbered until the 17th, but since then we have served our country well. We steadied the ship during the years of the Civil War, the Commonwealth and after the Restoration. We took the fight to the Jacobites to stabilise the monarchy of the United Kingdom of Great Britain and Ireland. We have fought in her wars, *against* the French right through to Waterloo, and *with* them against the Russians in the 1850s. Who can forget the charge of the Light Brigade? Not I. We stood against the Germans in 1914 and prepared for them in '39. We watch over this nation still, and we do what we can. We have lost many of our brothers, may they rest in peace, but the rest of us remain together, and we are still strong. I raise a toast then, to our accomplishments and our legacy!' Arthur concluded.

The gathered knights took up the toast, but then Tristan, who had remained seated, raised his glass again.

'To absent friends,' he whispered, thinking of Geraint, Gaheris, Galahad, Lamorak, of King Mark, Isolde and of Rozenn.

Once more, humbled, the company drank a toast.

◈

February 2020
Branok has been killed and the UK has voted to keep the monarchy. At the round table, Arthur is addressing his knights.

'Once, when we were but children, you heeded my words and followed me into battle, and I became king. Your king, king of a little land, still struggling to make its way in the world after the Romans left, dealing with the Norsemen and the Saxons. I was king for the blink of an eye, and then we rested and slept, duty done for a time.'

Tristan sat back in his chair, folding his arms across his chest, listening to Arthur speak.

'We were ripped from our rest and put back in that little land, finding it a changed place, beyond both our understanding and our reach, yet we have done what we could, and, in some small way, the prophecy was fulfilled.'

Tristan locked eyes with Arthur, who continued.

'But at what cost to our company? The silence in this room is a sound in itself, and none add to it more than do those who once sat upon the empty chairs,' Arthur said, his words soft and sad and sorrowful. He raised his mug in toast. 'To absent friends.'

'I will not throw away a lifetime of duty,' said Tristan. 'My oath holds.'

'We are a brotherhood,' said Gareth, and Dagonet nodded.

'And that will never change,' said Arthur. 'We are closer than brothers, and it is not right that I should be set apart on high any longer. Each of you has as much wisdom as do I, has seen this country change and quicken as the weary years rolled by. We have spilled much blood for

Britain, and it is time that each of you took some joy for yourselves.'

Tristan was about to object, but Arthur held up his hand.

'I will not turn away from this decision,' said Arthur. 'It is done. You are all free to go where you wish and do as you desire. Carve out lives for yourselves. Love. Have families, if that is what your heart wants.'

He took up his coffee and sipped again.

'The company will continue our work, but we will not take up arms any longer. Let us enjoy this England. To that end, I have divided our funds amongst us, transferred it to each of your accounts equally. I will not turn you out into the cold as beggars,' said Arthur.

Tristan shook his head, but Arthur continued.

'This is not an end to friendship or brotherhood, nor am I dismissing you from this house or my company. But you are no longer beholden to me. And that is how true friendship should be. How family should be.'

Tristan scowled at Arthur and then Dagonet spoke up.

'Thank you, Arthur,' he said, and Tristan was surprised to see the smile on his friend's face.

After Arthur had set out on his walk to rid himself of Excalibur before going on to see Caitlyn, the knights were left to process all he had said and the choices that lay before them.

Tristan had remained alone at the round table and was still sitting there, staring through the floor when Lucan came back in.

'Are you alright?' he asked.

Tristan blinked, daydream interrupted.

'How could I be?' he asked. 'He's ended it. Thrown us aside.'

Lucan frowned.

'Arthur's set us free, brother, surely you can see that?'

Tristan didn't, and he lashed out.

'So after everything, you'll just go? Our long years of friendship mean nothing to you? We swore oaths to Arthur and to one another.'

'Which he has held fulfilled, Tristan. It is long, long overdue. We have served him for centuries though he was no longer a king. It is our time now. A chance to have our own lives,' said Lucan, smiling. Tristan shrugged the knight's hand from his shoulder, and he shook his head.

'I won't leave him,' said Tristan. 'Not after everything I've given up for the love I bear him.'

Lucan did not reply.

'And you?' said Tristan, meeting his friend's sad eyes.

'It does not mean the end of our brotherhood. We will always be friends and will always come when called, you know that. But it will be a choice, not an obligation. Do you see the difference?' asked Lucan.

'I choose to honour my word. I choose to live and die for Arthur. I choose to remain,' said Tristan, and he pointed at Lucan. 'If you leave, you have turned your back on us, and I will not forget it. Things will never be the same.'

Lucan sighed, and it saddened Tristan, diminishing his anger just a little, for he loved the knight dearly, and in that moment he felt pulled in so many directions.

'If this friendship ends, it will not be because of me, brother,' said Lucan. 'But there is a world out there and endless possibilities, and I mean to explore them while I still have the time.'

Over the coming weeks, it became clear that in time, all would go, but Lucan, Ector and Gawain were the first, departing together to first travel the isles and then, they thought, around the world in due course. Tristan could not bring himself to see them off, and instead, he sat alone in his room, brooding.

When Bedivere, Dagonet and Bors moved out, they stayed local, and by now he had softened a little and they meant to stay nearby. He was not happy to see them go, but the men stayed in touch and were constantly visiting.

Soon, with Arthur spending so much time at

Hunter's Cottage, it was just Tristan and Kay rattling around the mansion, but he too was preparing to find a place once he'd got used to his prosthetic leg.

Tristan's life went on, unchanged except for the deepening of an old loneliness. He continued the watch, he maintained his weapons and he waited for the day when Arthur would have need of him again. He slept alone. He kept no company save for the knights when they were around. He read, he exercised, he remembered.

Each night he slept alone, and each morning he saw the faces of the loves he had lost, before getting up to waste another sixteen hours before he slipped between the sheets once more.

The grandfather clock in the hall ticked on.

Chapter Thirty-Nine

2021

The pain in Tristan's head faded away, and he let go of his hair, lying back and looking up at the ceiling. He felt … different.

'Don't ever do that to Mummy again.' He could hear Kayleigh shrieking at Simon.

Tristan pushed up on to his elbows as the boy replied through his tears,

'I'm sorry, but she's gone now. The bad woman.'

'Are you alright?' Gareth offered him a hand and helped to haul Tristan to his feet.

'I think so,' he said, looking at Arthur, whose face was grave, and he realised all the heat of emotion he had been feeling was gone. His former words seemed empty and inexplicable to him now. He wiped blood from his face and neck. 'What's the boy talking about?'

'He took me inside your mind,' said Arthur, sinking into his chair. 'Told me there was another voice in there. It was Morgana, whispering for mutiny and dissent, trying to make you betray me.'

'She's gone now,' said Simon, wiping away a tear, 'I sent her away.'

Tristan knelt down before the boy.

'I'm not sure what you did, but I think I owe you thanks, Simon,' said the knight, and he was relieved to see the boy smile.

'Better take him up for a while?' said Tristan to Kayleigh, and she nodded.

'Me and mister here are going to need to have a little chat, I think. And you guys need to regroup,' she said, getting her crutches into position and leading Simon into the hall.

'Sir, what … ' started Gareth.

'Give us the room,' said Arthur, to which Bors and Gareth protested, but as Tristan pulled out a chair and looked up, he caught the king's stare and the knights reluctantly nodded before they filed out.

'Did you hear me?' asked Arthur, and Tristan looked up from the surface of the round table at his liege lord, whose cheeks were still red. The man looked beaten up and defeated, but somehow, Tristan couldn't feel sorry for him, even if he was shocked at his own words and actions just a few moments before.

'I didn't, I'm sorry,' said Tristan, feeling the impulse to call Arthur 'sir' but holding back.

'How are you feeling?' said Arthur.

Tristan considered the question and took a mental inventory.

'I'm alright, but something is different. Something's missing,' he said.

'Morgana, it would seem. Will we never be rid of her influence?' asked Arthur, sitting back in his chair and sighing.

'She can't have been in my head all this time, can she?' said Tristan.

'Tell me, how do you feel about Caitlyn now?' asked Arthur. 'Honestly.'

Tristan knew the answer immediately, and there was no need to hold anything back.

'Ten minutes ago I was falling in love with her. I could feel it. I've felt it before. But now, that all seems like, I don't know, like I was drunk and I've sobered up in an instant, if that makes any sense.'

'Simon took me into your mind. I heard your true thoughts being manipulated by Morgana, as though she has been dwelling there,' said Arthur.

'Like Malagant and Agravain?' asked Tristan, horrified by the prospect of being possessed since the 5th century, but Arthur shook his head.

'I don't believe so. Morgana was always one for manipulation. If I had to name it, I'd guess she laid a curse upon you. Merlin spoke of her doing so before the two of them parted ways in anger prior to Mordred's conception. She was playing on your admiration and gratitude to Caitlyn, stirring up feelings and when you tried to rationalise what was happening, she began to whisper against me, as an obstacle to your love,' said Arthur.

Both men fell silent, as Tristan dropped his gaze to the table once more.

'A curse that makes me fall in love and betray my loyalties,' said Tristan, after a while, not looking up.

How long had the sorceress been working on him without his knowledge?

He felt nothing for Caitlyn, he knew that now. And Rozenn? And Isolde?

He could not tell, remembering only the love he bore them. But he also remembered the love of his uncle and the struggles he had endured, trying to decide where his loyalties lay, with his kin and king or with the object of his heart's affection. That had been the first time he had been swept away and to devastating consequences.

And Morgana had been at Tintagel. All had fallen apart after they spoke that first night she was there, the day before he set off to Ireland.

Could it be true? Had she slipped something into his drink or cast a spell upon him? His mind whirled. He had betrayed King Mark and for what? A whim of Morgana? Had he been part of a long plan to give Cornwall to Mordred and to distance Arthur and Mark?

'You always did fall hard and fast, loving fiercely. I knew something must be wrong. You have always been the most loyal of my knights,' said Arthur.

Tristan looked up, realisation dawning.

'But would I have been if it wasn't for Morgana? It must have been at Tintagel, Arthur, before I set out to fetch Isolde to marry Mark. I loved my uncle, and my desire for his wife took even me by surprise. I fought so hard against it, but it was as though I turned against him for some slight that never existed,' said Tristan. He began to pace the room, agitated and unable to expel the energy even as his body moved and his voice grew louder.

'If it weren't for your sister, Lucan and I would have lived out our days at Tintagel in service of our king and his new queen. Christ, perhaps Cornwall would never have fallen? Who knows what she did to Mark and Isolde!'

'We will never know,' said Arthur, 'but if one good thing came of it, it was that you found your way to my court and became Sir Tristan. You have been my trusted right hand for centuries.'

'Why have I been so?' shouted Tristan. 'I threw myself into my new duties as carelessly as I did when I pursued Isolde. We all know the myths and legends don't reflect the truth, Arthur. What were you but a wizard's pupil and the mightiest of warlords? I was honoured to serve, but at what cost? I threw away my marriage. Left Rozenn to follow you into what? Sleep? Death? And what of her? Did I ever truly love her?'

He stopped then, as the certainty of it gripped him, which comforted him a little, but intensified the feelings of injustice and loss all the more.

'I did love her, even now, looking back, I still love her, but Isolde? No! It was never real, just like what happened with Caitlyn! Morgana made me throw it all away and run to you! We always wondered where the stories of Lancelot and Guinevere came from and now we know, don't we?'

'What do you mean?' asked Arthur, his face red and taut, suppressing an outburst, Tristan knew, but was not perturbed from saying what needed to be said, now that it was all so clear to him.

'King Arthur's greatest knight, Lancelot, famed for saving Queen Guinevere from Malagant,' said Tristan, his eyes wild. 'She had sown the seed, Arthur. She drove a wedge between Mark and I, and when she knew I'd joined your company of knights, she knew something like this would happen before long. That I'd turn on you for love's sake. She made them both up, Lancelot and Guinevere, her or Malagant or someone else he took with him down the ages after her death. They've been playing the long game and we didn't even realise. Arthur's court was brought down by love and betrayal from within in the legends, and now, here we are! We've been idiots,' said Tristan.

Arthur did not reply.

Tristan turned his back on the king and leant his forearm against the window, breathing hard, his head hanging.

He'd never spoken to Arthur like that before and would never have tolerated it from anyone else, but he was doubting so many things. Had the anger he had felt at Agravain for leaving the company been unjust? Why was he so shocked that Lucan, Ector and Gawain moved away after Arthur told the knights they were free to leave his service?

He thought of all he had sacrificed and denied himself over the years. He had left Rozenn for the love of Arthur, he had avoided personal connections, all to ensure he never turned on the king as he had betrayed his uncle.

He turned back to face Arthur, who was still in his chair, staring into nothing.

'The feelings I had for Isolde and Caitlyn are gone, and when I look at you now, thinking about my life of service, I realise the love I bore you has been manipulated by this curse as well. You were the best of them when we were young, but I did not owe you eternity, nor should I have denied myself a life of my own. She stole that from me, Arthur, and you reaped the benefits. You are my friend, but I have given you more of myself than ever I should have. My friends, you and the knights, you mean the world to me, but this brotherhood, for me at least, has been a lie. What man in his right mind would condemn himself to what we've been through, floating through history without an anchor?'

He heard his raised voice nearing a shout, and for the first time saw the pain in Arthur's eyes. He had shaken his friend to the core. Friend? Was that the right word? In one day, Arthur had descended from king, to sir, to friend to … the man for whom he gave up his own life.

Tristan crossed the room to the door.

'Kings and queens today are nothing more than the beneficiaries of a line of warlords who fought their way to the top when the world was young, who turned into politicians and proclaimed themselves instruments of God. You were just a warlord. You *are* just a man, Arthur. You ruled us well and with honour, but Merlin and Morgana, who wielded the true power, are long dead now, and all of this,' he looked about the room, then pointed first at Arthur then back at himself, 'it should have died with them. I cannot stay a servant living his life in deference one moment longer.'

He left Arthur sitting at the round table, alone, and made his way up to his room.

Chapter Forty

2021

Days passed and the stillness of Arthur's mansion felt all the more profound.

Quiet, private funerals for Agravain, Nimuë, Kay, Dagonet, Bedivere and the fallen Hektor employees were held at a local crematorium after hours, but only Arthur, Gareth, Bors, Kayleigh and Simon attended, though they waited outside well past the scheduled start time, waiting to see if Tristan, or by some miracle, given that none of them had replied to messages or calls, Ector, Lucan and Gawain would show.

'It's time, Arthur,' said Bors, and Arthur felt a hand take him by the shoulder.

'Just a few moments more,' he replied.

'They're not coming, sir,' said Gareth.

'It's time,' Bors repeated.

Arthur looked up the long drive to the crematorium gates, manned by Hektor, and seeing nothing but leaves blowing across the tarmac, he sighed and went into the chapel to honour his fallen followers.

The service was brief and impersonal, and Arthur caught himself shaking his head, eyes fixed on the chaplain's shoes, though it was not the man's fault that he had not stood up to speak himself.

Gareth drove them all back to the house, and on the way home, Arthur stared out of the window, watching the low industrial buildings then commercial properties pass by, trying to remember his last moments with each of the knights, but growing increasingly angry with himself as he realised that he had been so consumed with getting Caitlyn back, he'd barely paid attention to any of the men who were, as always, giving their all to serve him.

Once home, Kayleigh and Simon headed up to their room and Arthur settled into the drawing-room with the knights and broke out his Scotch. They drank into the night, sharing memories and reminiscing.

Tristan did not join them.

Arthur woke with a hangover a little after dawn, the sun coming in through the window, as he'd left the curtains open when he went to bed in the early hours. He winced, shielded his eyes and looked out over the woods beyond his walls, as his head began to ache and the sinking feeling renewed.

He rolled over, away from the light, and, sighing, he closed his eyes, taking some time to go back to sleep, knowing if he moved, his stomach would begin to lurch.

He woke up feeling a little better, but still hungover. He

checked his watch and saw it was already late morning.

Arthur sighed and sat up with an effort, still fully dressed in yesterday's clothes, shoes and all. He leant on his cane and washed his face in the bathroom before following the sound of voices and the smell of cooking bacon to the ground floor.

He found Gareth and Bors eating breakfast seated at the island in the kitchen. An excess of bacon, sausages and fried eggs sat on serving plates on the counter, ready to be washed down with black coffee.

Bors looked up at the sound of Arthur's cane.

His 'morning, sleepyhead,' chafed against Gareth's, 'coffee, sir?'

Arthur nodded, and immediately regretted it. He steadied himself against the counter.

The three men perched on stools around the island while they ate. Gareth was the first to finish, and after fetching and downing a glass of orange juice, the knight asked,

'What's next for us, sir? One of the Order's vans is still unaccounted for, and we don't know how many of them are left.'

'Yeah, next move, boss?' asked Bors.

Arthur looked from one knight to another then drained his coffee cup while he considered what they should do.

'I've no idea what they're up to, but for all we know, Malagant's death has put an end to the threat from them. They had already kidnapped Caitlyn, perhaps they were continuing with the plan, but leaderless,' said Arthur.

'Or they're regrouping,' said Bors. 'We can't just let our guard down and hope for the best.'

Arthur saw Gareth nodding in his peripheral vision.

Exhausted, hungover and emotionally drained from the recent losses, as well as the sorrow of Caitlyn and Tristan walking away, Arthur just wanted to give up and forget about the whole ordeal. He was angry with Tristan. Furious that Caitlyn did not understand the necessity of him withholding the truth. He had lost so many people in just a few days, Agravain being but the first.

As always, he felt that call to duty, a responsibility to pick himself back up and press on, despite his desire to go back to bed, pull the covers over his head and shut out the world.

Later that day, Arthur released his hounds, Cynbel and Drust, from the kennels, taking some time to fuss the affectionate dogs and, after checking in on his horse, Hunter, he set out into the woods, in spite of his discomfited stomach and pounding head. The cool air and the sunlight through the trees did something for him as he wandered with no destination in mind. Before long though, perhaps inevitably, he found his feet on the path to Hunter's Cottage, but stopped and considered the road ahead. Caitlyn hadn't visited, called or sent word in any way. Should he leave her to think and maybe even recover? If he did, would it be easier for her to put him aside and decide to move on? Should he remain passive and allow her to do so or intervene and try to influence her back to him?

Cynbel nuzzled his hand, and Arthur scratched behind his ear. He took a deep breath and asked,

'What do you two think? Shall we go and see Samson?'

Drust looked up at him, tail wagging, and Arthur smiled, his mood lifting a little.

'Faint heart never won fair lady, eh?' said Arthur.

He mustered his courage and trod the path to Caitlyn's home.

⁌⁍

He passed through the gate and stood on the brink, or as it's more commonly known, the doorstep, poised to either knock or run.

Another deep breath, and he knocked. Samson barked somewhere within and then again, closer. Arthur's heart leapt as he heard the muffled sound of Caitlyn's voice through the thick wood of the door, but it did not open. He stood back and a movement caught his eye. Caitlyn was at a window, peeking from behind a curtain, then disappeared when she recognised him, which Arthur supposed made sense, being careful after what she had gone through.

The door opened, and Caitlyn stood, wrapped in a black cardigan, her hair tied in a high ponytail, wearing no make-up and with Samson at her heel. Cynbel and Drust rushed forward and mutual licking commenced.

Arthur hesitated, unsure how to begin, and he was already questioning whether it was a mistake to take the fight to her.

Caitlyn hunched her shoulders against the cold, frowning slightly, and she closed the door a little more, but said nothing.

They just looked at one another, both unwilling to start

the conversation, neither having anything to say.

But Arthur broke first. He owed her that, he thought.

'I hope you don't mind me stopping by,' he ventured.

No reply, but she sighed and tucked a strand of loose hair behind her ear.

Arthur took a step back, pointing the way he had come. 'Shall I …?'

'Not yet,' conceded Caitlyn. She leant against the door jamb and looked up at the clouds.

Arthur tucked both hands in his coat pockets.

'You lied to me. Or you kept things from me,' said Caitlyn.

Arthur nodded, dropping his eyes to her feet.

'I'm sorry. I didn't want to, but I didn't seem to have a choice,' he said.

'You did though,' she snapped.

'I did. I know it, but you must understand now how absurd the truth would have sounded. I couldn't think of how to say it without you dismissing me as a madman. I didn't want to lose you,' Arthur admitted.

'I do think you're a madman,' she said, 'but after what happened with that woman at your house. The things she knew about me, I … ' she stopped, covering her mouth as though to stifle her reaction. Arthur moved in to comfort her, but she held up a hand to stop him, and she regained her composure. He was tempted to ask her what Kayleigh had pulled from her memory, but thought better of it.

'Do you want to come in?' she asked quietly, opening the door just a little wider.

'If you'll have me,' said Arthur, not moving.

'Promise me you'll leave immediately if I tell you to go? No asking me to wait or trying to explain in a different way? You're on thin ice. I'm this close,' she said, the pads of her thumb and index finger millimetres apart.

'I promise,' he said, and she nodded.

'Good. Remember I have a Rottweiler, and he doesn't care if you're King Arthur or a burglar. If I say the word, he'll have you,' said Caitlyn, pushing open the door. Cynbel and Drust rushed in, and Arthur followed.

Caitlyn seated Arthur in an armchair in the living-room and fetched coffees before they spoke again, her huddled at one end of the sofa, the rest of it taken up by the sprawling Samson, his great head in her lap, his eyes closed, but opening occasionally to stare at Arthur and remind him of his place in this pack. Cynbel and Drust lay at his feet.

'Do you understand why I'm struggling? Can you get it?' she asked.

'I understand that you *are* struggling, but I can only really guess what it must be like for you,' Arthur replied, choosing every word carefully.

She didn't take her eyes from him, as though watching for any minute reaction.

'So … let me get this straight, just so we're clear. Not only are you and your friends carrying guns, but I'm expected to believe you are King Arthur. *The* King Arthur,' she asked, eyebrows raised. She shook her head slightly and sipped her coffee.

'Let me ask before answering, I know it was unpleasant

for you, but what did you make of Kayleigh Turner's ability?' asked Arthur.

Caitlyn sighed.

'It's hard to explain. She, you … someone … is either a better investigator than … ' she shook her head, 'but, no, it's just not possible. I've never told anyone some of the things she knew.'

Arthur nodded.

'Such abilities exist. They aren't common, and I suspect they have less than natural origins in the distant past, but they do exist. I've known only … ' Arthur counted in his head, looking up at the ceiling as he did so, 'eight such individuals in my lifetime, all with different abilities. Two survive.'

'The girl and her son?' asked Caitlyn, and Arthur nodded.

She stroked Samson's head absent-mindedly before, not looking up, she said,

'Your lifetime.'

'Another difficult thing to explain and for you to believe,' said Arthur. 'I know.'

'Go on then. How old? The nine-year age gap doesn't seem so wide now,' she smiled, but looked more nervous than good-humoured.

'I was born in the 5th century. I was the age I looked when we first met when one of the individuals I mentioned used his abilities on me and my brethren. We stopped ageing, could not be felled by illnesses or anything but violence or bodily damage,' said Arthur, watching her carefully. She was nodding slowly, letting it wash over her.

'But we weren't awake all of that time. I was badly injured or maybe even killed in the 5th century. I don't know which, but Merlin held me at that brink somehow and set me to slumber until, well, allegedly, until England needed me most, if you believe the legends, but England didn't exist back then. I don't really know what Merlin was thinking. He was not the most forthcoming man. Why didn't he just restore me back then rather than put me under? I don't know, I will never know. Perhaps he thought my return would usher in some great age, but in reality, when I did finally live again, it was clear to me that I was an irrelevance. I did what I could as the nation grew, but I'd never lead her again. That idea is nothing but myth and fairy tales. Like the King Arthur you've probably read about,' said Arthur. He looked into the fireplace, feeling overwhelmed by it all. '*I'm* just a man.'

'I'm more of a Stephen King fan, but I've probably seen the films,' she replied. 'I liked The Sword in the Stone when I was a kid. The Disney cartoon. Have you ever been turned into a squirrel?'

He heard the good-natured mocking return to her tone and it comforted him, even if that came from false hope. He smiled.

'Often. It was me that knocked off your bird feeders in the spring.'

'Of course,' said Caitlyn. She sighed then closed her eyes and pinched the bridge of her nose, massaging it between thumb and forefinger. 'I feel like I'm going nuts.'

He resisted remarking on the no doubt unintentional pun, but it took an effort. Time and a place.

'Jesus, I let you talking about Merlin just fly by me without a reaction. I can't decide whether I'm buying into this because it's real, whether I'm being gaslighted or perhaps I'm dreaming,' she said, and there was no humour in her voice now.

'Merlin was one of the eight, yes. Perhaps the first. We lost him a little after you and I met. When I told you about an old friend who had passed away from cancer?'

'Merlin died of cancer?' she asked.

Arthur said nothing.

'No, of course not,' said Caitlyn. 'Another lie.'

This was beginning to feel like a losing battle, although he had expected nothing else.

'He put you and your knights to sleep and you woke up when?'

'The 17th century. During the English Civil War. A student of Merlin persuaded him that it was the time when England needed us most. It didn't play out as he expected. I couldn't get involved. Can you imagine? A lone madman takes the field, claiming to be King Arthur? What do you think would happen if I tried that in Parliament today?' asked Arthur.

Caitlyn was watching him and looked thoughtful, so he pressed on.

'We built a life together, my brothers and I, as the centuries passed by, trying to right the ship where we could, fighting in England's wars and putting down threats where they arose. Merlin had sought to unite Briton when I was young, and I did what I could to bring stability and peace, even if it was just from the shadows, after we awoke. There were many more of us, but,' Arthur dropped his eyes to the floor, 'we lost so many. Only seven of us left of the original sixteen.'

'Seven?' she asked. 'Tristan, Mike, Gareth and you. Who else?'

'Mike's real name is Bors. After Merlin died, we began to age normally, and I told the knights they were free to pursue normal lives. After all, I wanted one with you,' said Arthur. 'Lucan, Ector and Gawain left before you could meet them, and we've not heard from them since.'

'You wanted a normal life after meeting me? I find that hard to believe,' said Caitlyn, her cheeks a little red, Arthur noticed.

'It's true. When our paths first crossed I was in the midst of events that would lead to the loss of my knight, Percival, and also Merlin. It was a difficult period, and yet for the first time in my life, I had met someone who made me want to build a home together and put aside this island's troubles. I decided I … we … had shouldered them long enough, and I wanted to give you my all. I did give you my all.'

'It felt like it,' she said. 'I believed in you.'

The words were a knife to the heart.

'But no longer?' he asked. She did not answer, but said, 'So what changed?'

Arthur sat back in his chair and chewed his lip, considering how to explain.

'It's complicated, but suffice to say that John Gravain, my friend in prison? His true name was Agravain. He was under the influence of … I don't quite know what he was … but his name was Malagant, and he not only fed on fear, but held an ancient grudge against me and mine. He was somehow dwelling inside Agravain and controlling him. Not knowing, we helped him escape from prison, and it became apparent Malagant was tormenting Agravain and hunting down his descendants. We stepped in, saving Kayleigh Turner and her son, Simon, but Malagant's people kidnapped you to get to me. I do not know their intention, and I suppose we will never know, but the knights and I did all we could to get you back. I'm devastated that you went through such an ordeal and heartbroken that my own lack of honesty may have destroyed the bond between us, Caitlyn,' he said, clasping his hands together.

'And Tristan dumped you right in the shit by telling me the truth, didn't he? Why?' she asked.

'We are not arcane practitioners, and I do not pretend to fully understand. Merlin could perhaps have discovered more, though even he was unaware of the curse laid upon Tristan back when we were young. But curse there seems to have been, now dispelled. Tristan was not himself, but he has received aid and is recovering, though I do not know if he will remain with me now,' said Arthur, the mansion seeming ever bigger, emptier and quieter in his mind as he thought of living there alone with Kay dead and Tristan gone, Bors and Gareth soon to return to their own homes.

Caitlyn rubbed her eyes as she replied.

'I'm making a mental list of things I have to wrap my head round. King Arthur, Merlin and his knights of the round table. By the way, your round dining table is a bit on the nose,' the hint of a smile, but still rubbing her eyes as she continued. 'Immortality, magic and curses. It's quite a list, my friend,' Caitlyn concluded, finally looking at Arthur, bleary-eyed. He only nodded. There was no denying it.

'Do you understand why I struggled to tell you?'

'I get it. I don't know how I feel about it, but I get it. I'm still not sure whether to believe you or get myself sectioned, but we'll burn that bridge when we're standing on it.'

'I suppose if you can forgive the deceit, I'd ask you to remember that I am just a man, and I always have been. I didn't write the legends nor are most of them even remotely related to the truth. I did lead men and I did govern, trying to unite the island, but it wasn't plate armour and glory like the stories would have you believe. That's all artifice, poetry and anachronism. When I returned, I did my duty as I interpreted it, and I built my wealth over long years of service and sacrifice. We did the best we could by the people of these lands while we whiled away our years. And now my life is finite, just like everyone else. I have comparatively few years left, but I want to spend them by your side, if you'll have me. I understand I may have forfeited the right.'

With that, he stood, leaning on his cane. The hounds lifted their heads.

'You're going?' she asked.

'You deserve time and space,' he said, leaning down to fuss Samson.

Caitlyn did not reply.

'Malagant is gone, but some of your kidnappers are still at large. There is business to conclude. I will do my part to end this story and condemn my enemies to the past, and when it is done, I will call on you again, if you'll permit it?'

She nodded, and he began to turn, but Caitlyn took his hand and pulled him into an embrace. She held him tight and he savoured the sensation, knowing he might never be in her arms again.

'I love you,' he whispered, and she held him tighter.

Arthur peeled himself away and after she showed him to the door, he set off home, not completely devoid of hope, thinking that perhaps there was still some of the ancient power in his voice after all.

Chapter Forty-One

2021

Still suffering from the hangover and emotionally drained from his conversation with Caitlyn, Arthur walked directly home, put Cynbel and Drust away and debated returning to bed. But he persuaded himself that, these days at least, life was short, and even if all he wanted to do was hide away, there were better things he could be doing and went in search of his knights.

The situation was, after all, *not* over, even if it was unclear how things would develop, who his enemies were, where they could be found and what they were doing.

It appeared that Bors, Gareth and Kayleigh shared his sentiment, as they were already at the round table, discussing options when Arthur returned. He assumed the boy was elsewhere, occupied with something technological, no doubt.

'How's Tristan?' he asked. Gareth shook his head and Bors said,

'Haven't heard a peep out of him. He's not come down except to bury Bobbi in the garden and to fetch food.'

'He buried Bobbi?' asked Arthur.

'Aye, found the grave this morning. Kayleigh was taking the boy to lay flowers. He was attached to that dog,' said Bors.

Arthur said nothing.

'It's difficult for Tristan,' said Gareth.

'What's so difficult about it? He was cursed and now he isn't! It's a good thing. Needs to stop sulking and pull his weight,' said Bors, stretching and yawning.

'Bit harsh,' said Kayleigh. 'There's probably a lot more to it than you think.'

'Nope, it's simple,' said Bors.

'Finding out you've given up everything because of a curse … imagine having had the life you've lived, the things you've endured and the things you've given up, but without making any of the decisions for yourself,' said Kayleigh.

Bors didn't reply.

'But he did decide for himself, didn't he?' asked Gareth, looking from Kayleigh to Arthur, who found himself wondering. Kayleigh threw up her hands.

'You tell me. But I've seen the man's life through his eyes, and it wasn't a picnic.'

'The curse enhanced his natural feelings for people and pushed them to extremes,' said Arthur, the full weight of Tristan's predicament hitting him for the first time. 'What if Morgana steered him into falling for Isolde to weaken Cornwall and undermine Mark? And, by lucky chance, Tristan moved on to my court and any loyalty he felt for me was amplified. Who knows whether he would have chosen to become one of my knights if not for the curse,' he concluded.

''Course he would,' said Bors. 'Who would have turned down that chance back then?'

'For the same reasons?' asked Arthur.

Bors looked as though he would respond, but fell silent, as did they all for a moment, lost in thought.

'It's more than that. I think if it hadn't been for Morgana, Tristan would have remained by Mark's side and remained a loyal servant of Cornwall until the end of his days, perhaps taking a wife and having children of his own, before passing into obscurity,' said Kayleigh. 'He never would have got out of the 5th century, and none of you would even remember him now.'

A heavy thought, but could it be true, that the most loyal of his knights had been compelled to be so? The notion sent Arthur's thoughts racing, a blow to his sense of security and family. Tristan was a pillar of his life. Someone who cared for him and upon whom he could always rely. But was it all a lie or, at least, the result of his sister's meddling, centuries ago? Sympathy awoke in him then, as he remembered seeing Tristan and Lucan approaching his throne for the first time. Younger men, tough and lean, and it had appeared Tristan was heartsore and almost defeated. But over time, that young man had rallied and served him more faithfully and with more devotion than any other, Arthur had thought, and didn't that do a disservice to Bors and Gareth, to Agravain, Percival, Kay, Dagonet, Bedivere and all the rest who had followed him into the future and remained by his side? Bors and Gareth were still here, sat at the latest of his round tables, of their own volition. But even they had moved into their own homes when Arthur released them. Not Tristan, who alone among the company had stayed for no other reason than loyalty, Kay simply taking some time to recover from his injuries in familiar surroundings before making his next moves.

If not for the curse, would Tristan have still remained by his side?

'Remember, he left a wife to join your sleep after Camlann,' said Kayleigh, quietly, 'which was a decision more difficult than perhaps you've ever considered, I'm guessing, you're so caught up in these men being 'your' knights. They had and, perhaps, *have* hopes and dreams of their own.'

'I know it,' said Arthur, a little stung, 'hence I released them once Branok was defeated and we began to age.'

'After centuries of slavery,' said Kayleigh.

Arthur pushed himself to standing, ignoring the pain in his leg, furious at the suggestion.

'Now, hang on, these men swore me their oaths,' he shouted, but then realised that neither Bors nor Gareth had leapt to his defence, and he scrutinised their guilty faces.

'Is that how you see it?' he asked them. Bors shook his head, and Gareth simply said,

'No, sir. We're here out of honour, loyalty to you and duty to our land,' he said.

Arthur was not sure that really constituted a no, though on any other day, he'd have thought so without question.

'Tristan has turned aside from everything but platonic love and love for you, as his king. Now the curse is gone, he can surely imagine all the great loves, children and passions he denied himself for a priority perhaps not entirely his own. No wonder he's sat up there for days. It's a lot to unpack,' said Kayleigh.

At that, the door creaked open and when Arthur turned, he saw Tristan standing in the entrance, dark circles under his eyes, but clean-shaven and wearing fresh clothes. His wet hair had been swept back to dry naturally.

'May I join you?' he asked.

Bors and Gareth stood, bowing their heads to him in acknowledgement as Arthur turned to face his knight squarely, leaning on his cane.

'You will always have a place at this table, my friend,' he said. 'I'm just grateful you can bear to sit at it.'

Tristan smiled weakly, closed the door and took up his place at Arthur's right hand.

'You alright?' asked Kayleigh, and Tristan nodded as the other men sat.

'We had just been considering the full implications of the curse, and its consequences on your life,' said Arthur.

'I've been thinking of nothing else,' Tristan replied, not raising his eyes from the table. 'I don't have the heart to discuss it now.'

Arthur nodded.

'But you are with us?' he asked.

'For now,' said Tristan. 'I owe you my allegiance. I swore my sword to you, Arthur, and no trick of my emotions discounts my word or my honour. I will remain by your side until this business with the Order is over. After that, well, that's for another time.'

Arthur thanked him, though the words fell flat, he thought, and Tristan would say no more about it, even when the others asked questions. They were forced to turn back to the matters at hand, but ultimately with no resolution.

The Order of Phobos and Deimos still existed, though it was unclear if they remained a viable organisation now that Malagant had died. The survivors of Tristan's attack at the farm had fled to a location not far from Tintagel, but there, the trail had gone cold. Arthur asked his people to prepare and to keep looking for clues, but it seemed there was little to be done until the cult reared its head once more.

They did not have to wait long.

A few days later, the phone rang in the hall while Arthur was in the drawing-room, cleaning his Colt, having already spent some time maintaining Excalibur.

The sound died away, replaced by the low murmur of a voice then footsteps and a knock on the door. When summoned, Tristan stepped into the room, frowning, still looking haggard, but as though he was making the effort to pick himself up.

'You're going to want to take this call,' said Tristan.

'What's happened?' asked Arthur.

'I don't know,' said Tristan, 'but I think we just found out what comes next.'

'Who's on the phone?' asked Arthur, but Tristan gestured towards the hall with his thumb.

'Hear for yourself, Arthur,' he said.

Arthur lifted the telephone to his ear, Tristan still at his side.

'Hello?' he said.

Nothing for a moment and then.

'Arthur?' The man's voice was familiar.

'This is he,' said Arthur.

Silence for a moment before the man spoke again.

'You don't recognise his voice?'

Arthur didn't reply. His stomach began to churn, and he braced himself against the wood-panelled wall.

'Lucan?' he asked.

'That's better, sire,' said Lucan, his tone mocking.

Something was wrong. Arthur could feel it in his bones, even if Lucan had not referred to himself in the third person. Not Malagant, surely? Another knight possessed?

'Who am I really speaking to?' said Arthur, keeping his response measured despite his beating heart and rising panic.

'We've never met,' said Lucan, 'but I have recently become acquainted with your friends. We were saving this, but we've had to escalate things somewhat. I'm calling to offer you an invitation. War is coming, but let's have the first battle on our ground and put an end to this. Do you have a pen?'

Arthur scribbled down the information as it was passed and then, finally, Lucan hung up and Arthur set down the handset. By now, all of the others had gathered in the hall.

'Well?' asked Tristan.

'The Order have Lucan and probably Ector and Gawain as well, if they're not dead already,' said Arthur. 'I have a journey ahead of me if they're to be released, it seems.'

'They won't release anyone!' Bors objected. 'They just want more of us!'

'Nevertheless, what choice?' said Arthur.

'We're not abandoning them,' said Gareth. 'We owe them that much.'

Arthur turned to Tristan, who had remained silent.

'We'd better get moving,' said Tristan.

'I can't ask any of you to come with me,' said Arthur. 'I have no idea what I'm walking into and there's every chance I won't get out alive. This is, I think, the moment where Morgana's long-awaited revenge is finally enacted, though she is long dead. I won't take you all down with me. And especially not you, Tristan, now that you've finally been granted your freedom.'

Arthur's thoughts turned to Caitlyn at that moment, wondering if he should bid her farewell before he set off to Cornwall or if he should spare her any pain.

'We are a brotherhood,' said Tristan solemnly. 'You have never and will never ride out alone, Arthur. I choose what I do with my own life now. My friends are in peril, and I will do what I can for them. Lord knows, I know now I've been unjust towards Lucan for moving on, and he deserves my aid.'

'We're all going,' said Bors.

'We entered this century together and we'll leave together if it comes to it,' said Gareth.

Arthur swallowed hard, stifling tears, then he nodded slowly, looking from knight to knight.

'Alright then, let's get about it,' said Arthur.

'What about me?' said Kayleigh. 'And Simon?'

Arthur shook his head.

'This is your time, Miss Turner, and the future is for your boy. I cannot put you at risk. It's time we put the past to bed. We must end any remaining threat to you and your son, let alone any of Agravain and Nimuë's remaining descendants. And I need you to guide your son well. He has the potential to be as powerful as Merlin and maybe more so. It's time you went home.'

Chapter Forty-Two

2021

With no time to waste, Arthur delegated tasks. Kayleigh and Simon were packed into a car to be driven home by Hektor Security, who would set up surveillance on the street and place a man within the house.

Arthur bade the young woman and the boy his farewells in the hall before excusing himself to make his own preparations, assuring them they would speak more when he returned. He passed a window a few minutes later and saw them standing beside a car deep in conversation with Tristan, which piqued Arthur's interest, but he was too busy to spend any time on it.

He had been given GPS coordinates by Lucan, and though the summons was certainly a trap of some kind, with his captured knights as bait, Arthur could think of no other option than to make the meeting, and as soon as possible. To that end, he asked Gareth to send for one of the corporate helicopters, which could get the company to Cornwall in a matter of hours. There would be little time before it landed in the grounds, and there was much to pack.

Having changed into practical clothing and boots, Arthur and the knights assembled at the round table, laying their swords, weapons and ammunition on its top. The king could not help feeling like an imposter as he laid down Excalibur, all too aware that his leg would betray him in any fight. But it was his sword, with him since he was an adolescent, the sword of the land, drawn from the land by his very hand, under the guidance of Merlin, who had been such a power then, before England even existed. Merlin, who had been felled by Mordred, wielding Excalibur.

This may be the last time that *I* wield her, thought Arthur.

What means had they to help Lucan, Ector and Gawain? They could have taken the Turners, but Arthur would not risk it and the others did not suggest such a measure. It was not their fight and they could not be put at risk, both for their own sakes and out of loyalty to Agravain.

Arthur heard the ominous heavy drone of the helicopter approaching with its blades, raising a swift thunder, and the company of four men trooped out through the kitchen and watched the Bell 222 land on the lawn.

After just a few minutes, the helicopter was in the air, heading for Cornwall.

Arthur looked at Tristan, still not yet recovered from his injuries, who was watching the countryside pass beneath them, and he wondered if his knight had any doubt about his involvement, despite the debt he owed Lucan. They were heading to the two men's homeland, and it was possible neither would return.

The helicopter set down on moorland near the coast, a few miles from Tintagel. Gareth jumped down first and reached up to help Arthur, who struggled out on to the grass.

He wore his Colt in a shoulder holster and carried Excalibur, still in her case, in his other hand.

'Where the hell do we go now?' said Bors.

Arthur looked around, scanning the moorland and the treelines, running his eyes over the line of the hills, but seeing nothing.

'We wait,' said Tristan, standing bent and breathing hard, beating Arthur to the punch. 'The terrain is so familiar, but so different. Lucan and I used to ride these lands in our youth.'

Arthur said nothing, impatient and looking all around for some sign of where they should go.

'There!' said Gareth, and Arthur saw him pointing towards a copse.

'Is that … ' started Bors, but Tristan finished his sentence.

'A white hart.'

The knight stepped in close to Arthur.

'This *has* to be Morgana's doing, somehow. Everything that went wrong at Tintagel began with her arrival and pursuit of the hart with King Mark while I went to Ireland to fetch Isolde.'

Arthur kept his eyes on the white hart.

'My sister is long dead,' said Arthur, barely audible and feeling somehow drawn to the creature of legend. He took a step forward.

'Death holds no bounds for her kind, we know that. We've lived it,' said Tristan.

'Are you suggesting we ignore it?' asked Arthur, finally turning to look at him, but he saw the knight shake his head.

'Of course not, but we follow with caution. What waits for us may be beyond our abilities. We need to accept that. We may not be able to save our friends this time, just put them out of their misery.'

Arthur met his gaze and nodded.

'Let's do this,' said Arthur, and he set off after the beast.

The white hart watched the four men approach, moving only when they were just a short distance away. The animal, eerie and seeming somehow not of that world, emerged from the trees and began to skirt them to the north, circling the copse. Arthur and the knights exchanged glances and, resigned to their fate, set off after the animal at a slow walk, neither side of the unspoken bargain in a hurry to reach their destination.

Arthur noticed the beast seemed to phase slightly as it moved, so that, just for an instant, he could see the landscape beyond through its body.

The white hart paid them no heed and continued to walk steadily on an invisible path, like a ghost fated to traverse the same nightly haunting route, a thought that made Arthur shiver.

After several hours had passed, during which both Arthur and Tristan had been forced to rest because of injuries both ancient and recent while the hart stood still and looked back towards them, continuing only once they were back on their feet. Gareth passed out some food and bottles of water from his bag during these intervals, and there was little conversation, each man considering what would come next and if this would be their final venture together.

Arthur's thoughts flew back to Caitlyn, and it occurred to him that he would never know whether she could forgive him and if they would have a future together, for he felt in his heart that this was one journey from which he would not return.

He had turned his back on that old life and set her free, in the name of both loyalty to his imprisoned friends and so that Caitlyn would not be shackled by the manacles of a quasi-supernatural life, bound to him, which could lead, he felt in that moment, to nothing but pain unless all threats were ended. And there was a good chance that in doing so, the possibility of being together was over.

'How's the leg?' asked Tristan.

'Well enough,' Arthur replied, and after a moment's hesitation, he added, 'I was thinking more of opportunities lost.'

'You are not alone in that,' said Tristan, and Arthur thought the knight sounded a little bitter.

'Do you blame me, Tristan? For the life or lives you never got the chance to live?'

Silence for a moment, and Arthur was conscious of Bors and Gareth standing just a little way off, pretending not to listen.

'I suppose I do, though I know I shouldn't,' Tristan confessed, meeting Arthur's gaze. 'I alone among your knights was compelled to love you as our king and a brother, but it was not of your doing. Would I have left Rozenn to stay by your side after Camlann had it not been for Morgana? Perhaps, we will never know. After all, these two are here by choice, are they not?' He gestured towards Bors and Gareth.

Bors sighed and turned to them.

'Are you still on this? We've lived the same life, you and I. You're a man of honour, Tristan, I'll admit it. You'd not have abandoned the brotherhood or your king,' he said.

'And yet I abandoned my wife,' said Tristan, briefly looking up at Bors before his eyes fell to the mud.

'As does every man who goes to war! As you did when you rode to Camlann to fight beside Arthur. Going with him beyond death is no different,' said Gareth. 'We all risk our lives for a cause, those of us who choose to fight. I believe you would still be one of us, curse or no. Did Lucan not come out of Cornwall with you? Did he not come into the long sleep for Arthur?'

'And yet he left us when free to do so,' said Tristan. 'I was angry about it, but now the curse is gone, I see more clearly. *He* held to his word as long as *Arthur* held him to it, then went to see his own life, free from duty.'

'His duty was done,' said Arthur. 'Had he been nearby when Malagant reared his head, he'd have returned just as Bors and Gareth did.'

'But he wasn't and he didn't. And he couldn't,' said Bors, pointing towards the hart. 'And he's in trouble. And so are the others. So let's get on with this, shall we?'

Arthur laughed and saw a smile had crept on to Tristan's tired face, even though he nursed his healing wounds with one hand.

Arthur groaned as he stood and called out to the hart.

'Lay on, Macduff, lay on.'

They followed the hart to the banks of a clear stream that ran down a slope from a rock face. As Arthur trudged upwards, Tristan beside him, he saw the animal disappear into a dark cavern at the base of a cliff, from which the stream emerged.

'I'll lead the way,' said Tristan as they entered the crevasse. 'You can concentrate on your footing, sir.'

Arthur did not object, but was heartened to hear the knight call him sir once more.

Tristan led the other three along the stream's bank, but suddenly stopped, and Arthur felt his stomach lurch, and he staggered, ducking slightly, as did the others, feeling for a moment as though the land beneath them had dropped away.

Tristan turned back, frowning, but seeing everyone was still on their feet, he once more led them on, deep into the darkness, accompanied by the dripping of water, the rock walls wet to the touch.

They pulled out torches to light their way, giving up on the idea of surprise.

What was now a tunnel turned to the right and a green glow became visible up ahead.

'Do you hear that?' said Tristan, turning off his torch. The others followed suit.

Arthur listened and, sure enough, he heard distant whispering voices.

They walked on together, mindful of their footing, until they reached the end of the tunnel, where Arthur saw Tristan had reached a curtain of hanging vegetation, through which light could pass.

'Ready?' said Tristan, turning back as though taking a moment to muster his courage, but when the others nodded, he pushed through, and Arthur followed.

The whispering voices stopped immediately.

At the sight of the underground lake with its glowing green waters and tiny islands, his memory stirred.

'I know this place!' he said, pointing towards the keep on an island. 'Merlin brought me here when I was a boy, but he blindfolded me on the last part of the journey here and the first part as we rode away.'

Arthur unfastened Excalibur's case and withdrew the sword, which felt light in his hand as it reflected the green glow of the lake.

'There's someone out on the water, fishing,' said Tristan. Sure enough, Arthur spied a man in a boat, rod in hand.

'How can he still be here?' he breathed. 'He ferried us to the castle and back, after I had drawn Excalibur from the stone within.'

'Arthur, look,' said Bors, pointing.

Before them lay a beach of white sand and lapping at the green water was the great white stag.

The creature looked up, and bowed its head to the humans.

Arthur felt compelled to return the gesture and as he did so, something changed so quickly that he did not perceive it. One moment the stag was receiving his bow and the next it had shifted form into a man, his skin burned by the sun, his beard and hair long and braided, his muscular body, some eight feet tall, covered in part by animal skins. From his head protruded the gleaming silver antlers.

'Cernunnos,' whispered Gareth, bowing his head. 'The Horned God, sire.'

Arthur felt rooted to the spot as the great antlered man advanced upon his company. He could not take his eyes from him, and he heard no sound nor caught any movement in his peripheral vision. His knights were not readying themselves either.

Instead, all four men dropped to one knee, bowed their heads then looked up at the creature before them.

'I was wrong to aid your sister, King Arthur. And this is the last time I will meddle in the affairs of mortals. But, you have a task ahead of you to heal the damage both Merlin and Morgana have wrought between them. Rise.'

King Arthur and his knights rose to their feet.

'Tell me,' said Arthur. 'It will be done.'

Chapter Forty-Three

2021

'Be not so sure, King Arthur,' said Cernunnos. 'This task will challenge not your ability as warriors, but the strength of your resolve, your moral courage and your hearts. Your friends are yonder, upon the Isle of Avalon, within Corbenic Castle, but they are not themselves.'

'Avalon,' said Arthur, an icy hand taking hold of his heart, knowing full well the implications for himself. The knights remained silent, but Arthur could hear their thoughts as loudly as the knelling of fate's bell, sounding in his mind.

Avalon — The Isle of Fruit Trees. Where legend told, incorrectly, that his sister Morgana had attempted to heal him after the battle of Camlann. Morgana's isle, then, perhaps. The place where King Arthur died, in many texts at least.

Arthur looked out to the island and as he did so, the name Corbenic came back to him.

He turned to Gareth, who among them enjoyed the legends more than the others, and was often found in the library making study of them.

'Corbenic Castle?' Arthur asked.

'The Grail Castle, sire,' said Gareth in a hushed, reverent voice, and Arthur noticed for the first time how the 'sir' had reverted to 'sire'. 'Which would make him,' Gareth pointed to the man in the boat, 'the Fisher King.'

'But there never was a Grail quest,' said Tristan. 'Not outside the stories.'

'Until now,' Bors huffed.

Arthur turned to Cernunnos.

'Is it true? The Holy Grail lies before us, on an island secured by the followers of Morgana?'

'I have heard the legend of the Grail and its arrival in Britain, but I can tell you I never led Joseph of Arimathea to this cavern. Who knows if it exists? Likewise the cauldron of Annwyn from which the idea of a grail was conflated along with the Christian myths. A cauldron, however, does lie yonder.'

'The cauldron of Bran the Blessed, whose living head is said to be buried beneath the Tower of London?' asked Gareth, who turned his attention to Arthur before continuing, 'The Welsh Mabinogion tells that the cauldron's waters were once used to revive the dead and could grant eternal life,' said Gareth.

Eternal life, thought Arthur. *Like Malagant. And Merlin. And … us, until Merlin died, at least.*

'Is it so?' Arthur asked Cernunnos, and the Horned God nodded, slowly.

'I know not of the cauldron's origins, but its waters do appear to grant eternal life, which the lake itself does not. Your wizard did not tell you of it then? Building mystery and his own legend was always Merlin's way. He knew of this place, sure enough, some say he created it or, at least, gave the castle its significance and its role. The cauldron's waters are not of this world, but of the one below, call it what you like, the Otherworld, the realm of fairy, Hades across the Styx. Time moves slowly there, scarcely at all, and it is the waters from the Otherworld that fill the cauldron.'

Arthur and the knights fell silent, thinking on all they had heard and wishing they had pressed Merlin on such matters when they had the chance, rather than relying on him as much as the old man desired.

'What business do Morgana's followers have here?' asked Arthur, gravely, continuing, 'What task would you have us do? We are here only to save or sacrifice our friends if it comes to it and to end the ongoing threat our enemies pose to the world without.'

'This lake was not always here,' said Cernunnos. 'This cavern filled from a river on the other side, ever so slowly as the centuries passed. The breach between the worlds lies now far below the surface and through it, some have passed. Merlin tore it open in the beginning, here where the barrier between the worlds is weak. Only he knew how to create a path to the world from which his powers came. The realm of Mab, of Hades and of a thousand others, has been open for passage since Merlin's ambition made it so, because of that,' said Cernunnos, pointing towards Arthur, who held up Excalibur, still reflecting the green light.

'Excalibur cut open the breach?' asked Arthur, but Cernunnos shook his head.

'Your sword was forged in Corbenic Castle and set within its stone, from which you drew it when Merlin deemed he had created the man he needed. But Excalibur's origins are not of this world. Merlin opened the rift below and found himself looking into a wall of water. When he returned through with ore from the other realm, it stayed open as long as part of the Otherworld remained within ours. That then, is part of the task you must complete to end this threat. Excalibur must be returned to its homeland if the breach is to be closed.'

Once more they all fell silent, and Arthur examined his blade closely, marvelling to hear of its origin.

'No offence, mate,' said Bors, 'but why should we bother? This breach has been here for … forever. No harm has come of it. Let's get on with what we came here for, Arthur, and finish the last of Malagant's people then go home.'

Cernunnos smiled, like a father watching his child throw a tantrum before intervening to soothe.

'Morgana's followers have not been idle. Long they sought to raise her and failed, though they have acquired most of the knowledge and arts. But Malagant was not the only spirit to come through the breach and even if you kill those who have possessed your two brothers, there are countless other creatures waiting to come through, many of whom will not require a captive host. An army has been assembling on the other side, Arthur, marching for the breach since the days of your sister's passage between the worlds. Malagant set things in motion now that they are close. Whether it be in your lifetime or a hundred years from now or a thousand, your sister's allies will come through and the weapons of humanity will be powerless to stop them. The breach must be closed, Arthur. And only Excalibur's return to the Otherworld can achieve it.'

Arthur licked his lips, nodding slowly.

'Two knights?' asked Tristan. 'We expected three.'

Cernunnos shook his head. 'Only two.'

Arthur begged Cernunnos's pardon and formed a circle with the knights for them to discuss the matter, but it did not take long for all to agree.

They would go to Corbenic and do what needed to be done for whoever was there with Lucan, whether it be Ector or Gawain. They would slay Morgana's servants and the remains of Malagant's cult. And then Excalibur would go below. Of that, they did not speak in more detail, forestalling the difficult discussion.

'You have our thanks, Horned God,' said Arthur, 'but will you aid us in this endeavour?'

'I have done all I can, for my power waned many long years ago, before even you were born. I aided Morgana out of spite, in folly, and I have shown you the way here as her followers asked of me, believing me still to be an ally.'

A second later and the white hart stood before the company once more. They bowed to Cernunnos and he to them, and he walked down to the shore and disappeared into the water, leaving Arthur, Tristan, Bors and Gareth standing in silence, contemplating what lay before them.

Arthur turned Excalibur over in his hands, a sword

forged from ore stolen from the Otherworld. What lengths Merlin had gone to in order to arm his chosen boy, the once and future king?

He would end this. Do his duty. See Excalibur went below whatever the cost.

Arthur led the company down to the shore and waved to the Fisher King, who put down his rod and began to row the boat towards them.

Arthur did not watch the approach with his knights. He closed his eyes and thought of Caitlyn, knowing full well there was every chance he would never see her again.

Chapter Forty-Four

2021

Tristan stood in his customary place, just behind King Arthur and to his right, as the company watched the Fisher King's boat approaching the shoreline. His back was to them, and he stopped a short way out. Bors and Gareth ran into the shallows, speaking to him, but getting no reply, and they hauled the boat up onto the white sand so that King Arthur did not have to try to wade through the water with his bad leg.

His heart felt heavy as he followed King Arthur, still conflicted, knowing there was a life beyond the cavern full of choices and honest passions, a life that he could control, but knowing full well his duty was to his friends and to their cause.

As King Arthur approached, the Fisher King turned his head and bowed to him.

'It has been a long time, Arthur,' he said as Tristan and Gareth helped Arthur into the boat. 'A long, long time.'

'It has,' Arthur replied, breathless as Tristan sat down beside him. Bors and Gareth shoved the boat out on to the lake and clambered inside, so that the craft rocked violently from side to side for a few seconds.

'It is said he waits for one who will heal his perpetual wound to replace him so that he can leave his boat and walk again,' whispered Gareth to Tristan, who noticed the bloody wound in the Fisher King's side for the first time.

'A long wait, it has been,' said the Fisher King, 'but necessary. For there must always be a boatman as long as there is a lake and a river beyond.'

Tristan shuddered at the old man's words, 'pay the boatman' running through his mind.

'Will you tell us how many we face?' asked Arthur, and the Fisher King frowned and looked up at the ceiling for a moment.

'Seven, I believe,' he said eventually. 'They come and they go. Some have been at Corbenic for centuries, and I have not seen them more than once. But others have come, from this age, I would imagine, judging by your attire. It's easy to forget how much time has passed, as it flows differently here, by the breach.'

The Fisher King rowed on, and Tristan ventured some tactical questions, but the old man merely smiled, and the knight gave up before long. Soon they had reached the other shore.

'Will you wait here for us?' asked Tristan once he'd helped Arthur to the shore of Avalon.

'Nearby,' said the old man. 'I may do some fishing.'

He gestured towards the lake with his head and Bors shoved the boat back on to the water.

The walls of Corbenic Castle loomed above them, exaggerated by the slope. Tristan scanned the surrounds, every window, along the ramparts and around the entrance to the keep with its portcullis raised. The place seemed to be anachronistic, in many ways, with features of architecture and technology from the distant past and yet also the middle years while they had slumbered, and yet Arthur had said he recognised the place from his childhood. Tristan couldn't understand it.

'Let us ready ourselves,' said Arthur and the company discarded their modern trappings, save for their weapons and torches. Tristan placed his own items in the pile of phones, keys, wallets and other items, and Arthur's coat and jacket landed in a heap atop them. Tristan looked up to see the king rolling up his white shirt sleeves, still wearing his waistcoat and pocket watch, his Colt visible in its holster. He had buckled a belt around his waist, as had they all, upon which hung their swords. Bors, Gareth and Tristan carried their MP5ks, while Arthur kept his cane in hand for the meantime.

Without a word, Arthur set off limping up the slope, and Tristan overtook him, dropping back to a slow walk, attempting to put himself in the line of fire should someone take a shot at the king; out of habit and duty, he realised, perhaps more than out of the fierce desperate need and love that had been there before.

As they approached the entrance to the castle, Tristan spied a man pass under the portcullis, dressed like a warrior from the 5th century, a sword hanging from his belt. Tristan held up a hand to halt the party and raised his MP5k.

'Who goes there?' he shouted. 'Put your hands in the air.'

The man looked vaguely familiar, but Tristan could not place him. He took aim with the MP5k, focusing on the front sight until everything fell into place.

'I am Treave, Castellan of Corbenic Castle and Lord of Avalon,' called the man. 'Well met, Tristan. You've aged but a little since I last saw you.'

'Who's he?' asked Bors, but Tristan shook his head. He couldn't place him.

'Don't waste our time,' he called. 'You summoned us for a reason, and we came to help our friends. Let's not pretend this will go well for either side. Where are they?'

Treave nodded.

'They are within, but I'm afraid there are none among you who can wrest them from our control, even if you somehow defeated Malagant.' Treave tilted his head. 'King Arthur, I assume, from your broken body and walking stick,' said Treave.

Bors took a step forward, muttering 'You … ' before Gareth held him back.

Tristan noted his own lack of reaction to the gibe, something that would have stirred a protectiveness just a few days ago. Instead, he remained steady and kept his aim true.

'I am Arthur, but I have not been a king for many an age outside this cavern, Treave. Why have you brought us here, knowing we will fight you?' said Arthur, moving to stand beside Tristan, still using his cane. Tristan would have been tempted to throw it aside, for pride's sake.

'If you hurt us, your friends die,' said Treave.

'So you expect us to throw down our arms and walk in to be executed, is that it?' said Arthur, and Treave smiled.

'It was my lady's wish to bring you to the edge of despair and to push you beyond it before the last, and even if Malagant failed in his part, I would have you know you are defeated even if I die in the attempt,' said Treave, and he turned back towards the entrance. Tristan recognised him then, remembered him at Morgana's side at Tintagel. He was about to speak when suddenly Arthur fell backwards and sand kicked up behind them. A shot echoed around the cavern and then another. Tristan fired his MP5k, but Treave was already running back through the entrance and disappeared.

Arthur's back hit the sand, and Tristan saw an entry wound in his chest where the bullet had pierced his waistcoat. Blood was spreading out from under it, turning his white shirt red at an alarming rate.

Gareth and Bors seized Arthur under his arms and were running forward, Arthur's eyes wide but his legs still moving as he leant heavily on his knights, leaving his cane lying in the white sand where it had fallen.

Tristan changed the magazine as he scanned the windows and another shot whizzed past him. He caught the muzzle flash in one of the windows this time, and he gave fire, causing their assailant to fall back. He continued to do so as Bors and Gareth bore Arthur to cover at the base of Corbenic's walls.

Bors and Tristan checked in with each other as Gareth called out.

'Through and through. There's an exit wound on his back.'

'How's he looking?' called Tristan over his shoulder. He could hear Arthur breathing hard and fast, spluttering and wheezing.

'Not good,' said Bors, standing beside Tristan. Behind them, the wall continued to meet the rock face with no obvious doorways and above them, the arrow slits were too small for someone to lean out and see them, but who knew what other modern technology was up there?

'We need to get to the cauldron,' said Tristan, but as he did so, he saw the same red mist rising from his body as Malagant had drawn from those whose fear and terror he fed upon. Looking back, he saw the same was happening to the others and even more was rising from Arthur, all drifting upwards and then spinning into an upward funnel, the cloud channelled over the ramparts and into Corbenic.

'The Dread Knight,' said Bors. 'He's still alive.'

'Or he's not the only one of his kind,' said Tristan. 'God knows what's gathering on the other side of the breach. What has come through already? We need to move,' he said to Bors. 'Shock and awe,' said Bors, nodding.

'I'll stay with Arthur,' said Gareth. 'Try to stop the bleeding.'

There was no time to say farewell or to disagree. He and Bors were all they had to enter Corbenic, and there was nothing else to be done.

'Ready?' asked Tristan and Bors nodded. 'Do or die.'

MP5ks in hand, they headed up the slope and approached the open entrance to Corbenic Castle, Tristan lagging behind, his body still objecting.

Chapter Forty-Five

2021

Tristan and Bors slowed as they approached the wall and, pressing his back against it, Tristan took a quick glance over his shoulder through the gateway, bracing for oblivion in case somebody was waiting to blow his head off.

Nothing. A missed opportunity to finish off the attacking knights, for sure.

Tristan went right, ducking into an alcove, while Bors took up position on the other side.

From there, they could see into the silent, deserted courtyard with a well at its centre, and Tristan saw a door swinging closed in one of the corner towers beyond.

He pointed towards the tower and broke cover, and the two knights moved carefully, methodically sweeping potential points of attack as they crossed the courtyard.

Tristan booted open the door, ready to fire at anyone on the other side, but again he saw nothing in the dimly lit void beyond, except for an impossibly steep stairwell, going both up and down.

Without a word, Tristan set off up the steps as Bors said

'Good luck' and he heard his brother knight descending the staircase.

The stairs wound so tightly that there was no possible way to fight in there or to be shot from above, so Tristan scrambled up, using hands and feet, as quick as he could manage, breathing hard, his way lit only by the green flames burning in sconces in alcoves on the walls, for there were no windows.

After several minutes, the stairwell opened up and Tristan got a brief glimpse of boots before a muzzle flashed, and he pushed off with his hands, falling down the stairs a short way before steadying himself, but not before ripping open his knees and banging his head against the stone. His ears were ringing as the shot echoed, and he rolled on to his front, aiming upwards with his MP5k. The boots and lower legs appeared, and Tristan fired, stitching across his assailant's limbs, shattering the bones so that the man collapsed into a heap and fell towards him, screaming and still holding his rifle, unwieldy at close quarters. The man fell to his knees and forward and as his head struck the stair before Tristan, the knight fired a burst along the man's spine. Tristan clambered over him, sending the corpse down the stairs and dashed up to the landing above him. He burst through the door and found himself out on the ramparts with yet another door visible ahead of him and the lake stretching out to his right. Tristan shuffled along the ramparts, intent on killing all in his path and finding the cauldron as quickly as he could in the hope of being able to heal Arthur. As he walked, Tristan noticed the red mist seeping from his body was drifting up towards a window of the tower ahead of him, which was built right up into the ceiling of the cavern, and he pushed himself to move faster, despite feeling blood coursing over his torso from opened stitches.

Lucan was in there, he realised now, possessed by a being such as Malagant. Perhaps Ector or Gawain as well, enemies wearing the bodies of his brothers.

What the hell could he do to help them?

As he approached, the door swung open and a woman with an AK47 stepped into view. Tristan fired first, and hit her in the chest and throat, but her wild spray was partially effective, and a bullet grazed his left leg, causing him to fall.

Through the door was another stairwell, similar to the first, going both up and down. The mist had been directed towards an upstairs window and so Tristan didn't hesitate in choosing his path, hobbling onwards.

Up he went, breathing hard, his leg bleeding and the wound in his shoulder aching. He changed the MP5k magazine, using the last one, and as he reached a landing with another door visible, he grabbed the handle, threw it open and then dashed into the room, throwing his back against the stone wall, under a glassless arrow slit through which the red mist was flowing, hoping to God that anyone up there was slower and less experienced with any firearms than he.

'Hello, Tristan,' said Lucan, his voice coming from the next room, shielded with a velvet curtain, through which the mist coming from Tristan, now green, was flowing. He edged sideways so he was clear of a direct line of fire.

He did not reply.

'We're coming through now, Tristan. If you shoot, you will be killing brother knights, and we will survive by occupying you. You can be the one to kill the rest of your friends.'

Both of you, Tristan wondered.

The curtain swept aside as both Lucan and Ector stepped into the doorway.

Tristan, MP5k at the ready, already knew what he had to do.

He pulled the trigger, emptying the magazine into his friends' chests.

Before the knights had hit the floor, the creatures rose as a mist from their bodies. They mingled in the air above Lucan and Ector, who disintegrated into nothing.

They flew towards Tristan, who pressed the muzzle of the MP5K to his temple.

The two creatures paused in mid-air as Tristan had hoped, guessing they would be unwilling to risk losing a host vital to sustain them. They hung in the air momentarily, already beginning to fade, but then poured out through the arrow slit, abandoning the tower.

'No!' said Tristan, realising his mistake.

He started back down the stairs, sometimes slipping as he did so, landing heaving on the stone stairs. He clambered over the fallen man in the stairwell and limped out along the rampart shouting warnings to the knights below.

Shots rang out, echoing up the stairwell.

Tristan descended the last steps, finally reaching the ground, then he limped across the courtyard, past some new corpses, cultists drawn out and killed by Bors, he assumed. His head was swimming, and he had to stop to catch his breath, leaning against the wall.

Go, he told himself, and he staggered out and along the wall.

There he saw Bors and Gareth kneeling over Arthur amid a swirl of mist that had descended upon them. Bors had a wooden goblet in his hand and was holding it to Arthur's lips.

Gareth fell on his side, clutching his head with both hands, his head thrashing as he screamed. Bors laid Arthur's head back in the grass, dropping the goblet, and leapt to his feet, one hand reaching for Gareth and the other holding his sword.

'It's taking him!' Tristan roared as he closed the distance, ignoring the pain. 'There's another.'

He dove forward and landed on top of Gareth, into whom red mist poured through his mouth, nose and into his eyes.

'Throw away your sword, Bors, quickly!'

Gareth stopped writhing and, eyes glowing green, he fought back with renewed strength. He forced Tristan off him, but the knight held on and they rolled away together as Bors dropped his sword and clutched his head as the spirit began to possess him. Tristan heard Bors scream as Gareth's hands closed around Tristan's neck and began to squeeze hard enough to constrict his throat and cut off his breathing.

'Morgana's dead, you crazy bastard,' roared Bors, his eyes now empty sockets filled with red smoke, and he punched Gareth in the back of the head, but the knight barely reacted, and Bors stood still, then grinned.

Gareth laughed, gripping Tristan's throat tighter with one hand and somehow stood, even with Tristan kicking him while he tried to pry his friend's fingers off him. Tristan felt the life going out of him, but he kicked out and still fought until Bors began punching him in the kidneys. Tristan cried out and, losing consciousness, he closed his eyes, fearing he had met his end.

And then he fell to the floor. He landed on his back, striking his head, and he opened his eyes, only to be blinded by a flash of white light. He caught movement above him, and rolled away to the side, blinking and shaking his head as he got to his knees.

The white light faded to nothing, and Tristan could see once more.

Arthur stood over Gareth's body, which was rent from shoulder to hip, with his knight's blood dripping from Excalibur. Bors collapsed in the grass, and his head rolled from his shoulders.

Tristan wheezed, stumbling as he tried to get to his feet, and landing on his knees. Arthur offered him his hand and when Tristan looked into his eyes, he saw the years had fallen away. His wrinkles were gone and before him, the grey was disappearing from Arthur's hair and beard. He stood straighter, and when back on his feet, Tristan grasped the king by the shoulders.

'Sire?' Arthur nodded gravely. He stood back and bent his leg then straightened it again, and Tristan's mouth fell open.

Arthur looked down at Bors and Gareth then dropped to both knees beside his fallen knights and wept.

'Be at peace, brothers,' he said.

Tristan looked back up the slope, and he saw Treave burst through the gates of Corbenic Castle, bearing a shield in his left hand and a sword in his right. He tore down the slope towards Arthur then saw Gareth and Bors and halted in just a few steps.

'Your friends are dead,' said Tristan.

'So many more are waiting to come through,' said Treave.

Tristan stood between Treave and Arthur, raising his sword.

'Throw down your arms,' said Arthur, standing, 'and I will let you live. I will close the breach. Your cause is lost.'

Treave raised his shield and sword once more.

'For my lady,' he growled and ran towards Tristan, knocking aside the knight's sword then swiping right towards King Arthur.

Arthur sprang back, avoiding the blow as Tristan lunged forward, barely keeping his feet, but Treave was a strong warrior, and he wheeled and parried, striking out at Tristan, who was forced to stagger back.

Tristan rallied, ready to give his life defending Arthur, but as Treave came at him, a gunshot sounded, and Morgana's man crashed to the grass, taken by a bullet to the chest.

Tristan watched as Arthur holstered his Colt and the echoes of the shot reverberated throughout the cavern and gradually faded away to nothing.

The knight's battered body could take no more, and Tristan's knees gave out.

Arthur knelt beside Tristan.

'Are you still with me?' asked the king, but dizziness nearly overcame Tristan, and he fell to coughing.

'It is nearly time for Excalibur to go home,' said Arthur.

'But what of Caitlyn,' asked Tristan before adding, 'let me go in your stead.'

But Arthur shook his head.

'With my youth and vigour renewed, can I condemn her to a life in which she ages, but I do not, now that I have drunk the cauldron's waters?' asked Arthur. 'No, I must let her go and fulfil my destiny. It was said King Arthur would return when Briton was in need, and perhaps it is so. I can do this last thing for the land I love. Perhaps I will be killed in the Otherworld, facing down the forces that wish to come through, but I do not wish to live forever, brother, going on alone when all of you have passed. I will go down fighting.'

Tristan again made an effort to stand.

'I will follow,' said Tristan.

Arthur smiled, sheathing Excalibur.

'You would not make it to the breach, my friend. Your shirt is sodden with blood and the wound in your lungs would betray you.'

Tristan felt Arthur's hands on his shoulders.

'You are free.'

With that, Arthur turned and walked down the slope. Tristan considered going after him, but instead, he stood and watched as his leader waded out into the waters of the lake.

When the glowing green lake reached his waist, the waters closing over Excalibur, King Arthur turned back and extended a hand in farewell.

Before he passed out, Tristan saw him smile, turn and dive beneath the surface.

Chapter Forty-Six

2021

Tristan awoke in the dark, his body aching. He fumbled in a pouch on his belt and withdrew his torch, and he immediately saw that the waters before him had receded, leaving only a slope downwards where the lake had been.

Standing, his head splitting, he made his way down to the lowest point of the bed where once the chasm had been and found no trace of it, just wet white sand. No glow. No water.

Tristan set off back up to what had been the shore and sweeping the torch beam around, he saw the Fisher King's boat resting in the sand a short distance from the top.

Tristan gripped the gunwale and cast the light of the torch on the old king's face, but he winced and turned away, holding up a shielding hand, so Tristan dropped the beam.

'Arthur has gone below,' said the king.

Tristan looked down at the Fisher King's wounded side.

'You would be healed and live forever?' he asked.

'I would have a life of my own, however long or short,' replied the old man.

Tristan nodded, understanding well.

'Gareth said the one who healed you would replace you,' said Tristan, frowning.

'The breach is closed. There is no longer any need for a boatman,' said the Fisher King, shaking his head.

'So be it,' Tristan said and he set off back to Avalon, retrieving the wooden goblet and other belongings from where they lay in the sand. He noticed for the first time that there was no sign of his friends' corpses.

After a while searching the castle, he returned with a single cupful of the cauldron's never-to-be-replenished waters.

The Fisher King did not hesitate, snatching the Grail from Tristan and gulping down the water. Tristan watched in wonder as youth and vitality returned to the old man and marvelled as he saw the gaping wound in his side seal shut.

The young man leapt from the boat and fell face first into the sand. Tristan started towards him, but the youth rolled over, laughing.

And when the mirth had subsided, they set off across the lake bed together, the Fisher King holding the wooden cup in his hands, staring at the object to which his fate was bound.

They climbed out the other side and, by the light of Tristan's torch, he led the way through the tunnel. He found himself in the sunshine once more, but as he stepped out from the crevasse and turned back to the Fisher King, there was a flash of bright light that somehow seemed to spring from the cup itself.

Tristan closed his eyes, staggering out into the world, temporarily blinded, and when his vision returned, he looked back and saw that the Fisher King, the chasm in the cliffs, the stream and the cup were gone.

Wandering back across the moor, Tristan took his phone from his pocket and called the pilot. There were questions, of course, when the Bell 222 landed and only one of the passengers returned aboard, but Tristan bade the pilot head for home, assuring him all would be explained in the fullness of time.

Ninety minutes later, the craft set down in the grounds of what had been Arthur's mansion, and Tristan disembarked, not looking back as the Bell 222 took off again.

He pushed open the door to the kitchen and stood there a moment, listening to the silent house.

Tristan was alone.

He made himself a mug of peppermint tea, thinking of Percival, and he wandered from room to room, passing his hand over the furniture, lamenting not only the dead, but the lost. He thought of Arthur, swimming down to the chasm at the bottom of the lake, passing through, and then what?

Arriving in some other kind of world, beyond his imaginings, perhaps facing innumerable foes, gathered and waiting to invade, as the breach closed behind them.

Was Arthur alive or dead? Tristan didn't know, and he knew he never would, though something deep down inside him suspected the answer was both.

Tristan took a long, hot shower and felt a little more

human once he was done. He knew he could not stay in the mansion, no matter what Arthur's solicitors might have arranged, and so he packed a rucksack, keeping his Glock 17 and spare clips on his person, then placed a call to extend the arrangements for the dogs and the horses, at least in the short-term.

Tristan set off out of the mansion and closed the door behind him, never to return. He pulled up his hood and walked up the drive, passed through the gate and considered his next move.

Money was no object. He had friends, connections and many ways to make his way in the world. And the choice of how he went about it was entirely his, he knew. But still some obligations remained, and he turned left, crossed the road and set off through woods towards Hunter's Cottage, to tell Caitlyn that Arthur was never coming back.

Later that evening, he paid the taxi driver and stood alone looking up at a house as the car pulled away from the kerb. He'd been there before, of course, but last time, he'd not waited to be invited in.

He walked up to the door and pressed the doorbell, but then his finger froze in position, and he heard Simon's voice in his head.

Hello, said the boy.

Hello, thought Tristan, and his body was his own once more. He heard the chain being taken off on the other side of the door, which, after the turn of a key, swung fully open, revealing Kayleigh Turner suspended between two crutches, wearing a fluffy dressing gown.

She looked concerned and seemed to be searching his face, then she nodded as though she already knew and understood.

'Come in,' she said. 'I'll put the kettle on. You can tell me all about it, yeah?'

Chapter Forty-Seven

Thirty Years Later

'Are you nearly ready?'

Robert's voice drifted up through Hunter's Cottage and found Caitlyn making the final adjustments to the angle of her hat. She grunted and resisted the urge to call back, as it was a long-standing rule that the Taylor family did not shout room to room, even though they all did, as long as they initiated - just never in reply.

She pulled on the new coat, bought especially for the occasion and, after checking herself in the mirror, she made her way downstairs. Robert looked rather fine, she thought, and he'd even had a decent go at getting his hair right, but she fussed over it for a moment, not because it needed it, but, unconsciously, to show she cared. She picked some lint from his coat and returned his smile.

'You look lovely,' said Robert, leaning in to kiss her on the cheek.

'Shall we?' she asked and, grasping her walking stick, she headed for the door, where she was greeted by their spaniel, Delilah.

'Be back soon, dopey. Don't fret,' Caitlyn told her, and the Taylors got into their car.

Robert drove and parked up behind the crematorium, then Caitlyn linked arms with him and they joined the mourners assembling at the front of the building, among them an old man in a black overcoat, a green band tied around his upper arm.

Robert wrapped his arms around her and held her close while they waited, and a few minutes later, a hearse passed through the gates and proceeded up the long drive, lined with flowers and overhanging trees, followed by the family in separate cars.

The hearse pulled up, and Caitlyn saw Simon, in his early forties now, she couldn't remember exactly, climbing out of the car in his black suit, looking much smarter than usual. He held the door for his younger sister, Rozenn, while his brother, Lucan, stepped out of the other side under his own steam. Simon leant in and after a moment of shuffling, Kayleigh Turner emerged on to the pavement at the front of the crematorium.

Simon, Lucan and Rozenn joined the other pallbearers to carry their father's coffin into the church. Dr and Mr Taylor fell in behind Kayleigh, who had barely raised her eyes, and once everybody was inside, the service began for the lately departed Tristan Turner.

Back at the Turner's house after the funeral, Caitlyn left Robert talking to a group of Tristan's friends and found

Kayleigh, Simon, Rozenn and Lucan gathered in the kitchen, drinking tea or something a little stronger. When she realised she was interrupting, she held up a hand and went to hurry away, but Kayleigh called her back and before a moment had passed, she had been presented with a glass and Simon was pouring her a whisky.

'To Dad,' said Simon, raising his glass, and they all chinked mugs and glasses, echoing the toast. Caitlyn downed the whisky, probably a mistake, she reflected, and crossed the room to give Kayleigh a hug. The other woman showed no sign of letting go, and the doctor settled in, feeling her loss all too keenly. After all, she'd lost a longstanding friend herself and there was the reminder there, too, of a man she had loved once, but who had become something of a myth all over again.

The afternoon wore on, and Caitlyn felt the time had come to head back to Hunter's Cottage. She found Kayleigh surrounded by mourners in the living-room, looking weary and sad, but she was holding up, with Simon at her side. She decided not to disturb them, but Simon looked at her, smiled and she heard,

We'll all come by tomorrow for a proper chat, Auntie Caitlyn. Losing Dad has brought out some new abilities in Rozenn, so it might be worth running some tests while the grief is fresh, as clearly as if he had spoken the words.

Caitlyn nodded and signalled to Robert, who caught the look and started rounding off his conversation.

She passed down the hall, its walls adorned with photographs of Tristan, Kayleigh, their children and their friends, and headed upstairs, where she knew Rozenn and Lucan would be hiding, if she was any judge of their characters. Sure enough, they were in Lucan's old room, lying next to each other on the bed, on their fronts, poring over a book.

They looked up as she pushed the door open, and they smiled, a little dutifully, as one does with one's parents' friends, and she offered a little wave.

'I just came to say goodbye, but I'll see you tomorrow, both of you.'

More polite smiles and Lucan got up to hug her goodbye. His sister followed suit, closing the book on her index finger to mark the page and when their brief, loving, hug was done, Caitlyn caught a glimpse of the cover before she closed the bedroom door.

Its title - *Tristan and Isolde*.

Chapter Forty-Eight

The Otherworld
Where Time Runs Differently

Arthur took a deep breath as his head broke the surface, and he coughed as he swam for shore. Under the starlight and interlacing branches, insects like fireflies flitting around them, he hauled himself up on the bank. He stood upon the grass and looked all around, seeing only trees.

'Well, I'm here,' said Arthur to nobody. 'Where's the horde of … fairies, or goblins, or spirits or … '

'The dead,' said a voice from behind him.

Arthur turned and looked across the wide river, but the other bank was lost to darkness. Starlight glittered on the surface of the river, and when Arthur leant in to peer closer, he swore he could see faces forming in the water, passing downstream with the current. Wispy hands reached out towards him.

'Who's there?' he called in the direction from which the voice had come, but there was no reply.

He turned back to look at the trees once more, and clouds of red and green mist that had newly emerged from the woods, spirited away, taking cover in the branches. Arthur heard trees falling in the far distance, and a roar, away to the right. He drew Excalibur and as he did so, the voice spoke again, this time from the woods.

An old man stepped from between two trees, his beard long and white, his robes green and splattered with blood.

'I knew you would come, boy, given time.'

Other figures gathered behind him, emerging from the darkness, clad for war and covered in gore, their faces scarred, but smiling.

Bors. Percival. Kay. Dagonet. Gareth. Ector. Lucan. Geraint. Bedivere. Galahad. Gaheris. Lamorak. Agravain and Nimuë with their children all about them.

Six ravens flew overhead.

'Forces of darkness are gathering, boy, and we have plans to make,' said Merlin.

King Arthur laughed, a tear rolling down his cheek, and he strode towards his lost friends. Bors laughed, clapping him on the back, while Gareth took a firm grasp of his hand. Together the company walked into a forest of the Otherworld, whatever *that* might be, but where we all must go to dwell in our own sweet time, the land where legends, myths and love never truly die.

The End.

Thank you for reading **Tristan's Regret.**
I hope you enjoyed it!
If so, please leave a review!

If you haven't already, sign up to the Jacob Sannox Readers' Club newsletter, and I will keep you updated about its release, other releases, giveaways and discounts. It will not cost you anything, you won't receive any spam, and you can unsubscribe at any time -
www.jacobsannox.com/readersclub.html

Why not try **Dark Oak**, a semi-finalist in the 2018 SPFBO competition, the first book of my dark epic fantasy series,
The Dark Oak Chronicles?
www.jacobsannox.com/dark-oak.html

Humanity has finally defeated the Dark Lord, but Morrick fought on the wrong side . . .

Though he was a slave, he is branded a traitor and must earn the trust of new lords in order to return to his family - if they are still alive.

Now that their common enemy is dead, the nobles begin to forget old loyalties, and Queen Cathryn's realm looks set to plunge into war once more. But there are older and more terrible powers dwelling within the forest, and when they are awakened, Morrick will decide who lives or dies.

Printed in Great Britain
by Amazon